DARTH BANE

RULE OF TWO

DARTH BANE

RULE OF TWO

DREW KARPYSHYN

NEW YORK

2021 Del Rey Trade Paperback Edition

Copyright © 2007 by Lucasfilm Ltd. & ® or ™ where indicated.
All rights reserved.
Excerpt from *Star Wars: Darth Bane: Dynasty of Evil*
copyright © 2009 by Lucasfilm Ltd. & ® or ™ where indicated.
All rights reserved.

Published in the United States by Del Rey,
an imprint of Random House, a division of
Penguin Random House LLC, New York.

DEL REY is a registered trademark and the CIRCLE colophon is a trademark of
Penguin Random House LLC.

Originally published in hardcover in the United States
by Bantam Spectra, an imprint of Random House,
a division of Penguin Random House LLC, in 2007.

ISBN 978-0-593-35881-8
Ebook ISBN 978-0-307-79586-1

Printed in the United States of America on acid-free paper

randomhousebooks.com

4 6 8 9 7 5

Book design by Edwin Vazquez

To my parents,
Ron and Viv, and my younger sister, Dawn

THE ESSENTIAL
LEGENDS COLLECTION

For more than forty years, novels set in a galaxy far, far away have enriched the *Star Wars* experience for fans seeking to continue the adventure beyond the screen. When he created *Star Wars*, George Lucas built a universe that sparked the imagination and inspired others to create. He opened up that universe to be a creative space for other people to tell their own tales. This became known as the Expanded Universe, or EU, of novels, comics, videogames, and more.

To this day, the EU remains an inspiration for *Star Wars* creators and is published under the label Legends. Ideas, characters, story elements, and more from new *Star Wars* entertainment trace their origins back to material from the Expanded Universe. This Essential Legends Collection curates some of the most treasured stories from that expansive legacy.

DARTH BANE

RULE OF TWO

PROLOGUE

DAROVIT MADE HIS stumbling way through the bodies that littered the battlefield, his mind numb with grief and horror. He recognized many of the dead: some were servants of the light side, allies of the Jedi; others were followers of the dark side, minions of the Sith. And even in his dazed stupor, Darovit couldn't help but wonder which side he belonged with.

A few months earlier he'd still gone by his childhood name, *Tomcat.* Back then he'd been nothing more than a thin, dark-haired boy of thirteen living with his cousins Rain and Bug back on the small world of Somov Rit. They had heard rumblings of the never-ending war between the Jedi and the Sith, but they never thought it would touch their quiet, ordinary lives . . . until the Jedi scout had come to see Root, their appointed guardian.

General Hoth, leader of the Jedi Army of Light, was desperate for more Jedi, the scout had explained. The fate of the entire galaxy hung in the balance. And the children under Root's care had shown an affinity for the Force.

At first Root had refused. He claimed his charges were too young to go off to war. But the scout had persisted. Finally, realizing that if the children did not go to the Jedi, the Sith might come and take them forcibly, Root had relented. Darovit and his cousins had left Somov Rit with the Jedi scout and headed for Ruusan. At the time, the children had thought it was the beginning of a grand adventure. Now Darovit knew better.

Too much had happened since they'd all arrived on Ruusan. Everything had changed. And the youth—for he had lived through too much in the past weeks to be called a boy anymore—didn't understand any of it.

He'd come to Ruusan full of hope and ambition, dreaming of the glory that would be his when he helped General Hoth and the Jedi Army of Light defeat the Sith serving in Lord Kaan's Brotherhood of Darkness. But there was no glory to be found on Ruusan; not for him. And not for his cousins.

Rain had died even before their ship touched down on Ruusan. They'd been ambushed by a squadron of Sith Buzzards only seconds after they broke atmosphere, the tail of their vessel shorn off in the attack. Darovit had watched in horror as Rain was swept away by the blast, literally ripped from his arms before plunging to an unseen death hundreds of meters below.

His other cousin, Bug, had died only a few minutes ago, a victim of the thought bomb, his spirit consumed by the terrible power of Lord Kaan's final, suicidal weapon. Now he was gone. Like all the Jedi and all the Sith. The thought bomb had destroyed every living being strong enough to wield the power of the Force. Everyone except Darovit. And this he couldn't understand.

In fact, nothing on Ruusan made any sense to him. Nothing! He'd arrived expecting to see the legendary Army of Light he'd heard about in stories and poems: heroic Jedi defending the galaxy against the dark side of the Force. Instead he'd witnessed men, women, and other beings who fought and died like common soldiers, ground into the mud and blood of the battlefield.

He'd felt cheated. Betrayed. Everything he'd heard about the Jedi had been a lie. They weren't shining heroes: their clothes were soiled with grime; their camp stank of sweat and fear. And they were *losing*! The Jedi whom Darovit had encountered on Ruusan were defeated and downtrodden, weary from the seemingly endless series of battles against Lord Kaan's Sith, stubbornly refusing to surrender even when it was clear they couldn't win. And all the power of the Force couldn't restore them to the shining icons of his naïve imagination.

There was movement on the far edge of the battlefield. Squinting against the sun, Darovit saw half a dozen figures slowly making their way through the carnage, gathering up the fallen bodies of friend and foe alike. He wasn't alone—others had survived the thought bomb, too!

He ran forward, but his excitement cooled as he drew close enough to make out the features of those tasked with cleaning the battlefield. He recognized them as volunteers from the Army of Light. Not Jedi, but ordinary men and women who'd sworn allegiance to Lord Hoth. The thought bomb had only taken those with sufficient power to touch the Force: Non-Force-using folk like these were immune to its devastating effects. But Darovit wasn't like them. He had a gift. Some of his earliest memories were of using the Force to levitate toys for the amusement of his younger cousin Rain, when they were both children. These people had survived because they were ordinary, plain. They weren't special like he was. Darovit's survival was a mystery—just one more thing about all this he didn't understand.

As he approached, one of the figures sat down on a rock, weary from the task of gathering the dead. He was an older man, nearly fifty. His face looked drawn and haggard, as if the grim task had sapped his mental reserves along with the physical. Darovit recognized his features from those first few weeks he'd spent in the Jedi camp, though he'd never bothered to learn the old man's name.

A sudden realization froze Darovit in his tracks. If he recognized the man, then the man might also recognize him. He might remember Darovit. He might know the young man was a traitor.

The truth about the Jedi had disgusted Darovit. Repulsed him. His illusions and daydreams crushed by the weight of harsh reality, he'd acted like a spoiled child and turned against the Jedi. Seduced by easy promises of the dark side's power, he'd switched sides in the war and thrown himself in with the Brotherhood of Darkness. It was only now that he understood how wrong he'd been.

The realization had come upon him as he'd witnessed Bug's death—a death for which he was partly responsible. Too late he had learned the true cost of the dark side. Too late he understood that, through the thought bomb, Lord Kaan's madness had brought devastation upon them all.

He was no longer a follower of the Sith; he no longer hungered to learn the secrets of the dark side. But how could this old man, a devoted follower of General Hoth, know that? If he remembered Darovit, he would remember him only as the enemy.

For a second he thought about trying to escape. Just turn and run, and the tired old man still catching his breath wouldn't be able to stop him. It was the kind of thing he'd once done all the time. But things were different now. Whether it was from guilt, maturity, or simply a desire to see it all end, Darovit didn't run away. Whatever fate awaited him, he chose to stay and face it.

Moving with slow but determined steps, he approached the rock where the man was sitting, seemingly lost in thought. Darovit was only a few meters away when the man finally glanced up to acknowledge him.

There was no glint of recognition in his eyes. There was only an empty, haunted look.

"All of them," the man mumbled, though whether he was talking to Darovit or himself wasn't clear. "All the Jedi and all of the Sith . . . all gone."

The man turned his head, fixing his vacant stare on the dark entrance to a small cave nearby. A chill went through Darovit as he realized what the man was talking about. The entrance led underground, through twisting tunnels to the cavern deep beneath the ground where Kaan and his Sith had gathered to unleash the thought bomb.

The man grunted and shook his head, dispelling the morbid state he had slipped into. Standing up with a weary sigh, his mind was once more focused on his duty. He gave Darovit a slight nod but otherwise paid him no further heed as he resumed the macabre task of rolling the corpses in cloth so they could be collected and given honorable burials.

Darovit turned toward the cave. Again, part of him wanted to back away and run. But another part of him was drawn to the black maw of the tunnel. Maybe there were answers to be found inside. Something to make sense of all the death and violence; something to help him see the reasons behind the endless war and bloodshed. Maybe he'd discover something to help him grasp some purpose behind everything that had happened here.

The air grew steadily cooler the deeper he descended. He could feel a tingling in the pit of his stomach: anticipation mixing with a sick sense of dread. He wasn't sure what he'd find once he reached the underground chamber at the tunnel's end. More bodies, perhaps. But he was determined not to turn back.

As the darkness enveloped him, he silently cursed himself for not bringing along a glow rod. He had a lightsaber at his belt; getting his hands on one of the fabled weapons was one of the temptations that had lured him over to the Sith. But even though he'd betrayed the Jedi just to lay claim to it, in the darkness of the tunnel, he no longer felt any desire to ignite it and use its light to guide him. The last time he'd drawn it had resulted in Bug's death, and the memory had tainted the prize he had sacrificed everything to gain.

He knew that if he turned back, he might never gather enough courage to make the trip down again, so he pressed on despite the darkness. He moved slowly, reaching out with his mind, trying to draw on the Force to guide him through the lightless tunnel. Even so he kept tripping over the uneven ground, or stubbing his toes. In the end he found it easier just to run one hand along the rocky wall and use it to guide himself.

His progress was slow but steady, the tunnel floor becoming steeper and steeper until he was half climbing down it in the darkness. After half an hour he noticed a faint light emanating from far ahead, a soft glow coming from the distant end of the passage. He picked up his pace, only to trip over a small outcropping of stone jutting up from the rough-hewn ground. He fell forward with a cry of alarm, falling and tumbling down the sharp slope until he came to rest, bruised and battered, at the tunnel's end.

It opened into a wide, high-ceilinged chamber. Here the dim glow that had drawn him forward was reflected from flecks of crystal embedded in the surrounding stone, illuminating the cavern so he could see everything clearly. A few stalactites still hung from the roof high above; hundreds more lay smashed on the cavern's floor, dislodged when Kaan had detonated the thought bomb.

The bomb itself, or what remained of it, hovered a meter above the ground in the very center of the cavern—the source of the illumination. At first glance it appeared to be an oblong, metallic orb four meters from top to bottom, and nearly three meters across at its widest point. Its surface was a flat, dusky silver that projected a pale radiance but at the same time devoured all light reflected back to it by the crystals trapped in the surrounding walls.

Rising to his feet, Darovit shivered. He was surprisingly cold; the orb had sucked all the warmth from the air. He took a step forward. The dust and debris crunching below his foot sounded flat and hollow, as if the thought bomb were swallowing not just the heat of the cavern, but the noise as well.

Pausing, he listened to the unnatural silence. He couldn't hear anything, but he definitely felt something. A faint, thrumming vibration running through the floor and up into his body, a steady, rhythmic pulse coming from the orb.

Darovit held his breath, unaware he was doing so, and took another tentative step forward. When nothing happened he let the air escape from his lungs with a long, soft sigh. Gathering his courage, he continued his cautious approach, reaching out a hand but never taking his eyes from the sphere.

He drew close enough to see dark bands of shadow slowly twisting and turning beneath the shimmering surface, like black smoke trapped deep within the core. Two more steps and he was close enough to touch it. His hand trembling only slightly, he leaned forward and pressed his palm against the surface.

His mind exploded with wails of pure anguish; a shrieking cacophony of voices rose from the orb, all the victims of the thought bomb screaming out in torment.

Darovit wrenched his hand free and staggered back, dropping to his knees.

They were still alive! The bodies of the Jedi and Sith had been consumed by the thought bomb, crumbling into dust and ash, but their spirits had survived, sucked into the vortex at the heart of the bomb's blast only to be imprisoned forever.

He had only touched the surface for the briefest of seconds, but the keening of spirits had nearly driven him mad. Trapped inside the impregnable shell, they were condemned to an eternity of endless, unbearable suffering. A fate so horrible that Darovit's mind refused to fully grasp the implications.

Still hunched over on the ground, he clasped his head in his hands in a gesture of helpless futility. He'd come here seeking answers and explanations. Instead he'd found an abomination against nature itself, one from which every part of his being instinctively recoiled.

"I don't understand . . . I don't understand . . . I don't understand . . ."

He muttered the phrase over and over again, huddled on the ground, rocking slowly back and forth on his heels and still clutching his head in his hands.

1

Peace is a lie. There is only passion.
Through passion, I gain strength.
Through strength, I gain power.
Through power, I gain victory.
Through victory, my chains are broken.

THE CODE OF THE SITH

DARTH BANE, the only Sith Lord to escape the devastation of Kaan's thought bomb, marched quickly under a pale yellow Ruusan sun, moving steadily across the bleak, war-torn landscape. He was two meters tall, and his black boots covered the ground in long, sweeping strides, propelling his large, powerfully muscled frame with a sense of urgent purpose. There was an air of menace about him, accentuated by his shaved head, his heavy brow, and the dark intensity of his eyes. This, even more than his forbidding black armor or the sinister hook-handled lightsaber dangling from his belt, marked him as a man of fearsome power: a true champion of the dark side of the Force.

His thick jaw was set in grim determination against the pain that flared up every few minutes at the back of his bare skull. He had been many kilometers away from the thought bomb when it detonated, but even at that range he had felt its power reverberating through the Force. The aftereffects lingered, sporadic bursts shooting through his brain like a million tiny knives stabbing at the dark recesses of his mind. He had expected these attacks to fade over time, but in the hours since the blast, their frequency and intensity had steadily increased.

He could have called on the Force to keep the pain at bay, cloaking himself in an aura of healing energy. But that was the way of the Jedi, and Bane was a Dark Lord of the Sith. He walked a different path, one that embraced suffering, drawing strength from the ordeal. He transformed the pain into anger and hate, feeding the flames of the dark side until his physical aspect seemed almost to glow with the fury of a storm it could barely contain.

The terrifying image Bane projected contrasted sharply with the small figure that followed in his wake, struggling to keep up. Zannah was only ten, a waif of a girl with short, curly blond hair. Her clothing was simple and plain to the point of being rustic: a loose-fitting white shirt and faded blue coveralls, both torn and stained from weeks of continuous wear. Anyone who saw her scampering along after Bane's massive, black-clad form would have been hard-pressed to imagine she was the Sith Master's chosen apprentice. But looks could be deceiving.

There was power in the child. He'd seen ample proof of that at their first meeting, less than an hour earlier. Two nameless Jedi were dead by her hand. Bane didn't know all the details surrounding their deaths; he had arrived after the fact to find Zannah crying over the body of a bouncer, one of the telepathic, green-furred species native to Ruusan. The still-warm corpses of the Jedi had been sprawled beside her, their heads lolling at grotesque angles atop broken necks.

Clearly the bouncer had been the child's friend and companion. Bane surmised that the Jedi must have inadvertently killed the bouncer, only to meet a similar fate when Zannah exacted her revenge. Unaware of her power, they'd been caught off guard when the child—driven by mind-numbing grief and pure, abject hatred—had unleashed the full fury of the dark side on the men who'd slain her friend.

They were victims of cruel misfortune: in the wrong place at the wrong time. Yet it would have been inaccurate to call their deaths pointless. In Bane's eyes, at least, their sacrifice had allowed him to recognize the young girl's potential. To some the series of events would have seemed preordained, as if the hapless Jedi had been inexorably drawn to their grim end with the sole purpose of uniting Bane and Zannah. No doubt there were even those who would profess that fate and the dark side of the Force had conspired to present the Master with a suitable apprentice. Bane, however, was not one of them.

He believed in the power of the Force, but he also believed in himself: He was more than just a servant of prophecy or a pawn of the dark side, subject to the whims of an inevitable, inescapable future. The Force was a tool he had used to forge his own destiny through strength and cunning. He alone among the Sith had truly earned the mantle of Dark Lord, which was why he alone among them still lived. And if Zannah was worthy of being his apprentice, she would eventually have to prove herself, as well.

He heard a grunt behind him and turned back to see that the girl had tumbled to the ground, falling in her haste to try to keep up with the relentless pace he'd set. She glared at him, anger etched across her features.

"Slow down!" she snapped. "You're going too fast!"

Bane clenched his teeth as a fresh bolt of pain ripped

through his skull. "*I* am not going too fast," he replied, keeping his voice even but stern. "*You* are going too slow. You must find a way to keep up."

She scrambled to her feet, swatting at the scuffed knees of her overalls to wipe away the most obvious traces of dirt. "My legs aren't as long as yours," she replied crossly, refusing to back down. "How am I supposed to keep up?"

The girl had spirit. That had been clear from the moment of their first meeting. She had recognized Bane instantly for what he was: one of the Sith, sworn enemy of the Jedi, a servant of the dark side. Yet she had shown no fear. In Zannah, Bane had seen the potential for the successor he needed, but she had obviously seen something she wanted in him, too. And when he had offered her the chance to be his apprentice, to study and learn the ways of the dark side, she hadn't hesitated.

He wasn't yet certain why Zannah had been so eager to ally herself with a Lord of the Sith. It could have been a simple act of desperation: She was alone, with nowhere else to turn for her survival. Or maybe she saw the dark side as a path to vengeance against the Jedi, a way to make them all suffer for the death of her bouncer friend. It was even possible she had simply sensed Bane's power and lusted to claim it as her own.

Whatever her true motivations, Zannah had been more than willing to swear fealty to the Sith and her new Master. However, it was neither her spirit nor her willingness that made her worthy of being his apprentice. The Dark Lord had chosen her for one reason, and one reason only.

"You are strong in the Force," he explained, his voice still betraying no hint of emotion or the agony he endured. "You must learn to use it. To call on its power. To bend it to your purpose. As you did when you killed the Jedi."

He saw a flicker of doubt cross her face. "I don't know how I did that," she muttered. "I didn't even mean to do it," she continued, suddenly uncertain. "It just sort of . . . happened."

Bane detected a hint of guilt in her voice. He was disappointed, but hardly surprised. She was young. Confused. She couldn't truly understand what she had done. Not yet.

"Nothing *just happens,*" he insisted. "You called upon the power of the Force. Think back to how you did it. Think back to what happened."

She hesitated, then shook her head. "I don't want to," she whispered.

The girl had already endured immeasurable pain and suffering since her arrival on Ruusan. She had no wish to revisit those awful experiences. Bane understood; he even sympathized with her. He, too, had suffered during his childhood, a victim of countless savage beatings at the hands of Hurst, his cruel and abusive father. But he had learned to use those memories to his advantage. If Zannah was to become the heir to the dark side's legacy, she had to confront her past. She had to learn how to draw upon her most painful memories. She had to transform and channel them to allow her to wield the power of the dark side.

"You feel sorry for those Jedi now," Bane said, his voice casual. "You feel regret. Remorse. Maybe even pity." The easy tone fell away quickly as his voice began to rise in both volume and intensity. "But these are worthless emotions. They mean nothing. What you need to feel is anger!"

He took a sudden step toward her, his right fist clenched before him to punctuate his words. Zannah flinched at the unexpected movement, but didn't retreat.

"Their deaths were not an accident!" he shouted as he took another step forward. "What happened was not some mistake!"

A third step brought him so close that the shadow of his massive frame enveloped the girl like an eclipse. She cowered slightly but held her ground. Bane froze, blocking out the pain in the back of his skull and reining in his fury. He crouched down beside her and relaxed his clenched fist. Then he reached out slowly with his hand and placed it gently on her shoulder.

"Think back to what you felt when you unleashed your power against them," he said, his voice now a soft, seductive whisper. "Think back to what you felt when the Jedi murdered your friend."

Zannah dropped her head, her eyes closed. For several seconds she was still and silent, forcing her mind to relive the moment. Bane saw the emotions crossing her face: grief, sorrow, loss. Beneath his massive hand on her frail shoulder, she trembled slightly. Then, slowly, he felt her anger begin to rise. And with it, the power of the dark side.

When the girl looked up again her eyes were open wide; they burned with a fierce intensity. "They killed Laa," she spat. "They deserved to die!"

"Good." Bane let his hand fall from her shoulder and took a step back, the hint of a satisfied smile playing across his lips. "Feel the anger. Welcome it. Embrace it.

"Through passion, I gain strength," he continued, reciting from the Code of the Sith. "Through strength, I gain power."

"Through passion, I gain strength," she said, repeating his words, responding to them. "Through strength, I gain power." He could sense the dark side building within her, growing in intensity until he could almost feel its heat.

"The Jedi died because they were weak," he said, taking a step back. "Only the strong survive, and the Force will make you strong." As he turned away, he added, "Use it to keep up. If you fall behind again, I will leave you here on this world."

"But you still haven't told me what to do!" she shouted after him as he marched away.

Bane didn't reply. He'd given her the answer, though she didn't know it yet. If she was worthy of being his apprentice, she'd figure it out.

He felt a sudden surge of power rushing toward him, concentrated on the heel of his left foot as she tried to trip him up to slow him down. Bane had braced himself for some kind of reaction the moment he'd turned his back on her. He'd pushed her to the edge; he'd have been disappointed if she had done nothing. But he'd been expecting a broader, more basic assault—a wave of dark side energy meant to hurl him to the ground. A focused strike against a single heel was much more subtle. It showed intelligence and cunning, and though he was ready for it, the strength of her attack still surprised him.

Yet even with as much power and potential as Zannah had, she was no match for a Dark Lord of the Sith. Bane drew upon his own abilities in the Force to absorb the impact of her attack, catching it and amplifying its strength before firing it back at his apprentice. The redirected blow struck Zannah in the chest, hard enough to knock her to the ground. A grunt of surprise escaped her lips as she landed hard on her backside.

She wasn't injured; Bane had no intention of harming her. The constant beatings inflicted on him by his father throughout his childhood had helped transform Bane into what he was today, but they had also caused him to hate and despise Hurst. If this girl was to be his apprentice, she had to respect and admire him. He could not teach her the ways of the dark side if she was not willing—even eager—to learn from him. The only thing Hurst's beatings had ever taught Bane was how to hate, and Zannah already knew that lesson.

He turned back and fixed his cold gaze on the girl still sitting on a hard, bare patch of dirt. She glared back up at him, furious at the way he had humiliated her.

"A Sith knows when to unleash the fury of the dark side," he informed her, "and when to hold back. Patience can be a weapon if you know how to use it, and your anger can fuel the dark side if you learn how to control it."

She was still fuming with rage, but he saw something else in her expression now: a guarded curiosity. Slowly she nodded as the meaning of his words became clear, and her expression softened. Bane could still feel the power of the dark side within her; her anger was still there, but she had hidden it below the surface. She was nursing it, feeding it for a time when she could unleash it.

She had just learned her first lesson in the ways of the Sith.

And she was wary of him now—wary, but not afraid. Just as he wanted. The only thing he needed her to be afraid of was failure.

He turned away from her again and resumed his march, suppressing a shudder as a fresh phalanx of blades carved their way through his thoughts. Behind him he felt Zannah gather the Force once more. This time, however, the girl directed it inward, using it to refresh and rejuvenate her exhausted limbs.

She sprang up and scurried after him, moving almost effortlessly at a full run. He quickened his pace as his apprentice fell into step beside him, easily able to keep up now that she was propelled by the awesome power of the Force.

"Where are we going?" she asked.

"The Sith camp," he answered. "We need supplies for the journey."

"Are the other Sith there?" she wondered. "The ones the Jedi were fighting?"

Bane realized he hadn't yet told her what had happened to Kaan and the Brotherhood.

"There are no other Sith. There never will be, except for us. One Master and one apprentice; one to embody the power, the other to crave it."

"What happened to the others?" she wanted to know.

"I killed them," he replied.

Zannah seemed to think about this for a moment before shrugging indifferently. "Then they were weak," she said with simple conviction. "And they deserved to die."

Bane realized he had chosen his apprentice well.

2

THE GREAT WARSHIP of Lord Valenthyne Farfalla—leader of the Jedi Army of Light since the loss of General Hoth—maintained a slow orbit high above Ruusan's surface. Fashioned so that her exterior resembled an ancient sailing barge, the vessel had an archaic elegance, a grandeur that some felt was a sign of vanity unbecoming in a Jedi.

Johun Othone, a young Padawan in the Army of Light, had once shared that opinion. Like many of Hoth's followers, he had initially regarded Lord Valenthyne as nothing but a prancing fool concerned only with brightly colored shimmersilk shirts, the long flowing curls of his golden hair, and the other trappings of garish and gaudy fashion. Yet in battle after battle against the Brotherhood of Darkness, Farfalla and his followers had proved their worth. Slowly, almost grudgingly, Johun and the rest of Hoth's troops had come to admire and even respect the man they once had scoffed at.

Now General Hoth was gone, destroyed along with the Sith in their final confrontation, and in his absence it was Lord Valenthyne who had taken up the banner of leadership. Following Hoth's orders, Farfalla had organized the mass evacuation of Ruusan before the detonation of the thought bomb, saving thousands of Force-sensitive Jedi and Padawans from its devastating effects by loading them onto the ships of his orbiting fleet.

It was mere chance that Johun had ended up here on the *Fairwind*, Valenthyne's flagship. The vessel was large enough to hold a crew of over three hundred comfortably, but crammed into the hold with nearly five hundred other evacuees, the young man was anything but comfortable. They were packed in so tightly, it was difficult to move; Jedi Masters, Jedi Knights, and Padawans were pressed shoulder-to-shoulder.

The other ships were just as full. In addition to the Jedi, the vast majority of the non-Force-sensitive troops who had joined Hoth's cause had also been taken offworld. One of the ships had even been loaded up with several hundred prisoners, the non-Sith followers of Lord Kaan who had quickly surrendered to the Jedi when their dark leader had abandoned them to embark on his final mad plan to destroy the Jedi. There wasn't any real danger for these ordinary soldiers; the thought bomb only affected those most attuned to the Force. But in the haste to evacuate it had been simpler to just take everyone.

Here on Valenthyne's personal galleon, however, Johun recognized nearly every face. He had fought beside them for many months, through ambushes, skirmishes, and full-scale battles. Together they had borne witness to death and bloodshed; tasted glorious triumph and endured crushing defeat. Each of them had seen many foes—and too many friends—die as they had waged a seemingly endless campaign against the forces of the dark side.

Now, as they huddled together in this ship, the war was finally over. Victory was theirs at last. Yet every being aboard wore a grim and somber mask. The extinction of the Sith had come with a terrible price. There was no doubt about what had happened, no hope that any of the Jedi still down on the surface had survived. Orbiting high above Ruusan, they had been safely outside the blast radius of the thought bomb. But through the Force they had heard the agonized screams of their fellow Jedi as their spirits were torn apart and swept up in the swirling vortex of dark side energy. Many of the survivors had wept openly. Most simply endured the suffering in stoic silence, reflecting on the sacrifice others had made.

Johun—like Farfalla and virtually every other member of the Army of Light—had volunteered to stay behind with General Hoth. But the general had refused. Knowing that those who stayed with him faced certain death, he had ordered all but a hundred of his Jedi followers off the world. None of the Padawans had been allowed to remain. Yet even though he was only following orders, Johun couldn't help but feel he had betrayed his general by fleeing the planet.

Across the densely packed hold he could just make out Farfalla, his bright red blouse standing out like a beacon among the sea of mostly brown-clad bodies. He was organizing the rescue parties that would be shuttled back down to Ruusan's surface to deal with the aftermath of the thought bomb, and Johun was determined to be among them.

It was difficult to move through the mass of Jedi, but Johun was small and slight. He was nineteen, but he had yet to fill out, and with his slender build, fair skin, and shoulder-length light blond hair—twisted into a tight braid, as was the custom for a young Jedi still in training—he looked at least two years younger. It could be frustrating to be mistaken for a kid, but now, as he twisted and slithered through the throng, he was grateful for his slim physique.

"Lord Valenthyne," he called as he drew near. He raised his voice further to be heard above the din. "Lord Valenthyne!"

Farfalla turned, trying to pick out the owner of the voice from the wall of bodies and faces, then gave a nod of recognition as the young man finally burst into view. "Padawan Johun."

"I want to join the rescue teams," Johun blurted. "Send me back down."

"I'm afraid I cannot do that," the Jedi Master replied with a sympathetic shake of his head.

"Why not?" Johun demanded. "Do you think I'm too young?"

"That is not—" Farfalla began, but Johun cut him off.

"I'm not a kid! I'm nineteen—older than those two for sure!" he insisted, waving his hand in the direction of the nearest rescue team: a group consisting of a middle-aged man with a short beard, a woman in her twenties, and two boys in their early teens.

"Be aware of your anger," Farfalla cautioned him, his voice stern.

Johun was about to reply, but instead bit his tongue and merely nodded. There was no point in getting upset; that would not convince Lord Valenthyne to let him go along.

"Your age has nothing to do with my decision," the older Jedi explained once he was assured that Johun had brought his emotions under control. "Fully a third of our forces are younger than you."

It was true, Johun realized. The mounting casualties of the Ruusan campaign had forced the Army of Light to accept younger and younger recruits into its ranks. His youth was not the issue; there had to be some other explanation. But instead of asking why he could not go, Johun simply remained silent. Patience would win him more from General Hoth's successor than incessant, thoughtless questions.

"Take a closer look at who I am sending down," Farfalla instructed. "These are brave volunteers, valuable allies in our battle against the Sith. But none of them is attuned to the Force."

Surprised, Johun took a second look at the shore party as they made their final preparations. The woman had dark skin and short black hair, and the Jedi realized he had met her once before. She was a Republic soldier named Irtanna, and she had joined their cause a little over a standard year earlier. It took him a moment longer to place the others, until he noticed the resemblance between the bearded man and the two teenagers. They were natives of Ruusan. The man was a farmer named Bordon who had fled before the advancing armies of Lord Kaan during the latest Sith offensive. The two boys were his sons, though Johun couldn't recall their names.

"We do not know the full extent of the thought bomb's effects," Farfalla continued. "There may be aftershocks that could harm or even kill a Jedi or Padawan. That is why you cannot go."

Johun nodded. It made sense; Valenthyne was just being cautious. But sometimes it was possible to be too cautious. "There are other risks on the surface," he noted. "We don't know that all the Sith are dead. Some of them may have survived."

Farfalla shook his head. "Kaan had some spell, some power, over his followers. They were enthralled to his will. When he led them down into the cave, they all followed him willingly. He had them convinced they could survive the thought bomb if they united their power . . . but he was wrong."

"What about the Sith minions?" Johun pressed, unwilling to let the matter drop. Like the Jedi, the Sith had their share of followers who were not attuned to the Force: soldiers and mercenaries who had allied themselves with the Brotherhood of Darkness. "We didn't capture them all," the young Padawan pointed out. "Some of them fled the battle. They'll still be down there."

"That's what this is for," the woman soldier assured him, patting the blaster on her hip. She gave a fierce smile, her gleaming white teeth contrasting sharply with her dark complexion.

"Irtanna knows how to take care of herself," Farfalla agreed. "She's seen more combat than you and me put together."

"Please, Lord Valenthyne," Johun begged, dropping to one knee. A vain and foolish gesture, but he was desperate. He knew Farfalla was right, but he didn't care. He didn't care about logic or reason or even the dangers of the thought bomb. He just couldn't sit by doing nothing! "Please! He was my Master."

Farfalla reached out with his hand and placed it tenderly on Johun's forehead. "Hoth warned me that his decision to send you away would not rest easily on your shoulders," he said softly. "But your Master was a wise man. He knew what was best for you, as do I. You must trust my judgment in this, even if you do not fully understand it."

Removing his hand from the young man's brow, the new leader of the Army of Light took Johun by the arm and helped him to his feet.

"Your Master made a great sacrifice to save us all," he said. "If we give in to our emotions now, if we allow ourselves to come to needless harm, then we dishonor what he has done. Do you understand?"

Johun nodded, a Padawan acquiescing to the greater wisdom of a Jedi Master.

"Good," Farfalla said, turning away to focus his attention on one of the other rescue teams. "If you want to help, give Irtanna a hand loading up their supplies."

Johun nodded again, though Farfalla didn't notice. He was already gone, whisked away by the responsibilities of his position.

Working in silence, Johun helped load the last few supplies into the shuttle: field kits filled with rations and water capsules; medpacs in case they came across any wounded; electrobinoculars and a sensor pack for scouting and recon; glow rods for when night fell. And, of course, spare power packs for the blasters Irtanna and the others carried in case they encountered any surviving minions from Kaan's army.

"Thank you," Irtanna said once they were done.

Trying to appear casual, Johun took a quick look around. Farfalla was nowhere to be seen.

"Did you want to fly us down, or should I?" he asked her. The words were easy, but as he said them he reached out with the Force to touch her mind. He did it gently, being careful not to cause her any harm as he planted the seed of a suggestion.

Her eyes glazed over momentarily and a look of blank confusion crossed her face. "Uh . . . I'll fly us down, I guess. You can take the copilot's chair."

"You're coming with us?" Bordon, the middle-aged father, asked. From his tone, it was obvious he had doubts.

"Of course," Johun replied amicably. "You all heard him say I should help you load up the supplies, right? Why else would he say that if I wasn't going with you?"

As he had done with Irtanna, he gave another slight push, adding the mind-altering power of the Force to the half-truth. Normally he would have abhorred the idea of manipulating friends or allies in this fashion, but in this case he knew the ragtag rescue team would fare better if he accompanied them.

"Yeah. Right," Bordon agreed after a moment. "Good to have you along."

"Makes sense to have a Jedi with us," Irtanna added. "Just in case."

Persuading someone through the Force was always easier when it was something they wanted to be convinced of, Johun noted. Still, he felt a slight twinge of guilt as he climbed into the small ship-to-surface shuttle.

That's only because you're disobeying Farfalla, he reassured himself. *You're doing the right thing.*

"Everyone strap in," Irtanna ordered, speaking over the pressurized hiss as the air locks sealed.

The shuttle's engines flared to life, lifting them off the docking platform.

"Back home to Ruusan. Or at least what's left of it," Bordon muttered glumly as they drifted through the cargo hold doors and out into the upper reaches of the planet's atmosphere.

3

D ARTH BANE FELT them long before he saw them.

Those ignorant in the ways of the Force saw it as only a weapon or tool: It could strike out against a foe in battle; it could levitate nearby objects and draw them into a waiting palm or fling them across a room. But these were mere wizard's tricks to one who understood its true power and potential.

The Force was a part of all living things, and all living things were a part of the Force. It flowed through every being, every animal and creature, every tree and plant. The fundamental energies of life and death coursed through it, causing ripples in the very fabric of existence.

Even distracted by the agonizing flashes of the blades slicing apart the inside of his skull, Bane was sensitive to these ripples. They gave him an awareness that transcended space and even time, granting him brief glimpses into the always shifting possibilities of the future. That was how, still two kilometers and several minutes away from where Kaan and his army had made their camp, he knew others were already there.

There were eight in total, all human—six men and two women. Mercenaries who had signed on with the Brotherhood for credits and a chance to strike at the hated Republic, they had survived the final battle with Hoth's troops. They had most likely fled the confrontation the instant Kaan had descended into the bowels of the planet's surface to lay his trap for the Jedi, displaying the loyalty of all followers bought and paid for. And now, like blood beetles picking the rotting meat off a bantha's corpse, they had come to scavenge whatever remnants of value they could find from the deserted Sith camp.

"There's someone up ahead," Zannah whispered a minute later. Less attuned to the subtle nuances of the Force than her Master, it had taken her longer to sense the danger. But given her lack of training, the fact that she had noticed anything at all was testament to her abilities.

"Wait here," Bane ordered, holding out a hand to freeze Zannah in her place. Wisely, she obeyed.

He didn't look back as he broke into a full run. The ground rushed by beneath his feet, a blur of motion as he called on the Force to drive him forward. The pain in his head vanished, swept away by the anticipation of battle and the physical exhilaration of his charge.

Within sixty seconds the Sith camp came into view, the outlines of the doomed mercenaries clearly visible as they argued over which objects were worthy of plunder. Six of the looters were gathered in the small clearing at the center of the camp, dividing up the spoils. The other two were on point: sentries stationed near the outskirts of the tents to watch for signs of trouble. Their posts were mere formality, however. The sentries should have been stationed on opposite sides of the camp to guard against assault from either direction. Instead the two men were standing less than twenty meters apart, more interested in having someone to pass the time with than in securing the perimeter.

Bane surveyed the scene with contempt as he bore down on them, the Force allowing him to take in every detail in one quick glance. The men on point were oblivious to his approach, their attention drawn by the angry shouts of disagreement coming from the other six bickering over their ill-gotten gains.

Altering his course slightly so his arrival would be hidden by a large supply tent until the last possible instant, Bane gave a final burst of acceleration and descended upon the camp in a storm of ruin. He drew and ignited his lightsaber in one smooth motion. The keening hum of the crimson blade preceded him, betraying his position a few precious seconds before his arrival. The advance warning gave just enough time for the nearest sentry to draw his blaster, but not nearly enough time to save him from the coming slaughter.

Bane materialized from behind the supply tent and fell on his first victim like a dark wind, slicing him diagonally from shoulder to hip. The man wore battle armor made up of composite plates stitched together on an interwoven padded underlay to allow for flexibility. The vest covering his chest was capable of absorbing several high-powered blaster shots from inside thirty meters, but Bane's blade sliced through the protective layers and carved a fatal five-centimeter gash through the flesh and bone beneath.

As the first victim toppled over, Bane leapt high in the air toward his next foe, instantly closing the ten meters between them and simultaneously evading the hastily fired shot from the second sentry's blaster pistol. As he came down virtually on top of his enemy, he delivered an overhead, two-handed descending chop—a classic move from Djem So, the fifth and most powerfully aggressive form of lightsaber combat. The heavy strike perfectly bisected the unfortunate man's helmet and drove deep into the skull beneath.

The gruesome ends of the first two mercenaries gave the others time to recognize what was happening. They drew their weapons and fired a full volley of blaster bolts at Bane as he turned to face them from across the camp. Smoothly transitioning from the attacking style of Form V to the more defensive style of Form III, Bane deflected the incoming bolts with two-handed parries of his lightsaber, flicking them aside with almost casual disdain.

Twirling his weapon in his right hand, Bane paused to relish the hopelessness and terror emanating from the half a dozen surviving mercenaries as they recognized the inevitable fact of their own deaths. Clustered together in the clearing between the tents, they did the only thing that gave any of them a chance of survival—they broke and ran.

They scattered in all directions: one of the women ran off to the left, two men ran off to the right; the other three turned and fled in a direct line away from the deadly interloper. Still twirling his lightsaber, Bane thrust his empty hand out before him, palm extended as he unleashed the Force in a wave of concussive power at the woman fleeing to his left. The wave cut a swath of devastation through the camp. Tents were uprooted from the ground, their material torn and shredded. Wooden supply crates exploded into kindling, the shattered contents spraying out in a shower of splintered shrapnel.

The Force wave slammed into the woman's back, pulverizing her spine and snapping her neck as it drove her facedown into the dirt and pinned her against the ground. Her corpse twitched once, then went forever still.

Clenching the fingers of his left hand tight against his open palm, Bane wheeled toward the two men on his right and thrust his fist up into the air. A dozen forks of blue lightning arced out from above his head to envelop the screaming soldiers, cooking them alive. Shrieking in agony, they danced and twitched like marionettes on electric strings for several seconds before their smoking husks collapsed on the ground.

In the few seconds it had taken to dispatch the others, the surviving three mercenaries had reached the far side of the Sith camp. A few meters beyond the edge of the tents a line of trees marked the start of the thick Ruusan forests. The concealing branches taunted them with offers of safety, giving even greater haste to their terror-filled flight. Bane watched them retreat with idle disinterest, savoring their fear.

A handful of steps from freedom, one of the men made the fatal mistake of glancing back over his shoulder to see whether their adversary was following. On a whim, Bane sent his light-saber hurtling toward him with a casual toss. The spinning blade sliced through the air in a tight loop, crossing the expanse of the camp in a fraction of a second before swooping back to be caught in the waiting hand of its Master.

Two of the mercenaries vanished into the forest, crashing through the underbrush. The third—the one who had paused to look back—stood still as stone. A second later his head toppled forward from his shoulders to bounce and roll across the ground, severed from the cauterized stump of his neck by the crimson blade of Bane's thrown lightsaber. As if the fallen head were a signal, the rigid limbs of the decapitated corpse went suddenly limp, and it fell over sideways.

Bane extinguished his lightsaber, the blade vanishing with a sharp hiss. For a brief instant he reveled in his victory, drinking in the last lingering remnants of his victims' emotions, drawing power from their fear and suffering. And then the moment was gone, fleeing like those who had escaped his wrath. He could have pursued them, but as much as he yearned to taste their panic, he understood the purpose of letting them live.

"You let them get away."

He spun around in surprise to see Zannah standing just inside the perimeter of the camp. Engrossed in the slaughter, he hadn't sensed her approach. Either that, or his young apprentice had taken pains to shield her presence from him.

Don't underestimate her, Bane reminded himself. *She has the power to one day surpass you.*

"You let them get away," Zannah repeated. She didn't sound angry, or disappointed, or even pleased. She just seemed puzzled.

"I told you to wait for me," Bane admonished her. "Why did you disobey?"

She didn't answer right away, weighing her words carefully until she could find an answer that would appease her Master. "I wanted to see the true power of the dark side," she admitted finally. "Can you teach me to . . . ?" She trailed off, unable to find the words to describe what she had just witnessed. Instead she simply waved her hand, indicating the totality of the carnage he had unleashed.

"You will learn," Bane assured her, attaching the hooked handle of his lightsaber back onto his belt.

She didn't smile, but there was an eager expression in her gaze, a hunger her Master knew well. He'd seen the same raw ambition in the eyes of Githany, his former lover and one of Kaan's doomed followers. He knew that if Zannah did not learn to temper and control her ambition, it would lead her down a path of destruction, just as it had with Githany.

"Prowess in combat is the simplest display of the dark side's power," her Master cautioned her. "Brutal and quick, it serves a purpose. Yet it is often less effective than subtlety and cunning. Ultimately letting those mercenaries live may prove more useful than killing them."

"But they were weak," his apprentice protested, throwing his own teachings back at him. "They deserved to die!"

"Few beings in the galaxy ever get what they truly deserve," he noted, choosing his words with care. The dark side was not easily understood; even he was still learning to work his way through its complexities and contradictions. He had to be careful not to overwhelm his young apprentice, yet it was important that she grasp the essence of what he had done here. "Our mission is not to bring death to all those unfit to live. We answer to a greater calling. All I have done on Ruusan, and all that we will do from this day forward, must serve our true purpose: the preservation of our Order and the survival of the Sith."

After a moment's consideration, Zannah shook her head. "I'm sorry, Master," she admitted, "I still don't get why you didn't just kill them."

"As servants of the dark side we revel in the vanquishing of our enemies. We draw power from their suffering, but we must balance this against greater gains. We must recognize that killing for sadistic pleasure—killing without reason, need, or purpose—is the act of a fool."

A frown of confusion crossed the young girl's face. "What purpose is there in letting scum like that live?"

"The Jedi believe the Order of the Sith died here on Ruusan," he explained patiently. "There are followers of the dark side on many other worlds: the Marauders of Honoghr and Gamorr, the Shadow Assassins of Ryloth and Umbara. But those with the greatest power—all those individuals with the potential to become true Sith Masters—had gathered together in Kaan's Brotherhood. As one they followed him into this war, and as one they followed him into death.

"But there will be those who doubt the totality of the Sith extinction. There will always be whispers that the Sith survive, hints and rumors that somewhere in the galaxy a Dark Lord lives. And if the Jedi ever find proof of our existence, they will be relentless in hunting us down."

He paused to let the implications of his last statement sink in before continuing. "We cannot live in isolation, cut off from the rest of the galaxy while cowering in fear. We must work to grow our power; we will need to interact with individuals of many species across many worlds. It is inevitable that some among them will recognize us for what we are, no matter our disguise. Eventually word of our existence will reach the ears of the Jedi."

Zannah was studying him closely, absorbing every word, seeking enlightenment in the murky logic of the dark side.

"Since we cannot hide the fact of our survival," Bane continued, "we must obscure it with half-truths. We must encourage the rumors, spreading them so thick they blind our enemies until they cannot separate myth from reality."

A glimmer of understanding illuminated Zannah's face. "A rumor is only as reliable as its source!" she exclaimed.

Bane nodded in satisfaction. "The survivors will spread the tale, but who will believe the likes of them? Everyone will know they are self-serving mercenaries who fled the final battle to save themselves, then came to loot the camp of their former allies. They will be spit upon as traitors and thieves. Nobody who hears their story will believe it, and the truth will be dismissed as a worthless rumor.

"And if there are any other witnesses to our presence on Ruusan," Bane added, spinning out the final thread of the convoluted tapestry of deception, "their accounts are now less likely to be believed. They will be tainted by their similarity to the so-called lies spewing from the mouths of cowardly looters."

"No use or purpose in their deaths," Zannah muttered, half to herself. She didn't say anything else, seemingly lost in thought as she mulled over all that she had been told.

Bane turned his attention away from his apprentice and focused on the items the looters had gathered in the center of the camp. He was the last of the Sith. If there was anything here of value, then by rights it should belong to him.

Most of what they had collected held no interest for Bane. Some of Kaan's Brotherhood had hoarded items of immense value, believing that the greed and envy they inspired in others could feed the power of the dark side. The mercenaries had grabbed these trinkets—ornate rings and necklaces fashioned from precious metals and set with glittering stones; ceremonial daggers and knives, their hilts inlaid with gleaming gems; intricately carved masks and small statues of remarkable skill shaped from rare and delicate materials—and thrown them haphazardly in a pile.

Surveying the invaluable treasures that were worthless to

his purpose, Bane felt another jolt of pain at the back of his head. In the same instant he saw a figure flicker at the corner of his right eye, then vanish from his field of vision.

He snapped his head around in the direction of the movement, but saw nothing. It hadn't been Zannah; this figure was much taller. He reached out with the Force, but felt only himself and his apprentice within the perimeter of the camp.

"What's the matter?" she asked, noting his sudden unease. "Is someone coming?"

"It's nothing," Bane replied. *Was it nothing?* he wondered. *Or is this another side effect of the thought bomb?*

Zannah made her way over to where he was standing, her eye drawn by the sun reflecting off the jewelry dumped on the ground. "What's this?" she asked, stooping to dig out something almost completely buried at the bottom of the pile.

She emerged with a thin, leather-bound manuscript. She turned it over curiously, examining it from all angles until Bane extended his hand. In response, she came dutifully forward and presented him with her find.

He recognized the style of the manuscript. There had been several similar volumes in the library at the Brotherhood's Academy on Korriban, though Bane had never seen this particular work before. The volume was thin, a few dozen pages at most, and the cover inscribed with arcane words traced in blood-red ink. Bane recognized the language. He had become familiar with the tongue of the ancient Sith during his studies at the Academy, turning to the wisdom of Masters long dead rather than trusting the fools who sought to instruct him in the tarnished "New Sith" philosophy of the Brotherhood.

He opened the volume and found that the same blood-red ink had been used to fill the pages with delicate script and elaborate illustrations. As with the words on the cover, the language inside was that of the ancient Sith. However, the margins of each page were filled with handwritten notes in Galactic Basic. He recognized the handwriting as that of Qordis, the former head of the Academy on Korriban and one of the many so-called Sith Lords serving under Kaan. Unlike the rest of the Brotherhood of Darkness, however, Qordis hadn't perished in the thought bomb's blast. He'd actually died several hours earlier when Bane had used the Force to crush the life out of his former teacher.

Why did Qordis bring this manuscript with him to Korriban? Bane wondered. Qordis had always been more concerned with hoarding wealth than studying the ancient texts. He wore only the finest silks and most expensive jewelry; each of the long, cruel fingers on both hands had been adorned with rings of incredible value. Even his tent on Korriban had been decorated with rare woven tapestries and ornate rugs. If he had carried this manuscript with him all the way from the Academy, Bane realized, it must contain knowledge of tremendous value

"What's it say?" Zannah asked, but Bane paid her no attention.

He flipped quickly through the manuscript, skimming both the original text and Qordis's notes. It seemed to be a compilation of the history and teachings of Freedon Nadd, a great Sith Master who had lived over three thousand standard years ago. Bane had read previous accounts of Nadd, but this one had something the other versions lacked: the location of his final resting place!

For many centuries the tomb of Freedon Nadd had been lost, hidden by the Jedi so that the followers of the dark side could not seek to gain guidance or power from the Sith artifacts sealed inside. But on the last page of the manuscript Qordis had made one final note, underlined for emphasis: *Seek the tomb on Dxun.*

How Qordis had come by this information signified little to Bane; all that mattered was that he now knew the location, too. The war on Ruusan had prevented Qordis from attempting to find Nadd's tomb on Dxun. Now that the war was over, there was nothing to keep Bane from making the journey and claiming Nadd's legacy as his own. But first he had to get off Ruusan.

The all-too-familiar jolt of pain shot through his skull, and once again he caught the flicker of a figure from the corner of his eye. This time the image seemed to sustain itself for nearly a full second. Tall, broad-shouldered, and clad in the robes of the Sith, it was a figure Bane recognized—Lord Kaan! And then, as before, it vanished.

Is this real? Was it possible that the leader of the Brotherhood of Darkness had, in some form, survived the thought bomb? Was it possible his spirit now haunted the world of his death?

He closed the volume and looked down at Zannah. She gave no indication that she had seen or sensed anything. *Just a trick of the mind,* Bane thought. It was the only explanation that made sense. Zannah would have felt the manifestation of a dark side spirit so close by, yet she had been oblivious.

The realization brought him an odd mix of relief and concern. When he had seen Kaan looming beside him, Bane had thought for an instant—just an instant—that he had failed in his quest to destroy the Brotherhood. But the affirmation of his mission's success was tempered by the awareness that the thought bomb had done even more damage than he'd first suspected. Hopefully the delusions and agonizing headaches were only temporary.

Zannah was still staring up at him, barely able to contain the flood of questions she had about what he had discovered inside the pages of the treasure she had found. Her expression of expectant curiosity turned to disappointment when he slid the manuscript into the folds of his clothes without offering any explanation. In time Bane would share all his knowledge, present and future, with her. But until he had a chance to explore Nadd's tomb himself, he was reluctant to tell anyone—even his apprentice—of its existence.

"Are you ready to leave this world?" he asked.

"I'm sick of this place," she answered, a hint of bitterness in her voice. "Things have gone bad ever since I got here."

"Your cousins," Bane asked, remembering a remark she had made earlier about the two boys with whom she had first arrived. "Do you miss them?"

"What's the point?" she replied with a shrug. "Tomcat and Bug are dead. Why waste time thinking about them?"

Her words were indifferent, but Bane recognized her callousness as a defense mechanism. Beneath the surface he could feel her passions burning: She was angry and resentful over their deaths; she blamed the Jedi for what happened, and she would never forgive them. Her rage would always be a part of her, simmering below the surface. It would serve her well in the years to come.

"Come with me," Bane said, reaching a decision.

He led her over to an abandoned swoop bike near one of the tents. He climbed aboard, and she clambered up onto the seat behind him. Her slim arms wrapped tightly around his waist as the swoop's engine roared to life and it lifted up into the air.

"Why are we taking the swoop?" she asked, shouting into his ear to be heard above the thrusters.

"We will travel faster this way. Time grows short," Bane called back over his shoulder. "Soon the Jedi will return to claim their dead and seek out the survivors of Kaan's army. But there is still one last lesson you must learn before we go."

He didn't say any more; some things could not be explained, but had to be witnessed to be understood. Zannah needed to see the remains of the thought bomb. She needed to see the true scope of Kaan's madness. She needed to grasp the finality of what Bane had accomplished here. And he needed to assure himself that the figure he had seen was nothing more than an aftereffect of his exposure to the thought bomb. He wanted to see with his own eyes undeniable proof that Kaan was truly destroyed.

4

DAROVIT LAY HUDDLED on the cold cavern floor, bathed in the eerie light emanating from the egg-shaped silver orb hovering in the center of the underground chamber. He hadn't moved for nearly two hours, paralyzed with the wonder and horror of it all. It was as if time had no meaning here at the epicenter of the thought bomb; as if Darovit himself were now suspended between life and death, trapped like the tormented spirits of Kaan's followers and the Jedi who had dared to face them.

Eventually, however, his shock began to fade. Slowly sanity crept back in, dragging the reality of the physical world with it. The air in the cave was damp and chilled; his body was shivering almost uncontrollably. His nose was running, and he reached up to wipe it away with a shaking hand, his fingers clumsy with the numbing cold.

"Come on, Tomcat," he said to himself. "Time to get moving. Up and at 'em."

With a great effort he managed to get to his feet, then fell back down with a cry as his calves and thighs cramped beneath him. The pain helped break the last lingering vestiges of the spell he was under, snapping him back to the present and focusing his mind on the here and now.

Frantically he massaged each of his legs, trying to restore the blood flow. He was anxious to leave this place now, desperate to get away from the evil presence of the silently pulsing bomb. Glancing up at it made his skin crawl, yet as repulsive as it was, he found it strangely compelling.

"Don't look at it," he berated himself in a sharp whisper, redoubling his efforts to ease the pain and tightness in his lower limbs. After another minute he dared to stand up again. Pins and needles shot through the soles of his feet, and his knees buckled briefly, but he stayed standing.

He looked from side to side, scanning the cavern by the light of the orb. There were at least half a dozen entrances leading out from the chamber, and Darovit swore when he realized he had no idea which would lead him back up to the surface.

"You can't stay here," he muttered.

Picking a tunnel at random, he made his way with slow, uneasy steps out of the cavern. The darkness quickly enveloped him once he entered the passage, until he drew out the lightsaber the Sith had given him. Using the faint glow of its ruby blade, he was able to pick his way along the uneven terrain.

It didn't take him long to realize he'd made the wrong choice. He remembered the sharp incline he had tumbled down on his arrival, but the floor here was relatively flat. It would have been a simple matter to head back and take one of the other exits. But the thought of returning to the main chamber—and the orb of trapped spirits—prevented him from turning around.

"This tunnel's gotta come out somewhere," he told himself. "Just follow it to the surface."

The plan sounded simple, but it became more complicated

when he reached a fork in the passage. He hesitated for several moments, studying the branch heading off to his left and then the one heading off to his right. Neither offered any clue as to which—if either—would lead him to freedom. With a resigned sigh and a shake of the head, he chose the one on the left.

Forty minutes and three more branches later he was regretting his decision. He couldn't go back to the cavern now even if he'd wanted to; he had become hopelessly turned around in the subterranean labyrinth. His stomach grumbled, and the realization that he might never find his way out began to creep into the corners of his mind.

He pushed on, his pace increasing with his rising panic. He was running now, his eyes darting from side to side, hoping that the dim illumination of the lightsaber's blade would reveal something—anything—that might show him the way. He darted down another side tunnel, stumbling along in his haste until he tripped and fell.

As he threw his hands forward to break his fall, the lightsaber flew from his grasp. It scored a gash along the wall, then bounced away from him across the uneven floor, extinguishing itself and casting all into total darkness.

Darovit had hit the ground hard. He lay facedown in the utter blackness of the tunnel, surrendering to the hopeless despair that crashed in on him. There was no point in going on; he would never find his way out. Better to just die here, forgotten and alone.

He rolled over onto his back, blind eyes staring up at the ceiling. And then he heard a sound. It was faint but unmistakable. A voice coming from a great distance, cutting through the oppressive silence.

Now you're hearing things, Tomcat, he thought. But a second later he heard it again, echoing through the tunnel. Someone else was down here!

He didn't know if it was a Jedi come to witness the fate of his fallen comrades, a minion of the Sith who had fled the final battle, or someone allied with a completely different group. He had no idea if whoever it was would welcome him, take him prisoner, or kill him on sight. But he didn't care. Even the fear of going back to the chamber and the unnatural, unholy silver orb didn't hold him back this time. Anything was better than dying of exposure or starvation in these dark tunnels beneath the planet's surface.

Crawling forward through the gloom, he felt around with his hands until his fingers closed around the hilt of the lightsaber. He thrust it triumphantly up in the air as it ignited, allowing him to see once more.

He had no way of knowing how far away the owner of the voice was. The acoustics of the tunnel were strange and unfamiliar. Sounds and echoes were unnaturally distorted as they bounced across the irregular stone walls of the underground maze. But he was certain the voice had come from somewhere up ahead, in the direction he had been going.

With the glowing blade to guide him, he moved with an eager confidence. Every minute or so he would catch another snatch of conversation coming to him from somewhere up ahead. He could tell there were two speakers now, each with a distinct voice: one a deep bass, the other a much higher pitch. Each time he heard the voices, they were slightly louder, and he knew he was headed in the right direction.

He noticed that the darkness of the tunnel was fading; he no longer needed his lightsaber to see his surroundings. But it wasn't the yellow light of the sun streaming in as he neared the surface; it was a cold silver glow. With a start he realized he had somehow circled back and was once more approaching the chamber of the thought bomb. Whoever the voices belonged to—friend or foe—he'd find them there.

The chamber was close, so close he could make out the words the next time the voices spoke.

"The Sith are only two now—one Master and one apprentice," the deeper one said. "There will be no others."

"What happens if I fail?" the other replied.

Sounds like a woman, Darovit thought, too focused on following the voices to pay much attention to the actual words. *No, not a woman,* he corrected himself a second later. *A girl.*

"Will you destroy me, too?" the girl asked.

With a shock, Darovit realized that he knew the voice! He didn't know how it was possible, but there was no doubt in his mind who this was.

"Rain!" he shouted, breaking into a run to meet the cousin he had thought was dead. "Rain, you're alive!"

THE TRIP TO the cave was quick and uneventful. Bane had noticed a few shell-shocked survivors of the final battle of Ruusan staring at him and Zannah as they roared past on their swoop, but he paid them little heed. He doubted any of them would recognize him for what he truly was. And even if they did, their tales of a surviving Sith Lord racing past them with a young girl in tow would seem as ludicrous and unreliable as the accounts of the mercenaries he had let escape back at Kaan's camp.

He brought the swoop to a stop outside the dark and forbidding tunnel that would lead them down to the chamber of the thought bomb. Small pebbles crunched loudly beneath the hard soles of his heavy black boots as he dismounted. Zannah was too small to simply step off the vehicle, but she leapt down from her seat without any sign of fear or hesitation, landing nimbly on the ground beside him.

Neither of them spoke as they made the descent, their way lit by one of the glow rods Bane had found in the supplies back at the Sith camp. The air grew colder and Zannah shivered beside him, but she didn't complain. They moved quickly down the rough-hewn passage; even so it took nearly twenty minutes for them to reach their destination due to the length of the tunnel. And for the first time Darth Bane actually saw what his manipulations of Kaan and his followers had wrought.

The pale, glowing orb floating in the center of the chamber was nearly four meters tall. It pulsed with raw power; it made the flesh on Bane's neck crawl and the hair on his arms stand on end. Dark veins of shadow swirled on the shimmering metallic surface in slow, hypnotic rhythms. There was something grotesquely compelling about it, something fascinating yet repulsive at the same time.

Beside him Zannah gasped, drawing a sharp breath in wonder then releasing it in a slow hiss of fear. He glanced down at her, but she didn't return his gaze—her wide eyes were transfixed by the remnants of the thought bomb. Turning his attention back to the orb, Bane stepped forward into the chamber. Zannah took a single step to follow him, then held back.

Approaching the globe, he reached out with his bare hand and pressed it firmly against the surface. It seared his palm with cold fire, but he was oblivious to the pain, enthralled by the object's mesmerizing call. Beneath his touch the dark swirling shadows within coalesced into a single mass. The thoughts of those trapped inside rushed up to meet him: faint whispers in the dark recesses of his mind, the words unintelligible but full of hate and despair.

Instinctively Bane's consciousness recoiled. He resisted, fighting the urge to pull his hand back. Instead he thrust his awareness forward, penetrating the surface of the orb to plunge into the unfathomable depths of its black heart. The hateful whispers erupted into shrieks of torment. But these were not the screams of sentient beings: they were bestial howls of primal, mindless fury. The identities of those the thought bomb had consumed—Lord Kaan, General Hoth, all their Sith and Jedi followers—had been destroyed, ripped apart by the thought bomb's explosion. Only torn bits remained, broken pieces of what once had been spirits, no longer capable of conscious thought, wailing in the shared suffering of their eternal madness.

They swarmed over Bane's consciousness, cleaving to his still-whole identity like parasites attaching themselves to a fresh host. The keening spirits enveloped him, clutching and clawing at his sanity as they tried to drag him down with them into their dark abyss.

Bane tore free with contemptuous ease, shredding the already frail and tattered spirits as he cast them aside, and let his mind drift back to the surface. An instant later he was free, leaving behind the prison from which the others would never escape.

He let his hand drop from the oblong sphere as he took a step back, satisfied at what he had learned. There were no ghosts haunting him; Kaan was no more. Not in any real sense. The figure he had seen at the Sith camp had been nothing but a delusion conjured up by his own wounded psyche.

"Are they trapped in there?" Zannah asked. She was staring at Bane with an expression of both awe and terror.

"Trapped. Dead. It makes no difference," he answered with a shrug. "Kaan and the Brotherhood are gone. They got what they deserved."

"Were they weak?"

Bane didn't answer right away. Kaan had been many things—ambitious, charismatic, stubborn, and in the end a fool—but he had never been weak.

"Kaan was a traitor," he said at last. "He led the Brotherhood away from the teachings of the ancient Sith. He turned his back on the very essence of the dark side."

Zannah didn't reply, but she looked up at him expectantly. The role of mentor was a new one for Bane; he was a man of action, not words. He wasn't used to taking the time to share his wisdom with another desperate to learn it. But he was smart enough to understand that the lessons would have far more meaning if his apprentice could figure out some of the answers for herself.

"Why did you choose to become my apprentice?" he asked,

challenging her. "Why did you choose the way of the dark side?"

"Power," she replied quickly.

"Power is only a means to an end," Bane admonished her. "It is not an end in itself. What do you need power for?"

The girl furrowed her brow. Her Master already recognized this expression as a sign she was struggling to come up with an answer.

"Through power I gain victory," she said when she finally spoke, reciting the final lines of the Sith Code she had learned only a few hours earlier. From her tone it was clear she was trying to work through her limited understanding of the dark side to arrive at the answer Bane wanted.

"Through victory my chains are broken . . . ," she continued, slowly searching for an answer just beyond her reach. A second later she exclaimed, "Freedom! The dark side sets us free!"

Bane nodded his approval. "The Jedi shackle themselves in chains of obedience: obedience to the Jedi Council; obedience to their Masters; obedience to the Republic. Those who follow the light side even believe they must submit themselves to the Force. They are merely instruments of its will, slaves to a greater good.

"Those who follow the dark side see the truth of their enslavement. We recognize the chains that bind us and hold us back. We believe in the power of the individual to break these chains. That is the path to greatness. Only if we are free can we reach our full potential.

"The belief that an individual must not bow down before anyone or anything is the dark side's greatest strength," Bane continued. "But it is also our ultimate weakness. The struggle to rise above those around you is often violent, and in the past the Sith were constantly at one another's throats."

"Isn't that a good thing?" Zannah interjected. "The strong will survive and the weak will die."

"Weak does not mean stupid," Bane countered. "There were those with less power, but more cunning. Several apprentices would band together to take down a powerful Master, hoping to elevate their own position among the Sith. Then they would turn on one another, making and breaking alliances until only one remained—a new Master, but one weaker than the original. This survivor would then be taken down in turn by another band of lesser Sith, further weakening our Order.

"Kaan recognized this. But his solution was far worse than the problem. Kaan declared all the followers of the dark side— all the members of the Sith Order—as equals in the Brotherhood of Darkness. In doing so, he betrayed us all."

"Betrayed you?"

"Equality is a lie," Bane told her. "A myth to appease the masses. Simply look around and you will see the lie for what it is! There are those with power, those with the strength and will to lead. And there are those meant to follow—those incapable of anything but servitude and a meager, worthless existence.

"Equality is a perversion of the natural order!" he continued, his voice rising as he shared the fundamental truth that lay at the core of his beliefs. "It binds the strong to the weak. They become anchors that drag the exceptional down to mediocrity. Individuals destined and deserving of greatness have it denied them. They suffer for the sake of keeping them even with their inferiors.

"Equality is a chain, like obedience. Like fear or uncertainty or self-doubt. The dark side will break these chains. But Kaan could not see this. He did not grasp the true power of the dark side. The Brotherhood of Darkness was nothing but a twisted reflection of the Jedi Order, a dark parody of the very thing we stood against. Under Kaan the Sith had become an abomination."

"And that's why you killed him," Zannah said, thinking the lesson had come to an end.

"That is why I manipulated Kaan into killing himself," Bane corrected. "Remember: power alone is not enough. Patience. Cunning. Secrecy. These are the tools we will use to bring down the Jedi. The Sith are only two now—one Master and one apprentice. There will be no others."

Zannah nodded, though something still seemed to be troubling her. "What happens if I fail?" she asked, glancing toward the thought bomb. "Will you destroy me, too?"

Bane's answer was cut off by a shout coming from one of the nearby passages.

"Rain! Rain, you're alive!"

A boy sprinted out of the shadows, no more than a year or two older than Zannah. He had dark hair and wore the black armor of the Sith. A lightsaber hilt was clutched tightly in his right hand. Despite these warrior's trappings, it was immediately obvious to Bane that this child posed no threat. The Force was barely alive in him. The power that burned so brightly inside Zannah was nothing but a dying ember of gray ash in this one.

"Tomcat!" Zannah shouted, her face lighting up with joy. She took a step forward, extending her arms as if she wanted to hug him. Then, as if suddenly remembering the presence of her Sith Master, she pulled up short and clutched her hands to her chest.

Oblivious, the boy kept coming. He didn't register her sudden change in mood; he hadn't even noticed the two-meter-tall figure looming in the shadows behind her. There was something pathetic about him, a desperate loneliness in his voice and his eyes that turned Bane's stomach.

"I'm so glad, Rain," the boy gasped as he skidded to a stop in front of Zannah, reaching forward to hug her. "So glad you're—"

She stepped back and shook her head, causing his words to catch in his throat. The happiness in his face vanished, replaced by a look of hurt bewilderment.

"I . . . I am not Rain," Bane's apprentice said, rejecting her childhood nickname and all it symbolized. "I am Zannah."

"Zannah?" A look of confusion crept across the boy's face. "Your real name? But why?"

Fumbling for answers, he finally tore his gaze away from the young girl and noticed Bane standing motionless in the background. His bewilderment became comprehension, and quickly turned into righteous rage.

"You!" he shouted, pointing an accusing finger at Bane. Then, as if suddenly remembering the weapon in his hand, he ignited his lightsaber. "You stay away from her!" he screamed. "I will fight you!"

The boy knew he was overmatched. He knew he had no chance to win a battle against a Dark Lord of the Sith. Yet he chose to stay and fight anyway—the actions of a complete and utter fool.

Darth Bane regarded his doomed adversary with contemptuous indifference. This boy was nothing to him—an inconsequential speck he would wipe away. If the boy wanted the vain and empty glory of a so-called courageous death, Bane would grant it.

He dropped his hand casually to his lightsaber, but before he could ignite his weapon, Zannah reacted. Just as she had done when she had broken the necks of the unfortunate Jedi who had accidentally killed her friend, the girl unleashed a wave of unstoppable dark side energy. She acted on pure instinct, drawing on her natural affinity for the Force with no forethought, preparation, or even training.

It happened so quickly Bane never even had a chance to put up his guard . . . but the attack wasn't directed at him. The right hand of the boy she had called Tomcat—her cousin and childhood friend—disintegrated. With a mere thought she obliterated everything below his wrist: flesh, bone and tendon vanished in a bloody explosion, leaving only a ragged stump.

With nothing left to grip it, the hilt of his lightsaber clattered to the floor, the blade extinguished. Howling in pain, the boy fell to his knees, clutching his mutilated limb to his chest. Small spurts of blood pumped out of the wound and splattered onto the cavern floor.

The Master glared down at his apprentice. "Why?" he demanded.

"Because there would be no use or purpose in his death," she answered, echoing his own explanation for letting two of the mercenaries survive.

Bane was smart enough to recognize what was happening. Zannah was trying to save her cousin's life. He knew that the emotions driving her—sentimentality, mercy, compassion— were weaknesses from which she must learn to free herself. But he didn't expect his apprentice to learn the ways of the dark side in a single day.

He looked down at the injured boy crumpled on the ground. The blood spurting from his stump had slowed; the blast that had taken his hand had also partially cauterized the wound. The flow was further stanched by dust and grime from the cavern floor as he rolled back and forth at Zannah's feet. Tears poured from his eyes and mucus ran from his nose to clog his mouth and throat, turning his cries into thick, blubbery whimpers. She regarded him with a cold and calculating eye, feigning disinterest.

The risks from letting this wretched creature live were small, Bane decided. Like the mercenaries, no one would believe his tales of surviving an encounter with a Sith Master. It was obvious that Zannah wanted the boy alive. But she hadn't begged or bargained for his life. Instead she had taken charge of the situation, unleashing the dark side and then defending her actions with Bane's own teachings. She had shown not only her power, but also her intelligence and cunning. It was important to reward such behavior—to encourage her when she displayed the gifts and talents that would allow her to one day take the mantle of Dark Lord from her Master's shoulders. More important than ending the life of one miserable, insignificant boy.

"Leave him," Bane said, turning on his heel. "He is nothing to us."

Zannah quickly fell into step beside him as they made their way from the chamber and began the long, slow climb through the tunnels back to Ruusan's surface. Bane noted with satisfaction that even though Tomcat's pitiful sobs echoed after them, his apprentice never once glanced back.

5

"PREPARE FOR REENTRY TURBULENCE," Irtanna warned them from the pilot's seat of their shuttle. With a crew of only five, she had no need to use the shipboard intercom. She simply spoke loud enough for everyone aboard to hear.

Although the *Envoy*-class shuttle carried only a handful of passengers, she was capable of comfortably transporting four times that many. The ship had been absorbed into the Jedi fleet sometime during the last few weeks of the Ruusan campaign, donated by an anonymous benefactor from Coruscant who had been charmed by Farfalla's urgent plea for resources to support the war effort. Christened the *Star-Wake*, she was a product of Tallaan Shipyards, a basic transport vessel capable of both suborbital flight and interstellar travel, thanks to her Class Twelve hyperdrive.

The fact that she had been pressed into service was proof of just how desperate the Army of Light had become. *Envoy*-class shuttles were known for being practical and affordable, making them a favorite choice of independent merchants and wealthy recreational travelers. Their most distinguishing feature was an easy-to-use navigation and autopilot system, allowing users to plot and engage hyperdrive routes to hundreds of known worlds across the Republic with a simple push of a button. Unfortunately they lacked heavy shielding or any significant armament, and were neither particularly fast nor maneuverable.

Johun would have preferred something in a more military vein; he doubted the autonav would be any use should a Sith Buzzard suddenly appear on the horizon. Logically, he knew this was highly unlikely. Every Buzzard in Kaan's fleet had been accounted for: either shot down, captured by the Army of Light, or seen fleeing the system at the tail end of the final battle. But scores of danger-filled flights through enemy-controlled airspace in the months before their ultimate victory had trained his mind to be on constant alert when approaching the planet's surface. From the way Irtanna was white-knuckling the shuttle's steering column, he knew he wasn't alone in his irrational fears.

There was the faintest bump as they passed from the cold vacuum of space into the upper layers of Ruusan's atmosphere and began their descent. Irtanna worked the controls with a confident hand, making subtle adjustments to their course as Johun studied the scanners skimming the ground below them, looking for signs of life. Four other craft were visible on the ship's monitors. Like the *Star-Wake,* each was crewed by a four- to six-person rescue team sent by Farfalla to help clean up the aftermath of the war.

"We've got movement on the ground," Johun called out as unidentified blips popped up on his screen. "Transmitting coordinates."

"Give me details," Irtanna ordered, banking the shuttle around in a wide arc that brought them in line with the people on the ground.

"Two walkers on foot," Johun informed her. "Can't tell if they're friendly from up here."

"Taking us down," Irtanna replied.

Locating and helping injured survivors was the team's first priority; providing reconnaissance reports to Fleet Command came second, and accepting the willing surrender of enemy troops was a distant third.

The shuttle nose dipped, and the acceleration pushed Johun back into his seat as they dived in to get a closer look at the figures. Irtanna took them in low and fast, a military maneuver that pushed the civilian vessel to her limits.

"I've got a visual," Johun reported as a pair of tiny, indistinct shapes on the ground became visible through the shuttle's cockpit viewpoint.

Bordon lifted himself up out of his seat and leaned forward over the back of Johun's chair to get a view as the shuttle plunged toward the rapidly growing figures. As it drew closer the details came into focus: a man and a woman, each wearing light armor and running hard.

The roar of the rapidly descending shuttle's engines caused the two on the ground to stop running and turn back to look up at them. An instant later they threw themselves face-first to the dirt as the shuttle swooped in less than ten meters from the ground and buzzed them.

Cursing under her breath as she struggled with the clumsy controls, Irtanna veered around sharply and brought them in to land less than fifty meters away from their quarry. Through the window Johun saw the pair slowly climb back to their feet as the pilot cut the engines. The woman said something to the man, who nodded in agreement. Then they raised their hands and began marching slowly toward the vessel.

They were dressed like members of Kaan's Brotherhood. But Johun didn't feel the presence of the dark side about them.

"Minions of the Sith," he said. "Mercenaries, probably."

"Could be a trap," Bordon warned. "Kriffing mercenaries have no honor."

"I don't think so," Johun replied. If there was any danger here, he would have felt some kind of disturbance in the Force. "I think they just want to surrender."

"Slag-sucking scum," Bordon spat. "Fire the engines up and run them over!"

"No!" Johun exclaimed when he saw Irtanna reaching for the ignition switch. "We need to question them," he reminded her. "See what they know."

"Then what?" Bordon demanded darkly.

"Then we take them to Farfalla and lock them up with the rest of the prisoners."

Bordon slammed his hand against the cockpit wall. "These schutta-spawn came to my world—my home—to kill my people for profit!"

"They'd cut our throats without a second thought if they had the upper hand," Irtanna agreed.

"We're not like them," Johun said. "We don't kill prisoners."

"My wife died fighting munk-whelps like these!" Bordon shouted. "Now you want to show them mercy?"

"Hate leads to the dark side," Johun replied, reciting the wisdom of the Jedi. But the words lacked power coming from the mouth of a nineteen-year-old Padawan, and even as he said them he knew how empty they sounded.

Bordon threw his hands up in frustration, then let himself fall back angrily into his seat. "Is that why you're here?" he grumbled in disgust. "To keep us in line? To make sure we don't stray from your precious light-side ways? Is that why Farfalla sent you along?"

He didn't send me. I came on my own, Johun thought. He turned in his seat to look back at Bordon, who stared intently at the floor, refusing to meet his gaze. His two sons, however, glared at the young Jedi with venom in their eyes. He understood their anger. The Sith had brought war to Ruusan, a war that had taken everything they knew and cared about: their homes, their livelihoods . . . and, of course, their mother.

What Bordon and his sons didn't see was that these nameless soldiers couldn't be held responsible for all the horrors and tragedies that had brought their world crashing down.

Whatever their crimes, these two didn't deserve to be made accountable for the actions of Kaan and his Brotherhood. It was the Sith Masters, the followers of the dark side, who were truly to blame. Yet as he looked into the boys' hate-filled stares, he knew there was no hope of making them understand. Not while all that they had suffered was still fresh in their minds.

Johun had come to Ruusan to hunt down any members of the Brotherhood who might have survived the thought bomb. He intended to continue the work of General Hoth—his Master and mentor—and eliminate the Lords of the Sith, ending the threat of the dark side forever. Now, however, he recognized a greater mission: He had to save Bordon and his sons from themselves.

These were honest, decent people. But driven by hate and anger, they would butcher their helpless foes in cold blood if he didn't stop them. Johun knew that once their anger faded, the memory of their bloody vengeance would haunt them. Guilt and self-loathing would eat away at Bordon and his boys until it eventually destroyed them. Johun wasn't about to let that happen.

Turning his attention back to Irtanna, he saw hate in her eyes as well. However, hers was a cold, calculated emotion—a professional soldier regarding an enemy. He recognized she wouldn't kill prisoners on her own, but she also wouldn't do anything to stop the others. And he knew what he had to do.

"This isn't why Farfalla sent you," he reminded the pilot in a low voice. "You're supposed to be helping the survivors."

Irtanna eyed him suspiciously but didn't say anything. Johun was reluctant to use the Force to bend her will to his own again. Subconsciously she might be more aware of his interference a second time and more likely to resist. Besides, it was important that she truly believe in what he was telling her. Compelling her obedience was a temporary solution, and one that could ultimately cause her to resent or mistrust him and the rest of the Jedi.

"Let me out and I'll take the mercenaries into custody,"

Johun said, offering up a plan. "Contact the fleet, and they'll send another ship to pick up the three of us."

The words weren't easy for him to say. He'd defied Farfalla—a Jedi Master—to come to this world. The last thing he wanted was to leave Ruusan now, so soon after arriving. Yet he was willing to make that sacrifice if it would prevent Bordon and his sons from giving in to their rash and reckless emotions. It was his duty as a Jedi to protect their lives, even if it meant abandoning his own personal crusade.

"You and the others should take the shuttle and head south to the battlefield," he continued. "Go help the injured. That's what you're here for."

Irtanna hesitated, then gave a curt nod of acknowledgment. Johun was barely more than a boy; the long thin braid in his hair clearly marked that he had not yet completed his Padawan training. But he was still a member of the Jedi Order. That counted for a lot among the Republic troops. He'd been relying on that to help her see the wisdom of his words.

Confident that Irtanna would keep Bordon and his sons out of trouble, Johun got up from his chair and made his way to the rear of the *Star-Wake*. He did his best to ignore the accusing eyes of the two angry young men as he waited for the shuttle's exit hatch to open. When it finally did, he leapt out and landed nimbly on the ground, then made his way quickly toward the pair standing patiently nearby, their hands still raised high above their heads. Once he was clear of the vessel, the engines roared to life and the ship lifted into the air and took off . . . much to the dismay of the two mercenaries.

"Where are they going?" the woman demanded, her voice a high-pitched squeak of panic. "No! They can't leave us here!"

Her arms dropped back to her sides, as did her companion's. For a second Johun worried that they might make a move for their weapons, but then he realized they were too distraught over the *Star-Wake*'s exit to even think about attacking him.

"Don't let them go!" the man shouted, turning away from

Johun to watch as the craft flew off and out of sight, then whirling back to implore the young Jedi once more. "Make them turn around! Tell them to come back!" There was a desperate urgency in his voice that mirrored the tone of his companion.

"Don't worry," the young Jedi assured them. "Another ship is on the way."

"We can't stay here," the woman insisted. "There's no time. He'll find us. *He'll find us!*"

"It's okay," Johun explained, holding up a calming hand. "I can protect you. I'm a Jedi."

The woman raised an eyebrow and gave him a skeptical glance. The slight young man widened his stance, placed his hands on his hips, and thrust out his chest, hoping it would make him appear noble and impressive. He tried to project the image of confident self-assurance he'd often admired in Hoth and the other Masters.

The man grabbed Johun by the arm, tugging it like a child clinging to his mother's apron. "We have to get off this planet," he said, the words coming out in a terrified whisper. "We have to go now!"

Johun shook free of the man's grasp with only minor difficulty. There was something unsettling about this whole encounter. From the way these two were dressed, it was clear they were experienced soldiers for hire. He suspected they were deserters from the recent battle—minions of the Sith who had fled the instant the Army of Light had broken their ranks. But their flight would have been an act of opportunistic preservation rather than fear or cowardice. Still, these combat veterans, accustomed to facing death and bloodshed, were acting like traumatized villagers after a slaver raid.

"Even if you are a Jedi, you can't save us," the woman muttered with a slow shake of her head. "You can't protect us from *him.*"

"Who?" Johun wanted to know. "Who are you talking about?"

The man glanced around quickly, as if he was afraid some-one might be listening. "A Dark Lord of the Sith," he hissed.

"One of the Brotherhood?" Johun asked, barely able to contain his eagerness. "Are you saying a Sith Master survived the thought bomb?"

The man nodded. "He killed Lergan and Hansh. Fried them with lightning from his fingers."

I knew it! Johun thought triumphantly. *I knew it!*

"He had a lightsaber, too," the woman added. "Sliced Pad and Derrin wide open." She hesitated for a moment, shudder-ing at the memory. "Rell got his head cut clean off."

Johun was about to ask for more details, but the sound of a rapidly approaching ship momentarily distracted him. He glanced up to see a Bivouac troop transport swooping in for a landing. Seconds after it touched down, three Republic soldiers jumped out, weapons at the ready. He recognized the senior of-ficer in the trio: Major Orten Ledes, one of the highest-ranking non-Jedi in the Army of Light's Second Legion.

"These the prisoners?" the major asked gruffly, pointing his blaster rifle at the mercenaries.

Johun nodded. Ledes gave a tilt of his head, and his subor-dinates moved in quickly to slap restraints on the enemy sol-diers. Neither made any attempt to resist. Once their wrists were secured they were frisked and stripped of their weapons, then marched off toward the vessel. The whole encounter was conducted with the efficiency and competence that were the hallmarks of all troops serving under Major Ledes's com-mand.

"You picked up Irtanna's message?" Johun asked as he watched the Sith minions being led away.

"We were in the area," the officer replied. "Farfalla sent me to come get you."

Something in his tone caught the young Jedi's attention. "Am I in trouble?"

The officer shrugged. "Hard to say. You Jedi tend to keep a tight rein on your emotions. But I bet the general wasn't too happy when he found out you disobeyed a direct order and snuck down here."

"Don't worry," Johun replied confidently. "He'll change his tune when he hears what those prisoners have to tell him."

BANE THROTTLED BACK the swoop bike's engine as they approached the small clearing that served as the *Valcyn*'s landing site. Originally presented as a gift to Lord Qordis, the vessel had been commandeered by Bane when he left the Academy on Korriban to seek out the knowledge of the ancient Sith. Qordis had never dared to try to take it back, and his cowardice had simply confirmed Bane's decision to abandon his studies and turn his back on the Brotherhood.

He brought the swoop to a stop twenty meters from the ship. Zannah released her grip on his waist and jumped off, then stood staring at the vessel.

Bane wasn't paying attention to her; the last ten minutes he'd had trouble focusing on anything but the pain carving up his skull. He'd hoped delving into the depths of the shimmering orb left behind by the thought bomb might somehow relieve the headaches, but if anything they'd gotten worse since their visit to the cave.

At least he'd been able to confirm that Kaan was truly dead. That made it easier for him to dismiss the ghostly form that materialized just then on the far side of the clearing. Pale beneath the late-afternoon sun, it was undeniably the image of the man who had founded the Brotherhood of Darkness.

Bane knew it was nothing but a hallucination, yet there was something compelling about the figure as it crossed the clearing to stop a meter or so away from the ship. The spirit turned and fixed him with a steady gaze, then reached out a beckoning hand.

"She's beautiful," Zannah breathed. Darth Bane snapped his head around in surprise. But his apprentice was staring raptly at the *Valcyn* herself. When Bane turned his attention back to where Kaan had been standing, the specter had vanished once again.

"I never thought I'd be leaving Ruusan in a ship like this," Zannah said.

"You aren't," Bane said as he stepped off the swoop. There was nothing he could do about the hallucinations other than act as if they didn't exist.

The young girl turned to look back at him, confused. "We're not taking your ship?"

"I am," her Master replied. "But you must find your own way off this world."

It took a moment for his words to register with the girl. When they did, her expression became one of utter shock. "I . . . I can't come with you?"

The big man shook his head. Spurred on by Zannah's discovery of the ancient tome in the Sith camp, he'd come up with a plan. He was heading to Dxun, Onderon's oversized moon, to seek out the lost tomb of Freedon Nadd. But he had other ideas for his apprentice.

"But . . . why not? What did I do?" the young girl choked out, clearly on the verge of tears. "Why are you leaving me?"

"This is part of your training," Bane explained. "To understand the dark side you must suffer through hardship and struggle."

"You don't have to abandon me to make me suffer," she countered. "Take me with you."

"The strength of the dark side lies with the power of the individual," he reminded her. "The Force comes from within. You must learn to draw on it yourself. I will not always be there to teach you."

"But you said there were always two," Zannah insisted. "One to embody the power, the other to crave it!"

She learned quickly, and Bane was pleased to see she had already committed so many of his lessons to memory. But reciting the words meant nothing if she didn't understand the truth behind them.

"Why do you follow me?" he asked, posing a question to lead her down the path of wisdom.

Zannah thought about her answer for several seconds, carefully considering everything he had already taught her. "To unleash my full potential," she said at last. "To learn the ways of the dark side."

Bane nodded. "And when I no longer have anything to teach you? What will happen then?"

Her brow furrowed in concentration, but this time the answer wouldn't come. "I don't know," she finally admitted.

"There will come a time when your training ends," he told her. "There will come a day when you have learned all the lessons, when all my knowledge of the dark side will be yours. On that day you will challenge me for the title of Master, and only one of us will survive the encounter."

The girl's eyes opened wide. Then they narrowed as she focused intently on what he was saying.

"You have the potential to surpass me," he continued. "If you achieve your potential I will cease to be of use to you. You will need to find new sources of knowledge. You will have to seek out a new apprentice so that you may pass on the secrets of the Sith Order to another.

"When your power eclipses mine I will become expendable. This is the Rule of Two: one Master and one apprentice. When you are ready to claim the mantle of Dark Lord as your own, you must do so by eliminating me.

"The confrontation is inevitable," he concluded. "It is the only way the Sith can survive. It is the way of the dark side."

Zannah didn't say anything. From her expression Bane saw she was still struggling to comprehend why her Master would train her knowing that she would ultimately betray him. But she didn't need to understand. Not yet. Right now she needed only to obey him.

"Make your way to Onderon," Bane instructed her. "I will meet you there in ten standard days." *After I find Nadd's tomb on Dxun.*

"How am I supposed to get there?" she protested.

"You are the chosen one, the anointed heir to the legacy of our order. You will find a way."

"And if I don't?"

"Then you will have proven yourself unworthy of being my successor, and I will seek out another apprentice."

There was nothing more to say. Bane turned his back on her and headed for his ship. Zannah merely watched him go, not speaking. As he walked away, he could feel her anger building, becoming a raging inferno of hate as he climbed into the cockpit. The heat of her fury brought a grim smile to Bane's lips as he fired up the engines.

The *Valcyn* took to the air, leaving Zannah behind—a tiny figure on the planet's surface staring after the ship, standing motionless as if she had been carved from cold, hard stone.

6

"THIS IS ALL just a misunderstanding," the man insisted from inside his cell.

"You're making a mistake," the woman with him agreed.

Johun took a deep breath, then let it out in a long, weary sigh. He'd arrived back on the *Fairwind* with his two prisoners over an hour earlier. His request for an immediate audience with Farfalla had been denied, as the acting general had been otherwise preoccupied with the cleanup efforts on Ruusan. So Johun had taken his prisoners down to the flagship's lower deck and placed them in a holding cell to wait. With nothing better to do, he'd decided to take a seat in a nearby chair and wait with them.

The young Jedi was now strongly regretting that decision.

"We were never part of Kaan's army," the woman called out to him from behind the bars of their cell. "We're just farmers."

"Farmers don't wear battle armor and carry weapons," Johun said, pointing to the corner of the room where the clothing and equipment confiscated from the mercenaries had been piled atop a small table.

"That stuff's not ours," the man explained. "We . . . we just found it. We were out for a walk this morning and . . . we came across this deserted camp. We saw all this equipment lying around and, uh, we thought it would be fun to dress up like soldiers."

The Republic guard standing watch over the prisoners with Johun barked out a laugh at the pathetic lie. Johun just closed his eyes and reached up to rub his temples. Back on Ruusan the prisoners had been all too eager to confess to their crimes. Fresh from their encounter with the unnamed Sith Lord, they had been temporarily scared straight. Now that they were safely away from the planet's surface, however, the sobering reality of a five-to-ten-year sentence on a Republic prison world was making them recant their earlier testimony.

"What about the others?" Johun asked, hoping to catch them in their own web of lies. "Your friends who died in the attack. Were they farmers, too?"

"Yes," the man replied, even as the woman said, "We didn't really know them."

"Well," the young Jedi asked coolly, "which is it?"

The two mercenaries gave each other a long, sour look, but it was the woman who finally answered. "We just met them this morning. At the Sith camp. They said they were farmers like us, but they might have been lying."

"Lying? Really?" Johun asked sarcastically. "Hard to imagine why anyone would do that."

The guard gave another short laugh. "You two should take this act on tour," he said. "You know . . . if you survive prison."

The man in the cell seemed about to say something biting in reply, but he held his tongue when his companion gave him a sharp elbow in the ribs. At that moment one of Farfalla's envoys poked her head into the room.

"The general can see you now," she said to Johun.

Johun leapt from his chair to follow her.

"Hey, tell him to let us out of here," the man called out after him. "Don't forget about us!"

No chance of that, Johun thought. To the guard he said, "Keep an eye on them. And don't believe anything they say."

The envoy led him on a long, winding journey through the various levels of the *Fairwind*. The holding cells were located in the bottommost depths of the great ship's hull; he was meeting Farfalla on the command deck at the top. Along the way they passed hundreds of faces Johun recognized, fellow Jedi and soldiers who had fought by his side during the campaign. Most gave a curt nod or a quick wave as they went by, too busy with their own duties to engage in any kind of conversation.

There were also many faces Johun didn't recognize: refugees from Ruusan. Many were evacuees brought here in the mad rush to escape the thought bomb, preparing to head back down to the surface to try to rebuild their lives. Others were men and women whose homes or families had been completely destroyed by the war; for them there was nothing to go back to but the painful memories of what they had lost. Farfalla had arranged for those people who didn't wish to return to Ruusan to be given transport back to the Core Worlds of the Republic, where they could find a fresh start away from the horrors they had witnessed.

So many people, Johun thought as he silently followed his guide. *So much suffering. And it will all be for nothing if any of the Sith manage to escape.*

When they reached the command deck, the envoy led him to Farfalla's personal quarters. She knocked once on the closed door, and a voice from the other side said, "Come in."

She placed a hand on the console and the door slid open, then she nodded at Johun. He stepped forward and into the room, and he heard the door *whoosh* closed behind him.

The room was larger than he had expected, and decorated in the lavish style for which Valenthyne Farfalla was famous. A brightly colored rug of crimson and gold lay spread across the floor, and the walls were hung with works that would not have seemed out of place in the finest art galleries of Alderaan. On the far side of the room was an enormous four-poster bed, the frame fashioned from the timber of a wroshyr tree—a gift from Wookiee tribal leaders on Kashyyyk. The covers and pillows were woven from shimmering silks of yellow and red, and each of the massive bedposts was emblazoned with a hand-painted mural depicting a major event from Farfalla's life: his royal birth, his acceptance into the Jedi Order, his ascension to the rank of Master, his famous triumph over the Sith forces on Kashyyyk.

The general was sitting at an oversized desk in the corner, reviewing reports on a monitor built into the surface. "You disappoint me, young Padawan," he said as he flicked off the screen and turned in his seat to face Johun.

"I am sorry I disobeyed you, Master Valenthyne," he replied.

Farfalla stood up and crossed the room, his feet padding softly on the luxurious carpet. "That is the least of my concerns," he said, placing a heavy hand on the young man's shoulder. His eyes were dark and sunken, and his normally joyful expression was hidden under a mask of worry and fatigue.

"Irtanna," Johun said, hanging his head in shame at the memory of how he had used the Force to trick the pilot into allowing him to join her crew.

"A Jedi does not use his powers to manipulate the minds of his friends. Even if your motives are pure, it is an abuse of your position and a betrayal of the trust others put in us."

"I know what I did was wrong," Johun admitted. "And I will accept whatever punishment you feel is necessary to atone for what I did. But there is something more important that we need to talk about first."

Farfalla gazed into Johun's eyes, then let his hand drop. The Padawan thought he saw a flicker of disappointment cross the Master's face as he did so.

"Yes, of course," Farfalla said, turning and walking back to his desk. He reached down and flicked the monitor back on. "The report from those prisoners you captured."

"You've seen it?" Johun asked in surprise.

"I read all the reports," he answered. "It is a leader's responsibility to know what his followers are doing. More important, he must stop them from making rash or misguided decisions."

"You still don't believe any of the Sith survived the thought bomb," Johun guessed.

"I lack faith in the credibility of your sources," Valenthyne replied. "These mercenaries are, to put it bluntly, the scum of the galaxy. How do you know they aren't just telling you what you want to hear?"

"Why would they do that?"

Farfalla shrugged. "Maybe they think you will stand up for them. Get them better treatment as prisoners. A lesser sentence for their crimes. These people are opportunists. They will seek every advantage they can find. Lying is second nature to them."

"I don't think they were lying, Master," Johun said with a shake of his head. "If you saw them on the surface . . . they were terrified! Something terrible happened to them."

"This is war. Terrible things are a matter of course."

"What about the details of their account?" Johun pressed. "The red-bladed lightsaber? The Force lightning? These are the weapons of the dark side!"

"If they were soldiers in Kaan's army, they would be well versed in the tools the Sith use against their enemies. It would be easy for them to add these elements to any story they wanted to tell."

Clenching his jaw in frustration, Johun spat out a harsh accusation. "You just want to believe the Sith are gone forever! That's why you refuse to see what's right in front of us."

"And you want to believe the Sith still exist," Farfalla countered, though his voice echoed none of the anger in the Padawan's challenge. "You want to strike out against those who killed your Master. Your desire to avenge him has blinded you to the facts. If you were thinking clearly, you would see that there is one part of the story that calls the entire account into question."

Johun blinked in surprise. "You have proof they're lying?"

"It's right there in the report you filed," Farfalla informed him. "They claim that a Dark Lord of the Sith slaughtered their friends. But somehow they survived the encounter. How is that possible?"

"They . . . they escaped into the trees," Johun stammered, knowing how foolish the words sounded even as he said them.

"You are a Jedi," Farfalla admonished him. "You know the power of the Force. Do you really believe they could have escaped the wrath of a Sith Master simply by running into the forest?"

He would have hunted them down and butchered them like zucca pigs, Johun admitted to himself. "Maybe he wanted to let them live for some reason," he suggested, still unwilling to surrender the point.

"Why?" Farfalla asked. "If a Sith Lord survived the thought bomb, why would he leave witnesses behind who could expose him to his enemies?"

Johun had no answer for this. It didn't make any sense. But somehow he knew—*he knew*—the mercenaries were telling the truth.

"Johun," the general said, sensing his inner conflict. "You must be completely honest with yourself. Do you really believe we can trust these mercenaries?"

Johun thought back to the prisoners in the cell and the endless string of lies pouring from their mouths. He thought about his own warning to the guard watching over them: *Don't believe anything they say.* And Johun finally realized what a fool he'd been.

"No, Master Valenthyne. You are right. They can't be trusted." After a moment he added, "I . . . I would like to speak with Irtanna and Bordon when they get back. To apologize for what I did to them."

"I'm glad to hear you say that, Johun," Farfalla said with a wan smile. "We Jedi are not infallible. It is important that we stay humble enough to admit when we make a mistake.

"Unfortunately, apologizing in person will not be possible," he continued. "I have been summoned to Coruscant to meet with Chancellor Valorum. Since you obviously cannot be trusted to follow my instructions in my absence, you will be accompanying me as my aide."

The proclamation had been framed as a punishment, but Johun's heart leapt at the words. In effect, Master Valenthyne was offering to take him on and mentor him.

"I . . . thank you, Master," was all he could say. Not sure what else to do, he gave a short bow.

"It's what Hoth would have wanted for you," Farfalla said softly. Then, louder, "We'll leave as soon as I finish making the arrangements for others to take over command of the fleet while I'm gone."

"Why does the Chancellor want to meet with you so urgently?" Johun asked, suddenly curious.

"Now that the Brotherhood of Darkness has been defeated, the Galactic Senate wants to put an official end to this war. There is important legislation on the table that could change the face of the Republic forever. Valorum wants to discuss it with me before the Senate votes."

"And this legislation will affect the Jedi as well?"

"It will," Farfalla answered grimly. "In ways you cannot even begin to imagine."

ZANNAH'S FEET HURT. Her calves ached. Her thighs burned with every step. Yet somehow she ignored the pain and pushed herself to go on.

She'd been walking ever since Darth Bane's ship had disappeared over the horizon, leaving her alone once again. Her mission was clear: make her way to Onderon. To do that, she had to find a ship to get her off Ruusan. That meant finding other people. But Zannah had no idea where any other people might be, and so she had simply chosen a random direction and started walking.

She was too small to pilot the swoop bike Bane had used to whisk them across the landscape. At first that hadn't mattered: She'd used her newfound talents in the Force to propel herself along, running so fast that the world passed by her in a blur of wind and color. But while the Force may have been infinite, her ability to draw upon it was not. Her skills were still developing, and fatigue had set in quickly. She had felt her pace slowing as her strength ebbed, and though she tried to summon the power of the dark side again by tapping into her deep reserves of anger and hate, her exhausted will could only call up the faintest flicker of a response.

Now she'd been reduced to a tired little girl plodding across the war-torn Ruusan landscape. Yet she refused to surrender to despair, instead focusing all her energy on putting one foot in front of the other. It was impossible to say how long she continued her forced march—how many hours or kilometers she endured—before she was rewarded with what she sought: the sight of a shuttle in the distance.

Hope gave new life to her weary limbs, and she managed a clumsy, limping run toward the vessel. She could see people milling about the craft: a young woman, an older man, and two teenage boys. As she drew nearer the woman noticed her and called out to one of her companions.

"Bordon! Tell the boys we've found someone who needs help."

Minutes later Zannah found herself inside the vessel's cargo hold, sitting on a supply chest while wolfing down nutrition bars from a ration kit and chasing them with a piping-hot cup of chav. One of the boys had thrown a thick blanket over her shoulders, and the entire crew was now hovering protectively around her.

"I've never seen someone so small eat so much," the woman said with a laugh.

She didn't look like she'd come from Ruusan originally. She had dark skin and short black hair, and she wore a bulky padded vest under her jacket. There was also a blaster pistol strapped to her hip, making Zannah fairly certain she was a soldier of some type.

"What did you expect, Irtanna?" the older man said. In contrast to the woman, he looked like he was probably a native of Ruusan. He had broad shoulders, leathery skin, and a short brown beard. He reminded Zannah of Root, the cousin who had raised her as a little girl back on her homeworld of Somov Rit. "The poor thing's nothing but skin and bones. When was the last time you had a decent meal, girl?"

Zannah shook her head. "I don't know," she said around a mouthful of food.

She'd only accepted their offer of a meal out of politeness. Ever since she had arrived on Ruusan she'd been living on roots and berries, her body constantly on the edges of starvation. She'd been doing it for so long that she'd gotten used to the pangs of a perpetually empty stomach, adapting to the point that she was barely aware of her hunger. But the moment that first bite of real food hit her tongue, she remembered her appetite, and now her body was determined to make up for weeks of poor nutrition.

"Where are your parents?" the woman called Irtanna asked.

"They're dead," Zannah answered after a moment's hesitation, setting down what remained of the ration kit. The food was delicious; the simple physical pleasure of eating was a glorious sensation. But she couldn't allow herself to be distracted by it right now. She had to be very careful with what she told these people.

The man crouched beside her, bringing himself down to her

eye level. When he spoke, his voice was soft and sympathetic. "Any other family? Brothers or sisters? Anyone?"

She answered with another shake of her head.

"A war orphan," Irtanna muttered sadly.

"My name's Bordon," the man told her. "This is Irtanna, and these are my sons Tallo and Wend. What's your name?"

Unwilling to reveal her true name, she hesitated for a second. "I'm . . . Rain," she finally offered, giving them her childhood nickname.

"Rain? That's a funny name. Never heard one like that before," the older boy, Tallo, said. He looked to be about sixteen.

"There are lots of names you've never heard," Bordon chided his son sharply. Then, in a softer voice, he asked Zannah, "Are you hurt, Rain? Or sick? We have medicine if you need it."

"I'm okay. I was just hungry is all."

"Should we take her with us?" Irtanna asked.

Bordon kept his eyes on Zannah as he replied, "Why don't we ask her. Rain, do you want to come with us?"

"I have to go to Onderon," Zannah replied without thinking. As soon as the words were out of her mouth she regretted them.

"Onderon? Nothing on that rock but monsters and beast-riders," Tallo chimed in. "You must be pretty stupid if you want to go there."

"Hush, boy," Bordon snapped. "You've never been off Ruusan, so how would you know?"

"I heard people talking," Tallo replied. "Around the camps and stuff."

"You can't believe every tale you hear around a campfire," his father reminded him. "Now take your brother and go wait up in the front of the ship."

"Come on," Tallo grumbled, grabbing his younger sibling by the arm.

"That's not fair!" Wend protested as he was led away. "I didn't do nothing!"

"Why do you want to go to Onderon?" Irtanna asked once

the boys were gone. "It's a very dangerous world. Not the kind of place for a little girl on her own."

"I won't be on my own. I . . . I have family there," Zannah lied. "I just need to find them."

Bordon rubbed his hand over his chin, tugging slightly at his beard. "It might be pretty hard finding them on a place like Onderon," he said. "Is there someone else we could contact for you? A family friend on Ruusan, maybe?"

"I have to go to Onderon," Zannah insisted.

"I see," the man said, then he stood up and turned to Irtanna. "Our young guest seems mighty determined to get off this world."

"We can't take you to Onderon," Irtanna said, "but we can take you with us when we leave Ruusan."

"Take me where?" Zannah asked, suspicious.

"We've got a whole fleet of ships orbiting the planet, Rain. You'll be safe up there. We'll find someone to get you cleaned up and look after you."

"I can look after myself," she answered defiantly.

"Yes, I can see that," Bordon interjected. "But I bet it's lonely being all by yourself." When Zannah didn't answer he continued, "Tell you what—it's getting dark outside. Why don't we take you with us up to the fleet for now? Then tomorrow we can figure out what to do next.

"If you still want to go to Onderon, we'll see if we can help. But if you change your mind, maybe you could stay here on Ruusan with me and my boys for a while. At least until we find your family."

Zannah's mouth dropped open at his offer.

Bordon reached down and patted her gently on the shoulder. "It's okay," he said. "You don't have to answer right now. Just something to think about."

Managing a slight nod, Zannah resumed eating her meal, her mind still reeling.

"I'll go get us ready for takeoff," Irtanna said as she left, heading up toward the front of the vessel.

Bordon grunted his agreement, then spoke to Zannah once more. "I have to go up front to help Irtanna. You just stay back here and finish eating, okay?"

Zannah nodded again. There was something comforting about the way Bordon spoke to her. He made her feel safe and important at the same time. She watched him disappear through the door separating the supply hold from the cockpit.

"You just holler if you need anything," Bordon's voice called back to her.

A minute later the engines roared to life and the shuttle lifted up into the air, but Zannah barely noticed. Her brain was overwhelmed with conflicting emotions. Part of her was silently screaming that she couldn't just sit there—she had to do something *now*! She couldn't let them take her back to the fleet. There were too many people there. Too many Jedi. Some-one was bound to notice her special gifts and start asking questions. They'd find out about Darth Bane, and everything he had promised her—all the knowledge and power of the dark side—would be lost.

Yet another part of her *wanted* to go back to the fleet. Bane had warned that her apprenticeship would be a long and diffi-cult struggle. She was tired of struggling. And Bane had aban-doned her. Bordon, on the other hand, had offered her his home; he'd offered to let her be part of his family. What would be so wrong about simply accepting his offer? Bane had said she was the chosen heir to the legacy of the ancient Sith, but was that really what she wanted?

Before she could come up with an answer she heard a noise, and looked up to see Wend, the younger of Bordon's two sons, coming in from the cockpit to talk to her. She guessed he was somewhere around thirteen—only a few years older than she was.

"Papa says you don't have any family," he said by way of greeting.

Zannah didn't know what to say, so she only nodded.

"Did they die in the war?" Wend asked. "Did the Sith kill them?"

She shrugged, unwilling to elaborate in case she inadvertently gave away some detail that would expose her façade.

"My mother was a soldier," Wend told her. "She was very brave. She went to fight the Sith when they first came to Ruusan."

"What happened to her?" She only asked the question because it was expected and it would have seemed odd if she hadn't. She didn't want to do anything to draw unwanted attention to herself.

"She died at the Fourth Battle of Ruusan. Killed by the Sith. Papa says—"

"Wend!" came Bordon's voice from the cockpit. "Get back up here. Let Rain have some peace and quiet."

The boy gave her a shy smile, then turned and left her alone again with her thoughts. Thanks to his words, however, she'd made her decision.

Bordon had offered to take her in. He'd offered to make her part of his family. He was tempting her with a simple but happy life. But his words offered nothing except empty promises. *Peace is a lie.*

What good were family or friends if you didn't have the strength to protect them? Bordon had lost his wife, and Tallo and Wend had lost their mother. When the Sith came they'd been powerless to save the one they most loved.

Zannah knew what it was like to feel powerless. She knew what it was like to have the things she valued above all else taken from her. And she had vowed to never let it happen again.

Bordon and his family were victims—slaves bound by the chains of their own weakness. Zannah refused to be a victim any longer. Bane had promised to teach her the ways of the dark side. He would show her how to unleash the power within and free herself from the shackles of the world.

Through power I gain victory. Through victory my chains are broken!

The realization of what she was—the acceptance of her destiny—spurred Zannah into action. She tried to call upon the Force to give her strength, but she was still too exhausted from her previous exertions to use her talents. Undaunted, she began to rummage through the supply crates in the cargo hold, looking for something she could use to stop the shuttle and her crew from bringing her to the rest of the fleet.

She found what she was looking for just as Tallo entered the hold, catching her red-handed.

"Papa wanted me to see if you—Hey! What do you think you're doing?"

Zannah wrapped her hand around the grip of the blaster a split second before Tallo crashed into her, tackling her to the ground.

"You kriffing little thief!" the boy swore at her, trying to pin her to the ground and pull the weapon from her hand. He outweighed Zannah by thirty kilos, but she fought with a savage desperation that kept him from getting a firm grip on her as they wrestled on the floor.

Drawn by the sounds of their struggle, Bordon came running into the room.

"What the blazes is going on here!" he shouted.

In that exact instant the blaster discharged. It was impossible to say whose finger had been on the trigger; Tallo and Zannah were each clutching at the pistol with both hands in their efforts to wrest possession of it from the other. But through ill luck or dark fate, when the bolt was fired the barrel of the weapon was pointed squarely at Tallo. The impact left a gaping wound in the center of his chest, killing him instantly.

The young man's hands went limp and fell away from the blaster. His body toppled forward, pinning Zannah's legs beneath its weight. Across the room Bordon's eyes flew wide in horror. With a scream of anguish he lunged forward to help his son.

Seeing the father of the boy she had just killed rushing toward her, Zannah acted on instinct and fired the weapon again. The bolt caught Bordon just above the belt, cutting off his cry and knocking him to his knees. He let out a low grunt of pain as he clutched at the smoking hole in his gut, then reached a bloody hand out toward Zannah. She cried out in fear and disgust and fired again, ending Bordon's life.

"Bordon!" Irtanna's voice came over the shipboard intercom. "I heard blasterfire! What's happening back there?"

Moving quickly, Zannah squirmed out from under Tallo's corpse and ran up to the cockpit. She arrived to find Wend still harnessed into his passenger's seat, trying to turn around to see what was going on. Irtanna was just rising from her chair to go help Bordon. She'd had to engage the autopilot before she could leave her seat, and the delay had given Zannah the precious seconds she'd need to gain the upper hand.

"Sit back down and don't move!" Zannah shouted, pointing the blaster at Irtanna. Her voice sounded thin and hollow in the tight confines of the cockpit—the voice of a panicky child.

Irtanna hesitated, then obeyed.

"What happened?" the woman asked, her tone carefully neutral. "Is anybody hurt?"

"Plot a course for Onderon," Zannah ordered, refusing to answer the question. She could barely hear herself speak above the deafening thump of her racing heart.

"Okay," Irtanna said slowly, reaching up to punch the coordinates into the ship's command console. "I'll do what you want. Just stay calm." The ship's autonav chimed to acknowledge the new destination, and the woman half turned in her seat so she could look the young girl holding her hostage square in the eye. "Rain, put the blaster down." There was a cool self-assurance in her words, and a grim determination on her face.

"I'm not Rain," the girl retorted through clenched teeth. "My name is Zannah!"

"Whoever you are," Irtanna said, standing up slowly, "you're going to give me that blaster."

"Don't move or I'll shoot!" Zannah warned, her voice rising shrilly. *How can she be so calm?* she thought, even as she struggled to slow her own breathing down. She was the one with the blaster, but somehow she felt like she was losing control of the situation.

"No," the young woman replied calmly, taking a single step toward her. "You won't shoot me. You're not a killer."

The memory of the two dead Jedi back on Ruusan flashed through Zannah's mind, followed quickly by the image of Bordon and his son lying lifeless in the cargo hold.

"Yes, I am," she whispered as she pulled the trigger.

Irtanna managed a faint gasp of surprise, then collapsed to the ground—a quick and clean death. Zannah waited a second to confirm she was gone, then turned to point the blaster at Wend. He had watched the encounter unfold as if paralyzed, not even bothering to undo the buckle of his safety harness.

"Don't kill me!" he begged, squirming beneath the chair's restraints.

She could actually sense the fear emanating from him. She felt the familiar heat of the dark side flare to life within her, responding to the plight of her victim, feeding itself on his terror. It flowed through her like a wave of liquid fire, burning away her guilt and uncertainty and strengthening her resolve.

Zannah's mind was filled with a great and sudden realization: fear and pain were an inevitable part of existence. And it was far better to inflict them on others than to suffer them herself.

"Please don't shoot," Wend whimpered, making one last plea for his life. "I'm just a kid. Like you."

"I'm not a kid," Zannah said as she pulled the trigger. "I'm a Sith."

7

BANE COULD HEAR the whine of the *Valcyn*'s engines as the ship sliced through the upper layers of Dxun's atmosphere, protesting as he pushed the vessel to her very limits. Normally the trip from Ruusan to Onderon's oversized moon would have taken a T-class cruiser like the *Valcyn* between four and five days. Bane had covered the distance in just over two.

Within hours of leaving Ruusan—and Zannah—behind, he had been cursed with the return of the almost unbearable headaches. And with them had come an unwanted and most unwelcome companion. The spectral shade of Lord Kaan loomed over him in the cockpit for the entire first day of the trip, a visible manifestation of the damage Bane's mind had suffered from the thought bomb. The spirit never spoke, merely watched him with its accusatory gaze, a constant presence on the edges of Bane's awareness.

The ghostly apparition had driven Bane to adopt an irresponsible, even dangerous, pace for the journey. He had pushed the *Valcyn* far beyond the recommended safety parameters, as if part of him was trying to use the speed of the ship to outrun his own madness. He was desperate to reach Dxun so he could find the tomb of Freedon Nadd and hopefully discover some way to rid himself of the torturous hallucinations.

Kaan had disappeared toward the end of the first day of his journey, only to be replaced by an even worse visitation. It wasn't the founder of the Brotherhood of Darkness that hovered beside him now, but Qordis—the former head of the Sith Academy on Korriban. Pale and semi-translucent, the figure was otherwise an almost perfect replica of what the Sith Lord had looked like at the time of their final meeting, when Bane had killed him. Tall and gaunt, Qordis had skeletal features that seemed more at home on a spirit than they ever had on a being of flesh and blood. Unlike Kaan, however, Qordis actually spoke to him, spewing forth an endless litany of blame, denouncing everything Bane had accomplished.

"You betrayed us," the phantom said, extending a long, thin finger topped with a talonlike nail. Bane didn't need to look at it to know the finger would be adorned with the heavy bejeweled rings Qordis had worn in life. "You destroyed the Brotherhood, you brought victory to the Jedi. And now you flee the scene like a craven thief in the night."

I'm not a coward! Bane thought. There was no point in voicing the words aloud; the vision was all in his mind. Speaking with it would only be a sign that his mental condition was further deteriorating. *I did what had to be done. The Brotherhood was an abomination. They had to be destroyed!*

"The Brotherhood had knowledge of the dark side. Wisdom that is lost forever because of you."

Bane was growing weary of the all-too-familiar refrain. He'd had this conversation with himself before he decided to destroy Kaan and his followers, and now he was reliving it again and again through the delusions of his wounded mind. Yet he refused to allow any doubts or uncertainties to weaken his resolve; he had done what was necessary.

The Brotherhood had lost its way. They had fallen from the true path of the dark side. All the study and training Qordis put prospective students through at the Academy was worthless.

"If that was true," the apparition countered, answering his unspoken arguments, "then how do you explain your current mission? Your claim to reject my teachings, yet I was the one who discovered the location of Freedon Nadd's lost tomb."

You didn't discover anything. You're just a hallucination. And Qordis may have stumbled on this information, but he didn't know what to do with it. A true Sith Master would have left Ruusan to seek out Nadd's tomb. Instead he decided to stay and help Kaan play army with the Jedi.

"Excuses and justifications," the spirit replied. "Kaan was a warrior. But you would rather hide from your enemies than fight them."

Bane gritted his teeth as the *Valcyn* hit the turbulence of Dxun's heavy cloud cover. The ship was still going too fast, forcing him to clutch the steering yoke so hard to keep his craft on course that his knuckles turned white. He heard the creaks and groans as the overstressed hull sliced through the thick atmosphere.

"You betrayed us," Qordis said again.

Bane swore under his breath, doing his best to ignore the ramblings of the image conjured up by his own mind. How many times had he heard this exact conversation in the past day? Fifty? A hundred? It was like listening to a busted holoprojector repeating the same message over and over.

"You destroyed the Brotherhood, you brought victory to the Jedi. And now you flee the scene like a craven thief in the night."

"Shut up!" Darth Bane screamed, no longer able to contain his rage. "You're not even real!"

He lashed out with the Force, releasing an explosion of dark side energy inside the cockpit, determined to blast the offending vision into oblivion. Qordis did vanish, but Bane's victory was short-lived. Emergency lights began flashing inside the ship, accompanied by the shrill whooping of a critical failure alarm.

The ship's console had been fried by the burst of power he'd unleashed. Cursing Qordis and his own reckless display of emotion, Bane began a desperate struggle to somehow bring the vessel in for a safe landing. From all around him he could hear the ghostly, mocking laughter of Qordis.

The *Valcyn* was in free fall, plummeting straight down toward Dxun's heavily forested surface. Bane yanked back on the yoke with all the strength of his massive frame, managing to redirect the ship into a shallower angle of approach. But if he didn't find some way to decelerate, it wasn't going to matter.

He punched at the controls, trying to restart the engine thrusters with one hand while the other still struggled to keep the yoke steady. Getting no response, he closed his eyes and reached out with the Force, digging deep into the burned-out circuits and melted wires of the ship.

His mind raced through the labyrinth of electronics that controlled all the *Valcyn*'s systems, reassembling and rerouting them to find a configuration that would restore power to the dead ignition switch. His first attempt resulted in a shower of sparks shooting up from the control panel, but his second effort was rewarded with the roar of the thrusters coming to life.

Bane managed to get the engines into full reverse only a few hundred meters above Dxun's surface. The ship's descent slowed, but didn't even come close to stopping. A split second before the *Valcyn* slammed into the forest below, Bane wrapped himself in the Force, creating a protective cocoon he could only hope would be strong enough to survive the unavoidable collision.

The *Valcyn* hit the treetops at a forty-five-degree angle. The landing gear sheared off on impact, tearing loose with a thunderous crack. Wide gashes appeared in the sides of the ship, the hull hurtling into thick branches and boughs with enough force to tear through the reinforced sheets of metal and peel them away from their frame.

Inside the cockpit Bane was flung against walls and ceiling. He was spun, tossed, and slammed against the sides of the cockpit as the vessel careened through the trees. Even the Force couldn't fully shield him from the devastating crash as the ship carved a kilometer-long swath of burned and broken foliage before slamming into the soft, muddy ground of a swamp and finally coming to rest.

For several seconds Bane didn't move. His ship had been reduced to a smoking pile of scrap, but miraculously he had survived, saved by the dark side energies enveloping his form. He hadn't escaped unscathed, however. His body was covered with painful bruises and contusions, his face and hands cut from fragments of shattered glass that had pierced his protective cocoon; his right bicep was bleeding heavily from a deep five-centimeter gash. His left shoulder had been dislocated and two ribs were broken, but neither had punctured a lung. His right knee was already swelling up, but there didn't seem to be any cartilage or ligament damage. And he tasted blood in his mouth, oozing from the gap where two of his teeth had been knocked out. Fortunately, none of his wounds was life threatening.

Bane rose to his feet slowly, favoring his injured knee. What was left of the *Valcyn* had come to rest on her side, turning everything in the cockpit at a disorienting ninety-degree angle. Moving gingerly, Bane made his way to the emergency exit hatch, his left arm dangling all but useless from his side. Given the ship's position, her exit hatch was now above him, facing the sky.

Strong as he was, Bane knew he wouldn't be able to pull himself to freedom with only one good arm. A Jedi might have been able to use the Force to heal his wounds, but Bane was a student of the dark side. Even if his ability to call upon the Force hadn't been temporarily exhausted in surviving the crash, healing was not a skill the Sith were familiar with. Before he became a Sith Master, however, Bane had served as a soldier, where he had received basic medical field training.

The *Valcyn* was equipped with an emergency medpac under the pilot's seat. Inside it were healing stims he could use to treat the worst of his injuries. But when he made his way over to look under the seat, the kit was gone.

Realizing it must have jarred loose during the crash, he rummaged around the cockpit until he found it. The outside of the kit was dented and slightly bent, but otherwise it appeared undamaged. It took him three tries to open the latch with only one good hand. When he finally succeeded, he was relieved to see that several of the health stims had survived intact.

He removed one and injected it directly into his thigh. Within seconds he could feel his body's own natural healing properties beginning to kick into overdrive in response to the healing shot. The blood flowing from his cuts began to clot. More important, the shot helped dull the pain from his swollen knee and broken ribs, allowing him to walk and breathe more freely.

His dislocated shoulder, however, required more direct treatment. Grabbing his injured left wrist with his right hand and gritting his teeth against the pain, Bane pulled with all his might, hoping the shoulder would pop back into place. Thanks to his size and strength, he'd been recruited more than a few times by field medics to help resocket the dislocated limbs of fellow soldiers during his military days. A simple procedure, it required a tremendous amount of torque to work effectively, and Bane soon discovered he simply couldn't get the leverage he needed to perform the maneuver on himself.

Grunting and sweating from his exertions, he realized he'd have to take more extreme measures. Lowering himself to a sitting position on the floor, he stretched forward and bent his knees so he could grip the wrist of his injured arm securely between his ankles. He took a deep breath, then thrust his legs straight while throwing his torso backward.

He screamed as the shoulder snapped back into the socket with an audible *pop*. The sudden jolt of pain was excruciating;

it took every bit of strength he had left to keep from passing out. As it was he simply lay on his back, pale and shivering from the ordeal. He was rewarded a few seconds later by the pins and needles of sensation rapidly being restored to the fingers of his left hand.

A few minutes and another healing injection later, he was able to use both arms to haul himself up through the exit hatch and clamber down the side of the *Valcyn*'s wreckage to stand, battered but not beaten, on Dxun's surface.

He wasn't surprised to find Qordis waiting there for him.

"You're trapped, Bane," the spirit mocked. "Your ship is destroyed beyond all hope of repair. You won't find another vessel here—there are no intelligent or civilized creatures on Dxun. And you can't wait for a rescue party. Nobody knew you were coming here. Not even your apprentice."

Bane didn't bother replying, but instead made a final check of his gear. He'd grabbed a pack of basic supplies from the ship and strapped it to his back. It contained food rations, glow rods, a handful of health stims, and a simple hunting blade that he slid into his boot. The pack and its contents, plus the lightsaber dangling at his belt, were the only things worth salvaging from the wreckage.

"The jungles of Dxun are filled with deadly predators," the spirit continued. "They will stalk you day and night, and the moment you let your guard down they will strike. And even if you survive the terrors of the jungle, how are you going to get off this world?

"There is no escape," the ghostly Qordis taunted. "You will die here, Bane."

"It's *Darth* Bane," the big man said with a grim smile. "And I'm not dead yet. Unlike you."

The reply seemed to satisfy whatever part of his subconscious was conjuring up the image, because Qordis abruptly disappeared.

With the distraction gone, Bane was free to examine his environment more closely. The thick forest canopy above blocked out most light; even though it was midday he found himself bathed in twilight. Still, he didn't need his eyes to see clearly.

Reaching out with the Force, he took closer stock of his surroundings. He was in the very heart of the forest; the trees went on for hundreds of kilometers in every direction. And as he probed the surrounding foliage for signs of life, he realized that the apparition had been right about one thing: the forests of Dxun teemed with a host of deadly and voracious beasts. Bane wondered how long it would be before one of the jungle denizens decided to figure out where he fit in on the food chain.

Yet he wasn't afraid. Even before Nadd's tomb had been hidden here, the ancient Sith had been drawn to Dxun. The Jedi had condemned it as a place of evil, but Bane recognized it for what it really was: a world infused with the power of the dark side. He felt strong here, rejuvenated . . . though he was smart enough to understand that the creatures prowling the wilderness would be drawing on that same power.

And then his mental explorations came across what he was looking for. Many kilometers away he sensed a concentration of power. He'd located the source of the dark side energy that permeated the forest around him, radiating power like a beacon emitting a homing signal.

It had to be Nadd's tomb, and now that he was here, Darth Bane felt the place calling to him. Leaving the wreckage of the *Valcyn* behind, he made his way toward the source. He marched in a perfectly straight line, taking the most direct route possible to his destination, using his lightsaber to hack and hew a path through the thick undergrowth that barred his way.

Keeping one corner of his mind focused on following the route to Nadd's tomb, Bane focused the rest of his awareness into a state of hypervigilance. As in most forest ecosystems, the creatures that had evolved on Dxun were masters of their environment. More than a few had quite likely developed the ability to camouflage themselves, blending not only into the branches and trees but into the ever-present hum of the dark side that hung over the forest, as well.

Even with his caution, Bane was almost caught unawares when the attack came. An enormous feline creature dropped down from above, silent save for the faint hiss of its forepaw slashing the air where its prey's throat had been a mere second before.

Bane had sensed the beast at the last possible instant, his Force awareness giving him a precognitive warning that allowed him to duck clear of the lethal claws. Even so, the massive body of the beast slammed into Bane, sending him reeling.

The Dark Lord of the Sith would have died right there had the creature not been momentarily stunned by the unexpected failure of its ambush. The beast's confusion gave Bane the second he needed to roll clear of his enemy and fall into a fighting stance.

With the beast no longer concealed by Dxun's forest, Bane got his first good look at the thing that had nearly killed him. It studied him with luminous green eyes that were definitely feline, though its fur was a metallic gray coat flecked with tiny bronze plates that shimmered as the muscles moved beneath the skin. It stood a meter and a half at the shoulder, easily weighing three hundred kilograms. It had four thick, muscular legs that ended in razor-sharp retractable claws. But the feature that drew Bane's immediate attention was the serpentine twin tails, each tipped with a deadly barb that dripped glowing green venom.

Bane retreated slowly until his back came up against the gnarled trunk of a tall tree. The nameless monstrosity advanced, then with a low growl that made Bane's skin crawl, it leapt at him again, twin tails whipping wildly. Bane lunged to the side, wanting to gauge his opponent's tactics before he engaged it in direct combat. He saw the front claws slashing and flailing through the suddenly empty air, and he watched as the twin tails arced up over the beast's back to stab at the space he had been standing in a moment before. The barbs slammed into the tree Bane had been backed up against with enough force to split the trunk, injecting their corrosive venom into the wood and leaving two smoking black circles.

The creature landed on all four feet simultaneously and spun to face Bane again before he had a chance to strike at its unprotected flank. Once more it began a slow advance. But this time when it pounced, Bane was ready.

The beast acted on instinct; it was a mindless brute that relied on strength and speed to defeat its enemies. Its methods of attack had evolved over countless generations until they were second nature, and it was inevitable it would use the exact same sequence of movements to bring Bane down a second time.

It came in high, leading with its claws just as he had expected. The natural reaction of most prey would be to retreat from those claws by leaping backward—only to be impaled by the deadly barbed tails lashing forward. Bane, however, ducked down under the claws and then stepped up to meet the creature's attack, his lightsaber held high above his head.

The blade sliced through the beast's underbelly, carving flesh and sinew and bone. Bane twisted the blade as it ran the length of the creature, redirecting it into a slightly diagonal stroke sure to cleave several vital organs. The move was simple, quick, and deadly.

The feline's momentum carried it over Bane's head and it crashed to the ground behind him, its body split open from midchest all the way to its still-twitching tails. The body shuddered once, the tails went motionless, and a milky film spread out to dull its luminous eyes.

Bane's heart was pounding from the thrill of combat. He stepped away from the corpse of his defeated foe, adrenaline still pumping through his veins. With a triumphant laugh, he threw his head back and shouted, "Is that all you've got, Qordis? Is that the best you can do?"

He looked around, half hoping to see the ghostly image of his former Master materialize. But it wasn't Qordis who appeared to him this time.

"You again," Bane said to the spectral image of Lord Kaan. "What do you want?"

Kaan, as usual, didn't speak. Instead the figure turned and walked away into the depths of the forest, its incorporeal form passing effortlessly through the branches and undergrowth. It took Bane a second to realize it was headed in the direction of Nadd's tomb.

"So be it," he muttered, using his lightsaber to hack a path in pursuit.

His illusory guide stayed with him the rest of the way, always just far enough ahead that Bane had to struggle to keep up. It took him nearly four hours of slogging through the jungle to reach his destination—a small clearing in the forest in which no vegetation grew. An irregular pyramid of flat, gray metal rose up to a height of twenty meters from the heart of the clearing.

Bane stopped at the edge. The ground ahead was nothing but dirt and mud; no living organism could flourish in the shadow of Nadd's crypt. Even the plants and trees bordering the clearing were stunted and deformed, corrupted by the dark side power that clung to the remains of the great Sith Master in death. The tomb itself was a disconcerting shape; the walls of the pyramid were set at odd and jarring angles, as if the stone of the crypt had been warped and twisted over the centuries.

There was a single entrance to the structure, a door that had once been sealed but looked as if it had been smashed open many centuries earlier by someone seeking the secrets of Nadd's final resting place. The ghostly figure of Kaan stood by the entrance, beckoning to Bane before disappearing inside.

Bane came forward slowly, senses attuned to any traps that might still be lying in wait. His mind flashed back to the ancient tombs in the Valley of the Sith on Korriban. Just before leaving the Academy, he'd ventured into those dark and dangerous crypts in search of guidance. He'd read accounts of Sith spirits appearing to share the secrets of the dark side with powerful apprentices who sought them out. But all Bane had found on Korriban was dust and bones.

He slid the backpack off his shoulders so it wouldn't encumber him. From inside he took half a dozen glow rods and crammed them into his belt, then left the pack on the ground near the crypt's entrance.

The ceiling inside the pyramid was low, and Bane had to duck as he went in. Using a glow rod for illumination, he found himself inside a small antechamber, with passages leading off in three different directions. Choosing the one on the left, he began his explorations. Room by room he searched the pyramid, finding nothing of value. Several of the chambers showed evidence that another had already been there, and Bane recalled the tales of Exar Kun, a Dark Jedi from a time long forgotten who was also rumored to have located Nadd's final resting place. According to the legends, Kun had emerged with power beyond his wildest imagining. Yet as Bane continued his fruitless explorations, doubt began to creep into his mind. Was it possible that this crypt—like the ones he'd searched on Korriban—was nothing but an empty, worthless tomb?

With mounting frustration he continued his search, winding his way through the passages until he reached an apparently insignificant chamber, almost buried at the very heart of the temple. Both Kaan and Qordis were there waiting for him.

They stood a meter apart, each on one side of a small doorway carved in the back wall. The door was only a meter high, and was blocked by a tightly fitted slab of black stone, giving Bane hope once more. The stone seemed to have been undisturbed by whoever had been here before him. It was possible no one had found this room, hidden at the end of the twisting maze of passages. Or maybe someone had found it but had been unable to move the stone slab. It was even possible that the small entrance had once been hidden by the lost arts of Sith sorcery, and the spell obscuring it had gradually faded over the centuries, making it visible only now.

Glancing quickly at the twin manifestations on either side

of the small doorway, Bane crouched down to examine the slab. Its surface was smooth, and it extended only a few centimeters out from the passage, making it impossible to get a firm grip. Of course, there was one other way to move it.

Summoning his strength, Bane reached out with the Force and tried to pull the stone toward him. It barely moved. The stone was heavy, but it was more than sheer mass that held it in place. There was something fighting his power, resisting him. Bane took a deep breath and tilted his head from side to side, loudly cracking his neck as he gathered himself for another attempt.

This time he went deep, plunging into the well of power that dwelled within his core. He reached back into his past, dredging up memories buried deep in his subconscious: memories of his father, Hurst; memories of the beatings; memories of the hatred he bore for the man who had raised him. As he did so, he felt his power building.

It started, as it always did, with a single spark of heat. The spark quickly became a flame, and the flame an inferno. Bane's body trembled with the strain as he fought to contain the power, letting the dark side energy build to a critical mass. He forced himself to endure the unbearable heat as long as he could, then thrust his fist forward, channeling everything inside him toward the stone blocking him from his destiny.

The heavy slab flew across the room and struck the far wall with a heavy thud. A long vertical crack appeared in the wall, though the dark stone block itself was undamaged. Bane dropped to his knees, panting from the exertion. He looked up to see the ghostly watchers still keeping their vigil beside the entrance. With a shake of his head, he crawled to the now-open doorway and peered in.

The room beyond was dark, so Bane pulled one of the glow rods from his belt and tossed it through the opening. It landed on the floor, illuminating the room. From what he could see, it was a circular, high-ceilinged chamber about five meters in diameter. A stone pedestal stood in the very center. Atop it was a small crystal pyramid Bane instantly recognized as a Sith Holocron.

The ancient Masters of the dark side had used Holocrons to store all their wisdom, knowledge, and secrets. A Holocron could contain ancient rituals of devastating power, or the keys to unlocking the magics of ancient Sith sorcerers, or even avatars that simulated the personality of the Holocron's original creator. The information inside was so valuable that for many centuries Holocrons had been the single most valuable tool in passing on the legacy of the great Sith Lords to future generations.

Unfortunately, the art of making Sith Holocrons had been lost several millennia past. And over the years the Jedi had scoured the galaxy to find all the known Sith Holocrons, then hidden them away at their library on Coruscant so no one could delve into their forbidden knowledge. To actually find a Holocron like this, one that might contain the teachings of Freedon Nadd himself, was good fortune beyond anything Bane had even imagined.

Crouching down, he squeezed his massive shoulders through the tight doorway. Not surprisingly, Kaan and Qordis were already waiting for him inside. Bane glanced over at them, then up at the five-meter-high ceiling. By the light of the glow rod he could make out movement, as if a carpet of living creatures was crawling across the surface above his head.

He stood motionless, his ears picking up wet slurping sounds. As his eyes became accustomed to the dim light he was able to make out a colony of strange crustaceans clinging to the roof. They were almost flat, and somewhat oval in shape—a circular shell that tapered to a point near either end. They varied in size from slightly smaller than a fist to as broad across as a large dinner plate, and their coloring ranged from bronze to a reddish gold. The slurping came as they dragged themselves along the ceiling, crawling over one another and leaving glistening trails of slime in their wake.

As he studied them, one of the creatures fell away from the

others and dropped down toward him. Bane swatted it aside disdainfully with one hand, sending its hard shell bouncing and skittering across the cavern floor.

A second later another broke free and tumbled down. Bane ignited his lightsaber and slashed at it. The blow batted the creature away, sending it flipping end-over-end into a far corner of the room. Bane stared in amazement—the lightsaber should have sliced the creature clean through. But his weapon hadn't even left a scratch on its hard, gleaming shell.

Suddenly realizing he was in grave danger, Bane made a lunge for the Holocron. As his hand closed around it, the colony of crustaceans broke free en masse and cascaded down on him in a chitinous swarm. With one hand clutching the Holocron, he swiped at them with his lightsaber and deflected others with the power of the Force. But there were too many to keep them all at bay; it was like trying to ward off raindrops in a storm.

One struck him on the shoulder and latched on, instantly burning through his armor and clothing with an acidic secretion before fastening itself to his skin. Bane felt a thousand tiny teeth burrowing into the thick meat of his back, followed by the searing pain of the acid secretion melting his flesh.

He screamed and slammed his back up against the wall hoping to jar the creature loose, but it held fast. As he struggled to dislodge it, a second struck him square in the chest. He screamed again as the burning acid and tiny teeth dug through clothes, skin, and even his thick pectoral muscles to fasten directly to his breastbone.

Bane staggered under the onslaught of pain, but managed to strike out with the Force. The rest of the creatures were sent hurtling away from him like leaves swept up by a fierce wind; they clacked and clattered as they struck the walls of the room. The brief reprieve gave Bane a chance to drop to his knees and scamper through the cramped opening and back into the small room from which he had originally entered.

Ignoring the agony of the two creatures still attached to

him, he reached out with the Force and hoisted the stone block on the far side of the room up into the air. His powers were enhanced by both pain and a desperate urgency, and the block moved easily for him this time, flying across the chamber to plug the entrance before any more of the strange crustaceans could scuttle out after him.

For a second he just lay there panting, clutching the Holo-cron and trying to ignore the pain coming from the two para-sitic organisms feeding on his body. He could hear the rest of the colony on the other side of the wall, the wet gurgles of their grasping mouths mingling with the sharp clacking of their hard shells as they crawled up the walls back to their roosts on the ceiling.

He imagined he heard another sound, as well: the harsh, mocking laughter of Qordis and Kaan echoing off the walls of Freedon Nadd's tomb.

8

"CHANCELLOR VALORUM WILL see you now," the Twi'lek assistant said from behind her desk.

Seeing Farfalla rise, Johun did the same, tugging awkwardly to reposition the unfamiliar ceremonial robes his new Master had insisted he wear for the meeting. Johun had protested that his wardrobe had nothing to do with who he was or why they were here, but Farfalla had merely replied, "On Coruscant, appearance matters."

Johun had never been to Coruscant before—or any of the other Core Worlds, for that matter. He'd been born and raised on Sermeria, an agriworld in the Expansion Region between the Inner and Mid Rims of the galaxy. His family had worked a farm a few kilometers outside of Addolis, one small cog in the great Sermerian agricultural complex that produced an overabundance of food and sold it to more developed worlds that lacked enough arable land to support their own populations.

He'd left Sermeria at the age of ten to begin his Jedi training. In the decade since he had accompanied General Hoth to dozens of worlds, though his former Master had preferred to stay on the Outer Rim, far from the politicians and urban culture of the Republic's capital. The planets they visited tended to be less developed rural worlds, much like Sermeria itself. As a result, Johun had never seen anything even remotely resembling the planetwide metropolis that was Galactic City.

On their initial approach to the world, Farfalla had tried to point out to him the location of important structures, like the Senate's Great Rotunda and the Jedi Temple. But to Johun's provincial eye everything blended into one unbroken ocean of permacrete, durasteel, and brightly colored flashing lights.

Upon landing, they had disembarked and boarded an airspeeder that had whisked them off toward their meeting with Chancellor Valorum. Johun had simply sat and gawked at the spectacle as they raced along the skylane, their speeder weaving in and out among skyrises so tall, the ground wasn't even visible beneath them. Occasionally they would dive down or swoop back up as their journey led them under and over pedestrian walkways, hovering billboards, and even other vehicles.

By the end of the trip, Johun's already bedazzled senses had been completely overwhelmed by the constant stream of traffic and the mind-boggling numbers of people who chose to live and work on Coruscant. The overall impression he took away from the experience was a sickening blur of motion set against a deafening cacophony of sound . . . all too much for a simple farm boy to handle.

Farfalla, on the other hand, was in his element. Johun had noticed his new mentor coming to life when they touched down, as if he were feeding on the energy of the great metropolis. The frantic pace and the madding crowds seemed to revitalize Valenthyne, the city washing away the weariness of a long military campaign on a dreary little frontier world. Farfalla even looked different here; set against the vibrant, cosmopolitan backdrop of the galactic capital, the clothes that had seemed so vain and garish back on Ruusan now looked to be the height of fashion and style.

Even at the center of the halls of power, Farfalla looked completely at ease. He gave a gracious bow of acknowledgment to the Chancellor's assistant, eliciting a flirtatious smile from the young woman, then moved with a confident yet purposeful stride through the doorway into Valorum's inner sanctum. Johun gave a bow of his own, stiff and forced, then scurried off after him.

The Chancellor's office was less ornate and more functional than Johun had expected. The walls, carpet, and furnishings were all a deep, dark brown, giving the room an air of significance. There was a large window in one wall, though much to the young Jedi's relief the coverings had been drawn for this meeting. In the center of the room were half a dozen comfortable-looking chairs set around a circular conference table; several monitors lined the walls, flickering with updates from various HoloNet news programs.

Tarsus Valorum was seated behind a large desk facing the doorway, and he rose to greet them. He was a tall man in his early fifties, though he looked ten years younger. He had dark hair; bright, piercing eyes; a straight, slightly pointed nose; and an almost perfectly square chin—a face many had called "honest and determined." It was these traits, along with his exemplary record of public service, that had led to Valorum being appointed the first non-Jedi Chancellor in over four centuries.

Johun had heard rumors that Farfalla had actually been the one in line for the position but had declined it, so that he could join the Army of Light on Ruusan. The young man wondered if his Master approved of the man who had been chosen to replace him.

"Master Valenthyne," Valorum said, clasping Farfalla's hand in an efficient, well-practiced gesture of welcome. "Thank you for coming on such short notice."

"You didn't leave me a lot of options, Your Excellency," Valenthyne noted.

"I apologize for that," the Chancellor replied, even as he turned and extended his hand to Johun. "And this must be your apprentice," he said, taking note of the long braid that marked the young man as one who had not yet completed his initial Jedi training.

"I am Padawan Johun Othone, Your Excellency."

Valorum's grip was firm but not overpowering—the perfect politician's handshake. He pumped Johun's arm twice, then pulled his hand free and indicated the chairs around the conference table.

"Please, noble Jedi. Make yourselves comfortable."

Farfalla took the end seat on the near side of the table. Johun sat down in the chair directly across from him, leaving the Chancellor the lone seat at the head of the table, between the two Jedi. Once everyone was in position it was Farfalla who initiated the discussion, turning slightly to better face Valorum.

"The message you sent me was most unexpected, Your Excellency. And the timing was somewhat inconvenient. We are still dealing with the aftermath of the thought bomb on Ruusan."

"I understand your position, Master Valenthyne. But you must also appreciate mine. News of the Brotherhood's defeat has reached the HoloNet. As far as the public is concerned, the war is over. And the Senate is eager to put this unpleasantness behind us."

"As are the Jedi," Farfalla replied. "But this motion you plan to put forward—the so-called Ruusan Reformation—calls for some rather extreme measures."

"That is why I brought you here to discuss the recommendations before we vote on them," Valorum answered. "I wanted you to understand why this has to be done."

Johun had not seen the details of the message Farfalla had received, nor had his Master spoken of it to him during their journey to Coruscant. As a result, he was having difficulty piercing their political double-talk. Fortunately, Farfalla chose to cut through the diplomatic niceties and address the issue directly in his next response.

"Do you realize the ramifications of what you are asking, Tarsus? Your proposal calls for the Jedi to renounce their military ranks and completely disband all our military, naval, and starfighter forces. You are asking us to destroy the Army of Light!"

"The Army of Light was created as a reaction to the Brotherhood of Darkness," Valorum countered. "With the Brotherhood gone, it no longer serves a purpose."

Johun couldn't believe what he was hearing. "Its purpose is to protect the Republic!" he burst out, unable to contain himself.

"Protect it from who?" the Chancellor challenged, snapping his head around to address him. "The Sith are gone."

"The Sith are never truly gone," Johun said darkly.

"And therein lies the problem," Valorum replied. "Over the past four centuries we have seen the Jedi declare war on the agents of the dark side time and time again. It is a struggle that never ends. And with each conflict, more civilians are swept up in your web of war. Innocent beings die as armies align with you or your enemies. Worlds loyal to the Republic break away, fracturing a once united galaxy. It is time to put a stop to this cycle of madness."

Farfalla held up his hand, cutting Johun off before the young man could say anything else. He waited for Valorum to turn his attention away from the Padawan, then asked, "Tarsus, do you really believe the changes you have proposed will do that?"

"I do, Master Valenthyne." There was undeniable conviction in his voice. "There are many good people who fear the Jedi and what they are capable of. They see the Jedi as instigators of war. You claim your actions are guided by the Force, but to those who cannot feel its presence it appears as if your order is not accountable to anyone or anything."

"And so you want the Jedi to answer to you." Farfalla sighed. "The Chancellor and the Senate."

"I want you to answer to the elected officials who represent the citizens of the Republic," Valorum declared. Then he added, "This is not an attempt to grab power for myself. The Jedi Council will still oversee your order. But they will do so under the supervision of the Senate's Judicial Department. It is the only way we can heal the scars left by your wars against the Sith.

"The Republic is crumbling," he continued. "For the past thousand years it has slowly been decaying and rotting away. A rebirth is the only way to reverse this process.

"Many of the measures proposed in the Ruusan Reformation are symbolic, but there is power in that symbolism. This will be the beginning of a new era for the Republic. We will enter a new age of prosperity and peace.

"Let the Jedi show their commitment to this peace. Cast aside the trappings of war and assume your rightful place as counselors and advisers. Instead of this endless battle to hold back the dark side, you should help to guide us toward the light."

Valorum finished his speech and looked expectantly at Farfalla. Johun held his breath, waiting for his Master's outburst of righteous indignation. He wanted to watch as Valenthyne expertly and eloquently refuted the Chancellor's arguments. He couldn't wait to witness the impassioned defense of all that the Jedi stood for and believed in that would justify everything General Hoth had done.

"I will speak to the Jedi Council and see that our order complies with your demands, Your Excellency," Farfalla said, his voice heavy. "And I will send the order to begin the dissolution of the Army of Light as soon as the Senate passes your proposal."

Johun's draw dropped, but he was too stunned to say anything.

"Your cooperation is greatly appreciated, Master Valenthyne," Valorum replied, rising to his feet. "Now if you will excuse me, I must call the Senate to session."

At first it seemed as if he was about to escort them from the room. But when he glanced at Johun, he obviously sensed the young man was not quite ready to let the matter rest. The Chancellor hesitated, giving him a chance to speak.

Johun, however, remained stubbornly silent. Valorum exchanged a brief look with Farfalla, then nodded in deference to the Jedi Master.

"Please see yourselves out when you are ready," the Chancellor said, before giving them each a cordial nod and leaving them alone in the room.

"How could you?" Johun demanded angrily the moment Valorum was gone, leaning across the table toward Farfalla.

The older man sighed and leaned backward, his hands clasped together and his fingers forming a steeple just below his chin.

"I know this is difficult to understand, Johun. But the Chancellor was right. Everything he said was true."

"General Hoth would never agree to this!" Johun spat at him.

"No," Farfalla admitted. "He never could understand the value of compromise. That was his great fault."

"And what's yours?" Johun shouted, slamming his fist on the table and jumping up so swiftly he knocked over his chair. "Betraying the memory of your friends?"

"Watch your anger," Farfalla said softly.

Johun froze, then felt his face flushing in shame and embarrassment. He took several deep, cleansing breaths—a Jedi ritual to calm and focus the mind. Once he had his emotions under control he turned and righted his chair, then took his seat again.

"I'm sorry, Master Valenthyne," he said, struggling to keep his voice even. "But this feels as if we are dishonoring him."

"Your Master was a man of great strength and steadfast conviction," Farfalla assured him, still sitting with his steepled hands clasped beneath his chin. "No other could have led us through our time of crisis. But the galaxy does not exist in a state of perpetual crisis.

"The Jedi are the sworn servants of the Republic," he continued. "We will fight to defend it in times of war, but when war is over we must be willing to set aside our weapons and become ambassadors of peace."

The younger man shook his head. "This still doesn't feel right."

"Since the earliest days of your training, you have known nothing but war," Farfalla reminded him. "It can be difficult for you to remember that violence should only be used when all other methods have failed.

"But you must always remind yourself that a Jedi values wisdom and enlightenment over all else. The great truths we seek are often difficult to find, and sometimes it is easier to seek out an enemy to do battle with . . . especially when we hunger to avenge those who have fallen. This is one of the ways even good people can fall to the dark side."

"I'm sorry, Master," Johun whispered. The words seemed to catch in his throat, even though his apology was sincere.

"You are still a Padawan. You are not expected to possess the wisdom of a Master," Farfalla consoled him. "That is why I brought you here: so that you could learn."

"I will do my best," Johun vowed.

"That is all I can ever ask," his Master replied.

THANKS TO THE Holocron he had discovered in Nadd's tomb, Bane now knew that the strange crustaceans that had attached themselves to him were called orbalisks. He had also discovered, through his own trial and error, that they could not be removed.

In the moments after his escape from the orbalisk chamber, he'd tried prying the one on his chest loose with the hunting knife from his boot, to no avail. Failing that, he had tried to dig it out by carving away the surrounding flesh. He'd drawn the knife across his chest in a long, straight line, feeling the agony of the blade slicing deep enough to cut through skin and muscle. And then he'd watched in amazement as the wound healed itself almost instantly, the creature having somehow caused his tissue to regenerate.

Bane had tried the Force next, probing deep inside to better understand what was happening to him. He could sense the creatures feeding on his power, gorging themselves on the dark side energies coursing through every fiber and cell of his being. But though they were parasites, they were also giving something back. As they fed, they pumped a constant stream of chemicals into his body. The alien fluids burned like acid as they were absorbed into his circulatory system; it felt as if every drop of blood were boiling . . . but the benefits were too powerful to be ignored. In addition to his miraculous healing abilities, he felt stronger than he ever had. His senses were keener, his reflexes quicker. And on his chest and back where the creatures had latched on, their virtually impenetrable shells would serve as armor plates capable of withstanding even a direct strike from a lightsaber.

The relationship, he had finally realized, was symbiotic—as long as he could endure the constant searing pain of the alien fluids being absorbed and metabolized in his bloodstream. A small price to pay, Bane had decided before turning his attention to the Holocron. Sitting cross-legged on the hard floor of the antechamber inside Nadd's crypt, he reached out tentatively with the dark side and brushed his hand against the small, crystal pyramid. Responding to his caress, it began to glow.

For the next four days and nights he lost himself in the secrets of the ancient artifact. As he suspected, it had been created by Freedon Nadd. Bane delved into the Holocron's secrets with the aid of the gatekeeper: a miniature hologrammic projection of the long-dead Sith Master responsible for its creation. The gatekeeper guided and directed his studies, serving as a virtual mentor to those who sought out Nadd's lost secrets inside the sinister pyramid.

Though Nadd had been human, his avatar was the image of a man who had succumbed to the physical corruption that sometimes affected those who delved too deeply into the power of the dark side. His skin was pallid, the flesh withered and sunken, and his eyes were glowing yellow orbs devoid of iris or pupil. Despite this, he still appeared as a formidable warrior: broad-shouldered, clad in heavy battle armor and the helm that had doubled as his crown when he had proclaimed himself king over the nearby world of Onderon.

Through the gatekeeper, Bane learned of the Dark Master's experiments with the orbalisks, and his only partly successful efforts to control their power. He discovered not only what they were called, but also all the details of their ecology. Some of the information merely confirmed what he already knew: once attached to a host the orbalisks could not be removed. But he also learned that, in addition to boosting a host's physical abilities, it was possible to tap into the parasites' ability to feed on the dark side to greatly increase one's own command of the Force.

However, Nadd's research also warned of several dangerous side effects of infestation that went beyond the constant physical pain. Should one of the organisms somehow be killed, it would release rapidly increasing levels of toxins, killing its host in a matter of days. The orbalisks would also grow over time, slowly spreading until they covered his entire body from head to toe. Fortunately, along with this disturbing revelation, Bane discovered blueprints for a special helmet and face guard designed to keep the parasites from growing over his eyes, nose, and mouth while he slept.

But the orbalisk research was only the beginning. Freedon Nadd had been a Jedi who turned to the dark side as the apprentice of Naga Sadow, the former ruler of the ancient Sith Empire. Sadow's power had been so great, it had allowed him to survive for six centuries, fueled by the energies of the dark side. As his apprentice, Nadd had absorbed all his knowledge and teachings, transferring them into the Holocron before murdering Sadow and taking his place.

Not surprisingly, most of the information inside the Holocron was hidden, locked away in the depths of its crystalline structure where it could be accessed only through time, meditation, and careful study. It would take many months, maybe even years, before Bane could lay claim to its greatest secrets. And right now there were more immediate concerns he needed to deal with.

Storing the Holocron safely away, he ventured forth from the crypt to find a way to escape the surface of Dxun. The specters of Kaan and Qordis were waiting for him outside.

"You are trapped here," Qordis said, falling immediately into his litany of failure and despair. "What good is the Holocron if you can never leave this moon?"

Bane reached inward to call upon the dark side, drawing it not only from himself but also from the orbalisks fastened to his chest and back. Feeling an incredible surge of power beyond any he had known before, he released it in a burst of energy. The hallucinations that had plagued his wounded mind ever since the detonation of the thought bomb vanished, instantly and utterly annihilated by his newfound power. He was stronger now than he ever had been, and he knew the visions of the dead Sith would haunt him no more.

Liberated from his tormentors, he still had to find a way off of Dxun. When he stared up into the sky he could see Onderon looming large above him, the planet so close to its moon that their atmospheres had occasionally passed through each other in centuries past. For a brief window of time, this had allowed the great flying beasts of Dxun to migrate to the other world, where some had been tamed and trained to become the fearsome mounts of Onderon's fabled beast-rider clans.

Staring up at the world that was almost near enough to touch, Bane could sense Zannah's imminent arrival there. Soon she would touch down on the dangerous and often deadly planet, and if her Master wasn't there with her, it was unlikely she would survive.

As he continued to gaze up he noticed an enormous winged creature circling high above, hunting for food. At the same time, the hunter noticed him. Folding its wide leathery wings tight against its body, it dropped into a dive headed straight for Bane.

He regarded the creature with a cool, analytical precision as it plummeted toward him. From the Holocron he knew it was called a drexl, one of the reptilian predators that ruled the skies of Dxun. Their appearance resembled that of a winged lizard: scaled, violet skin; a long, thick tail; and heavily muscled body and legs. A blunt, oversized head sat atop an extended, sinewy neck. It had tiny avian eyes; a flat, pushed-in snout; and a wide jaw full of jagged yellow teeth. Bane estimated this particular specimen to be ten meters in length from nose to tail with a wingspan of nearly twenty meters—a full-grown male easily large enough to suit his needs.

An instant before the beast swooped in to snatch him up with its razor-sharp talons, he reached out with the Force and touched the drexl's mind, attempting to dominate the brute's will with his own. He had done this once before, to a rancor on the dying world of Lehon. But the drexl's mind was stronger than he anticipated, and the beast shrugged off his efforts as it let loose a bloodcurdling shriek and slammed into him.

One of the drexl's feet lunged forward to impale him with its enormous claws, only to be deflected by the impenetrable orbalisk carapace on his chest. Instead of being skewered and carried away, Bane was sent flying backward by the momentum of the creature's dive. He hit the ground and rolled several times before springing back to his feet, uninjured thanks to his newfound physical prowess.

He saw the drexl swooping back up toward the sky, readying itself for a second attempt to dive down and seize its prey. Bane reached out to touch its mind again, bringing his will down with the crushing force of the sledgehammers he'd used in the mining tunnels of Apatros.

The drexl's body shuddered under the impact of his mental assault, and it screamed a piercing cry of protest that split the sky and reverberated over the treetops. This time, however, Bane succeeded in his efforts to subjugate the beast's thoughts to his own.

It circled twice more before coming in to land beside him. At an unspoken command from its new Master, it crouched and allowed Bane to climb atop its back. An instant later it spread its wings and took to the air, climbing higher and higher.

Bane pushed his mount, urging it into the uppermost reaches of the breathable atmosphere. Above them the nearby world of Onderon grew in size until it completely filled the horizon. Only a few hundred kilometers separated Dxun from its neighbor, an insignificant sliver of distance on the scale of worlds and solar systems.

Already he could feel the faint gravitational pull of Onderon trying to draw them in, the larger planet's mass battling for dominance with that of its slightly smaller satellite. Driven by Bane's relentless will, the drexl pumped its wings furiously, gaining speed and elevation with every beat.

Bane began to summon the Force, letting it build until the last possible instant. Then, gathering the dark side around him and his mount like a protective cloak, he spurred the drexl forward, and a second later they broke free of Dxun's atmosphere and plunged into the frozen vacuum of space that separated him from Onderon and freedom.

9

THE SOUND OF THE *Star-Wake*'s autonav update jarred Zannah awake from a restless slumber. She had curled herself awkwardly into the pilot's chair, and now her neck was stiff from sleeping in an uncomfortable position. There were plenty of places to lie down and stretch out properly in the cargo hold at the back, but Zannah couldn't sleep in there. Not with all the bodies.

She had removed Wend and Irtanna from the cockpit in the first few minutes after their deaths. It had been a struggle getting Wend out of his chair, but her adrenaline levels had still been high from the confrontation with Irtanna and she had managed to drag him down the hall to the cargo hold where his father and brother lay.

Relocating Irtanna had been more difficult. She had a soldier's physique, lean and muscular, and easily weighed twice what Zannah did. At first the girl hadn't even been able to budge the corpse. By the time she realized she would have to call upon the Force to aid her, the excitement of the moment was gone. In the aftermath she'd found it much more difficult to summon the dark side; each time she tried to draw upon her inner anger, her conscience had fought against her. Instead of the familiar heat of power, she'd felt only guilt and doubt. Images of Bordon and his sons lying side by side on the cargo room's floor had clouded her thoughts, making it difficult for her to concentrate.

Zannah had tried to block the images and allow the dark side to flow through her, but she'd been only partly successful. In the end she had relied more on determination and sweat than the power of the Force. Grunting and straining, she had eventually managed to drag Irtanna for half a meter before having to stop and catch her breath. She had repeated the process again and again, slowly pulling the body down the ship's corridor until Irtanna lay beside the others.

There had been very little blood; apart from the first glancing shot to Bordon's gut, all the wounds had been cauterized by the heat of the blaster bolts. Yet the lack of gore had done nothing to make the bodies' appearance any less unsettling. Their lifeless eyes had stared up at nothing, compelling Zannah to bend forward and close the lids, her hand trembling as she brushed against the clammy skin. Still not satisfied, she'd hunted around until she found several large blankets to drape over the corpses. Even under the sheets, the profiles of her victims were still somewhat recognizable, but there was nothing more she could do about that. She had only come back to the cargo hold one other time since then, grabbing as many ration kits as she could carry and taking them up to the front, trying not to look at the shrouded bodies at her feet.

In the ensuing seven days she had been both praying for and dreading an end to her journey, when she would be reunited with her Master and begin her training in the ways of the Sith. She never left the cockpit except to use the ship's refresher. Whenever she tried to sleep, she could never manage more than a fitful doze plagued with nightmares in which she relived her killing spree over and over.

Each time she woke she would tear open a ration kit and pick at the food, her body slowly replenishing what it had lost during her weeks on Ruusan. But the rations were meant for a full-grown adult, and she could never finish them. When she was done, she would toss the uneaten portion along with the container down the hall toward the cargo hold. After a few days the smells of a dozen half-finished meals began to mingle into a sickly sweet aroma that hung like a thin curtain in the air. Zannah actually welcomed the cloying scent of rotting food; it covered up the mounting stench of the decaying bodies in the back.

To fight the boredom, she'd tried to imagine what her future would be like as Bane's apprentice. She would focus on everything he'd promised her: the ability to call upon and command the Force at will; the mysterious secrets of the dark side; the power to reach her true potential and fulfill her destiny. Her mind, however, kept returning to the *Star-Wake*'s dead crew. And each time it happened she wondered what her Master would think about such weakness.

The autonav chimed again. Zannah glanced at the readout: The ship would be entering atmosphere in five minutes. She was being prompted to select landing coordinates.

Zannah sat up straight in the pilot's chair, furrowing her brow as she studied the onscreen display. She'd been hoping that the automated systems that had carried the vessel from Ruusan to Onderon would also be programmed to land. Unfortunately, it seemed that task now fell to her . . . and she had no idea how to bring the ship down safely.

She punched a button on the screen labeled LANDING ZONES. A long list of unfamiliar locations and coordinates began to scroll across the display. She had no clue what any of the numbers meant, and no idea how to select one anyway.

As she stared at the readout—they were entering atmosphere now—Zannah felt the familiar bump of turbulence. Caught between frustration and panic, she reached out and began randomly poking buttons. She stopped only when the autonav beeped twice: Destination accepted.

Heaving a sigh of relief, she collapsed back into her seat and buckled up for touchdown. She tried to peer over the console to get a view through the cockpit window of where she was headed, but she was too short to see clearly. All she could make out was kilometers of thick, green canopy stretching out in every direction. Evidently she had selected a landing zone in a less civilized part of the world.

A sobering question crossed her mind. *Does the autopilot know how to land in the middle of a forest? Or will it smash me to bits against the treetops?*

As if reading her thoughts, the autonav chimed angrily. Zannah read the update: "Suboptimal conditions detected at selected landing zone. Seeking nearest available alternative site."

She felt the ship bank slightly, veering and leveling off to skim the forest in search of a large-enough clearing to land in.

"Alternative landing zone located," the screen assured her a few moments later, and she felt the nose dip as the vessel began her final descent.

She heard a loud bang and the heavy, staccato pounding of branches striking the exterior of the hull as the *Star-Wake* plowed through a thin layer of branches en route to her chosen destination on the surface. A second later the ship rocked hard to one side, deflecting off a tree trunk too thick to smash through. Next came a series of heavy, jarring thumps as the ship skipped and skidded across the ground before finally coming to a stop.

Shaken but uninjured, Zannah undid her safety harness and opened the exit hatch. As she descended the vessel's loading ramp, she noticed she was on one end of a large clearing that had been carved from the forest to create a circle nearly two hundred meters in diameter. Much to her surprise, someone was in the middle of the clearing waving her over.

"Whoever's flying that ship of yours must be the worst pilot in the galaxy," the man said, eyeing her up and down as she approached him and stopped a few meters away.

He looked to be in his late twenties, though it was hard to tell because of his scrawny and somewhat scraggly appearance. His long copper-colored hair was full of mats and tangles, and his red beard was patchy and uneven across his grimy face. He wore loose pants and a torn shirt that might have been white beneath the mud and other unidentifiable stains. Over the shirt he wore a short leather vest that was fraying at the edges, and a pair of heavily scuffed boots. He gave off a sour odor.

"What's the matter, girlie?" he asked. "You don't speak Basic? I said whoever's flying your ship is the worst pilot I ever saw."

"Nobody's flying it," Zannah answered carefully, glancing back at the ship that was now a good thirty meters behind her. "She was set on auto."

"That explains it," he said with a nod. "Auto's only good at landing on a permacrete runway. Not worth bantha poodoo out here."

The man took a step toward her, and Zannah instinctively took a step back. There was something very wrong about finding this man waiting for her at the heart of a clearing in the middle of the forest. But she wasn't worried about the strangeness of the situation. Instead her mind was desperately trying to think of a way to keep him from discovering the bodies in the *Star-Wake*'s cargo hold.

"Why you using the autopilot out here, girlie? You don't got a pilot on that ship with you?"

Zannah shook her head. "No. There's nobody else on board. Just me."

"Just you?" he said with an arched eyebrow. "You sure about that?"

"I stole it," she said defiantly. Maybe if she could convince him she had been alone on the vessel, he wouldn't go in and find the bodies.

The man let out a low chuckle. "Stole it, you say?" Then, in a louder voice he called out, "Looks like we got ourselves a thief!"

A dozen men and women stepped out from the thick trees on the edges of the wide clearing the *Star-Wake* had landed in. They were all human, and most of them seemed to be about the same age as the redhead Zannah had first spoken with. Like him, they were clad in a motley assortment of soiled, ragged clothing. Several of the new arrivals had appeared from behind the redhead, but more than a few had emerged from the trees on the other side of the clearing behind Zannah, effectively cutting her off from her ship. And, unlike the man who had first greeted her, the newcomers were all armed with vibroblades or blaster rifles.

"How . . . how did you find me?" she demanded, glancing from side to side as she began to realize she was surrounded.

"Scouts saw your ship flying over our territory," the redhead answered. "Figured if you were looking for a place to touch down, you'd end up here on our landing pad."

"Landing pad?" Zannah repeated in surprise, momentarily distracted from her dangerous situation. "You made this place so ships could land here?"

"Who said anything about ships?" the man answered with a sly grin. He put two fingers to his lips and gave a sharp whistle so loud and shrill it made Zannah wince.

The air above was filled with the sound of a great roaring wind, and a dark shadow blotted out the sun. Zannah looked up in amazement as four enormous winged reptiles swooped down from the sky to land on the far side of the clearing. The creatures were outfitted with bridle and reins, and each wore a large saddle on its back that looked big enough to carry up to three people at once.

"You're beast-riders," she gasped, remembering Tallo's warning when she'd first mentioned Onderon.

"Skelda clan," the man said. "And like I already told you, you're in our territory."

"I'm . . . I'm sorry," Zannah said. "I didn't know."

The man shrugged. "Doesn't matter if you knew or not. You want to use a Skelda clan landing pad, you got to pay us for the privilege."

From the corner of her eye Zannah noticed his companions slowly drawing in tighter around her.

"I don't have any money," she said, taking a half step backward.

"That's okay," the man replied nonchalantly. "We'll just take your ship."

Zannah spun on her heel and tried to run for the forest as the man lunged for her. He'd been expecting her to make a break for it, and he was quick. He was on her after only a few steps, tackling her from behind. He knocked her to the ground, his weight slamming her to the hard dirt. And the next instant he was flying backward through the air.

He hit the ground with a hard grunt, the wind knocked out of him as he landed on his side five meters away. Zannah scrambled back to her feet. The other members of his clan had rushed forward when she started to run; now they all took a quick step back, weapons raised high above their heads. They were staring at her with wide-eyed expressions of fear and disbelief.

She turned back to the leader when she heard him laughing. He picked himself up off the ground and winked at her.

"Looks like we got ourselves a little Jedi in training," he said, loud enough for his companions to hear. "What brought you to Onderon, little Jedi? Decided to run away from your Master?"

"I'm not a Jedi," Zannah said in a cold whisper.

"That's right," he agreed. "You don't know how to control your power, do you? It only comes out when you're mad or afraid. Isn't that right?"

Zannah clenched her jaw and narrowed her eyes, but didn't say anything.

"Listen, little Jedi," he said, pulling a small blade from his boot and beginning to walk slowly toward her. "There are twelve of us and only one of you. You really think you can take us all on?"

"Maybe," Zannah said, thrusting out her chin.

"What about them?" he asked, tilting his head in the direction of the flying beasts as he continued his cautious advance. "One command from any of us and the drexls will rip your pretty little blond head clean off your body. Do you really think your powers will be enough to stop them?"

"No," Zannah admitted. In the back of her mind she felt something twitch, almost as if someone was calling out to her.

"It's time for you to give up, girlie," the redhead told her with a cruel grin. He was only a few steps away from her now, his blade held out before him. "You're all alone."

Zannah smiled back at him. "No, I'm not."

As the words left her lips a dark shadow fell across the two of them. The man had just enough time to look up before he was plucked from the ground by the swooping talons of a drexl far larger than any of the four he had called down earlier. It let loose a scream that shook the ground beneath Zannah's feet as it arced back up toward the sky. Astride the great beast's neck sat the familiar figure of Darth Bane.

The drexl climbed to a height of thirty meters, then released its deadly grip on the redheaded man. His limp body plunged to the ground below, landing with a dull thud and the sharp crack of bones.

The sight of their leader's mangled corpse dropping from the sky spurred the rest of the clan into action. With whooping cries and shrill whistles, they raced to their mounts to take the battle to the air, all thoughts of the little girl on the ground forgotten.

The first drexl off the ground had only two riders. The woman in front handled the reins, focusing all her attention and energy on the difficult task of steering and controlling the mount. The man seated behind her served as her eyes and strategist, shouting out instructions she followed without question—when to climb, when to dive, when to bank, and when to strike. The empty seat behind them was no doubt where the redheaded man would have sat had he not been killed.

The remaining drexls each carried a full complement of three riders—one to work the reins, one to give the orders, and one armed with a large blaster rifle. The bolts would have little effect against a drexl's thick hide, but a well-placed shot could bring down an enemy rider from long range. However, the offensive advantage of the third rider was offset by the extra weight that made the mount slower and less maneuverable.

With only two passengers, the first drexl was able to quickly outdistance the others. It climbed into the clear blue sky where Bane and his new pet circled defiantly, issuing a challenge that could not be ignored.

As this first opponent drew near, the Dark Lord's flier screamed its war cry and veered to intercept it. From the ground Zannah watched as the two reptavians clashed, the beasts seeming to throw themselves at each other in midair. Grappling together, they plunged planetward in a short but savage confrontation. The two great bodies twisted and writhed against each other, buffeted by wings and slashed by claws that glinted in the sun. Tails lashed out, attempting to blind the enemy flier or dislodge a rider. Jaws bit and snapped as the drexls' oversized heads danced and weaved atop the serpentine necks.

The beast-riders had counted on their skill and experience in aerial combat to carry them to victory against a lone rider overwhelmed by the struggle to control a flier by himself. They didn't realize that the Force gave Bane complete and total command of the creature. Without this advantage, their defeat was never in doubt. Bane's mount was larger and stronger, it carried the weight of a single rider, and it had no reins, bridle, or saddle to encumber its movements.

Less than twenty meters above the ground, Bane's drexl twisted, ducked, and tore out the throat of its enemy. Ten meters above the ground it disengaged from its foe, pulled out of the deadly free fall, and soared victoriously upward. The other drexl, mortally wounded, crashed to the dirt, a landing that killed the mount and both riders instantly.

The entire sequence had taken less than ten seconds, yet it had allowed the other Skelda clan flier teams to get high above their quarry, giving them a tactical advantage. With powerful flaps of its mighty wings, Bane's mount rose up to meet them. They responded with a barrage of blasterfire aimed at the mysterious lone rider, only to see the Sith Master ignite his lightsaber and deflect the incoming bolts.

One of the enemy fliers swooped in toward him, a feint meant to draw Bane's attention from the other two. The beast dived past him, a few meters too distant to actually engage in combat, then banked away sharply as the rider yanked hard on the reins. As they flew by, Bane reached out with the Force and ripped away the harness securing the saddle to the drexl's back. There was a trio of startled and then terrified screams as the saddle broke free and the riders plummeted hundreds of meters to the ground below. The mount, oblivious to their plight, continued to circle upward in preparation for another dive.

Bane didn't take the time to revel in the fear of his fallen enemies. Before they even hit the ground he'd turned his attention to the third opponent, unleashing a storm of Sith lightning that reduced the riders to ash and the drexl into a hunk of charred and smoking flesh that dropped from the sky.

With a single thought Bane directed his mount's attention to the lone remaining flier team . . . a tactical error on his part. For even though its riders had been slain, the second drexl was still alive. Acting on primal instinct, it had veered back to attack the unfamiliar male invading its territory.

The riderless drexl slammed into Bane's flier the exact instant he engaged the final team. The three beasts intertwined with one another, becoming a single, screaming mass of flesh, claws, and teeth hurtling toward the ground below. A spray of hot, foamy blood splashed across Bane's face as the creatures ripped one another apart. For a brief instant he glimpsed one of the other riders through the flailing wings and limbs of their mounts, her features frozen as she realized they were all tumbling toward a gruesome and inescapable end.

Bane released his hold on the drexl's mind and concentrated his awareness on the terror of the other three riders. He drank in their fear, using it to fuel his own emotions. He focused his power and channeled it through the orbalisks, letting them gorge themselves on the dark side. In return they pumped a fresh dose of adrenaline and hormones into his blood, allowing him to generate even more power in a cycle he repeated over and over until the moment before impact.

Zannah saw the last three flying creatures lock onto one another. As they dropped from the sky, spiraling down faster and faster, she watched them, waiting for one to break free and mount back up to the heavens. None ever did.

She screamed in horror as they all slammed into the ground together. The sound of the crash was like an explosion; the shock wave knocked Zannah off her feet and launched a great cloud of dust and debris into the air. The cloud rolled quickly over the ground to envelop her.

The would-be Sith apprentice struggled to rise, coughing and choking as small chunks of dirt and stone rained down on her. Through the haze she stared in wonder at the twenty-meter-wide, two-meter-deep crater left behind. In the center was a gore-covered mountain of pulverized flesh: the individual bodies of mounts and riders compacted into a single pulpy, quivering mass. And walking toward her from the carnage was the blood-soaked form of her Master.

He was limping and hunched over, with one arm clutched at his side. Yet even through the obscuring dust Zannah recognized him immediately. She could only stare in utter disbelief as he drew nearer, his gait becoming more sure and steady with every stride. With each step he stood taller and straighter, and when he let his arm fall away from his side, her heart began to pound with excitement.

Darth Bane was alive! And the power that had let him survive this incredible ordeal—the power of the dark side—would one day be hers to command! Overcome with emotion, she stepped forward to embrace her Master . . . only to recoil when she saw the alien growth protruding from his chest.

"They are called orbalisks," Bane said, offering an explanation rather than a greeting. "Creatures that feed on the power of the dark side. Without them I could never have survived what you just witnessed." He gasped faintly as he spoke, though whether from pain or the recent exertion of using the Force—or possibly both—she couldn't tell.

He stopped in front of her, and Zannah reached out slowly to touch the cold, hard shell. She pulled her hand back with a start when she felt it twitch beneath her fingers.

"They feel the power of the dark side within you," Bane said, speaking like a proud father.

"How do you get them off?" Zannah asked, her question an equal measure of curiosity and revulsion.

"I don't," Bane replied. "This armor is permanent."

"Will I have to wear them, too?" she asked softly.

Bane considered before replying. "The orbalisks give me great power, but there is a cost. The physical demands can be . . . taxing. It would be too much for you to bear as a child. Maybe too much for you to ever bear."

Relieved, Zannah only nodded. Her Master seemed to be almost fully recovered now, though his face and armor were still drenched in blood.

She noticed him looking past her at the *Star-Wake* on the far edge of the clearing.

"I stole a ship," she told him. "I . . . I had to kill the crew."

"You did what was necessary to achieve your goal," Bane said. "You showed the power and the strength of will to destroy those who stood in your way. You saw what you wanted and you took it, no matter what the cost.

"You acted like a Sith."

The young girl felt a surge of pride well up within her. "What happens now, Master?"

"Now your real training will begin," Bane said, marching off toward the *Star-Wake*.

She quickly fell into step behind him. The doubts and fears she had experienced during her time alone on the ship were gone, swept away by the words of her Master and the display of raw power she had witnessed. No longer was she afraid or uncertain about her future; she finally accepted who and what she truly was. She was the chosen apprentice of Darth Bane. She was the heir to the legacy of the dark side. And she was the future Dark Lord of the Sith.

"YOU SENT FOR ME, Master Valenthyne?" Johun said as he entered Farfalla's private quarters.

It was three days after the Senate had passed the Ruusan Reformations, and they were still on Coruscant. Johun was eager to leave the city-world behind them, but after his shameful outburst in Chancellor Valorum's chambers, he was determined to show that he could control his emotions and that he trusted in the wisdom of his Master. As long as Farfalla felt they were needed here, he would serve without further complaint.

"Sit down, Johun," the Jedi Master said softly, pointing to a nearby chair. From his tone it was clear he had bad news to deliver.

Johun did as he was instructed, dreading what was to come.

"We've located the *Star-Wake*."

For a brief instant Johun's heart leapt. Sometime after he had left Irtanna and her crew, their ship had gone missing. Search parties had been sent out but had come back with nothing. Now, nearly two weeks after she disappeared, she had been found!

Then Johun's elation vanished when he realized that his Master had specifically said the ship had been located; he'd made no mention of those aboard.

"What happened?" Johun asked, almost too afraid to get the words out.

"We think it may have been mercenaries," Farfalla explained. "The ship was discovered floating in the Japrael sector, abandoned. Everything of value had been taken. Everyone aboard was dead, shot with a blaster at close range."

"Everyone? Irtanna? Bordon? Even his sons?"

Farfalla could only answer with a solemn nod.

There is no emotion, Johun thought, reciting the Jedi Code as he fought to control the sudden burst of anger that flared at their senseless deaths. *There is only peace.*

"I know this is difficult for you to accept," Farfalla said, taking a seat across from Johun so he could face him. "But there is nothing we can do for them now. And whatever happens, you must not take it upon yourself to try to avenge their deaths."

"I understand, Master," Johun said, choking back tears. "Yet I cannot stop myself from grieving for their loss."

"Nor should you, my young Padawan," Farfalla said, giving him a reassuring pat on the knee before rising to stand. "It is only natural that you feel sorrow over what has happened. Grief alone holds no danger."

Farfalla stepped away to the far side of the room and studied a painting on the wall, giving the young man some privacy and allowing him time to collect himself. When Johun stood a few minutes later, his Master turned to face him again.

"This news sits heavy upon my heart, Master Valenthyne," the young man offered. "But I understand that it is not my place to seek out their killers. And I am grateful you brought me here to tell me."

"That is not the only reason I sent for you," Farfalla admitted. "I have a mission for you."

"Tell me, Master. I am ready to serve." Johun thought that truer words had never been spoken. He was desperate for something, anything, to take his mind off thoughts of Irtanna and her crew.

"The Senate has passed the Ruusan Reformations. You already know what this means to our order, but there are many other aspects to this legislation. As Chancellor Valorum has said, the Republic must be reborn."

Johun nodded to show he understood.

"There will be many people across the galaxy who are opposed to this new legislation," Farfalla continued. "Some see Valorum's efforts to reunite the Republic as an attempt to reestablish Senate control over worlds that have declared their independence . . . or worlds that were just about to."

"You fear for the Chancellor's life," Johun guessed.

"Precisely. And I also feel it is important for the Jedi to show our support for the Chancellor and the Ruusan Reformations. We must take a leading role in protecting him from those who would do him harm."

Johun struggled to keep his emotions under control. Farfalla had said he had a special mission for him. Maybe he was sending him to the Outer Rim Territories to infiltrate a radical separatist movement, or deploying him to the front lines of a battle against some dangerous rebel faction!

"I have chosen you to serve as the Jedi representative among Chancellor Valorum's personal guard," Farfalla continued, and Johun felt as if he had been punched in the gut.

The last thing he wanted was to stay on Coruscant, and now he had been condemned to remain here until the end of the Chancellor's term. Plus four more years, if the Chancellor won his bid for a second term.

"You seem upset, Johun."

"Not upset, Master," the young man answered carefully. "Disappointed. This was not what I was hoping for."

"Our order is sworn to serve. Often we must sacrifice what we most value for the good of others. This is what it means to be a Jedi."

Johun felt no desire to argue the point. As usual, his Master was right. If this was his duty, if this was the role he was asked to serve, then he would not only accept it but embrace it.

"Master Valenthyne, I humbly accept this great honor you

have given me. I will serve Chancellor Valorum with all my heart and spirit, to the best of my abilities."

"It gives me great pleasure to hear you accept your fate so willingly, Johun," Farfalla answered with a mischievous smile. "But there is still one more small matter.

"I will have to leave Coruscant in the next few days to attend to other business. As you can imagine, this is a difficult time for our order."

"Of course, Master."

"But you must understand that I cannot leave a Padawan here on Coruscant unsupervised."

It was true. All Padawans were required to be under the constant care and watchful eye of a Jedi Master until they completed their training. "I'm afraid I don't understand. If you are leaving, then what new Master will I serve?"

"I think your period of service is over, my young Jedi."

For a moment Johun just stood there, unable to wrap his mind around what he had been told. Only when he realized Farfalla had used the honorific *Jedi* instead of *Padawan* did it become clear.

"You mean . . . I am to be knighted?"

"That is precisely what I mean," Farfalla confirmed. "I have met with the Council and they agree that you are ready."

Involuntarily Johun's hand dropped to brush against the hilt of his lightsaber. He had constructed it on Ruusan at Hoth's insistence only weeks before his first Master's death. He realized the general must have been preparing him for this moment even then. However, building a lightsaber was only one step on the path to Jedi Knighthood.

"What about the trials?" Johun asked, trying to contain himself. "I must still pass the final tests of the Council."

"I have spoken with them about this, too, and they agree that you have already proven yourself many times over during your service on Ruusan. Assigning you to Valorum's guard was your final test. In accepting the position as you did, you have demonstrated beyond all doubt that you are willing to sacrifice your own wants and desires for the greater good."

"I . . . I don't know what to say, Master," the young man stammered.

"You earned this, Johun," Farfalla assured him. "General Hoth would be proud."

The Jedi Master's lightsaber appeared in his hand, igniting with a clean, crisp hum. Johun bowed his head and turned it slightly to one side. Farfalla flicked his wrist, and the lightsaber sliced away the dangling apprentice's braid. The young man felt the weight of it tumbling away as it fell to the floor, then raised his head with tears in his eyes.

He was unable to speak, his mind still swirling with all that had happened: his ascension to the rank of Jedi Knight; his posting to Valorum's guard; the tragic news of Irtanna and her crew.

"You will forever look back on this day as one of great joy, but also one of great sorrow," Farfalla told him, offering one final piece of advice. "It will help you to remember that, in life, the two are often closely linked."

"I will remember, Master," Johun vowed, realizing that for the first time he was offering his word not as a Padawan, but as a true Jedi Knight.

DAROVIT MOVED WITH a slow but steady pace across the cracked soil of the sunbaked field. His left hand clutched a walking stick while the stump where his right had been was wrapped in heavy bandages. A hovering bouncer matched his pace on either side; their round bodies bobbed along like a pair of furry green balloons tethered to his shoulders. They had wide, soulful eyes but no visible nose or mouth. Their long, flat tails streamed out behind them like ribbons fluttering on the breeze.

The bouncers had first come to him in the cave, where he had lain for days in a near-catatonic state. Huddled and clutching at his maimed limb, he had given up all hope. When they found him, he had wanted nothing more than to die.

The compassionate, telepathic creatures had circled above him, speaking directly to his mind, offering words of comfort and assurance. They had soothed his troubled spirit, and though they could not heal his wounds they were able to ease his physical pain.

They had guided him safely out of the underground tunnels and back up to the bright sun and fresh air of the surface. They had led him to a grove where he found cool water to slake his thirst and sweet berries to sate his ravenous hunger. They'd even shown him where to find an abandoned cache of medical supplies, so he could properly clean and dress his amputated stump to stave off infection.

For several days the young man had stayed hidden at the bouncers' grove, gathering his strength and recovering from his terrible wound. He was too afraid of being recognized as one of the Sith to seek out others of his own species, too ashamed by his actions and his mutilated limb to face others of his own kind. But more powerful than either his fear or his shame was his rage—Rain had taken his hand! His own cousin had betrayed and maimed him! Thoughts of vengeance and retribution consumed him; images of hunting her down and destroying her filled his restless dreams.

Yet as his body began to heal, his anger began to fade. Desperate to cling to his hatred, he had replayed the encounter with Rain over and over in his mind . . . only to have the truth suddenly dawn on him. Rain had been trying to save him!

Surrounded by the gentle bouncers and their calming presence, Darovit was finally able to understand what she had done. The Sith at his cousin's side would have killed him without a second thought. By crippling him, Rain had spared his life; a final act of mercy before she fell under the sway of her new dark side Master.

And with understanding came acceptance. Darovit's hand

was gone. Rain was gone. His dreams of joining the Jedi—or the Sith—were gone. All he had left were the bouncers.

Darovit was grateful for their kindness, but he couldn't understand why they had helped him. Perhaps it was because everyone else was gone: The Sith were destroyed, their minions had fled the world or been taken away as prisoners of war. The Jedi and Republic soldiers serving in the Army of Light were all gone. Two nights earlier he'd seen the telltale flicker of ships making the jump to hyperspace in the starry sky as their fleet had left orbit. Even those who lived on Ruusan had gone back to their farms and villages, abandoning the site of the great battle between the darkness and the light. For several days now he had seen no living creature other than the bouncers who had saved him.

He understood that they had given him a second chance at life. He could put his past behind him and start again. But to what purpose? To what end? The bouncers spoke often of the future, as if they had some ability to see glimpses of what was to come. Like most oracles, however, they used words that were couched in vague riddles and generalities, words that offered him no clue to his own fate.

Darovit sad, one of the creatures projected into his mind, a statement more than a question.

"I just don't know what I should do now," he answered out loud. While the bouncers could project their thoughts and empathically sense broad emotion in others, they weren't able to read minds. It was necessary to actually speak to carry on a conversation with them.

"What kind of future is there for me?" he continued, giving voice to the problem he had been struggling with internally. "I failed as a Jedi. I failed as a Sith. What could I hope to become now?"

Man?

The answer actually made him stop short. "A man?" he repeated.

Not a Sith, not a Jedi. Not a mercenary, not a soldier. Not anything but a simple, ordinary man. He nodded and resumed his march across the empty, open field, feeling as if a great weight had been lifted from him.

"Just a man. Why not?"

10

TEN YEARS LATER

THE OUTER RIM WORLD of Serenno was one of the wealthiest planets in the Republic. It was also a breeding ground for anti-Republic sentiment and radical separatist movements, often secretly funded by the vast wealth of various Serenno noble families eager to free themselves from the political yoke of the Galactic Senate.

Yet despite the dangerous revolutionary undercurrents of its culture, or perhaps because of them, the great outdoor market of the planetary capital of Carannia had become renowned as a hub of interstellar mercantilism. Shoppers of two dozen different species mingled freely beneath the tents and awnings of a thousand vendor stalls. From dawn to dusk the cries of merchants hawking goods imported from every corner of the galaxy mingled with the shouted bids of haggling customers. Even the affluent and privileged braved the masses of the crowded plaza, willingly reducing themselves to part of the unruly mob pushing and shoving its way through the stalls in search of rare or valuable treasures that could be found nowhere else.

Zannah stood motionless in a secluded corner of the market square, trying to avoid notice. It wasn't easy for her to blend in with a crowd; although she was of average height, she was a strikingly attractive young woman. It was necessary for her to take precautions when she didn't wish to draw the appreciative stares of males, or the envious glances of other females. In this particular instance she had donned a loose black cloak that covered her from head to toe, obscuring her lean, athletic figure. The hood was pulled up to conceal her flowing mane of long, curly blond hair, and the shadows it cast across her features hid her bright, fierce eyes.

She had also wrapped herself in a faint aura of insignificance, an illusion of the dark side that allowed her to hide in plain sight when she ventured out in public. It wouldn't shield her from the eyes of anyone looking for her, but as long as she didn't draw attention to herself she would remain unnoticed and unremembered by the vast majority of weak-minded common folk.

Even with these precautions, she would occasionally notice someone giving her a second glance. There was something about her, a hard edge to the way she moved and even the way she stood, that set her apart from others. Yet it was far easier for her to remain inconspicuous than it was for her Master. Over the past decade, the orbalisks that had attached themselves to Bane's torso had spread until they covered virtually his entire body. Only his feet, hands, and face remained free of the infestation, and only because he took extreme precautions: He wore special gloves and boots at all times, and when he slept he donned a special helmet that resembled a cage, meant to keep the parasites from growing over his face.

Cloaks and thick layers of clothing couldn't fully hide what he had become. Anyone who happened to catch a glimpse of the shiny carapaces beneath his garments would definitely remember. As a result, Bane rarely left their camp on Ambria. He relied on his apprentice to be his eyes and ears to the outside world. He counted on her to act as an agent of his will, to coordinate and oversee the intricate plans he orchestrated from behind the scenes.

That was why she was here now, waiting for a young Twi'lek she knew as Kelad'den. It was unlikely that was his actual name, however. After all, he didn't know *her* real name . . . despite the fact that they were lovers.

Kel was a political revolutionary—a self-styled freedom fighter battling tyranny as a high-ranking member of a small extremist group determined to bring down the Republic. It had taken Zannah several months to win his trust, but he had finally succumbed. Last night, as they had lain intertwined in the rough sheets of the small bed in Zannah's rented apartment, the Twi'lek had promised to meet her at midday in the plaza to bring her to one of his organization's clandestine meetings.

From the height of the sun in the afternoon sky it was obvious Kelad'den was late. Still, Zannah continued to wait. She had learned the value of patience early on in her studies . . .

"Secrecy. Cunning. Patience. These are the weapons of the Sith," her Master told her.

They had left Onderon eight days before, abandoning the Star-Wake *and acquiring another vessel from a Neimoidian merchant to bring them to Ambria. It was here on this remote world that Bane would begin her training.*

"Act in haste and you give the advantage to your enemy," Bane explained. "Sometimes the proper, and more difficult, course is not to act. Even the greatest warrior often fails to wait until the moment is right before striking out. That is a mistake we cannot afford to make."

She nodded, absorbing his words and committing them to memory. But words were only part of her training. Her Master also gave her a task—a test that would prove she had truly learned her lesson.

In one of the caves near the shore of Lake Natth, a few kilometers from their camp, lived a small family of neeks: small, reptilian herbivores native to Ambria. Only a meter in height, they stood upright on their hind legs, using their tails for balance and support. Their forelimbs were short and underdeveloped, good only for digging up shallow roots or carrying small nuts back to their nests. They had long necks and tiny heads with small, toothless jaws that resembled beaks.

The first day she and Darth Bane had arrived on the world, Zannah had noticed them scurrying and darting about on the hot sands of the beach. As the first part of her training, Bane had tasked her with bringing one of the neeks to him, alive and unfettered.

The mission proved to be much harder than she first imagined. A common food source for the large carnivores that often prowled the shores of Lake Natth, neeks were skittish by nature. They would flee at the sight of her, scampering off to disappear into the small cracks and crevices in the rocks surrounding the caves where they made their home.

She couldn't simply set a trap for one; Bane's instructions required her to bring him one that came of its own free will. At first Zannah had tried luring them back to the camp by leaving a trail of food, but the creatures were mistrustful and spurned her offerings. Next, she tried dominating one's mind as she had seen Bane do with the drexl. But at Lake Natth an ancient Jedi had once bound the dark side power of his enemies. That same power had emanated from the depths of the poisonous waters over the centuries, mutating the neeks and making them immune to her clumsy efforts to control them with the Force.

In the end she realized she would have to tame one, training it to grow accustomed to her presence. So early each morning she made her way down to the entrance of the cave, where she would sit cross-legged and practice the meditation exercises Bane was teaching her.

She would stay motionless for hours, then calmly get up

and return to the camp in the late afternoon, only to repeat the process the next morning. For the first three days she was completely alone, but on the fourth day the neeks began to show themselves. Cautious at first, they would dart out into view and scamper past her, well beyond her reach. By the middle of the second week they began to grow used to her presence, and would sit and stare at her, only a few meters away. Occasionally one would bark out a squeaking yip in her direction, or emit a low, tremulous chirping from the back of its throat. By the third week one particularly curious youngling, not even as tall as Zannah's knee, came close enough to her that she was able to reach out and touch it.

After that she started bringing food to her vigil, letting a small morsel sit in the open palm of an upturned hand at her side. The same bold little neek would approach her with trepidation each time, balancing its fear against the alluring scent of the nuts wafting up from the young girl's hand. She would coo to it softly, and eventually it would gather its courage enough to rush in and snatch the morsel away before scurrying off to the safety of its cave, peeping with excitement.

Zannah started positioning herself farther from the cave for her meditations. Each day the neek would come looking for her, ranging beyond the familiar borders of its territory in its quest to find her. Bit by bit she drew it closer and closer to the camp until one day, when she got up to leave, the neek began to follow her.

She made a point of taking soft, slow steps so as not to startle it. Moving with small strides so she wouldn't lose her balance, she gingerly shifted her weight from one foot to the other as she led the tiny creature all the way back to her Master.

It was near nightfall when she arrived, her pace turning the relatively short distance from the lake back to the camp into a four-hour journey. There were several tents in the camp; in addition to the ones she and Bane slept in, there was one for storing food, another for clothing and equipment, and still others for weapons and fuel for their starship and land half-track. The tents were arranged in a three-quarter circle, facing inward toward the cooking fire.

Bane was sitting by the blaze waiting for her, stirring at a bubbling pot of bland-smelling stew. He had taken off his shirt in the summer night's heat. In the flickering glow of the flames, his apprentice could see that the orbalisks were beginning to spread. The one on the back of his shoulder had traced its way across his bicep to the elbow of his heavily muscled arm, while the organism on his chest now extended halfway down his abdominal muscles and partway up his throat. Several narrow, dark bands of softer-looking flesh bisected each shell vertically, and the girl realized that in addition to growing, the creatures were about to split apart and multiply.

Suppressing a shudder, Zannah called out softly to him. "I have completed my first lesson, Master."

Bane glanced down at the small neek trailing into the camp behind her, visible proof that his apprentice had fulfilled the task he had given her. Zannah followed his gaze, turning toward the tiny creature. It looked up at her and chirped expectantly. She bent down to pet it, and Bane reached out with the Force and snapped its long, thin neck.

"You have done well," he muttered as she stared in horror at the tiny body twitching at her feet. "Now toss it in the stew."

Zannah took a moment to steel herself, pushing away the grief that threatened to well up inside her. When Bane had first given her this task, she realized, he must have known she would develop a fondness for the little neek. If she had been wiser she would have foreseen this, and viewed the creature simply as a tool—something to be used then tossed aside—rather than allowing herself to become emotionally attached. The pain she felt now over its death was a warning—a reminder that her only allegiance was to her Master.

She picked up the body and carried it over to the bubbling pot. Tossing it in, she looked Bane square in the eye.

"I see you decided to teach me two lessons today, Master."

His only response was a grim smile. . . .

"Rainah," she heard a voice shouting above the din of the market, using the false name she adopted for all her missions. After a moment she was able to pick Kelad'den out of the crowd, motioning her to come over and join him on the far side of the square.

Twi'lek complexions came in a wide variety of colors, but Kel was of the extremely rare red-skinned Lethan race. Like most Lethans, he was undeniably gorgeous. He was tall and broad-shouldered, with a hard, flat stomach and perfectly proportioned limbs. He wore tight black pants and a loose-fitting tan tunic that hung open at the front to expose the lean muscles of his chest and abdomen. He had sensuous, perfectly symmetrical features: soft, full lips and dark, smoldering eyes that seemed to draw you in if you stared at them too long. His firm, shapely lekku coiled around his neck and shoulders, winding their way suggestively down the front of his open tunic and exposed chest.

"Rainah!" he cried out a second time, causing more than a few people to stop and look at him curiously. Zannah cursed under her breath, and moved quickly through the crowd to his side.

"Keep your voice down," she hissed when she got close. "Everybody's staring at us!"

"Let them stare," he said defiantly, though he did lower his voice to match hers. "They're commoners. Their opinion means nothing to me."

Kel was a child of position and privilege. In addition to being of Lethan stock, he came from a family that ranked among the nobility of the Twi'lek warrior caste. His entire life he had been told by all those around him how special he was; it was only natural he would grow up believing others to be beneath him.

At times Zannah admired his haughty arrogance. It was a sign of power: He knew he was a superior specimen, and he wasn't afraid to show it. But it was also his great weakness. She had discovered early on that Kel was easily manipulated through flattery or challenges to his pride and ego, and she wasn't afraid to exploit that knowledge in the pursuit of her mission.

"You're late," she told him. "I don't like to be kept waiting."

"I shouldn't even be doing this," he snapped back at her.

"I'm sorry," she said, pressing herself close and wrapping her arms around his neck and shoulders. "I was beginning to think you were with another lover," she purred. "If I ever find you with another female, I will cut her heart out."

Kel pulled her even tighter against his body. "You are more than enough for any male," he whispered into her ear, sending a shiver down Zannah's spine.

She kissed him on the lips, then broke the embrace. "We don't have time for this," she protested. "Your friends are waiting for us."

Licking his lips as if he could still taste her, Kel nodded and grabbed her hand. "Let's go," he said, pulling her through the crowd of shoppers.

As DUSK FELL over the camp on Ambria, Darth Bane reached out toward the tiny crystal pyramid he had carefully positioned on the small pedestal in the center of the otherwise empty tent. Moving slowly, he brushed his fingers gently against its cold, dead surface, then pulled his hand back when he saw it tremble. An instant later his fingers started twitching spasmodically as tingling jolts of sharp pain laced their way from his elbow down to his wrist. Swearing a silent oath, he gritted his teeth and closed his eyes, trying to ride it out.

Because of the orbalisks that encased his body, he was used to living in constant pain. It was always there, a dull throbbing just above the level of subconscious awareness. Normally he could shut it out, bearing the torments of his infestation with no visible effects. However, if he wasn't careful—if he pushed himself too far—the physical demands could overwhelm him. The tremor had been a warning, the first sign that he was reaching the edges of his endurance.

Three times before he had attempted to create his own Sith Holocron, and each time the project had ended in failure. He wasn't about to fail this time. He knew that one false move at this stage and all his work, literally years of preparation, would be undone. Yet he also knew that he had no choice but to find a way to deal with the pain and continue his work.

He had made his first attempt five years before. Using Freedon Nadd's Holocron as a blueprint, he had re-created the intricate matrix of lattices and vertices that were the key to storing nearly infinite amounts of knowledge in a data system small enough to fit in the palm of a hand. It had taken months to gather and fashion the rare crystal into the filaments and fibers of the interlaced network, followed by weeks of delicate and painstaking adjustments. The matrix had to fall within highly exacting specifications, and Bane had spent hundreds of hours making thousands of precise, subatomic alterations through the power of the Force to ensure that each crystalline strand was properly in place.

Once the crystal matrix inside the Holocron was ready, he had carefully transcribed the ancient symbols of Sith power onto the pyramid's surface. The markings were part of a powerful ritual that was critical to maintaining the stability of the matrix after it was infused with the energies of the dark side. Unfamiliar with the exact purpose or meaning of the arcane glyphs, Darth Bane had once again used Nadd's Holocron as his guide, studying the markings etched on the surface, then copying them exactly on his own creation.

But when he tried to activate the Holocron by channeling his power through it, the matrix imploded, collapsing in on itself and reducing the artifact to a pile of glimmering dust in a crackling white flash.

He had tried again several months later, only to be met with the exact same result. Forced to admit that the secret of crafting Holocrons was still beyond him, Bane had begun a campaign to discover everything he could about the powerful talismans. With Zannah's aid, he accumulated a vast wealth of knowledge on the subject.

He devoured every datacard, historical account, and personal memoir he could find that theorized on the steps needed to create one of the fiendishly complex pyramids. He came across thousands of veiled references to, and hundreds of theoretical speculations on, the art of crafting a Holocron. However, he was unable to find a single source that explicitly set out the spells and rituals required, and their secrets still eluded him.

Bane refused to give up. He continued his research, seeking out rare tomes, hidden documents, and forbidden works of lore. It took three more years until he learned the purpose and meaning behind the glyphs . . . and in doing so he found an answer to why his first efforts had failed. He discovered that each Holocron was emblazoned with symbols that were uniquely tied to the Sith Lord responsible for the artifact's creation. The miniature pyramids were far more than a simple collection of raw data. Learning was imparted through the wisdom of a gatekeeper—an advanced simulated personality that mimicked the creator's own identity. The right combination of symbols, applied in conjunction with specific sorceries and spells of the ancient Sith, would allow Bane to capture his appearance, knowledge, and cognitive processes. Within the structure of the Holocron they would be transformed into a three-dimensional hologram to guide and direct anyone who used the artifact. The cognitive network that fueled the gatekeeper also stabilized the interwoven lattices and vertices of the matrix, keeping it from collapsing as it had done on Bane's previous attempts.

Armed with this new understanding, Bane had made a third attempt to create his own Holocron two years ago. He had proceeded carefully; the Rituals of Invocation required to divine and inscribe the proper symbols onto the pyramid's surface were mentally and physically exhausting. Ever wary of making a mistake, he had drawn the process out over two long weeks. Ironically, his caution proved to be his undoing. As he began manipulating the inner structures of the crystal matrix during the final phase of the project, he sensed that the power of the symbols had faded. The cognitive network of the gatekeeper had degraded to the point that it lacked the ability to support and stabilize the matrix.

In desperation, he had sought some way to restore it, only to realize his efforts were futile. Enraged at yet another failure, he had crushed the useless pyramid to dust with his bare hands.

Before beginning his fourth and most recent attempt, Bane had vowed that he would not fail again. Time was the real key. He had to finish aligning the matrix and infuse it with his dark side energies within a few days, before the cognitive functions of the gatekeeper began to degrade. Now, after months of gathering the rare materials, weeks of meditations to focus his power, and three straight days and nights of intense focus and concentration, he was finally nearing the end. Only a few dozen minor adjustments still needed to be made, but Bane was keenly aware that time was running out.

Three days of constantly drawing upon the Force without food or respite had left him exhausted in body, mind, and spirit. He was particularly vulnerable to the orbalisks in this state. Normally they fed off the dark side energies that naturally flowed through him, but the creation of the Holocron demanded that he channel all his power directly into his work. The parasites were slowly starving, and in response they were flooding his bloodstream with chemicals and hormones intended to drive him into a mindless fury so they could gorge themselves on the dark side as he unleashed his rage.

The spasming muscles of his hand and fingers were a direct result of their efforts, and there was nothing Bane could do but wait for the tremor to pass. He had only a few hours left to complete his work, yet he couldn't risk making a mistake and damaging the delicately interwoven crystal fibers of the Holocron's internal structure.

Slowly he was able to reassert control over his convulsing digits, ruing each precious second that slipped away as he did so. When his hand at last became still, he took a slow, deep breath to refocus his mind, then reached out with the Force to touch the matrix once more.

A ribbon of electric blades raveled itself around the muscles and nerves of his spine, causing him to arch backward as he screamed in agony. The pain momentarily broke his concentration, and an uncontrollable surge of dark side energy shot through him and into the Holocron. An instant later it exploded, spraying Bane with a shower of crystal fragments and dust.

For several seconds he simply stared at the empty pedestal, feeling the pulsing hunger of the orbalisks and his own gathering rage. A red veil fell across his vision, and Darth Bane surrendered himself to the fury.

11

"WHO'S THIS?" THE MAN at the door demanded, eyeing Zannah with suspicion. He was human, though his face and shaved head were covered with green and purple tattoos that made it difficult to pick out his features. He wore a light blue shirt and dark blue pants. He was shorter than Kel, but much thicker through the waist and chest.

"She's with me, Paak," Kel replied, pushing him aside and passing through the door, pulling Zannah along with him.

The unfurnished room beyond was small and dark. Music and loud laughter could be faintly heard from the cantina on the floor above them, but those gathered in the cellar spoke only in low, conspiratorial whispers. Inside the room were four others gathered in a tight circle: two more young men, a woman only slightly older than Zannah, and a blue-skinned, red-eyed Chiss female.

Paak trailed after them, unwilling to let the matter drop. "You can't bring her here!" he insisted.

"She works at the embassy," Kel assured him, relaying the

false backstory Zannah had offered at their first meeting. "She can help us."

The heavier man grabbed Kel by the elbow and spun the Twi'lek around to face him. "You don't get to make that decision! Hetton is our leader, not you!"

"Hetton put *me* in charge of this mission," Kel reminded him angrily.

"Only because you offered to purchase those forged passes to get us past the embassy guards!" Paak snapped back. "He put you in charge because he needed your credits!"

"Hetton doesn't need anyone's credits," the red-skinned Twi'lek replied contemptuously. "He put me in charge because he was tired of dealing with oafish thugs like you."

Paak's lips curled up in a menacing snarl, but Kel had already turned away, dismissing his underling. Zannah waited to see if the tattooed man would go after Kel, but he only shook his head and went back to his position guarding the door.

Kel marched over to the others, who widened their circle to accommodate him. Zannah hung back slightly, noting the others regarding her with curious stares. She stared back, though she was already well aware of everything she needed to know about them.

Like Kelad'den they were revolutionaries: young, idealistic, and pitiful. Easily swayed and manipulated by fiery speeches and impassioned rhetoric, they had been recruited by the mysterious "Hetton" into joining the Anti-Republic Liberation Front—one of a hundred small, insignificant separatist movements scattered across the galaxy.

For a small radical group, however, the ARLF was particularly well funded, and the membership included an inordinate percentage of highly skilled and dangerous individuals. Elite warriors like Kel, or beings with advanced military training, were the norm rather than the exception. For one reason or another, they had all sworn allegiance to Hetton and his organization.

Zannah imagined they believed themselves to be heroes or

even eventual martyrs to their glorious cause. Yet she felt nothing but disdain for them. Despite their martial backgrounds, they were little more than overgrown children gathering in tiny, dark rooms to whisper secret plans and plot petty terrorist actions against a galactic government that didn't even know they existed.

Even Kel wasn't above her contempt. Still, she did have to admit that there was *something* appealing about him. Allowing him to fall in love with her hadn't been necessary to complete her mission, yet she had been willing—even eager—to have his attention. The attraction went beyond his mere physical appearance. There was a wild energy about him. He burned with a savage arrogance; its fire enveloped her whenever they were together.

She knew she was drawn to his warmth in part because her Master was always so cold. Bane had served as her guardian for ten years; he had raised her and protected her and trained her in the ways of the Sith. Yet she didn't think of him as a father figure. While he hadn't been cruel or abusive, neither had he shown any affection toward her, not even a trace of empathy or compassion. He valued her not as a person but as his heir; she was nothing but a mechanism to continue the Sith legacy after his death.

Encased in his orbalisk armor, Bane was barely even human anymore. Anger, hate, love, desire—they were nothing to him now but a means to fuel his power. Yet Zannah still needed to feel. She hungered for the raw passion of real emotions. She craved them.

She had found them in Kel. He had given her the one thing her Master could not. But she never considered betraying or abandoning Darth Bane. She had seen his absolute command of the Force; she had tasted the power of the dark side in him. He was the Dark Lord of the Sith, and Zannah would one day tear the mantle from his shoulders and seize it for her own. Nothing—not fanciful notions, not the temptation of emotional fulfillment or even love—would keep her from claiming her rightful destiny.

Compared with this, Kel and the other separatists gathered in the room were tiny, insignificant people leading small, meaningless lives. Their only worth was that Bane saw a potential use for them, and it was her duty to make sure that whatever they had planned fit into her Master's grand design.

Kel had revealed their intended scheme to her during a romantic dinner: They planned to kidnap minor local officials and hold them for ransom. They actually believed the media interest generated by their actions would be the catalyst that would unite the people of the Outer Rims to rise up as one and overthrow the Senate.

They were pathetic in their naïveté; fools Zannah had chosen to become pawns in her own mission. They were tools to be used and then discarded once they had served their purpose . . . and that purpose was to die so that she could fulfill the directive of her Master.

"My fellow patriots," Kel began, his voice rising in the manner of a professional orator giving a public performance. "We are united in a single cause—the complete and utter destruction of the Republic. Yet what have we done so far to accomplish this?

"We speak of revolution yet we are afraid to do what is necessary to make it happen. But that will soon change. In three days, we will force the Republic to stand up and take notice of us!"

"Three days?" Cyndra, the Chiss protested. "What are you talking about?"

"Hetton wants us to strike during the Armistice Celebrations," Paak added. "It will draw more attention if we act on the anniversary of the Ruusan Reformations."

"Why wait months when the perfect opportunity is right before us?" Kel asked, using the same arguments Zannah had used to persuade him. "Nobody will care about the fate of a single ambassador. We must find a target that will make the entire galaxy sit up and take notice!"

"Who?" one of the young men demanded.

"Chancellor Valorum."

"Chancellor Valorum's term ended two years ago," Paak spat out from over by the door.

"He still serves the Senate as a diplomatic emissary. And it was his so-called Unification Policies that have drawn so many worlds back into the web of Republic influence. He is responsible for everything we are fighting against, the symbol of everything we wish to destroy. He is the perfect target."

"How do we get to him?" Cyndra asked.

"He has scheduled a secret meeting with the heads of Serenno's most powerful noble families. We believe he is going to try to persuade them to take steps to put down the separatist movements on this world—movements like our own."

"How did you find out about this?" the young woman asked.

Kel nodded in Zannah's direction, his head-tails twitching slightly. She stepped forward and began to speak.

"My name is Rainah. I'm an administrative assistant at the Republic embassy."

This was the lie she had first used to draw Kel's attention, and it was a convenient cover for the information she had purchased from one of Bane's mysterious underground contacts . . .

"Everything is in place, Lord Eddels," the Muun croaked, handing a datapad to her Master. "Everything you will need is in here."

Zannah had never seen a Muun before, and she found something inherently off-putting about this one's appearance. He was tall enough to look Bane in the eye, but his head, body, and limbs were elongated and thin, as if he had been horribly stretched to reach his current height. His skin was pale, pasty white with a disconcerting hint of a sickly pinkish hue. His features were flat, his eyes and cheeks appeared sunken, the corners of his mouth turned down in a perpetual frown, and he didn't appear to have a nose. His head was hairless, and he wore drab, brown clothing. He looked extremely uncomfortable beneath Tatooine's twin suns, but he was too professional to give voice to his complaint.

Earlier, Bane had explained that this meeting in the sandy wasteland of the Dune Sea was the culmination of a plan set in motion nearly a year before, shortly after they had first touched down on Ambria. A plan she had inadvertently been the catalyst for. Scribbled in the back cover of the manuscript she had discovered and presented to her Master at the Sith camp on Ruusan had been a long list of cryptic numbers: anonymous accounts with the InterGalactic Banking Clan.

Lord Qordis, Bane told her, had been a collector of rare and expensive treasures. Over the years he had siphoned off an incredible fortune from the combined wealth of Kaan's Brotherhood of Darkness and secreted it away, drawing on it whenever he purchased another item to feed his avarice. With the Brotherhood gone, Bane was the only one left who knew about, and could lay claim to, those accounts. But material wealth had no appeal to her Master beyond what use he could put it to.

"Information is a commodity. It can be traded, sold, and purchased. And in the end, credits are only as valuable as the secrets they can buy."

Over the past year Bane had begun to spend the credits. Key administrative officials were bribed to gain access to classified files. Government spies and well-connected criminal figures were hired to be his agents. Using his newfound wealth, he carefully built a network of informants to be his eyes and ears across a hundred different worlds.

However, Bane never had any direct contact with any of these people. As the last of the Sith, it was vital that he remain shrouded in anonymity. Everything he'd accomplished had been through the use of a broker—the Muun who now stood before them.

"You followed my instructions exactly?" Bane asked the Muun.

"*Precisely, Lord Eddels. All payments will be made through tertiary accounts, completely untraceable to the source,*" *the Muun assured him.* "*In return you will receive regular dispatches and a constant stream of legal and illegal information. Any instructions you wish to pass on to your agents will be delivered through secure messaging services. Completely anonymous.*"

"*And no one else knows I am involved?*"

"*You are well aware of my reputation,*" *the Muun reminded him.* "*I pride myself on discretion. That is why people like you come to me, Lord Eddels.*"

"*Then our business here is done.*"

Glancing briefly down at Zannah, the Muun turned and made his way slowly across the sand toward his waiting ship. The young girl watched, eagerly anticipating the manner of his death. The idea that her Master would allow the Muun to leave this meeting alive never entered her mind. He alone knew the identity of the individual responsible for creating the galaxywide web of spies and informants. He alone had seen Bane's face.

The Muun reached his ship without incident and climbed aboard. She continued to watch as the engines flared to life and the vessel began to climb in the sky. When it disappeared beyond the horizon unharmed, she turned to her Master in disbelief.

"*You let him live?*"

"*He still has value to us,*" *Bane answered.*

"*But he's seen you! He knows who you are!*"

"*He knows only as much as he needed to: a wealthy man using the name Lord Eddels hired him to set up an anonymous information network. He has no knowledge of who I really am or what my true purpose might be. And he has no knowledge of where or how to find me unless I contact him with a location for another meeting.*"

Zannah recalled a story her Master had once shared with her about a healer on Ambria named Caleb. Bane, near death,

*had come across the healer and ordered the man to help him.
But Caleb, sensing the power of the dark side in her Master,
had refused. Ultimately Bane had compelled Caleb's obedience
by threatening the life of his daughter. Once the Dark Lord
was healed, he had taken no action against the man who had
dared to defy him. The healer had power, and her Master knew
that the value of letting him live outweighed the risks—and
petty pleasure—of ending his life.*

*"No purpose in his death," Zannah muttered, chewing her
lip thoughtfully. . . .*

"Rainah can provide us with the exact times and locations
of Chancellor Valorum's schedule," Kel explained to the rest
of the small group. "When his shuttle touches down, we'll be
there waiting for him."

"He'll have guards," Paak warned.

"Only his personal security detail," Zannah countered.
"Anything more would draw unwanted attention."

"He wants to keep his arrival here secret," Kel added. "The
Senate refuses to officially acknowledge that separatist movements even exist, so his mission has been classified as a personal visit."

"Three days is too soon," Cyndra objected. "We need more
time to prepare."

"Everything we need is right here," Kel replied. "We have
the weapons, and we're all trained to use them. We know where
and when the Chancellor is coming. What else is there?"

"An order from Hetton," Paak muttered.

Kel turned on him angrily. "Do we really need Hetton's *permission*? Are we children? Are we incapable of acting on our
own?"

"He's our leader," Paak muttered sullenly. "He tells us what
to do."

"So does the Republic Senate," Zannah chimed in. "Isn't
this the very thing you're fighting against? Obedience to a
master—any master—is still slavery."

She said the words with utter conviction even though she

didn't believe them. At the same time, she reached out with the Force to touch the minds of everyone in the room. It was possible to use the dark side to dominate another's will, but that would not serve her purpose here. The effects of mental domination would begin to fade after a few hours. By the time of Chancellor Valorum's arrival, any direct influence she exerted over Kel and his friends would be completely gone.

Zannah preferred a more subtle and insidious approach. Instead of using the Force to bend them to her will, she was gently prodding their collective psyche, pushing their thought patterns to make them more emotional, more aggressive. By itself the process was useless, but combined with persuasive words to further stir the blood, the effects could be more powerful—and more permanent—than the brute force of simple mind control.

However, the words couldn't come from her. She was a stranger here; they didn't trust her. Their natural instincts would be to reject her arguments; in their artificially induced hyperaggressive state they would quickly turn against her. They needed to be convinced by someone they knew. Someone like Kel.

"You say you want independence," the handsome Twi'lek told them. "You say you will fight for your freedom. Yet when I offer you this chance, you want to slink away like a Kath hound banished from its pack."

"We should wait for the Armistice Celebrations," Cyndra insisted. "We need to stick to the original plan."

"A plan is nothing until you act on it," Kel replied. "We talk about what we will do in the future, but when the Armistice Celebrations come, how easy will it be to find another excuse to wait yet again?

"Secret meetings will not bring change to the galaxy. Plans alone will not make the Senate tremble or bring the Republic to its knees. We must take action, and the time for action is now!"

Zannah recognized her words being spoken with Kel's

voice. She had fed them to him over weeks of intimate conversations, planting the seeds of ideas, then watching them grow. Now he spoke the words with passion and fire, delivering them as if he truly believed they were his own.

Bane would be pleased. This was true power: to twist another to your purpose, yet have him believe he was in control. Kel was her puppet, but his pride and ego had blinded him to the strings she used to make him dance.

"We stand on the precipice of a momentous event," he continued. "In three days we will strike a great blow against the tyrants of the Republic, the first step in our long and glorious march to independence and true freedom!"

A spontaneous cheer of assent rose up from the room, and Zannah knew Kel had won them over. Only Paak and Cyndra showed any signs of reluctance, but as the rest of the group began working on the details of the plan to capture Chancellor Valorum, even they set aside their hesitations.

The meeting lasted long into the night, and when it was over she and Kel went back to the small apartment she had rented as part of her cover story.

"You were magnificent tonight," she breathed.

"This is the last time I can see you until all this is over," Kel warned. "The others are counting on me. I can't have any distractions."

As an answer she reached out and grabbed his wrist, then pulled him close in a tight embrace.

He left the next morning. Zannah kissed him good-bye and went back to sleep. Later, she rolled out of bed and began to gather her things. Her mission here was over; she knew she would never see Kel alive again. It was time to return to Ambria.

THE CAMP WAS IN RUINS. The tents were leveled, their canopies shredded and torn. Wooden supply crates had been smashed into sawdust and splinters, their contents tossed and scattered on the wind. Hundred-kilogram fuel cells lay strewn about the campsite, some thrown fifty meters from where they had been stored.

The ground was littered with debris and marred by dozens of still-smoldering black scorch marks Zannah recognized as the remnants of a terrible storm of unnatural lightning. The air still crackled with the power and energy of the dark side that made her tingle in fear and anticipation.

It was easy enough to guess what had happened. Bane had failed yet again in his attempt to create a Holocron, then in a blind rage lashed out at the world around him with all the power of the Force.

If she had been here when it happened, Zannah wondered, could she have stopped him? Would she even have been able to survive?

She saw Bane seated on the far side of the camp, his back to her as he stared out to the horizon, meditating on his failure. He turned to face her as she approached, rising up to his full two-meter height so that he towered above her. His clothes had been torn and burned away, revealing the full scope of the orbalisk infestation. Hundreds of the creatures clung to him; except for his face and hands, his body was now completely covered. He looked as if he were wearing a suit of armor fashioned from the hard, oblong shells of dead crustaceans. Yet she knew that beneath the shells, the parasites were still alive, feeding on him.

Bane claimed the orbalisks enhanced his power, granting him unnatural strength and healing abilities. Yet witnessing the aftermath of his failure with the Holocron, Zannah wondered at what cost those abilities came. What use was greater power if it could not be controlled?

To her relief the fury seemed to have passed, and Zannah knew better than to ask him about it. Instead she offered news of her mission.

"It's done. When Chancellor Valorum's shuttle lands, Kel and his followers will be waiting for him."

"You have done well," Bane answered.

As always, she felt a surge of pride and accomplishment at her Master's praise. But her satisfaction was tempered by memories of Kel, and the knowledge that he was lost to her forever.

"Is there any chance they will succeed?" she asked.

"No," Bane said after a moment's consideration.

"Then what purpose do they serve?" she demanded, finally giving in to her frustration. "I don't understand why you send me on missions like this! Why waste all this time and effort if we know they're going to fail!"

"They don't need to succeed to be of value to us," Bane answered. "The separatists are only a distraction. They draw the attention of the Senate, and blind the eyes of the Jedi Council."

"Blind them?"

"The Jedi have surrendered themselves to the will of the Senate. They have let themselves sink into the morass of politics and bureaucracy. The Republic seeks a single, unified government to maintain peace throughout the galaxy, and the Jedi have been reduced to nothing more than a tool to make it happen.

"Each time radicals strike against the Republic, the Jedi Council is called upon to take action. Resources are wasted on quelling rebellions and uprisings, keeping their focus away from us."

"But why must the separatists always fail?" Zannah asked. "We could help them succeed without risking exposure!"

"If they succeed, they will gain support," Bane explained. "Their power and influence will grow. They will become harder to manipulate and control. It is possible they might even become strong enough to bring down the Republic itself."

"Isn't that a good thing?" Zannah asked.

"The Republic keeps the Jedi in check. It maintains control and imposes order across thousands of worlds. But if the Republic falls, a score of new interstellar governments and galactic organizations will rise. It is far easier to manipulate and control a single enemy than twenty.

"That is why we must seek out radical separatist groups, identify the ones that have the potential to become true threats, then encourage them to strike before they are ready. We must exploit them, playing them off against the Republic. We must let our enemies weaken one another while we stay hidden and grow strong.

"One day the Republic will fall and the Jedi will be wiped out," he assured her. "But it will not happen until we are ready to seize that power for ourselves."

Zannah nodded, though her mind was reeling as she tried to comprehend the true complexity of her Master's intricate and convoluted political machinations. She thought back to all her past missions, trying to see how each one played a part in his plans.

"You have never questioned your missions before," Bane noted. He didn't sound angry, but rather curious.

She didn't want to tell him about Kel. Even though she had accomplished everything Bane had demanded of her, she knew he would view her feelings for the Twi'lek as a sign of weakness.

"Even if I didn't understand the purpose behind my missions, I never had reason to doubt your wisdom, Master," she answered, realizing she could turn his question to her advantage.

"Yet you doubt me now?"

She took a long, slow look around, letting her eyes linger over the wreckage of the camp surrounding them.

"I've never seen you lose control of your power like this before," she whispered, shrouding her deceit in a kernel of truth. "I feared the orbalisks could be impairing your judgment. I feared they might have finally driven you mad."

Bane didn't answer right away, and when he did his voice was short and gruff. "I control the orbalisks. They do not control me."

"Of course, Master," she apologized. But she knew from his reaction that she had successfully planted the seed of doubt. Attempting to manipulate her Master was a dangerous game, but it was a risk she had to take. If the orbalisks drove him into another rage, he might kill her. Convincing Bane to seek out some way to rid himself of the infestation was a matter of self-preservation.

"Clean up the camp," Bane commanded. "Then head back to Serenno. We need more supplies."

She acquiesced with a bow and began gathering up debris as Bane resumed his meditations. As she slowly restored some semblance of order to their camp, Zannah began to see that the doubts she had planted in Bane's mind could have one other valuable, long-term benefit.

It was inevitable she would one day challenge him for the title of Sith Master, but Bane was incredibly strong—both physically and in the Force. Encased in a suit of living armor that augmented his powers and protected him from virtually all known weapons, he was nearly invincible.

Convincing Bane to shed his orbalisk coat, Zannah realized, might be the only real hope she had of defeating him and achieving her destiny.

12

JOHUN SHIFTED IN HIS SEAT, trying to find a more comfortable position and thinking how much easier it had been to bear the burden of starship travel in his youth. But he was no longer a teenager on the cusp of manhood. He was taller, for one thing—a full 1.85 meters in height. And his slight frame had become corded with taut, wiry muscle. The only remnant of the young man he had been was the blond hair that still hung down to his shoulders—a sharp contrast with the scruffy black beard that covered the line of his jaw.

He shifted again and glared pointedly at Tarsus Valorum, resting easily in the seat across from him. The Chancellor was in his sixties now, though apart from a slight graying of his hair around the temples he looked very much as he had the first day Johun had met him. Tarsus met the Jedi's fierce gaze with a smile and a shrug . . . the closest thing Johun would ever get to an apology for having to endure the long interstellar flight aboard this second-rate vessel.

The *New Dawn* was an *Emissary*-class shuttle—serviceable,

but far from luxurious. It would have been a simple matter for Tarsus Valorum, former Supreme Chancellor of the Galactic Republic, to request a more extravagant ship for his personal use: one of the new Cygnus *Theta*-class shuttles, or possibly even the magnificent Consular space cruisers so popular among the diplomatic community. Given his previous position, there was little doubt the Senate would have approved the funds for the purchase. But Valorum had insisted that the tiny *New Dawn*, with her two-person crew, passenger seating for six, and Class Six hyperdrive, was more than adequate for his needs now that he had officially stepped down from his position.

It was a small gesture of modesty and practicality that spoke volumes about the man himself. Over the years Johun had observed the Chancellor in public and in private, and the more he got to know him the more respect he had for him. But that wasn't to say the man couldn't be stubborn and even obstinate, as he'd proved when he refused the Senate's offer of an honor guard accompaniment for his diplomatic missions.

A retired politician is no threat to anybody, he'd argued. *And I'm certainly not important enough anymore for others to put themselves in harm's way for my sake.*

Johun still traveled at his side, but that was by his choice, not the Chancellor's. He knew how valuable Valorum remained to the Republic, and he knew there were enemies who would do him harm if given the chance. He had tried several times to convince Tarsus to travel with more security, with no success. So until his stubborn friend agreed to a personal guard detail, Johun was determined to accompany him on every mission.

"I hope we get there soon," Johun muttered, giving voice to his discomfort.

"You could always enter one of your meditative trances to pass the time," the Chancellor said jokingly. "You're not one for idle conversation anyway."

Tarsus only permitted Johun to accompany him because of

the long-standing relationship between them. The Jedi had been a member of the Chancellor's Guard through most of Valorum's first four-year term and the entirety of the second. Now his official position was Jedi adviser, though Johun would never presume to "advise" the Chancellor about anything.

Tarsus Valorum was known throughout the galaxy as the man who saved the Republic. Spearheading the Ruusan Reformations through the Senate, he had ushered in a new age of peace, prosperity, and expansion. Yet it wasn't what he had accomplished that made him a great man in Johun's eyes; it was how he had done it.

Serving at the Chancellor's side, the Jedi had seen the true power of words and ideas. Tarsus Valorum was a man of deep conviction—that rare breed of politician who truly believed his own words. Determined to create a Golden Age for the citizens of the galaxy, he had pursued with tireless vigor his dream of a reborn and reunited Republic. Hundreds of worlds that had fallen away during the last few centuries of war and galactic turmoil were brought back into the Republic fold during his reign. And when his term of service ended and the time came for him to pass his position over to his successor, he made sure everything was in place for her to continue his work.

Most amazingly, the great reunification had been accomplished with a minimum of bloodshed and battles. Relying on ambassadors and treaties, he had accomplished what could never be done through armies and war. *To win a world, you must win the hearts and minds of its people,* the Chancellor had once explained, shortly after Johun had been assigned to him. Now, after a decade of witnessing all Valorum had achieved, he knew truer words had never been spoken.

"Estimated arrival in five minutes," the voice of the pilot crackled over the shipboard intercom. "Prepare for landing."

Johun gave an exaggerated sigh of relief, and the Chancellor chuckled softly. It was a familiar routine to both men. Even though he was retired, Tarsus was not a man to simply step aside from the realm of politics. He remained a vigorous advo-

cate for the Republic. In the two years since his term of office
had ended, Johun had accompanied him on over fifty personal
diplomatic missions . . . like the one they were on now.

The planet of Serenno was an important world to the Republic. The ruling noble families were among the wealthiest
individuals in the galaxy. In addition to donating enormous
sums to highly visible charitable and political organizations,
they had the financial capital to help underwrite massive government infrastructure projects.

More important, their vast resources also enabled them to
fund groups that were opposed to the Republic, should they so
choose. Separatist factions often sought out wealthy benefac-
tors in Carannia, Saffia, and Fiyarro, Serenno's three largest
cities.

Valorum had come to meet with the heads of the six most
powerful families on the world. He hoped to convince them to
use their influence to persuade the other families to cut off all
funding to anti-Republic factions. It was a difficult mission, as
the Counts of Serenno were not known for acceding to the
demands of outsiders.

To make negotiations easier, the visit was being conducted
through unofficial channels. Valorum had once explained to
Johun that many rulers and politicians behaved quite differ-
ently when their actions were exposed to the public eye. Too
often they would simply give the appearance of meeting expec-
tations, a tactic Tarsus personally despised. In a public forum
officials would frequently offer promises of support to a cause
they did not believe in, only to reverse their position once public awareness of the issue faded.

Conversely, rulers might oppose or reject an idea they supported so as not to appear weak-minded or easy to manipulate. Such was the case on Serenno. If it was widely known that
a representative of the Republic was coming to pressure them
into action, they would oppose him on mere principle.

Never trust a promise made in front of a holoprojector, the
Chancellor often warned. *If you want to get anything done,*

*you need to meet behind closed doors and look a person right
in the eye.*

"Making final approach," the pilot announced, and Johun
felt their shuttle bank slightly to port.

They were scheduled to touch down at the private spaceport of Count Nalju, head of one of Serenno's six Great
Houses and a staunch ally of the Republic. Landing at a secluded location on the Nalju family estate, they would take a
landspeeder to prearranged meetings with representatives
from each of the Great Houses in turn so Valorum could plead
his case.

They felt the slight bump of touchdown and heard the
whoosh of the exit ramp descending. Eager to get out and
stretch his legs, Johun jumped to his feet.

"Shall we disembark, Your Excellency?" he asked, using the
honorific to which the Chancellor was still entitled even in re-
tirement.

Valorum rose from his chair, then made one last check of
his appearance. Johun was dressed in the traditional brown-
and-tan garments of his Order, but Tarsus was wearing an
elaborate outfit in the custom and fashion of Serenno royalty.
He had been fitted with dark blue trousers and a loose white
shirt, both handmade by master tailors. Draped over his shoulders was a silken cape of midnight black—a gift from Count
Nalju. The edges of the cape, along with the collar and cuffs
of his shirt, were embroidered with a repeating pattern of
three overlapping white circles set against a blue background,
the emblem and colors of House Nalju.

The entire outfit had been fashioned from only the finest
and most expensive materials; Johun shuddered to imagine
what it had cost. Yet the garment was a symbol of the unwav-
ering support House Nalju gave to the former Chancellor's
cause. Without the sponsorship of a powerful and long-
standing House, the nobility would simply dismiss Valorum as
an outsider or inferior.

Johun knew that Tarsus could have asked the Senate to reimburse him for the expense. However, as was his nature, Valorum had chosen to pay for it himself.

They disembarked to find themselves on a small landing pad constructed atop a tall outcropping of stone rising up like a pillar from the ocean. Fifty meters away stood the towering cliffs of the shoreline, their tops the same height as the landing pad. A single two-meter-wide durasteel walkway connected the landing pad to the clifftops. Halfway along the walkway, perfectly centered between the cliffs and the landing pad, was a wider five-by-five-meter platform, supported underneath by a crisscrossing skeleton of reinforced girders.

There were no railings on either the landing pad or the catwalk. Johun knew the lack of railings—like so many other aspects of Serenno's culture—were symbolic. There was a long-standing tradition of fierce independence among the nobility. Railings on the walkway or the landing pad would have been a sign of weakness, an admission of frailty and mortality that would have undermined House Nalju's pride and position. Even so, the Jedi couldn't help but worry about the Chancellor's safety when he contemplated the fifty-meter fall off the edge to the cold waters below.

The sole purpose of their arrival was to avoid fanfare and attention, so it was no surprise that there were only a handful of people waiting to meet them. Johun guessed they were servants from Count Nalju's household retinue, as they wore clothing similar to Valorum's custom-made cape.

Four figures were huddled together on the platform in the middle of the walkway waiting for them, buffeted by the stiff ocean breeze that tugged at their clothes and made their capes flutter out behind them. Three of them were human—two men and one woman. The fourth was a male Twi'lek with bright red skin; Johun wondered if it was some type of status symbol for the nobles to employ a Lethan among their household staff.

Waiting on the clifftops beyond the platform were two more servants, standing beside the landspeeder that would whisk them away to their appointed meetings. Unlike those on the platform, they were too far away for Johun to make out any details that might indicate species or gender.

The *New Dawn*'s engines shut down, only to be replaced by the crashing rhythm of the surf as it pounded itself relentlessly against the face of the cliffs.

"Not my first choice of places to touch down," Johun noted, raising his voice loud enough that Tarsus could hear him over the waves and wind.

"Well, I did ask Nalju to let us land someplace remote," Tarsus shouted back with a laugh. "I see they only came out halfway to meet us," he added, nodding his head in the direction of the four figures waiting on the platform.

"Would you go any farther out on this walkway than you had to?" Johun asked.

"I guess not," the Chancellor admitted, then put his head down against the rising wind and made his way out onto the walkway.

Johun followed a moment later, though he felt a sudden uneasiness about the entire situation.

"Be careful," he called ahead to Valorum. "If you go over the edge I can't promise I'll catch you."

The other man either didn't hear him or was too busy concentrating on making his way safely across to respond.

They were only a few meters away from the platform's edge when Johun was hit with a powerful premonition, an undeniable disturbance in the Force that warned him something terrible was about to happen. To this point his attention had been focused on Valorum's progress across the treacherous walkway. Now he opened up his awareness and allowed the Force to flow through him, painting a perfect picture of their entire surroundings.

The four figures waiting for them on the platform were armed with blasters and vibro-weapons. The two by the landspeeder—a short, heavyset man whose arms and neck were covered in green and purple tattoos and a Chiss female—were also armed. More alarmingly, the Chiss seemed to be concealing something in her hand.

Even without turning around, his heightened awareness allowed him to see the *New Dawn* resting on the landing pad behind him. Around the circumference of the pillar, just below the edge and carefully hidden from view, he sensed something explosive. He guessed that what the Chiss held in her hand was a remote detonator.

Johun took in every detail of the scene in the blink of an eye. Even so, he wasn't fast enough to save the *New Dawn* or her crew. The Chiss flipped the switch in her hand, and the charges wired around the landing pad exploded. The blast ripped through the ship's exterior, leaving great smoking holes in her unarmored hull. The shrapnel fragments shredded the pilot and navigator inside, killing them instantly.

The top half of the landing pad's stone column crumbled away, sending the *New Dawn* tumbling down. It ricocheted off the pillar's jagged rock face then hit the water with an echoing smack, sending a spray of foam shooting skyward; it sank almost instantly beneath the cold, frothing surface.

As the landing pad fell away the durasteel walkway buckled and bent, sending Valorum toppling over the edge. Empowered by the Force, Johun leapt forward and landed on his stomach, his arm shooting out over the edge to catch Valorum by the corner of his cape an instant before he plunged to his death. The Chancellor dangled there for a second before Johun heaved him up with one hand, swinging him by the cape so he dropped safely on the listing walkway behind the Jedi.

Johun ignited the green blade of his lightsaber just in time to deflect a blaster bolt fired at him by the woman on the platform, then scrambled to his feet to face his attackers. They hesitated at the sight of his trademark weapon, considering their chances against a Jedi.

Their delay gave Johun a chance to evaluate the situation. Retreat was impossible: the section of the durasteel walkway they stood on now jutted out at a descending angle from the platform where their enemies gathered; the far end had been sheared away and now dropped off into empty sky. The only escape was to go forward toward the cliffs—even if it meant going through his enemies.

"Don't move!" he shouted to Valorum as he leapt forward, landing on the platform even as the woman and both men drew their vibroswords and attacked. Only the Twi'lek held back.

All three wielded weapons laced with cortosis, allowing their blades to clash with Johun's lightsaber without being sliced in two. It only took the first pass for him to realize each one was a highly skilled opponent. Deflecting a quick slash intended to disembowel him by the first man, Johun wheeled to intercept a hard swipe at his neck from the woman. He delivered a spinning round kick to her side, sending her reeling even as he reached behind his back with his lightsaber to parry a savage thrust by the third man at his unprotected flank.

Johun's training in lightsaber combat was limited to the strikes and parries of Form VI, Niman, the most balanced of all the styles. Colloquially known as the Diplomat's Form, Niman had no specific strengths or weaknesses. Its general versatility had served him well during the unpredictable grand melees of the Ruusan battlefields. But over the past decade he had made only the most basic efforts to maintain his skill with the blade. Instead he had focused his attention on developing diplomatic talents. Yet he was still a Jedi, and a formidable foe for anyone to face.

He may have been outnumbered, but his enemies attacked as individuals, unable to coordinate the timing of their strikes. The woman regained her balance and rushed in, but Johun spun to the side and shoved her toward the first man. Her momentum sent her crashing into her partner, both of them tumbling to the ground in a tangled mess of limbs.

Knowing that the other two were momentarily incapacitated, he focused all his attention on the second man. Attacking as a trio, they had forced Johun onto the defensive.

One-on-one, however, he was able to press the action. He came at his lone opponent aggressively, holding nothing back, knowing he was fighting to save not just himself but the Chancellor, as well. His blade danced and sizzled, moving too swiftly for the eye to follow.

The man fell back under the assault, frantically parrying the blows and retreating until he felt his heels dangling over the platform's edge. In desperation he lunged forward with a clumsy stab at Johun's chest. The Jedi simply slapped his blade aside and ended the assassin's life with a single cut of the lightsaber across his chest.

The other two were back on their feet now. The woman rushed toward him recklessly yet again. This time Johun stood his ground, ducking under the wide, flat arc of her blade sweeping in from the side. He reached out with his left hand and seized her wrist as he rolled onto his back, using the momentum of her own charge against her. Pulling hard on her wrist, he tumbled backward and brought both feet up, planting them in the middle of her stomach. He completed the move by kicking out with both legs, sending her flying up and over the platform's edge. She screamed all the way down, her cries ending abruptly when she struck the water and rocks below.

Johun was already back on his feet, bracing for the first man's next attack. But rather than face him alone, his remaining adversary turned to flee, making a break for the walkway leading from the platform back to the shore.

He passed the Twi'lek at a dead run, then stopped as his body went rigid and his hands flew to his throat. He turned around slowly so he was facing Johun, clutching the bloody gash just beneath his jaw as he toppled forward and fell facedown on the platform.

It happened so fast it took a moment to register on Johun. Then he noticed the small, crescent-shaped blades clutched in each of the Twi'lek's hands. They looked like miniature sickles; the one in his left hand was a bright silver, the one in the right dripped with red.

The Chiss and the tattooed man had been making their way toward the platform to join the battle. Seeing the Twi'lek cut their escaping accomplice down, they abruptly reconsidered. Faced with a wrathful Jedi Knight and an ally who would kill them if they tried to flee the confrontation on the platform, they made the only logical choice and raced back up the walkway to their waiting vehicle. Piling in, they fired up the engines and sped away, wanting no part of a plan that had gone so wrong.

Stepping over the still-gasping body of the accomplice he had just killed, the Twi'lek dropped into a fighting crouch. He didn't seem to know or care that the other two had abandoned him. His lekku hung down behind him like twin tails, the tips twitching and curling in anticipation.

"I've always wanted to test my skills against a Jedi," he said, issuing the challenge.

Johun was more than willing to accept. He leapt forward, moving with the blinding speed of the Force as he stabbed his lightsaber squarely at the Twi'lek's chest to put a quick end to their confrontation. With an almost casual grace, the red-skinned Twi'lek merely leaned backward and twisted out of the way, slashing out with the strange crescent blades at Johun's throat.

The Jedi turned his body at the last second, avoiding the first blade completely, but catching the other with the meat of his right shoulder. It sliced deep into the muscle, eliciting a grunt of pain from Johun.

He wheeled back around to see the Twi'lek in the same low crouch, holding the crescent blades up in front of him like a boxer. Johun approached more cautiously this time, recognizing that this opponent was far more dangerous than the other three put together.

Using tight slashes and quick cuts, he probed his enemy's defenses with his lightsaber, trying to learn the patterns and rhythms of his foe's unfamiliar weapons. The Twi'lek slapped each blow aside with contemptuous ease, alternating hands so he could always leave one of the crescents up in a defensive position.

The unusual weapons sacrificed reach for speed and maneuverability, Johun realized. He was vulnerable if he let the Twi'lek get in close, but if he could keep him at a distance he had the advantage. The Twi'lek seemed to realize this, too, and began to move in slowly.

Johun tried to force him back with a sequence of aggressive attacks, but he was unable to penetrate the Twi'lek's defenses. No matter what he tried, his enemy was always able to keep at least one of the crescent blades back to parry his blows.

Frustrated, Johun overextended on one of his strikes, bringing the lightsaber in a fraction of a centimeter too high and wide and putting too much weight on his front foot. The mistake nearly proved fatal.

The Twi'lek swatted Johun's blade aside and stepped forward, closing the distance between them to less than a meter as he slid inside the arc of the lightsaber's effective range. The sickle of his left hand sliced down in a high vertical strike as the one in his right carved a low horizontal slash. Johun was able to backpedal and avoid the initial blows, but he wasn't so lucky when his opponent reversed his attack, allowing the crescent blades to retrace their original paths in the opposite direction.

One of the blades sliced upward, opening a gash in Johun's cheek and narrowly missing his eye. The other left a long, shallow cut along the left side of the Jedi's ribs—painful but not debilitating.

His enemy was in too close for Johun to bring his lightsaber to bear effectively; all he could do was butt with his head, sending his brow smashing hard into the Twi'lek's face. There was a wet crunch as the cartilage of his enemy's nose crumpled beneath the impact. The Twi'lek staggered back, then dropped once more into his fighting crouch. Blood flowed freely from his nostrils, the dark crimson flow visible even against his bright red complexion.

Johun tried to gather the Force to hurl his opponent off the platform's edge. But gathering the Force required concentration, and for a fraction of an instant it drew his focus away from the battle. His enemy sensed his momentary lapse and sprang forward, the sickles carving deadly semicircular arcs through the air.

Johun threw himself backward at the last instant, the power he'd accumulated disappearing harmlessly as he fell into a full retreat to avoid the lethal assault. Dropping low to the ground, he tried to swipe the feet out from under the Twi'lek. His opponent anticipated the move and leapt nimbly over his outstretched foot, bringing his knee up to strike Johun square in the jaw.

Seeing stars, Johun rolled clear, narrowly avoiding decapitation, as the crescent blades swooped in again. He regained his feet and took a wild swipe at his opponent. Dodging the blow, the Twi'lek swooped in close, and Johun was forced to give ground yet again to survive another series of lightning-fast blows.

The Twi'lek pressed the attack, staying close enough to Johun that the Jedi's only options were blocks and parries. Darting from side to side he cut off Johan's paths of retreat, slowly backing him up until he was balanced on the platform's edge.

Johun knew he couldn't beat the Twi'lek. His opponent was faster, his skills honed by years of intense training. He could continue to fight, but the outcome was inevitable—he was going to die on this platform. He could not escape his fate—yet he could still sacrifice himself to save the Chancellor.

There is no death; there is only the Force.

The Twi'lek had braced himself in preparation for a desperate counterattack, expecting Johun to try to fight his way clear of the platform's ledge. Instead the Jedi dropped his weapon and both hands shot forward to clutch tightly onto the front of his opponent's shirt. The handle of Johun's lightsaber clattered on the platform's durasteel surface, the blade extinguished the moment it fell from his hand.

The unexpected move caught the Twi'lek completely off guard, and he hesitated for a split second before his eyes went wide with fear and dawning comprehension. He slashed frantically at Johun's wrists and forearms, carving deep gashes into the flesh. But the Jedi's grip never faltered.

With his heels already dangling over the precipice, Johun simply had to let himself fall backward, dragging his enemy with him. The Twi'lek screamed as they plunged toward the deadly rocks jutting up from the waves fifty meters below; Johun felt nothing but a serene inner peace.

They seemed to fall forever, the world moving in slow motion as Johun surrendered himself fully to the power of the Force. It flowed through him, stronger than he had ever felt it before. The instant before they hit the water he looked into the terrified eyes of his foe and smiled. He had never felt more at peace than he did in that moment.

Dropping from fifty meters into the ocean was nothing like diving into a pool; the surface tension of the water struck them with the impact of a sledgehammer. During the fall they had turned slightly, so the impact took Johun on the right side. He felt his ribs crack, and then a cold shock as the freezing waters enveloped them.

It took Johun several seconds to realize he wasn't dead. Even missing the rocks, a fall from that height should have been lethal. Yet somehow he had survived, though he was now sinking quickly into the ocean's angry depths. *The Force*, he thought in amazement. He had given himself over to its power during the fall; in return it had spared his life.

He realized he was still clutching tightly to the front of the Twi'lek's shirt. Through the murky waters he could see his opponent's head lolling to the side at an unnatural angle, his neck broken when they had slammed into the unyielding ocean surface.

Releasing his grip he swam toward the surface, pulling with powerful strokes. Just as his lungs threatened to give out, he breached, gasping and swallowing huge gulps of air. The girders supporting the platform rose up out of the water before him, only a few meters away. He kicked his legs and reached out to grab the slick, wet durasteel with hands already going numb in the chill waters, then began the long slow climb back to the top.

Blood poured freely from the cuts to his forearms. But though the wounds were deep, they hadn't struck any critical nerves or tendons, and he was able to use his hands to help him along as he clambered up the girders.

He had reached the halfway point when he paused to rest, shivering in the wind. A voice called his name; looking up, he saw the face of Chancellor Valorum staring down at him. Knowing he needed to save his breath for the rest of the climb, Johun's only response was a weak wave of acknowledgment.

Half a meter from the top Valorum's arm reached down over the edge to clasp his own. The exhausted Jedi was grateful for the aid as the Chancellor helped him clamber up and back onto the safety of the platform. Johun tried to stand, but his limbs betrayed him. All he could manage was to roll onto his back and stare up at the sky, panting and wheezing as he tried to catch his breath.

"You saved my life," the Chancellor said, sitting down beside him to wait for the Jedi to recover from his ordeal. "I can never repay you for what you have done, but if there is ever anything you want of me you need only ask."

"There is one thing." Johun gasped from his back, still too tired to even try to sit up. "Hire yourself a kriffing security team."

13

Zannah made her way slowly through Carannia's market square, purchasing supplies to replace those Bane had inadvertently destroyed. Only a week had passed since she'd last been here, but in that short time a great many things had changed.

Kel was dead, for one. The HoloNet was buzzing with the news of the failed attempt to kidnap Chancellor Valorum, and all the accounts made specific mention of the red-skinned Twi'lek and his end at the hands of a Jedi Knight named Johun Othone.

Three of the others from the small group were dead as well, though reports indicated that two of the terrorists had fled the scene. From the descriptions given it was obvious to Zannah that Paak and Cyndra were the two surviving fugitives.

The attack had prompted immediate condemnation from the Senate and the rest of the Republic. More important, the Counts of Serenno had promised swift and decisive action to stamp out the separatist organizations that plagued their fair world. Based on the enormous rewards being offered for information leading to the capture of those involved in the attack, it seemed the nobles intended to keep their promise.

Even had Kel and his friends succeeded, Zannah now realized, the reaction of the Counts would have been the same. In the aftermath of the violence, the bodies of several members of Count Nalju's household staff were discovered near the landing site. They had been sent to greet Chancellor Valorum on his arrival, only to be murdered by the radicals who had set the ambush.

The deaths of several long-serving followers was a great tragedy for House Nalju, but it paled in comparison with the horror elicited by the attack itself. The Count had personally sponsored the Chancellor's visit; an assault upon his esteemed guest was an insult to family honor, and a crime tantamount to attacking the Count himself. Always willing to protect their own, the other Great Houses had rallied to the Nalju cry, vowing to hunt down and exterminate those responsible for this atrocity.

No doubt Darth Bane had foreseen this outcome. For the next several years the eyes of the Republic would be focused intently on Serenno and its campaign to snuff out the separatist elements that had infiltrated its culture.

"Don't move," a familiar female voice hissed in her ear, and Zannah felt the muzzle of a blaster press itself hard into the flesh of her lower back.

"I'm surprised you'd dare to show your face in public," Zannah whispered without turning around to face the Chiss standing close behind her. "There's a lot of credits being offered for your head."

"Thanks to you," Cyndra snapped back, jabbing her painfully with the weapon. "Now start walking. Slowly."

There were a dozen ways Zannah could turn the tables on Cyndra, but each of them involved a display of dark side power she wasn't willing to make in the crowded market square. So she did as ordered, making her way past the vendor stalls as she waited for the right moment to make her move. Cyndra followed close, pressing tight up against her to shield the blaster at Zannah's back with her own body.

"Where are you taking me?" Zannah asked her.

"We're going to see Hetton," Cyndra snarled. "He's got some questions for you."

How convenient, Zannah thought. *I've got some questions for him, too.*

Cyndra took her down a narrow alley leading away from the market square to a deserted side street.

"Stand still or I shoot," she warned Zannah, then pulled a comlink from her belt. "I've got her," she said. "Come pick us up."

In less than a minute an airspeeder swooped down to land on the far side of the street. Zannah wasn't surprised to see Paak sitting in the pilot's seat. He jumped out as the Chiss marched her prisoner over to the vehicle.

"Told you she'd come back," he said to his companion.

"Just search her for weapons," she answered.

Paak leered at Zannah as he roughly patted her down. "What have we here?" he exclaimed, discovering her only weapon and holding it up for inspection.

The handle of Zannah's lightsaber was slightly longer than normal to accommodate the twin crystals required to power the blades that extended from either end. However, while most traditional double-bladed weapons had blades each measuring a meter and a half or more, those of Zannah's lightsaber were slightly under a meter in length. This small but significant difference was critical to the way in which she used her weapon . . .

"The smaller blades give you greater speed and maneuverability," her Master explained as the fourteen-year-old Zannah twirled her newly constructed lightsaber in her left hand, focusing on mastering the feel of its unique balance and weight.

"Grip the handle lightly in your fingers. Control the weapon

with your wrist and hand rather than the muscles of your arm. You will sacrifice reach and leverage, but you will be able to create a shield of impenetrable defense."

"Defense will not slay my enemy," Zannah remarked, smoothly transferring the spinning crimson blades from her left hand to her right and back again.

"You lack the physical strength required for the powerful attacking strikes of Djem So or the other aggressive forms," her Master explained. "You must rely on quickness, cunning and, most of all, patience to best your enemies."

He ignited his own lightsaber and took a long, looping swing in her direction. Zannah intercepted the blow with her own weapon, easily deflecting it to the side.

"Form three allows you to parry incoming attacks with minimal effort," he told her. "Your opponent must expend precious energy with each blow, slowly tiring while you remain fresh and strong."

Bane seized the hook-handled grip of his own lightsaber with both hands and raised it high over his head, then brought it straight down in a fierce chop. Using the techniques he had made her practice for two hours each day over the past year, Zannah met her Master's blade with one of her own. Had she tried to meet it head-on, the strength of his attack would have driven her own weapon back into her, or knocked the lightsaber from her hand. Instead she clipped his blade with a glancing contact, rerouting it so that it continued its downward arc at an angle, passing harmlessly a few centimeters from her shoulder.

"Good," Bane said approvingly, winding up for another heavy-handed swipe. "Do not block. Redirect. Wait for opponents to become weary or frustrated. Let them make a mistake, then seize the opening and make them pay."

To illustrate his point Bane took a wild swipe that she easily picked off. The momentum of his swing caused him to lean too far forward, exposing his shoulder and back to her counterattack. With a flick of her wrist Zannah directed her own *weapon toward the opening. She scored a direct hit, one of her twin blades tracing a ten-centimeter-long slash across his shoulder that would have severed the arm of any other opponent.*

In Bane's case, however, the blade only cut through the cloth of his shirt and left a small scorch mark on the impregnable shell of the orbalisk beneath.

"You're dead!" she exclaimed triumphantly, still twirling her blade so that it never lost momentum.

Bane nodded in approval. But it was early, and the day's lesson had only just begun.

"Again," he commanded in the stern taskmaster's voice he always used during their drills and practice sessions. . . .

"What is this? A lightsaber?" Paak muttered, turning the handle over in his hands. "Where'd you get this? You steal it off a Jedi or something?"

Zannah didn't bother to answer. There was nobody else in view; the three of them were alone in the deserted street. She could easily have ended their lives right there and escaped. But they had said they were taking her to Hetton, and she was most eager to meet the founder of the Anti-Republic Liberation Front.

"Hetton's going to be very interested in this," he remarked. "Very, very interested."

"Come on. Let's get moving," Cyndra told him. "I don't want to keep Hetton waiting. He's mad enough at us already."

Paak tossed the lightsaber onto the passenger seat in the front, then climbed into the pilot's chair.

"Get in the back," Cyndra ordered Zannah, waving the blaster's nose threateningly.

She did as she was told, and a second later Cyndra climbed in beside her, still keeping her weapon trained on Zannah. The airspeeder lifted off the ground, whisking them through the city and out to the countryside beyond.

"How long until we get there?" Zannah asked.

"Shut your kriffing mouth," Cyndra answered. "There'll be

plenty of time to talk when you explain to Hetton why you betrayed us."

"Kel always was a sucker for a pretty face," Paak said, glancing back at her over his shoulder. "Always knew it would be the death of him. If he was smart he would have just stuck with you, Cyndra."

Cyndra's red eyes narrowed angrily. "Shut up and drive, Paak."

"You and Kel?" Zannah said, legitimately surprised. "I'm sorry. I didn't know."

"Neither did Cyndra," Paak said with a laugh. "At least not until you showed up at our meeting. She wanted to kill you right there. Lucky for you she's a professional."

The rest of the ride passed in silence as they made their way farther and farther from the city. Soon they passed into the country estates of the noble families, confirming Zannah's suspicion that Hetton was a member of a powerful Serenno house. She wondered what would happen to him now that the political climate of Carannia had turned so strongly against the separatists.

The speeder continued on, passing over lavish rose gardens that stretched for acres, the irrigation provided by exquisite fountains while armies of staff clipped and pruned to keep each individual flower in a perfect, pristine state.

An enormous mansion loomed in the distance; in truth it looked more like a castle than a home. The flag flying from one of the many turrets was a bright red, emblazoned with a single eight-pointed star of gold. Zannah suspected it was derived from the five-pointed star of the Demici Great House. Apparently Hetton's family were distant relations of the Demicis that had earned the right to create their own variation on the family crest.

When they landed they were met by six guards clad in long red robes. Each wore a full helmet that completely covered the head and face, and they all carried force pikes. The meter-and-a-half-long metal poles were equipped with stun modules at the tip, capable of discharging an electrical current to stun or incapacitate opponents . . . or even kill if set to a high enough power. She recognized the exotic weapon from Bane's teachings; it had been a favorite of the Umbaran Shadow Assassins, though the members of the group had gone into hiding with the fall of Kaan's Brotherhood.

"Get out," Cyndra demanded, gesturing once again with her blaster. A small part of Zannah pitied the Chiss—Kel had used her then tossed her aside—while another part of her resented her blue-skinned romantic rival. But she was not about to let either emotion affect her thoughts or actions in any significant way.

She did as she was told, exiting the vehicle and submitting to another search by one of the red-robed guards before passively holding her hands out before her and allowing them to slap a pair of binder cuffs on her wrists. Only then did Cyndra finally put away her blaster, stuffing it into her belt and grabbing Zannah by the arm to pull her along after Paak and the guards.

The procession made its way through a high archway and into the marble-lined hall beyond. Paintings and sculptures lined the walls; floating holographic artworks hovered near the ceiling. The display of wealth would have impressed or even intimidated most visitors, Zannah suspected. She, however, saw the collection as nothing but a waste of funds that could have been better spent elsewhere.

The mansion was enormous, and it took them five full minutes to pass from the airspeeder landing pad to the reception chamber where Hetton awaited them. Zannah knew they were near their destination when they stopped before a pair of towering doors, closed and barring their progress. Two of the guards stepped forward, one on each door, and pushed them open.

The room beyond was thirty meters long and twenty meters wide. Like the halls, the walls were lined with art, and a long red carpet led to a small staircase and a raised dais at the far end. The room was devoid of furniture except for a large chair atop the dais, though Zannah thought it could more properly be described as a throne.

Sitting there, flanked by two more of the red-robed guards, was a man who could only be Hetton himself. He was small in stature, and older than she had suspected; he looked to be in his late fifties. She had expected him to be garbed in the colors of his house, but instead he wore black pants, a black shirt, black boots, and black gloves. Crimson striping trimmed the tops of his boots and the cuffs of his gloves. A hooded cape, also black with crimson trim, was draped across his shoulders, though the hood was thrown back to reveal his face.

He had fine gray hair, cropped very short. He had a long, pointed nose, and his pale blue eyes seemed small and too close together. There was a cruel tilt to his thin lips that made it almost appear as if he was sneering. As they entered, he leaned forward in his seat and clutched at the arms of his oversized throne; he looked hunched, sinister.

Although he was not conventionally attractive or physically imposing, there was an undeniable air of importance about him. Zannah suspected it was a natural confidence born of wealth and privilege, but as she was marched down the red carpet toward him, she realized it was something far more impressive: Hetton radiated with the power of the dark side!

They approached until they were ten meters from the steps leading up to Hetton's seat, then stopped at a signal from one of the guards flanking the throne. Their escort stepped to the side, leaving Zannah, Paak, and Cyndra alone before Hetton.

"And who are you, my dear?" Hetton asked, his words sharp and clipped as they echoed thinly off the walls of the great room.

"My name is Rainah," Zannah answered. "I am—I was—a friend of Kel's."

"Of course," Hetton said with a knowing smirk. "Kelad'den had many female friends."

"She's the one who betrayed us to the Republic!" Cyndra

said angrily, shaking the still-cuffed Zannah by her elbow as she spoke.

"I didn't betray anyone," Zannah protested, stalling for time as she tried to gauge Hetton's power.

During the war between the Brotherhood of Darkness and the Army of Light, both sides had actively sought to recruit those with power into their ranks. But it would have been a simple enough matter for a family as obviously rich and powerful as Hetton's to shield one of their own from both the Jedi and the Sith.

"You knew every detail of our plan," Cyndra insisted. "Who else could it have been?"

"You and Paak seem to have survived somehow," Zannah remarked, letting the unspoken accusation hang in the air as she continued her subtle probing of Hetton.

His power didn't have the raw, untamed feel of one who had never been trained. Was it possible he'd once had a tutor or mentor? Had someone knowledgeable in the Force taught him the ways of the dark side, then abandoned him to follow Kaan? Or was there some other explanation?

"I am not a traitor!" the Chiss shouted angrily.

"Calm down, Cyndra," Hetton said, sardonically amused at her outrage. "Chancellor Valorum had a Jedi Knight with him. Your mission was doomed to failure from the start.

"And even if you had succeeded," he added, his voice dropping to a low and dangerous whisper, "you still would have brought the wrath of the Great Houses crashing down on us.

"What were you thinking?" he demanded with a sudden shout that made both Paak and Cyndra jump. Zannah could feel the air crackle as the small man called upon the Force, gathering the energies of the dark side. His power was undeniable, yet as she felt it building she was confident his abilities would be no match for hers.

"Hetton, wait!" Paak shouted, sensing the peril they were in. "We've got something for you."

He held up Zannah's lightsaber, waving it above his head so

Hetton would be sure to see it. The effect was immediate and instantaneous; the building power of the dark side vanished as Hetton froze, his eyes riveted on the hilt. After a moment he seemed to regain his composure and sat back down, signaling for one of his guards to bring the treasure to him.

When it was placed in his hand he studied it carefully for a full minute before setting it reverently in his lap.

"Where did you find this?" he asked softly, though there was a dangerous undercurrent in his voice.

"On her," Paak said. "She wouldn't tell us how she got it."

"Is that a fact?" Hetton muttered, suddenly staring at Zannah with renewed interest, running the fingers of one hand idly over the lightsaber's handle. "I would be most interested to learn how she acquired this particular specimen."

"Give me five minutes alone with her," Cyndra said. "I'll get her to talk."

Zannah decided that the game had gone on long enough. It would have been a simple matter to snatch the lightsaber back to her shackled hands using the Force, but she had other weapons at her disposal . . .

"The Force manifests itself in many different ways," Darth Bane told her. "Every individual has strengths and weaknesses— talents they excel at and others that are more difficult."

The twelve-year-old Zannah nodded. Several months before, Bane had unlocked a new data bank of information in Freedon Nadd's Holocron. Though he wouldn't tell her what he had uncovered, he had added a new element to her training shortly after his discovery. Every two or three days he would put her through a series of rigorous tests and challenges designed to evaluate her command of different aspects of the Force.

Until today he had refused to discuss the results of his experiments with her, and Zannah was beginning to fear she had somehow failed him.

"Some possess raw elemental power; they can unleash storms of lightning from their fingertips, or move mountains

with their mere thoughts. Others are more gifted in the subtle intricacies of the Force, blessed with the ability to affect the minds of friend and foe alike through the arts of persuasion or battle meditation."

He paused and fixed her with a long stare, as if considering whether to say more.

"A rare few have a natural affinity for the dark side itself. They can delve into the depths of the Force and summon arcane energies to twist and warp the world around them. They can invoke the ancient rituals of the Sith; they can conjure power and unleash terrible spells and dark magics."

"Is that my gift?" Zannah asked, barely able to contain her excitement. "Am I a Sith sorcerer?"

"You have the potential," Bane told her. From inside his robes he produced a thin leather-bound manuscript. "Hidden deep inside the Holocron, I discovered a list of powerful spells. I transcribed them into this tome. They will help you focus and channel your power for maximum effect . . . but only if you study them carefully."

"I will, Master," Zannah promised, her eyes gleaming as she reached out to take the book from his hands.

"My ability to guide and teach you in the ways of sorcery are limited," Bane warned her. "My talents lie in another direction. To unleash your full potential you will have to do much of the study and research on your own. It will be . . . perilous."

The thought of exploring the dark and dangerous secrets of Sith sorcery alone filled her with dread, but the chance to achieve a power beyond the abilities of her Master to comprehend was a temptation she could not resist.

"I will not disappoint you, Master," she vowed, clutching the tome tightly against her chest.

"And if you ever try to use one of your spells against me," Bane added as a final caution, "I will destroy you."

Zannah shook her elbow free of Cyndra's grasp and raised her shackled hands before her face. Weaving her fingers in a complex pattern in the air, she reached out with the Force and plunged deep inside the Chiss woman's mind to find her secret, most primal fears. Buried in her subconscious were nameless horrors: abominations and creatures of nightmare never meant to see the light of day. Drawing on the power of Sith sorcery, Zannah plucked them out and brought them to life one by one.

The entire process took less than a second. In that time Cyndra had drawn her weapon, but instead of pointing it at Zannah she suddenly screamed and aimed it high in the air above her, firing wildly at demons conjured from her own mind that only she could see.

The illusions grew more real and more terrifying the longer the spell continued, but Zannah had no intention of ending it yet. The Chiss shrieked and threw her weapon to the ground. She flung her head wildly from side to side, covering it with her arms and screaming "No!" over and over before collapsing on the floor. Weeping and sobbing, she curled up into a tight little ball, still muttering "No, no, no . . ."

Everyone else in the room was staring at her in horror and bewilderment. Some of the guards took a step back, afraid they might somehow become infected by her madness.

Zannah could have ended it then, dispelling the illusion and allowing Cyndra to fall into unconsciousness. She would wake hours later with only the most basic recollection of what had happened, her mind instinctively recoiling from the memories of what it had witnessed. Or Zannah could push the illusion even farther, driving her victim to the edge of insanity and beyond. An image of the Chiss romantically entangled with Kel sprang unbidden to her mind—and Zannah pushed.

Cyndra's cries of terror became animal howls as her sanity was ripped apart by the ghastly visions. Her hands scratched and clawed at her own eyes, tearing them out. Blood poured down her cheeks, but even blindness couldn't save her from the nightmares crawling through what was left of her mind.

Her howls stopped as her body went into seizure; her mouth foamed as her limbs convulsed wildly on the floor. Then, with a final bloodcurdling shriek, she fell suddenly limp and lay still. Her conscious mind completely and irrevocably obliterated, her catatonic body was now nothing more than an empty shell.

The body shivered once, and Zannah knew that somewhere in the deepest core of Cyndra's subconscious a small part of her still existed, silently screaming, trapped forever with the horrors inside her own mind.

Though everyone had borne witness to the Chiss's gruesome and terrifying end, Zannah was the only one who knew what had really happened. Yet even she was never quite certain just what her victims saw. Based on their reactions she figured it was probably better not to know. She coolly regarded Cyndra's body on the floor, still trembling occasionally, then glanced up to see Hetton staring at her intently.

She turned away when she heard Paak shouting at her from across the room.

"You did this!" He pointed an accusing finger at her. "Stop her or she'll kill us all!" he cried.

Several of the guards took a step toward her, only to pull up at a slight shake of the head from Hetton.

"She's not dead," Zannah announced. "Though whatever's left of her mind surely begs for death."

The answer did nothing to calm Paak's mounting hysteria. Reaching into his boot, he pulled out a short vibroblade and rushed at Zannah with a scream.

The spell she had unleashed on Cyndra was powerful but exhausting. Zannah doubted she'd be able to effect a similar reaction in Paak before he ran her through with his blade. So instead of sorcery, she turned to more conventional means to dispatch him.

Extending her shackled hands, she used the Force to draw the lightsaber from Hetton's lap, sending it flying across the room and into her waiting palm. As the blades ignited she casually snapped her restraints with a single thought.

Paak had come in expecting to skewer a helpless prisoner;

he wasn't ready to face an armed foe. She could have slain him right then and there, but she noticed that Hetton was still sitting passively in his seat, observing the action. Zannah decided she'd give him a show.

Instead of decapitating her overmatched opponent, she simply toyed with him, twirling and spinning the lightsaber through intricate, hypnotic patterns as she easily parried his ham-fisted blows. Paak was a brawler, all muscle and no technique, making it ridiculously simple for her to repulse his attacks. He came at her three times, hacking and slashing as he tried to bowl her over. Each time she would nimbly skip to one side and redirect his blade with her own, turning their combat into a dance where she was most definitely taking the lead.

After three failed passes, the tattooed man threw his blade down in frustration and scooped up Cyndra's fallen blaster. He took aim and fired twice from point-blank range, but Zannah didn't even flinch.

Using the precognitive awareness of the Force, she was easily able to anticipate the incoming shots and intercept them with the crackling crimson blades of her lightsaber. The first bolt ricocheted harmlessly up into the ceiling; the second she sent back at Paak.

It struck him square between the eyes, leaving a smoking hole in his forehead. His body went rigid, then toppled over backward.

Still twirling her weapon, Zannah turned to face Hetton again. He had not moved from his throne; nor had he made any signal to his guards. As she stared at him he rose slowly to his feet and walked down the stairs of the dais until he was standing only a few meters in front of her. Then he dropped to his knees before her and bowed his head.

In a trembling voice he whispered, "I have been waiting for someone like you my entire life."

14

J OHUN WALKED WITH LONG, quick strides down the dormitory corridors of the great Jedi Temple. He passed halls and staircases leading to the various wings that had been constructed to house the Jedi Knights and Padawans who chose to dwell here on Coruscant, making his way toward the base of the Spire of the High Council and the private chambers reserved for the Masters-in-residence.

He nodded curtly to those who waved or called out to him as he marched briskly past, but Johun had no time to stop and exchange pleasantries. He had received a summons from Valenthyne Farfalla immediately after landing, and Johun had a pretty good idea what his old Master wanted to talk to him about.

When he arrived at his destination he was surprised to find the door to Farfalla's private quarters standing open, the Jedi Master seated at a desk inside, deep in study.

"You wanted to see me?" Johun said by way of greeting, stepping inside and closing the door behind him.

The room was decorated much as Farfalla's private cabin had been aboard the *Fairwind,* the flagship of the now disbanded Jedi fleet. Fine art adorned the walls, and expensive rugs covered the floor. In one corner sat the four-poster bed depicting the key stages of Valenthyne's rise to the rank of Jedi Master.

"Johun," Farfalla said with mild surprise. "I did not expect to see you so soon." He turned in his seat and motioned to one of the other chairs in the room, indicating that his guest should sit.

"Your summons sounded urgent," Johun answered. He spread his feet and stood stiffly, refusing the offer of a chair.

"I need to speak with you," Farfalla said with a weary sigh.

"As my friend, my Master, or a representative of the Jedi Council?"

"That depends on what you have to say," Farfalla answered, ever the diplomat. "I have heard that Chancellor Valorum intends to petition the Senate for funds to create a memorial to Hoth and the other Jedi who fell on Ruusan."

"No doubt he believes this to be a fitting tribute to the people who gave their lives to keep the Republic safe," Johun remarked. "A tribute some would say is long overdue."

Farfalla raised an eyebrow. "So you had nothing to do with this request? Valorum came up with this idea on his own?"

"I never said *that,*" the Jedi Knight replied. The truth, as both he and Valenthyne were well aware, was that Valorum had agreed to do this to show his gratitude toward Johun for saving him during the attack on Serenno.

"As I suspected," the Master said with another sigh. "The Jedi Council does not approve of this, Johun. They see it as an act of pride and arrogance."

"Is it arrogant to honor those who made the ultimate sacrifice?" Johun asked, staying calm. He was a Jedi Knight now; the Padawan who would fly off the handle at the slightest provocation was long gone.

"Requesting a memorial to honor your former Master

smacks of vanity," Farfalla explained. "In elevating the man who first trained you, you in effect elevate yourself."

"This is not vanity, Master," Johun explained patiently. "A memorial on Ruusan will serve as a reminder of how one hundred beings willingly marched off to face certain death so that the rest of the galaxy might live in peace. It will be a powerful symbol to inspire others."

"The Jedi do not need symbols to inspire them," Farfalla reminded him.

"But the rest of the Republic does," Johun countered. "Symbols give power to ideas, they speak to the hearts and minds of the average person, they help transform abstract values and beliefs into reality.

"This monument glorifies the victory on Ruusan: a victory that came not through the strength of our army, but through the courage, conviction, and sacrifice of Hoth and those who perished with him. It will serve as a shining example to guide the citizens of the Republic in their thoughts and actions."

"I see Valorum's flair for speeches has rubbed off on you," Valenthyne said with a rueful smile, recognizing that he would not be able to convince Johun to change his position.

"It was you who chose to assign me to the Chancellor's side," Johun reminded him. "And I have learned many things in my years of service."

Farfalla rose from his seat and began to pace the room.

"Your arguments are eloquent, Johun. But surely you know they will not sway the Jedi Council."

"This matter falls outside the Council's authority," Johun reminded him. "If the Senate approves funding for Valorum's request, construction on Ruusan will begin within the month."

"The Senate will never refuse Valorum anything." Farfalla snorted. He stopped pacing and turned toward Johun. "And what will your role be in this project?"

"That, too, is for the Senate to decide," Johun answered evasively. However, after a moment he relented and told Farfalla the truth. "The Chancellor has agreed to travel with a full security complement on future diplomatic missions so that I will be free to go to Ruusan and oversee construction of the memorial."

Farfalla sighed and sat back down in his chair.

"I understand why you are doing this, Johun. I do not fully approve, but neither I nor the Jedi Council will stand in your way." After a moment he added, "I doubt we could stop you now even if we tried."

"At times I can be most stubborn," the Jedi Knight replied with the hint of a smile.

"Just like Hoth," Farfalla noted.

Johun chose to take his words as a compliment.

"MY FATHER DIED when I was only an infant," Hetton said, his voice low enough that Zannah had to strain to hear it over the clacking of their footsteps on the polished marble floor. "Burdened with the responsibilities of being the head of our house, my mother left it to the servants to raise me. They knew of my special gifts for many years before word of it ever reached my mother's ear."

"Perhaps they feared what she might do to them if they told her," Zannah suggested.

She and Hetton were alone now. After her performance in the throne room, he had insisted on bringing her to see his vast collection of Sith manuscripts and artifacts, located in his inner sanctum on the far side of the great mansion. He had also insisted that his guards stay behind. To pass the time on the journey through the seemingly endless halls and rooms of his manor, he had started to tell her his personal history.

"My mother was a strong and intimidating woman," Hetton admitted. "Perhaps the servants were afraid of her. Whatever the reasons, I was already in my early twenties before she finally discovered my affinity for the Force."

"How did she react?"

"She saw my talents as a tool we could use to further the

fortunes of our house. She had no use for the Jedi—or even the Sith, for that matter—but she wanted to find someone to help teach me to better master my skills.

"This was many years before the Brotherhood of Darkness came to power," he reminded her before resuming his tale.

"After a number of discreet inquiries and many substantial bribes and payments, she finally settled on a Duros named Gula Dwan."

"He became your Master?"

"*Master* was a title he never deserved," Hetton replied with just a hint of bitterness. "He was nothing but a bounty hunter and assassin who had the good fortune to be born with the ability to touch the Force. Over the years he had gleaned a simple understanding of the most basic techniques to access his power, allowing him to levitate small objects and perform other similar tricks.

"But he had no allegiance to the Sith or the Jedi; Gula's only fealty was to whoever paid him the most credits. And my family could afford to pay him more credits than he had ever dreamed of."

They had reached another set of large double doors, though these were sealed and locked from the other side. Her host reached out and placed his palm on the surface, then closed his eyes. Zannah felt the soft whisper of the Force; then the lock clicked and the door swung open to reveal Hetton's inner sanctum.

The room was part library, part museum. Shelves of ancient manuscripts and scrolls, and endless lines of old datatapes lined the walls, and there was a data terminal and large viewscreen in one corner. Several long glass display cases ran lengthwise down the center of the room, displaying the collection of Sith treasures Hetton had spent the past three decades acquiring: strange glowing amulets, small jewel-encrusted daggers, a variety of unusual stones and crystals, and the handles of at least a dozen different lightsabers.

"Gula's instruction gave me a foundation on which to build,

but most of my learning came from the books and manuscripts you see before you," Hetton said with pride.

They walked slowly along the length of the display cases, Zannah splitting her attention between Hetton's words and the intriguing array of Sith artifacts. She could still feel faint remnants of dark side energy clinging to them: fading memories of the incredible power they once contained.

"Early on in my apprenticeship I recognized Gula for the fool he was. At my urging, my mother used the wealth and resources of our house to scour the galaxy in pursuit of every record, object, or trinket even remotely associated with the dark side so that I could further my learning without having to rely exclusively on my so-called Master.

"As you might expect, much of what came to us was worthless rubbish. But over the years a number of rare and valuable items found their way into my possession."

Hetton turned to the shelves, running his hands lovingly over the cataloged volumes.

"The knowledge here allowed me to quickly surpass Gula. Once my mother realized he was no longer of any use to us, she had him killed."

Zannah started and blinked in surprise. Hetton laughed softly at her reaction.

"My mother was a woman driven by ambition and ruthless practicality. She had worked hard to keep my existence hidden from the Jedi and Sith; if Gula were allowed to simply leave our service, it was inevitable he would reveal our house's great secret."

"A necessary death," Zannah said with a nod, realizing that Bane probably would have done the same thing. Then, hit with a sudden flash of insight, she said, "You were the one who killed him, weren't you?"

Hetton smiled at her. "You are as perceptive as you are powerful. When the order came down from my mother, I was more than happy to comply. Gula had become a burden and an impediment to my own research into the ways of the dark side."

"You speak of your mother as if she is gone," Zannah noted. "What happened to her?"

Hetton's eyes narrowed, and his expression grew dark.

"About fifteen years ago, when Kaan first began to assemble his Brotherhood of Darkness, my mother urged me to reveal myself and join their cause. She believed they would succeed in their quest to destroy the Republic, and she sought to ally our house with the rising new power in the galaxy.

"But I refused to become part of Kaan's cult. He preached that all who followed the dark side would serve as equals— a democracy of Sith. I found the concept repugnant, a perversion of everything I had studied and believed in.

"However, my mother still thought in terms of governments and political alliances. Through my study of the dark side I had transcended such mundane interests, but she could not grasp my objections. In the end, I was forced to eliminate her."

This time Zannah wasn't surprised. "She would have ignored your wishes and tried to forge an alliance with the Brotherhood," she said, showing that she understood—and even approved of—Hetton's matricide. "She would have exposed you. You had no other choice."

"I poisoned her in her sleep," Hetton explained, his voice betraying just a hint of regret. "It was a peaceful death; I never wanted her to suffer. After all, I'm not a monster."

There was a moment of silence as he let his thoughts linger over what he had done. Then he shook his head and resumed speaking as he led Zannah over to the monitor and data terminal.

"With the fall of the Brotherhood and the reformations of the Jedi Order, I became more bold. In addition to my quest to seek out the knowledge and artifacts of the ancient Sith I also began to assemble an army of followers. Under the separatist banner, I drew those individuals with unique skills and talents into my service. We were united in our hatred of the Republic and the Jedi, yet I was still wary of revealing my true purpose: the resurrection of the Sith!

"And now you are here," he said, concluding his tale. He reached down and removed a datacard from the terminal they were standing beside. "The timing could not be more perfect."

Zannah wasn't quite sure what he meant by that, but before she could ask a question he had placed the datacard in her hand. "What's this?"

"Do you know the name of Belia Darzu?" he asked her. Zannah shook her head. "She was a Dark Lord of the Sith who reigned over two centuries ago. She was a student of Sith alchemy; it was said she learned the secrets of *mechu-deru*, the ability to transform the flesh of living beings into metal and machinery. She used this power to create an army of technobeasts: organic–droid hybrids bound to her will."

Zannah vaguely recalled a passing mention of technobeasts from her studies, though the name *Belia Darzu* still didn't sound familiar.

"Many also believe that before her death she discovered the secret of creating Sith Holocrons," Hetton added, and Zannah's thoughts flashed back to Bane and his failed attempts to do the same.

"Ultimately, Belia was betrayed and murdered by her own followers," Hetton continued. "A familiar occurrence in the histories I have read. When she fell all her secrets were lost, though there is speculation that much of what she discovered is still stored in the archives of her stronghold on Tython."

"Tython?" Zannah exclaimed, recognizing the name. "Isn't that one of the Deep Core worlds?"

The Deep Core was a small cluster of densely packed stars centered on a black hole in the very heart of the galaxy. The worlds of the Deep Core—planets like Tython—typically appeared only in myths and legends, or in the wild tales of half-mad explorers who claimed to have visited them. Unstable solar masses, large pockets of antimatter, and gravity wells powerful enough to warp the space–time continuum made it virtually impossible to chart safe hyperspace routes into the region.

"I know what you're thinking," Hetton said. "I was skeptical myself at first. But the more I learned about Belia, the more evidence I found to support the theory that her stronghold was on Tython."

"Even if it's true," Zannah protested, "nobody knows how to get to Tython."

"I do," Hetton said with a sly smile. "In my research I discovered the coordinates for a long-forgotten hyperspace lane into the Deep Core. But I never dared to make the trip. I feared the defenses of Belia's stronghold would be impenetrable. And then I met you."

"I don't see what this has to do with me," Zannah said.

"For many years I have studied the dark side, but my power has plateaued. I will learn nothing further on my own. I need a new Master—one with the power to penetrate the defenses of Belia's stronghold and lay claim to her secrets."

"You want to become my apprentice?" Zannah asked, her voice rising in disbelief.

"Everything I know about Belia Darzu, including the hyperspace route to Tython, can be found on that datacard," Hetton said, speaking quickly. "I am presenting it to you as a gift, a sign of respect and admiration and proof of the seriousness of my offer."

"You're at least twice my age!" Zannah exclaimed, still unable to wrap her mind around the bizarre turn of events.

"Age has little relevance in matters of the Force," Hetton assured her. "Your power is far greater than mine. I am asking you to teach me the ways of the dark side. In exchange, I offer you access to all the knowledge I have collected over the past thirty years."

"I am only an apprentice myself," Zannah admitted. "And my Master would kill us both before he accepted your offer. For the Sith to survive, there must only be one Master and one apprentice."

"Then how does the Sith line continue?" Hetton asked, puzzled.

"When I surpass my Master, I will kill him and take his place," Zannah explained, relaying the beliefs that Bane had drilled into her over the past decade without even thinking. "Then I will find my own apprentice to carry on the legacy of the dark side."

Hetton was silent for a moment, considering what she had said. "Perhaps that time is now," he said softly. "Together, we could end your Master's reign."

Zannah actually laughed at the suggestion. Hetton's eyes narrowed momentarily, stung by her reaction.

"I have more resources at my disposal than you might imagine," he said, raising his hand and snapping his fingers.

Two of his red-cloaked guards appeared beside him, seeming to materialize out of thin air. Zannah let her hand drop to her lightsaber, wondering if she had been lured into a trap. She couldn't figure out where the guards had suddenly come from; even if they were somehow cloaked, she should have been able to sense their presence through the Force.

The guards made no move to attack her, however, and a second later she relaxed once more and looked questioningly at Hetton.

"As I told you before, I have recruited a number of individuals with unique and specialized talents to my side," he explained. "Included among them are eight former students of the Sith Academy on Umbara."

Through Bane, Zannah knew those students sent to Umbara were trained in stealth and assassination, learning to use the Force to mask their presence from all manner of detection. That was why she had been unable to sense them in the room.

"Should you accept me as your apprentice, my guards will swear fealty to you as well," Hetton told her. "You will have a squad of eight unstoppable, undetectable killers at your command."

Zannah was silent for several minutes, thinking about everything he had said.

"We cannot risk the Jedi learning of our existence," she

warned at last. "If you become my apprentice, you must leave all this behind."

"I could not stay here much longer anyway," Hetton reminded her. "It won't be long before the Great Houses discover I am the founder of the Anti-Republic Liberation Front. They will seize my assets and condemn me for a traitor.

"I have already begun the process of transferring my library onto datacards in preparation for my flight."

In her mind Zannah weighed all she knew of Darth Bane's strength and power against Hetton and his eight Shadow Assassins, trying to determine which side had the upper hand. In the end she couldn't accurately predict who would survive such an encounter, but she decided she wanted to find out.

"How soon can you and your assassins be ready?"

"We can leave within the hour."

"And after Bane is dead we will go to Tython?"

"If that is your wish, Master," Hetton said with a bow.

15

NIGHT HAD FALLEN over Ambria, but Bane was not interested in sleep. Instead he was sitting cross-legged in what remained of their camp, waiting for Zannah to return with supplies so they could rebuild. As he waited, he meditated on his most recent failure with the Holocron.

The dilemma offered no easy solution. If he pushed himself too hard, his body would betray him, causing him to make mistakes during the precise adjustments of the Holocron's matrix. If he went slowly, conserving his strength, he would be unable to finish before the cognitive network began to degrade. The two factors worked at cross purposes, and Bane had racked his mind to find a way to balance the requirements of both time and effort.

His most recent attempt had pushed his power to its limits, bringing him to the edge of complete exhaustion. Yet even if he hadn't made the critical error that caused the matrix to collapse, he doubted he would have been able to complete the final adjustments in time.

The more he contemplated the process, the more frustrated he became. He had failed on both sides of the spectrum, unable to finish in the allotted time and lacking the necessary strength to complete his task without error.

Was it possible there was some other essential element in the process that he was missing? Was there one more secret waiting to be unlocked that would finally allow him to create a Holocron so he could pass his wisdom and knowledge on to his successors? Or was the failure in him? Did he simply lack power? Was his command of the dark side somehow less than that of the ancient Sith Lords like Freedon Nadd?

It was an uncomfortable line of speculation, but it was one Bane forced himself to consider. He had read the histories of the great Sith Lords; many were filled with feats almost too incredible to be believed. Yet even if these accounts were true, even if *some* of his predecessors had had the ability to use the dark side to destroy entire worlds or make a sun go nova, Bane still felt that his power measured up to the described abilities of many of those who had successfully created Holocrons of their own.

But how much of your power is wasted on the parasites infesting your body?

The question sprang unbidden to his mind, posed not in his own voice but that of his apprentice. Zannah had expressed her concerns about the effect the orbalisks might be having on him; it was possible she was right.

He had always believed the drawbacks of the orbalisks—the constant pain, the disfiguring appearance—to be offset by the benefits they provided. They healed him, made him physically stronger, and protected him against all manner of weapons. Now he began to question that belief. While it was true that he could channel his power through the creatures for a temporary increase in his abilities, over the long term they might actually be weakening him. They were constantly feeding on the dark side energies that flowed through his veins. Was it possible that, after a decade of infestation, his ability to draw upon the Force had been subtly diminished?

It was an idea he would have once dismissed out of hand. But his continued failure with the Holocrons had forced him to reevaluate his symbiotic relationship with the strange crustaceans. He could feel them even now, feeding, drawing on the Force that flowed through his veins.

The orbalisks suddenly became agitated. They twitched and trembled against his flesh; he felt their insatiable hunger growing as if in response to the nearby presence of a fresh source of dark side power.

Bane glanced around, expecting to see Zannah approaching the camp beneath the brightness of the full moon. He saw nothing; he sensed nothing—not even the small creatures and insects that came out at night to hunt for food, flying overhead or crawling across the sand. The normal awareness he had of the ambient world around him seemed strangely muted or . . . masked!

He leapt to his feet and drew his lightsaber, the blade blazing to life with a crackling hiss. A burst of red light exploded around him, illuminating the darkness and burning away the illusions cloaking his unseen enemies.

Eight red-robed figures surrounded the camp, their identities hidden by the visors of their helmets. Each carried a long metal rod that Bane recognized as a force pike, the traditional weapon of the Umbaran Shadow Assassins.

Specially trained in the art of killing Force-sensitive adversaries, Shadow Assassins preferred to rely on stealth and surprise. Exposed by Bane's energy burst, they suddenly found their greatest advantage taken away. And even though there were eight of them, Bane never hesitated.

He leapt forward and cut the first red-robed figure down before he—or she—had a chance to react, a single slash of his lightsaber bisecting the unfortunate opponent horizontally, just above the waist.

The other seven swarmed him, thrusting their force pikes forward to deliver the deadly electrical charge stored in the tips. Bane never even bothered to parry the incoming blows, relying on his orbalisk armor to protect him as he adopted a strategy of pure offense.

His unexpected tactics caught two more of the assassins completely unprepared, and they walked right into a sweeping two-handed cut that disemboweled them both.

The remaining five struck Bane almost simultaneously, their force pikes sending a million volts of current through his body. The orbalisks absorbed most of the charge, but enough filtered through to jolt him from his teeth down to his toes.

The Dark Lord staggered and fell to his knees. But instead of rushing in to finish him off, the assassins simply stood their ground. The idea that anything smaller than a bantha could withstand a direct hit from a force pike set to maximum charge—let alone five pikes at the same time—was inconceivable. Their miscalculation gave Bane the second he needed to shake off the effects and rise to his feet, much to the amazement and horror of his enemies.

"Zannah was right about you," a voice from behind Bane called out.

He whirled around to see a small man in his fifties, clad all in black, standing on the far edge of the camp. In his hand was a green lightsaber, though it was obvious from the way he gripped it that he had never received any proper training in how to handle the exotic weapon.

At the man's side was Bane's own apprentice; she had not drawn her lightsaber.

Bane snarled in anger at her betrayal, his rising anger fueled by the chemicals the orbalisks were pumping into his system.

"Today is the day you die, Darth Bane," the man said, charging forward to attack.

At the same time, the five red-robed figures rushed in from behind him. Bane spun and thrust his open palm toward them, lashing out with the power of the dark side. Like the Jedi and Sith, one of the first techniques Shadow Assassins learned was the creation of a Force barrier. Channeling their power, they could form a protective shield around themselves to negate the Force attacks of their enemies. But if an opponent was strong enough, a concentrated attack could still breach the barrier. Darth Bane, Dark Lord of the Sith, was definitely strong enough.

Two of the assassins were stopped in their tracks, knocked to the ground as if they had run into an invisible wall. Two more, weaker and less able to defend themselves against Bane's power, were sent flying backward. Only the fifth was strong enough to resist the Sith Lord's throw and continue his charge.

However, without his brethren at his side to harry and distract his foe, he found himself the sole focus of Bane's wrath. Unable to defend against the savage sequence of lightsaber cuts and thrusts, he fell in a matter of seconds, half a dozen fatal wounds scored across his chest and face.

While the four remaining assassins regained their feet, Bane wheeled back to their leader. Wisely, the man in black had stopped his own charge and was gathering the Force. As Bane stepped toward him the man unleashed it in a single long, thin bolt of indigo lightning. Bane caught the blast with his lightsaber, the blade absorbing the energy. In retaliation he struck back with lightning of his own—a storm of a dozen bolts arcing in toward his target from all angles.

The man leapt high in the air, flipping backward to avoid the deadly electrical conflagration. He landed on his feet ten meters away, a small, smoking crater marking the spot where he had been standing only an instant before.

"Zannah!" the man shouted. "Do something!"

But Bane's apprentice didn't move. She merely stood off to the side, biding her time and observing the action.

The assassins fell on Bane again, but instead of repelling them with the Force, he allowed his body to become a conduit, turning himself into a physical manifestation of the dark side's tumultuous power. As he spun like a whirlwind, his blade seemed to be everywhere at once: hacking, slashing, and slicing his enemies to ribbons.

All four assassins died in the attack, though one managed to land a single blow with his force pike before his throat was slit, the wound so deep it nearly severed his head. Fueled by rage and fury, Bane shrugged off the deadly electrical shock like a rancor shrugging off the bite of a venn-bug.

Once again he turned his attention to the man in black. Bane marched slowly toward him as his adversary stood frozen in place, paralyzed by the terrifying knowledge of his own imminent death.

"Zannah!" the man cried out to her again, holding his lightsaber vertically before him as if it were a talisman that could hold the approaching demon at bay. "Master! Help me!"

Bane chopped down with his own weapon, severing the man's sword arm at the elbow. The man screamed and dropped to his knees. An instant later his voice went silent as Bane ran him through with a single hard thrust, the lightsaber entering his chest just below his heart and protruding a full half a meter out the back of his shoulder blade.

Bane slid his blade back out. As the old man's body fell face-forward into the dirt, the Dark Lord turned to his apprentice. Zannah merely stood there, watching him.

"You betrayed me!" he roared and leapt at her.

ZANNAH HAD WATCHED the battle with interest, taking careful note of Bane's tactics and tendencies and storing them away for later. Her Master easily dispatched Hetton and his minions, as she had expected . . . though there had been a brief instant near the start of the battle when Bane had appeared vulnerable. Apparently the orbalisks were not able to fully protect him against the electrical current of the force pikes— another fact she made a point of filing away for later.

When it was over her Master turned to face her. She waited for him to demand an explanation, but instead he let loose with a cry and flew at her. Zannah barely had time to ignite her twin blades to meet his completely unexpected attack.

She fell into a defensive posture as she so often had during their training sessions. But this was no drill, and her Master came at her with a speed and ferocity she had never faced before. Giving in to his orbalisk-fueled bloodrage, he was like a wild animal, raining savage blows down on her from all angles, the strikes coming so fast it seemed as if he wielded a dozen blades at the same time. Zannah fell into a full retreat, desperately giving ground beneath the overwhelming assault.

"I did not betray you, Master!" she shouted, trying to make Bane see reason before he cleaved her in two. "I lured Hetton here so you could kill him!"

She ducked under a horizontal cut from his lightsaber, only to catch a heavy boot in her ribs. She rolled with the kick, narrowly avoiding the return cut of his blade. She parried a sharp descending blow, gathered her feet under her, and launched herself backward, flipping ten meters clear.

"Listen to me, Master!" she shouted now that she had put some distance between them. "If I wanted to betray you, why didn't I help them during the—oooffff!"

Bane hit her with a powerful Force throw, sending her hurtling backward. Only the barrier she had instinctively thrown up at the last second to shield herself saved her bones from being shattered by the concussive force of the impact.

She scrambled to her feet and twirled her lightsaber before her, creating what she hoped would be an impenetrable wall of defense. Instead of trying to pierce her guard, Bane leapt high in the air and came down almost right on top of her. She deftly parried his blade, redirecting it to the side as she spun away to keep his body from slamming into her. But Bane caught her on the chin with his elbow as she turned, the blow snapping her head back. Her body went limp, her weapon dropped from her nerveless fingers, and she crumpled to the ground.

For a second she saw nothing but stars. Her vision cleared to reveal the image of Darth Bane looming above her, his blade raised for the coup de grâce.

"I only did this for you, Master!" she shouted up at him, ignoring the throbbing pain in her jaw. "I only wanted to bring you the key to creating a Holocron!"

Bane hesitated, her words finally piercing the bestial madness that had enveloped him. He stared down at her on the ground, his head tilting to the side as his bloodlust slowly faded.

"You did this for me?" he asked suspiciously.

Zannah nodded frantically, even though it made her head spin. "Hetton recognized me as a true Sith. I had to find some way to eliminate him and his minions to keep our existence secret."

"So you led them here to ambush me," he said, his skepticism obvious.

"I had to win his trust," Zannah explained, speaking quickly and reaching into the folds of her clothes to pull out the datacard Hetton had given her. "I had to trick him into giving me this, so I could then give it to you."

She held the datacard up toward her Master, marveling at the fact that it had survived the punishment he had inflicted on her during their confrontation. Bane reached out to take it from her grasp, lowering his lightsaber and extinguishing the blade.

He gave a brief nod and took a step back, allowing her room to stand. Zannah retrieved her own lightsaber from where it lay on the ground, then rose slowly to her feet. Her head was still swimming from the elbow to her jaw, making it difficult to stand without swaying slightly.

"I knew you had the strength to defeat them, Master," Zannah said. "That was why I didn't come to your aid during the battle."

"And what if you were wrong?" Bane asked in a quiet, menacing voice. "What if they had somehow killed me?"

"Then you would have been weak, unworthy of being the Dark Lord of the Sith," Zannah answered boldly. "And you would have deserved to die."

"Precisely," Bane said with his familiar grim smile, and Zannah knew her Master approved.

16

WINTER WAS STILL a new—and not entirely welcome—
phenomenon on Ruusan. Originally it had been a
temperate world, its climate controlled and moderated by the
vast boreal forests that dominated the planet's surface. But
during the prolonged conflict between the Brotherhood of
Darkness and the Army of Light, millions of hectares of old-
growth trees had been decimated, turning a huge swath of
Ruusan's northern hemisphere into a desolate and arid wasteland.

Alone, the dramatic changes in the geographic features of
the world might not have been enough to affect a significant
climatic shift. However, the damage to the environment left the
world more vulnerable to the terrible devastation of the
thought bomb. In the wake of Kaan's ultimate weapon, a powerful Force nexus was created: an invisible maelstrom of dark-
and light-side energies capable of permanently altering the
planet's weather patterns.

As a result, even in the regions of the planet where the forests still stood, snow—a rarity in generations gone past—became a regular yearly occurrence. The unprecedented winters typically lasted only a few months, but they were particularly brutal on an ecosystem that had evolved in a much warmer clime. Some of the flora and fauna of Ruusan, like the humans who still inhabited the world, had learned to adapt. Other species simply died off.

Over the years Darovit had learned there were three keys to surviving the harsh cold. The first key was to always dress in layers. His hooded overcloak was a gift from a farmer he had treated for a bad case of fungal rot. The thick sweater beneath had been offered as payment by a miner after Darovit mended the man's foot; he'd accidentally crushed it with his own pneumatic jack. In fact, every garment on his person—the long-sleeved shirt, his heavy trousers, his warm padded boots, the fur-lined glove on his left hand, and the custom-made cuff covering his amputated stump—had been given to him by locals who had come to his isolated home seeking aid from the "Healing Hermit."

The second key to surviving the winter wind and snow was to stay dry. He learned to watch the sky, seeking shelter at the slightest sign of precipitation. If he allowed his clothes to become wet, hypothermia could easily set in before he was able to find help. It was one of the disadvantages that came with living alone deep inside the forest, but Darovit had become too accustomed to his life of solitude to give it up now.

In his first years he had been a wandering vagabond, exploring the wilds of Ruusan as he traveled between the small pockets of civilization scattered across the land. But as he learned to hunt and forage for himself, he found fewer and fewer reasons to venture into the towns and villages he came across.

Six years ago he had wearied of his nomadic existence. Locating a suitably remote location beneath a large stand of sheltering trees, he had constructed a simple hut of branches and mud. The hut gave him a sense of permanence and stability while still allowing him to enjoy the inner peace he had found in his self-imposed isolation.

There were no other human settlements within ten kilometers of his home, and even the closest bouncer colony was almost five kilometers away. Yet that didn't mean he was without visitors. From the teachings of the bouncers and the experiences of his youthful travels, he had become wise in the lore of herbal medicines and natural remedies. Three or four times a month he would be visited by someone imploring him to treat some malady or injury. Darovit never turned these people away, asking only that in return they respect his privacy . . . though often patients bestowed small gifts on him, like the clothes he now wore, as tokens of their gratitude.

The third key to surviving the inhospitable Ruusan winters was to never venture out at night. Bone-chilling temperatures, the chance of becoming lost and unable to find shelter, and even the occasional predator made risking the darkness a dangerous and foolish proposition.

Yet here Darovit was in the dead of night, his feet crunching over the wind-crusted snow. He'd left the warmth of his hut many hours behind him as he set out to see with his own eyes if the rumors he'd heard from many of his recent patients were true.

Darovit angry?

"No," he whispered to the small green-furred bouncer hovering above him. "Just curious."

For reasons he still didn't fully understand, the bouncers had developed a particular fascination with him. During the day there were always two or three of them circling his domicile. And each time he left his hut at least one of the unusual creatures accompanied him.

Perhaps they felt responsible for his well-being after rescuing him from the cavern of the thought bomb. Or maybe they were drawn to him by their shared vocations: the bouncers eased the mental anguish of those suffering or in pain, and Darovit had chosen to share his healing talents with any who came to him seeking succor. It was even possible they simply found him entertaining or amusing, though in truth Darovit didn't know if bouncers had a sense of humor.

He had quickly grown used to their constant company. They were gentle companions, and they seemed to sense when he was in the mood for conversation and when he just wished to be left alone with his thoughts. Most of the time he found their presence calm and soothing, though some bouncers were less soothing than others. The young female accompanying him now, Yuun, seemed to be more talkative than her compatriots.

Darovit home now.

"Not yet," he whispered.

Two of Ruusan's Three Sisters moons were waxing full tonight, their light reflecting off the silver layer of frost and the white blanket of snow that had accumulated over the past few weeks. Darovit was crouched behind a copse of trees, leaning on his walking stick for support and reaching out with the stump of his right hand to push the branches aside so he could peer through without being spotted. Through the vapor clouds of his own breath, he studied the scene that confirmed the rumors were true: the Jedi had returned to Ruusan!

Darovit had openly scoffed the first time a patient mentioned that the Republic was going to build a monument to honor those who had fallen on Ruusan. It made no sense to undertake such a project now, Darovit had argued, a decade after the battle. Yet there was no denying what he saw through the branches.

A large plot of land on the edge of the forest had been cleared of snow, revealing the frozen, scrub-covered fields beneath. The perimeter had been marked with stakes and surveyor's chains, and the groundbreaking had already begun. The deep furrows of soil dug up by the construction droids to lay the foundations struck Darovit as a wound upon the planet itself.

Several dozen large stones were scattered about the site, each brought to Ruusan from the birth world of one of the dead Jedi the monument was meant to honor. To Darovit's eye the alien rocks stuck out like a Wookiee in a crowd of Jawas: unwelcome interlopers defacing the Ruusan landscape.

"They have no right to be here," he whispered angrily.

Hurting nobody, Yuun suggested.

"This land is only just now beginning to heal itself from their kriffing war," he answered. "It's taken ten years for the people to put this all behind them. Now the Jedi want to open old wounds."

Senate approved. Not Jedi.

"I don't care what the official story says. I know the Jedi are behind this. It will lead to trouble."

Trouble?

Yuun was too young to remember the war that had ravaged her world. She hadn't witnessed the senseless death and suffering that drove hundreds of bouncer colonies into madness. Damaged beyond all hope of salvation, the wounded bouncers had projected thoughts of pain and torment, attacking and even killing other living creatures until they were slain by Jedi teams sent to wipe them out.

"The Jedi and their war nearly destroyed Ruusan," Darovit told her. "Countless thousands of men, women, and children died. The forests burned. And your species was hunted almost to extinction."

Sith started war.

"The Sith couldn't have had a war on their own. They needed someone to fight, and Hoth was more than willing to throw his Jedi followers against them," Darovit argued, wondering how much the bouncers—and Yuun in particular— knew of his past. "Both sides were equally to blame."

Darovit guilty.

It was a statement of fact, rather than a question. "Maybe," the young man admitted, leaning on his walking stick. "But trouble seems to follow the Jedi wherever they go. And I'm not going to sit back and watch so they can destroy this world a second time."

Apart from the construction droids the dig site was deserted; the organic crews only worked during the light of day. Crouching low and holding his walking stick parallel to the ground at his side, Darovit crept out from the cover of the trees.

Peace. Calm, Yuun projected after him, trying to soothe his anger. But she wasn't bold enough to follow him out into the open, and he ignored her pleas until he had crossed beyond the range of her telepathic communication.

Darovit wasn't strong in the Force; that was part of the reason he failed in his attempts to join both the Jedi and the Sith. But he did have a minor affinity for it, enough to allow him to creep through the dig site unseen and unnoticed by the semi-intelligent construction droids.

Construction droids were employed only for simple, basic tasks. The majority of the work on the monument would be done by a crew using heavy machinery and hoversleds. Moving quickly, Darovit made his way to the nearest sled, crouching down out of sight behind it.

He had come well prepared, stashing a large supply of powdered tass root and two handfuls of crushed petals from the flowers of the scintil vine in the pockets of his overcloak. Individually the two substances were harmless, yet when mixed together and dampened they had a startling interaction.

With his good hand he pried open the sled's maintenance panel just below the control box and stuffed four scintil petals into the repulsor coils. Next, he sprinkled a pinch of powdered tass root over the petals. Then, as a final touch, he scooped up a handful of snow, letting it melt in his glove so it would drip down onto the mixture.

There was a soft hiss and a sharp alkaline smell as the elements combined to form a highly corrosive paste that began to eat its way through the repulsor coils. Darovit snapped the sled's maintenance cover back in place; wispy tendrils of brown-green smoke wafted out from underneath it.

Darovit spent the next hour moving from sled to sled, paus-

ing whenever a construction droid wandered past in its prepro-
grammed assignments, oblivious to the vandal in their midst.
By the time he got back to where Yuun was still waiting for
him, every single hoversled had been disabled.

Temporary solution. Will replace.

"Repulsor coils are expensive," Darovit said. "And they're
always in high demand. This should set them back at least a
week."

Then what?

"I've got a few more tricks up my sleeve for our Jedi friends,"
he assured the little bouncer. "This was only the beginning."

Light soon. Home now?

Darovit glanced up and saw the faint glow of the first of
Ruusan's twin suns peeking over the horizon.

"Home," he agreed.

THREE WEEKS HAD passed since Zannah had presented her Master with the datacard that had almost cost the young apprentice
her life. Bane had used that time to study the datacard's contents
carefully, analyzing every tiny scrap of information Hetton had
assembled about Belia Darzu. He cross-referenced much of the
data with his own sources, verifying everything he could to au-
thenticate Hetton's research. And Bane was now confident that
everything the old man had discovered was true.

Belia's experiments in Sith alchemy had revealed the secrets
that allowed her to surround herself with a technobeast army.
Even more impressive, at least from Bane's perspective, Belia
had successfully created her own Holocron. And there was
strong evidence to support the theory that the Holocron she
created—the repository of all her knowledge—was still hidden somewhere in her stronghold on Tython.

Bane ran the final diagnostics check on his vessel: he
couldn't afford to have anything break down on the upcoming
journey. The hyperspace route into the Deep Core was treacherous, and if something went wrong there was no chance of

anyone coming along to find him. He would die a cold and lonely death—a frozen corpse floating in a metal coffin around the black hole at the galaxy's heart.

The *Mystic*'s systems all appeared to be in perfect working order. One of the new Sienar-designed Infiltrator series, the *Mystic* was a medium-sized long-range fighter Bane had anonymously acquired through his network of front-men and shadowy suppliers. Built to carry up to six passengers, Infiltrators were armed with light weapons and equipped with minimal plating, the focus of the model being on speed and maneuverability. The *Mystic* had been customized with the addition of a Class Four hyperdrive, enabling her to outrun virtually any other vessel she encountered.

Though there was room on the vessel for both Master and apprentice, Bane had decided Zannah would not accompany him on his trip to Tython. But she was not going to simply wait on Ambria for his return.

Along with his study of the datacard Bane had also spent a great deal of time thinking about the orbalisks clinging to his flesh. Though it was possible that he would discover new information on Tython unlocking the final secrets of creating a Holocron, it was also possible that Belia had succeeded using the exact same process he had employed in his failed attempts. Bane still could not discount the theory that the orbalisks were responsible for his failure, bleeding him of the dark side energies he needed to draw on to complete the procedure.

There were other considerations, as well. Twice now he had lost himself in a bloodrage, thought and reason replaced by the mindless urge to destroy anything and anyone in range. The first time it happened he had left their camp in ruins: a foolish and pointless waste of resources.

The second time had almost been far more costly. Had he succeeded in killing Zannah, he still would have found Hetton's datacard on her. But he would also have been forced to find a new apprentice. A decade of training would have been lost, thrown away because of his temporary madness.

Zannah had saved herself by explaining the motives behind her actions. She had acted in perfect accordance with her Master's teachings—a fact Bane should have realized on his own. But the orbalisks blinded him to her skilled machinations, and he now understood that the raw power they granted him came at the expense of subtlety and cunning.

So while he went to Tython to face the dangers and defenses of Belia's lost stronghold, Zannah was undertaking a mission of her own.

HETTON'S SHIP WAS MAGNIFICENT. A custom built cruiser eighty meters in length, she could comfortably hold twenty passengers, yet only a single pilot was required to operate her. Every detail of her construction and design had been made to Hetton's precise and lavish specifications. Equipped with enough firepower and armor plating to take on a small capital ship, the interior was still luxurious enough to host a formal dinner for planetary dignitaries. No expense had been spared, the vessel being as much a symbol of his incredible wealth as it had been a mode of transportation. There was only one thing Zannah disliked about it: He had called it the *Loranda,* after his mother.

She reached forward and punched the controls, marveling at the smooth takeoff and responsiveness of the yoke as she guided the ship up and out of Ambria's atmosphere. In two days she would be touching down on Coruscant; no doubt she'd have to bribe a spaceport administrator to keep her arrival off the official books. The *Loranda* was still registered to Hetton, and her arrival would draw immediate attention if it was logged with the proper authorities.

Fortunately it was common practice for the nobles of Serenno to make frequent unscheduled—and unreported—landings, even on Coruscant. The wealthy weren't bound by the rules of the average Republic citizen, and portraying herself as a servant sent to bribe a port administrator upon landing wouldn't strike anyone as unusual. Arriving onworld without drawing undue attention would be the easy part of her mission. Gaining access to the Archives in the Jedi Temple would be much more difficult.

Bane was taking a tremendous gamble in sending her there. They had spent the past decade hiding from the Jedi, and now she was about to enter the very heart of the order. But she couldn't second-guess his decision, not when she had been partly responsible. It was she who had planted the first seeds of doubt in her Master's mind about the orbalisks, and now her scheme had come to fruition. Bane had decided—for her sake and the sake of the Sith—that he had to free himself from the infestation.

Nothing in Freedon Nadd's original experiments indicated that the orbalisks could be extracted from the host, and Bane's own research into the subject had failed to uncover anything to the contrary. But the Jedi Archives were the greatest single collection of assembled knowledge in the known galaxy. If an answer existed, they would find it there.

Her Master had taken every precaution to keep her true identity hidden while she visited the Archives. Through his network of mysterious informants and shadowy contacts, he had assembled a list of names and background portfolios for virtually every member of the Jedi Order. From this list, he had chosen one name that suited their purpose: Nalia Adollu.

Nalia was a Padawan of approximately Zannah's age under the tutelage of Anno Wen-Chii, a famously reclusive Pyn'gani Jedi Master on the Outer Rim world of Polus. Over the past week Zannah had memorized every detail of her profile and history, along with the history of Master Anno, so she could pass herself off as the young woman.

The cover story was simple: Zannah would claim her Master was studying a rare breed of parasitic organism that lived beneath the ice-covered surface of Polus. Eager to compare the newly discovered life-form with similar species from other worlds, but loath to leave the quiet of his homeworld, he had sent his Padawan to gather research materials from the Jedi Archive.

Yet she would need more than a plausible cover story to maintain her disguise when she presented herself to the chief librarian and asked for permission to view the Archives. Zannah and Nalia were of the same age. They were roughly the same height and shared the same athletic build. They both had long, flowing hair—though Zannah had dyed her locks a deep, lustrous black to match those of the other woman.

It had been five years since Nalia had last left her Master's side on Polus, so there was little chance of running into anyone who knew her well enough to recognize Zannah as an imposter. But even if her appearance didn't give her away, there was one final element to consider.

Throughout her mission, she would be surrounded by servants of the light; if they sensed the dark side in her, she would be instantly exposed. The secrecy she and Bane had worked so hard to preserve would be destroyed. Everything they had labored for over the past decade, everything they had accomplished, would be for naught. She would surely be captured, possibly condemned to death, and her Master would be hunted down and slain.

The only way the plan would work was if she could use the power of Sith sorcery to mask her strength while simultaneously projecting an aura of light-side energy. It was a complicated spell, one she had never tried before. It required a balance of strength and delicacy, and she had practiced it continuously in the weeks leading up to her departure. Yet despite her best efforts, there were still moments when her concentration slipped and her true nature showed through.

She just had to hope that, if it happened on Coruscant, none of the Jedi would be close enough to notice.

17

A CHILL WIND BLEW through the forest, dropping the temperature well below freezing, but Johun was able to draw upon the Force to warm himself and keep away the worst of the cold.

The Jedi Knight was frustrated. Little progress had been made in the construction of the monument on Ruusan over the past weeks, the project the victim of a campaign of vandalism and sabotage.

It had begun with the destruction of the hoversleds, the repulsor coils eaten away by some type of toxic substance smeared across their surface. It had taken four days to arrange for the shipment and installation of the replacement coils.

The second incident had seen all the heavy equipment coated with a thick, sticky sap that turned out to be a powerful adhesive. Gloves, boots, and other clothing of the workers had stuck fast, becoming permanently attached to any surface they even brushed against; luckily nobody had made contact with bare skin. It had taken hours to find and apply chemical solvents strong enough to break the bond, and two full days to clean the gummy residue off the equipment.

Johun had considered posting some of his crew as guards through the night. But the monument site was remote; each morning the crews were flown in by air shuttle. Anyone assigned to watch over the site would be left completely alone, and if the unknown vandals were armed, the guards might be injured or even killed. That was something the Jedi was not willing to risk.

For a few nights after the second incident he'd hired a private security team to patrol the region, hoping they could catch whoever was responsible. Those nights had passed without incident, however, the would-be saboteur likely scared away by the show of force. But funding on the project was limited, and Johun was already overbudget because of the previous setbacks. Ultimately, he'd ended the contract with the security patrols . . . and two nights later the vandals had struck again.

The third incident began with the crew arriving in the morning to find that someone had spread pungent pollen around the entire construction site. As the suns rose, a great flock of tiny birds—tens of thousands of the squawking, screeching creatures—descended on the site, drawn by the scent. Their numbers blotted out the twin suns as they swooped and dived at the crew, making it impossible to work. Even after the pollen was gone, the smell lingered for two days, drawing the birds back each morning to put a halt to construction.

Johun had decided to take matters into his own hands. Whoever was behind the mischief was cautious, and a security team marching the perimeter was too visible to be an effective deterrent. So for the past three nights, when his crew boarded the waiting flier and returned to the comfort of their beds, he had remained behind, determined to catch the vandals in the act and bring them to justice.

As a Jedi, he could go several days without sleep, instead throwing himself into light but restful meditative trances that allowed him to remain aware of his surroundings. And if the perpetrators turned out to be armed and even hostile, Johun was confident he wouldn't be in any danger.

He was hunkered down behind a camouflage blind hidden in the trees that surrounded the construction site. Located atop a small bluff that overlooked the site and armed with night-vision goggles, he had a clear view of the entire area. The first two nights had passed without incident, and Johun had begun to fear that whoever was behind the attacks must have known he was there. If something didn't happen tonight, he decided, he'd have to try some other course of action.

Nearly two hours later his patience was finally rewarded when, through the goggles, he saw a single figure creep out from the trees less than a hundred meters from where Johun was hiding. At its side was a long, thin object that could have been a weapon, a walking stick, or possibly even both.

Johun scanned the surrounding forest, looking to see if the person was alone. The only companion showed up in the night-vision goggles as a small green blob, hovering in the shelter of the branches. Johun recognized it as one of Ruusan's indigenous bouncers, and he felt an involuntary shudder as he remembered the terror the species had inspired in the Jedi after a powerful Sith ritual had destroyed their forest homes and driven them mad.

It would make sense if the bouncers turned out to be behind the vandalism. To protect his troops, Hoth had, in the last days of the war, given standing orders to shoot the creatures on sight, and hundreds had died at the hands of the Jedi. Though the surviving members of the species had returned to their peaceful, healing ways, it was possible they still bore a grudge against the order for what had happened. But that still didn't explain the involvement of the humanoid figure making its way slowly toward the camp.

Johun broke from his hiding place. He knew the bouncer would flee at his approach, launching itself on the forest limbs high into the air where he couldn't follow. Short of killing it—

which he wasn't about to do—he wouldn't be able to bring it down. But the bouncer's companion would have to escape on foot, and Johun was confident he could outrun any non-Jedi.

He raced toward his prey and the figure turned its head, alerted by the loud crunching of Johun's boots in the snow. Johun caught enough of a glimpse of the face beneath the hood to know he was chasing a young man. The man threw down the walking stick and bolted for the trees, the long robes he wore to protect against the cold fluttering out behind him.

Johun had fifty meters of ground to gain; with the power of the Force flowing through his limbs he had expected to make up the distance in a matter of seconds. But his adversary moved with surprising speed, and the Jedi realized that his quarry was, at least on some small level, attuned to the Force as well.

Across open ground Johun was still faster, but he was a good ten meters behind when the man reached the forest's edge and plunged into the undergrowth. He cut a path that would have shaken off almost any pursuit: weaving and darting in and out of the densely packed tree trunks, ducking under sharp branches, and leaping over thick, protruding roots at a breakneck pace. Drawing heavily on the Force, however, Johun was able to match his progress, swatting away the limbs and leaves that threatened to smack him in the face and nimbly avoiding the roots that would have sent him crashing to the ground.

They sprinted through the forest for several kilometers, neither able to gain ground in their contest. The chase ended when they broke into a small clearing with a tiny mud hut built in the center, and Johun realized that his quarry, blinded by panic, had instinctively run for home.

The man raced to the door, as if hoping to escape by locking himself away inside. Then he stopped, suddenly realizing the mistake he had made. With slumping shoulders he stood by the door, making no attempt to flee as Johun cautiously approached.

"I didn't think anyone could keep up with me through the

forest," he said, defeated as he opened the door to his small hut. "You might as well come inside and get out of the cold."

The interior was simple but clean, and just large enough for the two men to share the space without feeling cramped. The only furnishing was a small sleeping mat in the corner. Glowing embers in a pit at the room's center threw off enough heat that Johun was able to remove his thick winter robe and lay it beside him as he sat cross-legged on the floor.

His host also shed the heaviest of his garments, peeling away multiple layers before kneeling across from his uninvited guest. Johun guessed the man was in his early twenties, only a few years younger than the Jedi himself. He had dark scruffy hair and a long scraggly beard; there was a wildness in his eyes. But it was only when Johun noticed he was missing his right hand that he recognized him as the famed Healing Hermit of Ruusan.

"Do you know who I am?" Johun asked.

"I know you're a Jedi," the hermit replied. "That's why I couldn't shake you."

"My name is Johun Othone. I'm in charge of the project to build a monument to those who sacrificed their lives here on Ruusan."

Johun waited, giving the other man a chance to respond or reply. But the hermit simply stared at the ground, his good hand resting in his lap, clasping the stump of his right arm.

"Why did you wreck our equipment at the construction site?"

He half expected the hermit to make some type of denial; after all, Johun hadn't actually caught him in the act. But instead he freely admitted what he had done.

"I wanted to stop you. I figured if I cost you enough time and credits you would give up and go back where you came from."

"Why?" Johun asked, puzzled at the venom in the hermit's voice.

"We don't want your kind on Ruusan," the younger man snapped. "You have no right to be here!"

"I served with General Hoth in the Army of Light," Johun answered, trying to stay calm despite the righteous indignation he felt. "I saw my friends die. I saw them sacrifice themselves to save the galaxy from the Sith."

"I know all about the Sith," the hermit sneered. "And the Jedi, too. I saw the war with my own eyes. I know what happened.

"Look at what your war did to this world!" he shouted, his voice accusing. "Every year the snow falls, and with each winter more and more animals die from the cold. Ten years after your so-called victory, entire species are still being driven to extinction by what you caused!"

"I am sorry for the suffering this world has endured," Johun said. "But the Jedi cannot be held responsible for everything. The greatest harm to this planet was done by the Sith."

"Jedi, Sith, you're all the same," the hermit spat. "You were so blinded by your hatred of each other you couldn't see the consequences of what you were doing. And in the end your general marched down into the underground caverns to face Kaan's followers, knowing he would unleash the devastation of the thought bomb on this world."

"Hoth sacrificed himself so that others could be saved," Johun protested.

"The thought bomb was an abomination! Hoth should have done everything in his power to keep Kaan from using it. Instead he intentionally forced his hand."

"There was no other choice," Johun answered, defending his former Master's actions. "The detonation of the thought bomb destroyed the Brotherhood and forever rid the galaxy of the Sith."

The hermit laughed loudly. "Is that what you believe? *The Sith are gone?*" He shook his head and muttered, "Poor, deluded little Jedi."

"What do you mean?" Johun demanded. He felt an icy fist closing around his guts. "You don't believe the Sith were wiped out?"

"I *know* they weren't wiped out," the hermit answered. "One of the Dark Lords survived, and he took my cousin as his apprentice."

Johun's head snapped back as if he'd been slapped. "Your cousin?"

It sounded crazy, completely implausible. But the hermit, despite his wild eyes, didn't strike Johun as mad.

"How do you know this?"

"After the thought bomb exploded, I went down into the tunnels to see what was left," the hermit whispered, his expression grim as he dredged up dark memories from his past. "I saw them there, my cousin and Lord Bane." He held his stump up before his face. "They gave me this."

Johun's mind was reeling. He remembered the mercenaries he'd encountered in the aftermath of the battle, and their tales of a Sith Master who had brutally slain their companions. Though he'd later recanted his position and dismissed their account in the face of Farfalla's irrefutable logic, part of him had always clung to the belief that their story was true.

With no evidence and no leads, he had abandoned his efforts to prove that a Sith Master had escaped Ruusan alive. Now, inside the walls of a tiny mud hut, he had stumbled across the proof that had eluded him a decade ago.

"You saw a Sith named Lord Bane?" Johun pressed eagerly, looking for greater confirmation. "How do you know it was him?"

"For a time I was part of Kaan's army," the hermit whispered softly. "We all knew who Bane was."

"This . . . this is unbelievable!" Johun stammered, all thoughts of the monument and the vandalism that had led him to the hermit gone from his mind. "We have to tell the Jedi Council! We need to go to Coruscant as soon as possible!"

"No."

The refusal was delivered with such simple finality, it stopped Johun cold. "But . . . the Sith are still out there. The Council must be warned."

The hermit shrugged. "So warn them. My place is here on Ruusan."

"They won't believe me," Johun admitted. "They'll want to question you themselves."

"I've seen what happens when the Jedi and Sith go to war. I won't be part of it again. I won't go to Coruscant."

"You were vandalizing Republic property," Johun reminded him. "I could arrest you and bring you there to face charges."

The hermit laughed again. "And then what, Jedi? Torture me until I confess what I saw? Use your powers to twist my mind and make me say the words you want to hear? I'm sure the Council will believe you then."

Johun frowned. The hermit was right; the only way the Council would believe him was if his testimony was freely given.

"Don't you see what's at stake?" Johun said, changing tactics. "You saw what happens when the Sith raise an army and go to war. If you come with me now, the Council will listen to your warning. We can seek out this Lord Bane and stop him before he has a chance to lure others to his cause."

As he spoke he reached out to touch the hermit's mind with the Force. He didn't compel him to agree to the request; that wouldn't serve his purpose here. Force persuasion was a temporary measure, and by the time they got back to Coruscant, the effects would have worn off and the hermit would know he had been manipulated, making him even more intractable. Instead Johun simply tried to make the man more willing to listen to reason, casting a veil of calm and tranquillity over his thoughts. He gently swept the other man's bitterness and resentment to the side, allowing him to weigh the logic of his arguments unclouded by passion and emotion.

"Bane has gone into hiding," he continued. "If we do not find him, he will reveal himself only when he has rebuilt the armies of the Sith, and the galaxy will be plunged once again into war. But if you come with me now, we can convince the Council to seek him out. Help me stop him, and we will prevent another war."

The hermit stared at him for a long time before finally nodding his agreement. "If it means stopping another war, I will go with you to Coruscant."

THE CHIEF LIBRARIAN of the Jedi Archives was a venerable Cerean named Master Barra-Rona-Ban.

"Welcome to Coruscant, Padawan Nalia," he said, rising from his seat to greet Zannah with a smile as she entered his room. "How was your trip from Polus?"

Master Barra's private quarters looked much as she had expected: a great number of journals, handwritten notes and datacards covered his small desk, organized into neat little piles. There was also a small viewscreen and a terminal that she suspected was linked to the main index catalog of the Archives, allowing Master Barra to reference it at will.

"The journey was long but uneventful," she replied.

Her voice was calm and relaxed, though inside her heart was pounding. The illusion she projected of being an apprentice of the light side had served her well so far, but now she was face-to-face with a Jedi Master. If she made even the slightest mistake, all was lost.

"It was good to get away from the cold," she added. Nalia, unlike her Master, had not been born on Polus: She had originally come from the tropical regions of Corsin.

The Cerean laughed, creasing up the wrinkles on his tall, cone-shaped forehead. "Master Anno would disagree with you, I suspect."

She replied with a gentle laugh of her own. "My Master sends his regards," she said, recalling from the profile that Anno and Barra had briefly studied together at the Academy here on Coruscant. "Do you have any plans to visit him on Polus in the near future?"

"I'm afraid such a journey would be impossible," he replied with a sigh. "The Archives require my constant attention."

"Master Anno warned me you would say that," she said, smiling. "He told me you would use any excuse to avoid ever visiting Polus again."

"Not everyone takes to the ice and snow with the ardor of the Pyn'gani," the Cerean admitted with a sly twinkle in his eye.

The exchange of pleasantries concluded, he returned to his seat and punched a key on his terminal, bringing up a large block of text on the screen.

"I have reviewed your request to access the Archives," he told her, "and I believe we can accommodate you."

He tapped the terminal again and inserted a datacard. The terminal hummed as encrypted data was loaded onto it.

"The Archives are available at all hours, day or night," he informed her. "You will have clearance to access the general collection, but please remember that the contents of the analysis rooms and the chamber of Jedi Holocrons are restricted."

"I don't think they'll be necessary for my research," she assured him. "Master Anno was very specific in what he wanted me to look for."

The datacard popped out of the terminal, the information download complete, and Master Barra handed it to Zannah.

"Insert this into any of the catalog terminals in the Archives whenever you wish to log in and look something up. Original works may not be removed from the premises, but you are free to copy any materials you find onto this disk for your personal use or collection.

"I've taken the liberty of preloading your disk with some seminal works that may be of interest to your research," he added, smiling at her once again.

"Thank you, Master Barra," Zannah said with a bow.

"How long do you expect to remain here on Coruscant?" he asked.

"A few days at most," she answered. She doubted she could maintain the illusion that shielded her dark side powers from detection any longer than that. "Master Anno is anxious to continue his research. He wants me to return as soon as I have the information he needs."

The Cerean nodded in understanding. "Of course. But while you are here, I hope you won't spend all your time studying parasites and symbionts. You have a rare opportunity to explore all the knowledge and wonders of the galaxy, and I hope you will take advantage of it."

"I will try, Master Barra," Zannah promised, though she had no intention of staying a second longer than was necessary.

"Good luck with your research, Padawan Nalia," the librarian said, dismissing her.

With another bow, Zannah turned and left his room, more confident in her mission than ever. If she could fool Master Barra, chief librarian of the Jedi Archives, into believing she was Nalia Adollu, she knew she could fool anyone.

18

THE *MYSTIC* DROPPED out of hyperspace with a jolt. Through the cockpit viewport a large planet loomed only a few thousand kilometers away, its surface concealed beneath a thick mass of rolling gray clouds. Bane checked the nav computer, confirming via the coordinates that he had arrived at Tython.

Like all planets in the Deep Core, Tython was a world shrouded in mystery and legend. Some accounts held that the Jedi had visited this world during the era of the Great Hunt, three thousand years ago, to cleanse it of the fearsome terentateks, monstrous creatures that fed on the lifeblood of those sensitive to the Force.

Much older legends identified Tython as the original birthplace of the Jedi Order over twenty-five thousand years before. According to the tale, priests and philosophers of the world had the ability to draw upon a mystical energy they called Ashla; a power that represented all compassion and mercy in the universe. They were opposed by a rival group that drew their strength from Boga, the manifestation of raw passion and pure uncontrolled emotion.

The stories said that a great war ensued between the two groups, with the worshipers of Ashla emerging victorious. The first Jedi Knights supposedly had evolved from the survivors of the war, creating the first lightsabers in their initiation ceremonies. Many years later, the legend continued, some of these Jedi left Tython and braved the unstable hyperspace routes to share their beliefs with worlds beyond the Deep Core. And as they met and mingled with other civilizations, Ashla and Boga became more commonly known as the light and dark sides of the Force.

Bane didn't know if the legend was true, but even if it was, it merely proved the superiority of the dark side and its inevitable conquest of the light. For though the followers of Ashla had supposedly defeated the followers of Boga, the dark side had prevailed in the end. Tython, revered by many as the birthplace of the Jedi Order itself, was now a bastion of dark side power, and the location of Belia Darzu's hidden fortress.

Bane knew it was possible that other people still lived on Tython: descendants of the early Jedi who had survived for eons in the isolation of the Deep Core. But he had no interest in seeking them out, even if they existed. Armed with the information from Hetton's datacard, he was heading straight for Belia's stronghold.

Pushing forward on the yoke, he sent the *Mystic* plunging down into the atmosphere of the cloud-covered world. Breaking through the mist, he saw that the surface below was the color of ash; barren fields stretched endlessly beneath an unbroken mantle of gray and sunless sky.

He brought his ship in low, only a few hundred meters above the ground, as he raced toward the only feature visible on the horizon: a massive, two-towered citadel constructed entirely of black durasteel.

The building was square and measured 150 meters on each side. The exterior walls rose up thirty meters above the ground, and the only entrance appeared to be a massive, twenty-meter-wide gate on the face of the front wall. The towers stood on either side of the front wall, rising up another ten meters from the corners.

As he closed to within a few hundred meters, a barrage of ion cannon fire erupted from the towers. Bane pulled hard on the stick, banking the *Mystic* ninety degrees to starboard, narrowly avoiding the unexpected attack. Except for her techno-beasts, Belia's stronghold was supposed to be empty.

He circled and brought his ship in again, setting the targeting systems to lock on to the first of the two towers. The ion cannons roared again, and Bane barrel-rolled out of the line of fire as he opened up with the *Mystic*'s lasers, reducing one of the towers to a heap of molten slag as he flew by.

The *Mystic*'s sensors had detected no life-forms present during his pass, suggesting that the ion cannons were likely part of an automated defense system still active after almost three centuries. This theory was confirmed twenty seconds later when Bane used the exact same barrel-roll maneuver on his next attack run to eliminate the second tower; automated defenses were nothing if not predictable.

He circled the citadel twice more, making a sensor and visual scan to confirm that there were no other threats before bringing his ship down to land on the barren ground a short distance from the stronghold's entrance.

Drawing his lightsaber, he leapt from the cockpit and moved carefully forward until he stood before the black gate. It loomed above him, a giant blast door without handles, hinges, or a visible control panel. Gathering his power, he placed his left palm against the surface. The gate exploded, rupturing inward with a sharp bang that reverberated down the long, dark hallway leading into the fortress.

Bane stepped forward, wary and watching for any trick or

trap that might await him. He could feel the power of the dark side in this place, but he detected no immediate threats to his person, and he proceeded cautiously.

Using glow rods to light his way, he explored the stronghold room by room, stirring up dust that had lain undisturbed for centuries. It was primarily a military base, the majority of the space taken up with the barracks and mess halls necessary to house and provide for an army of followers. But the rooms were deserted. Not even the vermin and insects one would expect in an abandoned building prowled the halls, though whether they were kept at bay by the dark side energy permeating the air or by some unknown means he couldn't say.

As he moved deeper into the fortress, he began to come across Belia's alchemy labs. Sealed beakers filled with strange-colored liquids rested atop long metal tables. Empty vats connected by coiled glass piping used to distill or separate mixtures lined the walls. In one room the hearts and brains of a dozen different species floated in specimen bottles, preserved forever in clear embalming fluid. Another lab contained notes and sketches tracking Belia's efforts to transform living creatures into organic–droid hybrids.

Bane paused at these, glancing through them briefly before continuing on his way. He was unable to make sense of the cryptic scrawl; he needed to find Belia's archives—and hopefully the Holocron where she had stored all her knowledge—if he was to comprehend her experiments.

Near the back of the building he came upon a narrow set of stairs leading down to the underground levels. One thing Hetton's research had not provided was a map of the stronghold's interior, but he could feel the power emanating from beneath him. There was little doubt that the source of the dark side energies hanging like smoke in the air of every room and hallway of the fortress was located at the bottom of the steps. It was here, Bane knew, that he would find Belia's inner sanctum.

He crept down the stairs. At the bottom was another long, narrow hall, and at the end of this corridor was a small, archaic wooden door. A sliver of pale fluorescent light shone out from beneath. Unlike the floor above, Bane realized, generators were still providing power to the room beyond—another sign that it was of critical importance.

Bane approached the door, pausing at the threshold. He was unable to get any sense of what awaited him on the other side; his Force awareness was overwhelmed by a great concentration of dark side power. Taking a deep breath, he gently pushed open the door and stared in fascinated horror.

The chamber beyond was enormous, at least fifty meters long and easily twenty wide. Standing alone in the center was a pedestal, atop of which rested a small, familiar four-sided pyramid: the Holocron of Belia Darzu. Yet this was not what had grabbed Bane's attention. The rest of the room had been completely overrun by an army of technobeasts.

They seemed to have come from all manner of species: a menagerie of humanoids and beasts from every corner of the galaxy that had fallen victim to Belia's technovirus. Once a mutated combination of flesh and technology, most of the technobeasts' living tissue had long since rotted and fallen away. What remained were desiccated strands of skin and sinew clinging to bone, supported and held together by rods, wires, and twisted scraps of metal.

The arms and hands of those creatures that had walked on two legs in life had been transformed into flat, jagged blades extending from their elbows. The larger creatures—like the technobeast bantha he saw across the room, or the rancor near the pedestal in the center—had become machines of war, with blaster cannons fused to their shoulders and their hides replaced with spiked, plated armor.

From Hetton's research, Bane knew that the technovirus attacked the frontal lobes of the brain, reducing its victims to mindless automata incapable of higher thought functions—

a grim fate for any sentient being. The creatures in the room were in an even worse state. Over the centuries what remained of their brains had been kept alive by the nanogenes of the technovirus, but the inevitable long-term degradation had impaired their motor skills and reduced them to shells of shambling, mummified metal.

Bane guessed that the army assembled in the chamber must once have roamed the halls and rooms of the stronghold, guarding it against attack and serving the needs of their mistress. With Belia's death—poisoned by the assassins of the Mecrosa Order when her alliance with them fell apart—they had been left to wander mindlessly, without any purpose or direction. Over the decades they'd been slowly drawn to this chamber by the dark side energies radiating from the Holocron, the last surviving remnant of their mistress, calling them to her side. Driven only by simple, primal instinct, they had been helpless but to obey until, one by one, the entire bulk of her technobeast army had assembled in this single chamber.

An eerie silence hung over the scene; the vocal cords of the unfortunate creatures had disintegrated hundreds of years earlier. The only sound was the faint whirring of mechanized joints and the rusty scraping of metal across the stone floor as they milled about in slow confusion. Occasionally they would bump one another with a hollow clank, their movements awkward and clumsy as they jostled for position to move ever closer to the Holocron in the center of the room. But though they were clearly drawn to it, none dared to come within three meters of its pedestal. Instead they congregated in a loose, scuffling circle, an army of the living dead awaiting orders that would never come.

Bane stepped into the room, lightsaber drawn. The technobeasts ignored his presence, their attention focused only on the Holocron. He made his way slowly through their legions, trying to estimate their number as he edged ever closer to the center of the room. Fifty? A hundred? It was impossible to count; their bodies of rusted metal and mummified flesh all seemed to blend together into a single ghastly mass.

Reaching the pedestal at the heart of their numbers, he paused, uncertain what would happen when he reached out to claim the Holocron as his own. Would the creatures bow down before him as their new Master, or would they fall upon him in single-minded fury to protect the idol they worshiped? There was only one way to find out.

As his fingers closed over the Holocron he heard a noise that caused him to pull his hand back with a start. It sounded like the moan of a long-dead god rising from the grave; a hundred mechanized limbs sprang to action with an angry hum as the monsters swarmed over him.

Bane thrust out with the Force, and a dozen of the oncoming creatures exploded into dust and tiny flecks of small, twisted metal. But the others surged forward like a wave, driving him under. Their feet stomped and kicked at him; their bladed arms slashed at him as he lay prone on the floor. But none of their attacks could pierce the chitinous shells of his orbalisk armor.

From his back, Bane slashed indiscriminately with his lightsaber, hewing off limbs with every swipe. There were no screams of pain or gouts of blood—the bodies of his enemies had been exsanguinated when their flesh had crumbled away centuries before. The only sounds of battle were the Dark Lord's own grunts of exertion, the clatter of metal falling to the stone floor, and the occasional small shower of sparks.

Even in their rage, the creatures were slow and cumbersome. Bane's vicious strokes quickly cleared enough space for him to find his feet again. He rose to see the wall of creatures pressing in on him, and he unleashed a wave of lightning through their ranks. The bolts arced through the mostly metal bodies; the nanotechnology that animated their frames and gave them life smoked and smoldered, and a dozen more of his opponents toppled over never to rise again.

A heavy blow suddenly struck Bane in the back, the metal rancor sending him flying with a swipe of one massive, club-like claw. He slammed face-first into what might once have been a human, and the technobeast opened its mouth and released a cloud of tiny metal spores directly into his face.

Bane breathed them in even as he cut the creature down, chopping it diagonally clean through from shoulder to hip. He could feel the technovirus inside him, its nanogene spores burrowing up to his brain to eat away his frontal lobes and begin the process of transforming him into an abomination that was neither droid nor alive.

Before he could reach out with the Force to save himself, he felt a surge of heat in his blood as the orbalisks released a burning chemical to destroy the microscopic invaders. His skull felt as if it were on fire as his heart pumped the searing chemical through his carotid artery and up into the capillaries of his brain, but he could feel the nanogenes wither and die in the heat almost instantly.

Using the pain in his head to fuel his rage, Bane spun and leapt at the rancor, slicing both its metal legs out from under it. The laser cannons on the creature's shoulders tried to fire at him, but in the more than two hundred years since its creation the power cells had lost their charge and the only result was a barely audible click. The torso fell to the floor, but the claws still clutched for him; Bane had to leap back out of the way before lunging forward to sever the arms at the shoulders.

That enemy vanquished, he used the Force to disintegrate two more advancing technobeasts, then felt something bump against his foot. He glanced down to see that the rancor's jaws had clamped shut on his boot; it was trying to gnaw off his leg. Once again his orbalisk armor protected him from harm, and Bane sliced the rancor's head from its body, relieved to see it finally go still.

There were still dozens upon dozens of the abominations in

the chamber, closing in on him from all sides. Bane now realized that they couldn't possibly harm him, but he also knew the technobeasts would not stop until he had reduced each one to pieces.

The slaughter lasted over an hour. He used his lightsaber to repeatedly dismember his enemies, conserving his Force abilities to stave off exhaustion in arms, legs, shoulders, and back. Three times during the one-sided melee he allowed himself to lose focus, his martial instincts thrown out of sync by the unnerving silence of his enemies as they were butchered. Each time his attention lapsed he was knocked to the ground by the blows of one of the lumbering creatures that got close enough to make contact and forced to battle his way back to his feet. Two other times during the battle he felt the burning in his brain as the orbalisks purged his system of yet another cloud of nanogene spores he had unknowingly inhaled.

By the time it was done every muscle in his body ached from hewing through hundreds of cubic meters of metal, bringing back memories of the long shifts he had endured in the mines of Apatros as a young man. From wall to wall the room was littered with the limbs, torsos, and heads of the technobeasts, the carnage made bearable only by the fact that there was no gore.

Kicking aside the remains with weary legs, Darth Bane slowly cleared a path back to the center of the room. He extinguished his lightsaber and hung it from his belt, then staggered forward, grasping the edges of the pedestal to keep from collapsing as his thighs and calves simultaneously cramped.

Gritting his teeth, he leaned heavily on the pedestal to take the weight off the locked-up muscles. Breathing deeply, he called upon what remained of his Force abilities to replenish his strength. After several minutes the spasms began to fade, and he was able to stand gingerly once more.

His body and will were exhausted; the smart thing would be to rest before attempting to use the Holocron. But he had come too far, and endured too much, to be put off any longer.

Still clutching the pedestal for support with both hands, the Sith Master stared at the talisman, focusing his will on bringing it to life. Slowly it began to pulse with a faint inner light of deep, dark violet, and Bane smiled.

Soon, all the secrets of Belia Darzu would be his.

19

"I THOUGHT YOU HAD put this madness behind you, Johun," Farfalla said with a disappointed shake of his head.

"It's not madness," Johun insisted. "He was there, Master. He saw it with his own eyes!"

Farfalla sighed and got up from his seat and began to pace, making small tight circles over the carpet of his private quarters. Johun remained in his seat, focusing on staying calm and letting his arguments be guided by logic and reason.

"How did Hoth deal with your headstrong ways?" Valenthyne asked, stopping to throw up his hands in exasperation.

"Your personalities are quite different," Johun remarked. "Hoth often accused me of being too passive."

Farfalla shook his head again and returned to his seat.

"Are you certain this witness is reliable?" he asked, alluding to the mercenaries Johun had wanted to bring forward ten years before.

Johun nodded. "All the details of his story check out. He calls himself Darovit now, but back then he was known as

Tomcat. Records confirm he was recruited on Somov Rit by Torr Snapit, and he came with his cousins to join the Army of Light."

"And one of these cousins is the girl he claims took his hand?"

"A girl ten years ago," Johun noted. "She'd be a woman now. The cousin's name was Rain. She was lost in an attack by the Sith shortly after they landed on Ruusan. She was missing and presumed dead, but she must have been found by this Lord Bane and taken as his apprentice."

"I've heard that name before," Farfalla admitted, leaning back in his chair. "It was mentioned in some of the statements given by Sith minions we took as prisoners. If I remember correctly, he was one of the last of the Sith to join the Brotherhood."

Johun nodded. "Darovit said the same thing. He said Bane was always reluctant to follow Kaan. If he refused to join the rest of the Brotherhood in the cave, that would explain how he survived the thought bomb!"

"It's possible," Farfalla admitted. "But how did Darovit recognize Bane?"

"He defected to the Sith near the end of the war."

Farfalla threw his hands up again. "A defector, Johun? A traitor to the Jedi? The Council will never believe this!"

"That is what makes his story even more believable," Johun countered. "If he was lying he could easily have found some reason to explain how he recognized Lord Bane. But he has freely admitted his crime to me because he has decided the time has come to speak the truth."

"And why is that?" Farfalla wanted to know. "Your report said he has lived as a healer on Ruusan for the past decade. Why did he suddenly decide to come forward now?"

"When I spoke with him on Ruusan I convinced him of the dangers the Sith represent. He wants to stop Bane before another war begins."

Farfalla raised an eyebrow. "You convinced him? After a decade of silence, one meeting with you and he is ready to come forward? How, exactly, did you achieve that?"

"I didn't use the Force to do it," Johun protested. "Not exactly. I didn't use the Force to compel him. I just made him more willing to listen to me."

"You are making this very difficult for me," Valenthyne said, reaching up with one hand to rub at his temple.

"I only ask that you speak with him yourself, Master," Johun implored. "Hear what he has to say. Listen to him, and then decide if you will bring him before the Council."

"Very well, Johun," Farfalla said, nodding. "I will meet with him. Where is he now?"

"He wanted to learn more about the healing arts of our Order," Johun explained. "Master Barra gave him access to the Archives."

Valenthyne slapped his hands on his thighs and rose to his feet. "Then I suggest we go find him before I come to my senses."

THE GENERAL COLLECTION of the Jedi Archives was arranged in four long halls built off a massive central rotunda. Each hall contained a wide primary aisle, with hundreds of smaller secondary aisles leading off either side. Lining the walls of the secondary aisles were the stacks: trillions of datatapes and datacards arranged under millions of categories, topics, and subtopics. Access to the disks of a particular hall could be gained via any of the terminals built along the center of its main aisle. Each terminal was equipped with a master index to help those seeking knowledge on a particular subject to find the proper hall, but to make things easier each hall also represented a specific, though very broad, branch of knowledge.

The first hall, the one all visitors passed through when they entered the Archives from the Jedi Temple, contained works of philosophy and historical records. Included in its stacks were the personal journals of Jedi, political leaders, and individuals

of historical significance. Basic treatises examining the Force
were also filed in this section, though Padawans were restricted
from accessing many of these works lest they misinterpret the
knowledge and become corrupted.

The second hall contained works dedicated to the mathe-
matical and engineering sciences, including theories of space–
time and hyperdrive construction, floor plans of official
government buildings, and detailed design blueprints of every
vehicle, weapon, or gadget ever made. The third focused on
the geography and culture of the millions of known planets in
the galaxy. Maps, both planetary and interstellar, as well as
detailed descriptions of every recorded civilization, past and
present dominated the stacks of the third hall.

However, it was the fourth hall where Zannah—still in the
guise of Nalia—was headed. The fourth hall contained zoo-
logical data and research on virtually all known life-forms of
the galaxy. This was her third day in the archives, and she had
yet to find what she was looking for. The preloaded works on
the datacard given to her by the chief librarian had helped to
narrow her search, but locating a specific piece of information
in an infinite ocean of knowledge was no simple task.

Had she gone back to Master Barra, or approached any of
the analysis droids roaming the Archives, and asked for information on orbalisks rather than the more general topic of
parasitic organisms, she might have made quicker progress.
But, this would have conflicted with her cover story and raised
unwanted questions. So Zannah had been forced to seek out
the information using only the skills she had developed while
studying various works during her apprenticeship under Darth
Bane.

Her efforts had quickly brought to light several thousand
articles and experiments that made at least some reference to
orbalisks, but she had yet to find any mention of how to remove
them without killing the host. She knew she was running out of
time, but as she made her way down the first hall toward the
rotunda, she was determined to find what she had come for.

There were always a number of other scholars in the Archives, but the primary aisles of each hall were wide, and the stacks were so numerous and deep that Zannah never felt crowded. This allowed her to work without fear of anyone accidentally discovering what she was investigating. However, she still felt a flash of apprehension whenever another of the Archive patrons passed her by, always worried that her projected aura of light-side power would falter.

She nodded at one of the analysis droids as she entered the central rotunda and turned to her right, heading for the fourth hall. She passed by the bronzium busts honoring powerful and memorable members from the Order's history. She paused as she often did in front of the busts of the Lost: the only twelve individuals who had willingly set aside the vows they had sworn upon becoming Jedi Knights and chosen to leave the Order.

The Lost served as a reminder to the Jedi that, despite their wisdom and talents in the Force, they were not infallible. The Jedi viewed each of the Lost as a failure of their Order, not as a failure of the individual. A plaque on each bust recounted the individual's history of service, praising what he or she had achieved and contributed before departing from the Jedi ranks. Curiously, though, none of the plaques offered a reason for leaving.

Zannah shook her head and continued. As a Sith, she couldn't imagine any reason to honor someone who abandoned her cause . . . though with only one Master and one apprentice, the Sith had been transformed into something very different from the Jedi Order and its vast numbers.

She made her way down the fourth hall, heading for the privacy of the last viewing terminal in the central aisle. She inserted the personal datacard Master Barra had given her to gain access to the Archive catalogs, and then resumed her search where she had left off the day before.

Gathering a list of index numbers, she typed in a passcode to lock her terminal from other users, then wandered off into the stacks to retrieve the half a dozen datacards she wanted to study in further detail. By necessity the datacards in the Archives were nearly twice the size of her personal datacard; each one contained the full text of hundreds—if not thousands—of different titles.

For five long hours she continued her research without a break. Time and time again she brought datacards back to the terminal and scoured their contents, only to find that they offered nothing new. Frustrated, she would eject the cards and compile a new list of possible sources, then return to the stacks to switch the old datacards for those promising better results.

It was the rumbling in her stomach that told her it was time to take a break. If she became distracted—too tired or too hungry—her spell might falter, exposing Zannah's true nature to those around her. It had happened once before, on the first day when she pushed herself too hard and worked long into the night. It had lasted only an instant, a momentary lapse, but that could have been enough to doom her. Fortunately, at that late hour the Archives had been mostly deserted, and nobody had been close enough to notice the Sith in their midst. Since then, however, Zannah had been much more careful.

There was one last datacard to check; then she would head down to the cafeteria and return once she had sated her hunger. She popped it into the terminal and quickly scanned the contents. When she found what she was looking for, she tapped a key; a block of text from an academic paper popped up onto the screen.

AN EXAMINATION AND EXPLORATION OF
A MOST DANGEROUS AND RESILIENT ORGANISM
BY DR. OSAF HAMUD

In my years of study I have encountered a number of life-forms that subsist primarily through symbiotic relationships established with other species. Some of these relationships are commensalist, in which neither species is significantly affected by the presence of the other. Others are mutualistic, enabling both species to benefit from their shared existence. And still others are parasitic, in which the host organism suffers while the symbiont thrives.

Of course, to properly classify any symbiotic relationship into one of these three categories, we must first explicitly define the meaning of words such as *harmful* or *beneficial,* a task that many have regarded as . . .

Zannah blinked twice to clear away the stupor settling in. The Archives' general collection included everything from explorers' journals that were as exciting to browse as any well-written piece of fiction, to academic papers so dry and boring they would test the limits of a Jedi Master's patience. Apparently the works of Dr. Osaf Hamud fell into the latter category.

For a brief instant she considered simply popping the data-card out and going in search of a meal, but then made a quick search for *orbalisk* instead. A dozen pages scrolled by on the viewer as it skipped to the relevant section.

. . . called orbalisks by the local Nikto populace. One warrior recounted how he had been infested for nearly a full year before ridding himself of the creatures because they so disfigured him that he could not find a mate.

This returns us to our earlier dilemma of how to define *harmful* and *beneficial.* Revisiting the previous discussion, we must now include capacity to find a mate in our discussions . . .

Zannah pulled her eyes back up to the top of the screen.

. . . one warrior recounted how he had been infested for nearly a full year before ridding himself of the creatures . . .

In desperation she typed in a new phrase, then hit SEARCH again.

It is a fact generally assumed by most zoologists that orbalisks cannot be removed without killing the host. However, my research has revealed that an infested host can be cured, though the process is both dangerous and extremely complicated, as I will detail here.

First, the host must be in excellent health. As one might expect, the very definition of excellent and even health must be expounded upon . . .

She had found it. She had found it! Zannah leapt to her feet, pumping a clenched fist in a quiet victory celebration, barely able to contain a fierce shout of triumph. And in her moment of elation, the spell concealing her true identity slipped.

Zannah quickly regained control, glancing to her left and right to see if anyone had noticed. Heart pounding, she slammed the personal datacard Master Barra had given her into the terminal to copy over the orbalisk article.

Behind her a voice said, "Rain? What are you doing here?"

DAROVIT WANDERED ALONG the wide aisle of the Jedi Archives' fourth hall, overwhelmed by the sheer volume of knowledge in the stacks.

He had briefly tried looking for information on the native flora and fauna of Ruusan, hoping to broaden his knowledge so he could better help those who came to him for aid. He was used to a simpler world, however, and found the technology of the Archives daunting. An analysis droid had explained how to use the search and retrieval systems to find information in the stacks, but his brisk tutorial had left Darovit even more confused than before.

Other scholars were there, and he could have approached one of them to ask for help. But as a man who valued his own privacy, he was loath to interrupt theirs. Ultimately, he had simply started to wander up and down the aisle, waiting for Johun to return.

Darovit was beginning to regret his decision to come to Coruscant. He had let himself get swept up in the moment by the Jedi Knight, the thoughts of stopping another war with the Sith appealing to the romantic ideals that had first led him to Ruusan as a teenager. But those were the dreams of a child; he was older and wiser now.

The Jedi moved through a world that was not his own. The concerns of an entire galaxy weighed upon their shoulders; their decisions affected trillions of lives. Darovit didn't want that kind of responsibility. Surrounded by the grandeur and glory of the Archives, all he wanted was to return to his simple hut in the forest.

Unfortunately, that might no longer be an option. He was here now, and Johun seemed determined to have him speak before the Jedi Council.

To take his mind off his plight, he began to study the other scholars. They were all Jedi: Padawans and Masters, young and old, human and otherwise. He noticed an attractive young woman with long, dark hair staring intently at her viewscreen, chewing on her lip as she delved into some work of academia.

There was something familiar about her, though Darovit was sure he had never met her before. Over the past decade he hadn't met anyone except those few individuals who sought him out in his hut, and the woman certainly didn't look like she had come from the farms or villages of Ruusan.

He crept toward her, not wishing to interrupt her studies but trying to figure out if he knew her. For several minutes he watched her; she was obviously frustrated, unable to find what she was looking for in the datacards. Suddenly she leapt up, clenching her fist victoriously, and Darovit felt a familiar presence wash over him.

For the first ten years of his life, that presence had been at his side constantly. As children, they had shared a bond that went beyond being cousins—they were as close as brother and sister. And though the figure before him had black, not blond, hair, there was no doubt in Darovit's mind who she was.

"Rain?" he called softly, so as not to startle her. "What are you doing here?"

The woman spun to face him, her eyes wide. She stared at him blankly, unable to recognize the man she had last seen as a boy ten years before. Then her eyes dropped to the stump of his right hand, and her jaw fell agape.

"Tomcat?"

He nodded, then added, "It's Darovit now. But sometimes I think I still like Tomcat better."

"You're a Jedi now?" she said, confused by his presence in the Archives.

"No," he answered quickly, unwilling to be mistaken for something he was not. "I stayed on Ruusan after . . . after this." He held up his stump. "I became a healer."

"What are you doing here?"

"I came to—" He stopped midsentence, suddenly realizing the danger Rain was in. The danger he had brought upon her.

"Rain, we have to get out of here! The Jedi are looking for you!"

"Tomcat, what are you talking about?"

"A Jedi came to Ruusan. I told him about you and Bane. That's why they brought me here!"

The young woman's eyes glowed with pure hatred and anger, and for a second Darovit thought she was going to kill him in the middle of the Jedi Archives.

"How much do they know?" she demanded. "Tell me everything you told them!"

"Rain, there isn't time," he protested. "I'm just waiting here for them to come get me. They could be here any minute. You have to get out of here or they'll find you!"

She turned and punched a key on the terminal; a small datacard popped out. She snatched it up and stuffed it beneath her clothes. Then she grabbed him by the wrist and dragged him back down the aisle toward the central rotunda. She moved as quickly as she could without drawing attention, her pace something between a brisk walk and a run.

Darovit made no move to resist, though he did ask, "Where are we going?"

"Tython," she whispered. "I have to warn my Master."

They reached the rotunda, but instead of turning down the first hall and heading toward the exit, she led him into the third hall.

"What are you doing, Rain?" Darovit asked, his voice rising slightly. "We have to get going!"

One of the other scholars—an older woman with coppery red hair sitting at a nearby terminal—turned to stare at them, her attention drawn by Darovit's exclamations.

"Quiet, Tomcat," Rain shushed him, nodding apologetically in the woman's direction. "You're disturbing the other patrons."

The old woman turned back to her viewscreen, dismissing them. Darovit's companion gave his arm a rough shake.

"I'm sorry," he whispered, just loud enough for her to hear. "But you have to get out of here. Leave for Tython before they find you here."

"I don't know where Tython is," she snapped back through clenched teeth. "We need to find a hyperspace route."

Taking the terminal one down from the red-haired old woman, Rain punched a series of buttons. A second later the screen came to life with a list of reference numbers.

"Got it," she said, shoving Darovit into the seat by the terminal's viewscreen. "Wait here."

She disappeared into the stacks, moving with the same half-walking, half-running stride. As Darovit waited for her to return, it occurred to him that his loyalties had suddenly shifted. He had been lured to Coruscant with the notion of helping the Jedi wipe out the Sith and prevent a war. But the abstract concept of widespread galactic suffering meant little when he had come face-to-face with his childhood friend. Now all he could think about was what would happen to Rain if she was caught, and he realized he was willing to do whatever it took to keep her safe.

Less than a minute later she returned and slapped a data-card into the terminal. Leaning across Darovit, who was still seated in the chair, she tapped away at the controls until an image of a cloud-covered world appeared on the screen.

"I need to copy this," she said, pulling out the datacard she had been using when he first saw her and jamming it into an-other slot on the terminal.

"Why not just take the original?" Darovit asked.

"Sensors on the Archive doors," she explained. "Removing an original will set off alarms."

The terminal beeped and the datacard popped out, the copying complete. Zannah stuffed it into her robes, then hauled Darovit up by his elbow.

"Let's go. Before your friends show up."

Not bothering to return the original back to the stacks, she half-led, half-pulled him away from the terminal. She whisked him to the rotunda, then down the main aisle of the first hall and out the exit, leaving the Archives behind them.

20

"I DON'T UNDERSTAND, MASTER VALENTHYNE," Johun said, casting his gaze from side to side as they made their way down the aisles of the Jedi Archives. "I left him here less than an hour ago."

He had expected to find Darovit sitting at a terminal in one of the four halls, or possibly examining the bronzium busts in the rotunda. But when he brought Master Valenthyne to speak with the young man, Darovit had vanished.

"He's probably just lost somewhere in the stacks," Farfalla assured him.

Johun signaled to a passing analysis droid. It turned and made its way toward them with quick, stiff-legged steps.

"May I be of assistance?" it inquired helpfully.

"I'm looking for someone," Johun explained. "A young man."

"Beings of all species and ages visit the Archives," the droid responded. "I would be better able to provide assistance if you could provide a description, Master Jedi."

"He is missing his right hand."

There was a soft whir as the droid accessed its recent memory banks.

"I believe I recently saw the man you are looking for in the third hall," the droid offered, turning to lead them in that direction.

Johun didn't bother to wait; he pushed past the droid in his haste. Farfalla followed closely at his heels.

There were many people examining the datacards located in the third hall, but the Healing Hermit of Ruusan was not among them.

"We've got to find him!" Johun said to his Master, then ran up and down the entire length of the hall, peering into the side aisles to see if Darovit was hidden among the stacks. His disruptive antics drew the ire of several of the other scholars.

Farfalla reached out and grabbed Johun as he ran past a second time, stopping him before he could make another lap of the hall.

"He's not here, Johun," he said.

There was a loud clearing of the throat, and two men turned to see an older redheaded woman glaring at them.

"Master Valenthyne," she said, "I respectfully remind you that the Archives is a place of contemplative research. Your young friend would be better served to resume his exercises out in the training yards."

"Our apologies, Master Qiina," he whispered. "But this is a matter of some urgency. We are looking for someone who has gone missing."

"It is easy to lose oneself in the wisdom of the Archives," Qiina replied. "I myself often disappear for days at a time."

Farfalla smiled politely at the jest. "This is somewhat different."

The analysis droid that had been helping them earlier toddled over toward them, having only just now caught up after they left it behind in their haste. Johun glanced at the droid, then back to Master Qiina.

"We're looking for a young man," he told her. "He's missing his right hand."

Qiina raised her eyebrows. "I saw him not thirty minutes ago. He was with a young woman."

"A woman?" Farfalla asked in surprise.

"They seemed to know each other," the old Jedi informed them. "They called each other by silly little nicknames. Tomcat and Rain, if I remember correctly."

Johun seized Farfalla's arm. "Rain was his cousin! The one he met down in the caves. She's here!"

"Do you know where they went, Master Qiina?" Farfalla asked.

The old woman shook her head. "They were using that terminal over there to look something up. Then they left."

Farfalla turned to the droid. "Is there any way we can find out which records they were viewing?"

"I am sorry, Master Jedi," the droid replied. "To protect the privacy of our scholars and to avoid compromising their research, the terminals do not store any data on which records they were used to explore."

"Your friends seemed to be in quite a hurry," Qiina offered. "I doubt they even bothered to return the datadisk to the stacks. It might still be plugged into the terminal."

Johun rushed over to the screen. It was still logged on, under the name *Nalia Adollu*. As Qiina had guessed, there was a datacard loaded in. He pulled up the disk's index as Farfalla came and peered over his shoulder.

"Tython," the Jedi Master remarked, picking out the common theme among the thousands of articles and papers referenced by the index. "Birthplace of the Jedi."

"That must be where they're going," Johun insisted. "Bane must have gone into hiding in the Deep Core!"

He turned to Farfalla, clutching his Master's arm in his urgency. "You have to convince the Council to let us go after them."

Farfalla's eyes were cold and hard. "I doubt the Council

will be in any great hurry to take action in this matter," he warned.

"But Master Valenthyne—" Johun pleaded, only to have the other man cut him off with a sharp wave of his hand.

"The Council will not help you, Johun. Therefore we must go to Tython ourselves."

Johun's eyes went wide in surprise.

"I swore a vow to General Hoth," Farfalla explained, his voice taking on the hard tone of military command he had not used since the disbanding of the Army of Light. "I promised I would not rest until the Sith had been cleansed from the galaxy. I still intend to honor that vow.

"Go find Masters Raskta and Worror," he added. "They also served with Hoth on Ruusan. They will join us in our cause. Tell them we leave within the hour."

THE FIRST THING Zannah did after the *Loranda* had escaped Coruscant's orbit and made the jump to hyperspace was wash the black dye out of her hair.

She'd engaged and locked the autopilot before heading off to the staterooms in the aft decks, leaving Tomcat to wander freely about the vessel. When she emerged, still drying her restored blond locks with a towel, he was calmly waiting for her.

He had settled in on one of the long, padded couches in the *Loranda*'s sitting lounge, reclining comfortably along its length. Judging by the drink in his hand, he had also located the collection of ales Hetton had kept on board. Still dressed in the ragtag robes of a hermit, he cut an image that was slightly comical.

"Even with the dye job gone, you still don't look anything like what I thought you'd grow up as," he told her.

It wasn't just her hair that Zannah had changed; she'd also replaced the drab Jedi robes with her more familiar and comfortable all-black garb. Being left-handed, she'd hung her lightsaber on that same hip, and the valuable datacard with the article on the orbalisks had been secured in a cargo pocket sewn into her trousers along the outside of her right thigh.

"This is the real me," she assured him.

She had often assumed character roles and disguises in her missions for Darth Bane, and she was usually comfortable in the act of deception. Yet for some reason she'd found the guise of Nalia repellent, and she'd been eager—almost desperate—to rid herself of all remnants of the Padawan façade.

"So am I your prisoner?" he asked as she sat down on the seat across from him.

"I don't think prisoners are allowed to drink tarul while they lounge on couches," she noted, tossing the towel onto the cushions beside her.

"Then why did you bring me along?" Tomcat asked, sitting up and leaning forward, suddenly serious and intent.

"I couldn't leave you behind. You were going to expose me and my Master to the Jedi Council. You were a threat to the Sith."

"Do you really believe you're a Sith, Rain?"

"Don't call me that," she said angrily. "Rain is dead. She died on Ruusan. My name's Zannah now."

"I guess Tomcat died on Ruusan, too," he agreed somberly, slowly swirling the glass in his hand. "You should probably call me Darovit now. But you never answered my question. Do you really believe you're a Sith?"

"I am Darth Zannah, apprentice of Darth Bane, Dark Lord of the Sith," she said, making no effort to hide the fierce pride she felt in the titles. "And one day I will destroy my Master and choose an apprentice of my own, continuing the legacy of the dark side."

"I don't believe that," Darovit told her, obviously unimpressed with her declaration. "I know you, Zannah. You're not evil."

"*Evil* is a word used by the ignorant and the weak," she snapped. "The dark side is about survival. It's about unleashing your inner power. It glorifies the strength of the individual."

"That's not you, either," Darovit countered. "Followers of the dark side must be brutal and ruthless. You care about others, Zannah."

"You don't know me," she sneered at him. "I've killed more people than you can possibly imagine."

"I've killed people, too. Bug died because of me," Darovit said softly, referencing the third cousin who had come with them to Ruusan. "But killing people doesn't make someone into a Sith," he said in a louder voice.

"Don't lecture me on the ways of my order," Zannah warned, getting to her feet and snatching up the towel off the cushion beside him. "What could you possibly know that I have not already learned?"

"I may not know the dark side," Darovit admitted, looking up at her. "But I know you. I know what you're capable of."

Zannah angrily threw the towel across the room, flinging it through the open door into the stateroom. She stepped forward and grabbed Darovit's right forearm, spilling his drink. Then she twisted his arm up so his stump was right before his face.

"Maybe you forgot who gave you this," she reminded him.

Darovit made no move to break free of her grasp, though she clutched his arm so hard that her nails were digging into his flesh.

"I'm not a fool, Zannah," he said calmly. "Your Master would have killed me in that cave. I know you did this to save my life."

She released her grip, tossing Darovit's arm back down into his lap in disgust. She turned her back on him and marched up the corridor toward the cockpit. The young man tossed the empty glass onto the couch and scrambled to his feet to follow.

"You risked yourself to save me, Zannah," he called out after her as she neared the cockpit. "You did it because you cared about me."

Wheeling around, Zannah reached out with the Force and yanked Darovit to the floor. He landed with a grunt, facedown at her feet.

"Things have changed since then," she said, then spun away from him again and threw herself angrily into the pilot's seat.

Darovit got up slowly and moved to stand behind her chair, hovering over her right shoulder.

"If you don't care about me anymore, then why did you bring me with you?" he asked quietly.

"I already told you," she said stiffly, staring straight ahead. "You would have exposed us. I couldn't leave you behind."

"You could have killed me."

"Ha!" Zannah barked out a laugh, turning her head and craning her neck to glare at him contemptuously. "Just strike you down with the power of the dark side in the middle of the Jedi Temple? Do you think the Sith are fools?"

"We're not in the Jedi Temple anymore," Darovit said softly. "Why don't you kill me now?"

Zannah snapped her head forward again so she wouldn't have to look at him. "You're a healer. We can use you."

"There are plenty of healers in the galaxy," her cousin pressed. "Ones who can't expose you to the Jedi."

"I don't have time to find anyone else. You were in the right place at the right time," she insisted. "You got lucky."

"That's not true, Zannah. How do you think I recognized you after all these years? There's a bond between us. There always has been. Ever since we were little."

Zannah didn't say anything, but merely shifted in her seat.

"Do you remember when we were kids? Everyone thought I was so strong in the Force, and nobody believed you had any power at all."

She didn't answer, but she did remember. As children Darovit was the one who could levitate objects, and bat away fruit tossed into the air with a stick while blindfolded. Her own powers hadn't manifested until she found herself alone on Ruusan.

"I didn't realize it then, Zannah, but the power I showed, all those tricks I did—that wasn't me, it was you! Even as kids you knew how badly I wanted to be a Jedi, and you wanted to help me. So you channeled your own power through me, allowing me to do all those things."

"That's not how I remember it," she said coldly.

"You didn't do it on purpose," Darovit explained. "The bond we shared was so strong, and you cared about me so much, that your subconscious took over."

"That's the stupidest theory I've ever heard." Zannah snorted, still staring straight ahead.

"Is it? Think about it, Zannah. After we lost you on Ruusan, it was like my powers disappeared. That's why I failed as a Jedi and as a Sith.

"My power is weak. That's why I survived the thought bomb when all the Sith and Jedi around me were destroyed by its power. It only affected those with a strong affinity for the Force.

"And what about you? You have so much power. Why do you think it took so long to show itself? You were always channeling it through me." He paused. "You won't become the Dark Lord of the Sith, Zannah," he added. "It's just not in your nature. Sooner or later you'll realize that."

"Shut up," she said flatly, still keeping her eyes riveted on the controls in front of her. "If you say one more word I'll take your other hand."

Darovit didn't reply, but his fingers instinctively went to his stump.

"I brought you along for one reason, and one reason only," she continued, her voice still completely devoid of emotion. "My Master is infested with parasites called orbalisks. And you are going to heal him."

"But . . . I don't know how," Darovit protested, forgetting her warnings to remain silent.

Zannah reached back with the Force, wrapping it around his windpipe. And slowly she began to squeeze. Darovit fell to his knees, his hands flying up to his throat as his oxygen was cut off.

"There is a data terminal in the back," Zannah said, ignoring his choking coughs. "Use it to go over everything in the article I took from the Archives."

She pulled the card from the pocket on her thigh and tossed it down in front of her suffocating cousin. He was rolling back and forth on the floor now, his hands clawing at his throat. His face had turned a bright red, and his eyes were starting to bulge from his sockets.

"If you can't find a way to help my Master by the time we get to Tython," she warned, "he will kill you."

She released Darovit from the Force choke, and he gasped and gulped down air in raw, ragged breaths. She turned to watch him with a cruel smile on her lips, making sure he knew she was enjoying his suffering. Eventually he recovered enough to pick up the datacard and head for the terminal in the back.

Once he was gone, Zannah got up from her chair and began to pace back and forth between the pilot's and copilot's seats. She knew Darovit was wrong. He had to be. She was confident in her commitment to the dark side, despite everything her cousin had said. But there was enough weight to some of his arguments to make her wonder what Bane would think about all this.

If her Master—like Darovit—believed her actions showed a lack of commitment to the ways of the Sith, things would go very badly for her when they reached Tython.

BELIA DARZU HAD been a Shi'ido in life, a changeling species whose members were capable of shifting their appearance, so it was not surprising that the projection that served as the gatekeeper of her Holocron similarly changed forms. At various times she appeared to be Twi'lek, Iridonian, Cerean, or human, occasionally even switching between genders.

"The process of creating a Holocron cannot be rushed," the gatekeeper explained. "The adjustments to the matrix must be made with precision and care."

She was currently in the form she most often assumed: that

of a tall human female with short brown hair. She appeared to be roughly thirty years of age, with a sly, almost crafty, look to her features. In this guise she was typically clad in a dark, formfitting flight suit, dark boots, and a pale yellow vest that left her arms bare. She also wore yellow gloves, a short black sleeve over each elbow, and a red flight cap and belt.

After his initial activation of the Holocron's power, Bane had brought it up out of the inner sanctum and into a large common room on the main level that once served as a mess hall for Belia's living followers. Here Bane had been exploring the Holocron off and on for the past several days. He had proceeded carefully, still drained from his battle with the techno-beasts. The slow pace allowed him to recuperate his energies and rebuild his strength as he probed the crystal archives.

Much of what he discovered focused on the rituals and practices of Sith alchemy—something he would explore in depth when he had more time. Other times he stumbled across Belia's own philosophical examinations of the Force, though in truth there was little there that Bane hadn't already discovered for himself. Only now had he finally found what he had truly been searching for.

"It can take weeks, or even months," Belia's image explained, "before the final stages of construction are completed."

Her form flickered, to be replaced by the image of a Holocron shown in cutaway. The filaments and strands of the crystal matrix in the image began to shift and move, illustrating the adjustments the gatekeeper was talking about. Bane didn't bother paying close attention; he already knew how to fine-tune the matrix's internal structures.

"You said the adjustments can take months. How is that possible?" Bane asked with a shake of his head. "The cognitive network degrades too quickly."

Belia's image flickered into view again. "The cognitive network must be trapped within the capstone before you begin," she explained.

"Capstone?" Bane asked, his nerves tingling with excitement. In all his research he had never heard mention of a capstone before.

An image of a Holocron appeared once more, though no longer in cutaway. The small black crystal built into the apex of the pyramid was flashing.

"The capstone is key to the process," Belia's voice said. "Without it the cognitive network will degrade before you complete your adjustments, and you will fail every time."

Bane stared in wonder at the image. He had known that the dark crystal was an essential part of the Holocron's construction. Yet he had believed its sole purpose was to channel the power of the symbols etched across the sides of the pyramid into the matrix. He never imagined it would serve another function as well.

"How do I trap the cognitive network inside the capstone?" he asked, eager to learn the secret that had eluded him.

"You must invoke the Rite of Commencement," Belia told him.

The projection shifted to show an incredibly elaborate and complicated Sith ritual, one that went beyond anything Bane had mastered so far. With subtle pushes from the Force he flipped through image after image after image, realizing it would take him many months of careful study to memorize the rite. Still . . . the secret was his!

Satisfied, he shut the Holocron down. It was time to leave Tython and return to Ambria. If all had gone well, his apprentice would be there waiting for him.

He made his way outside, where the *Mystic* waited. But as he prepared to board his ship, he saw another vessel in the distance racing toward him. He reached out with the Force, and felt the presence of Zannah inside . . . and one other.

The *Loranda* came in to land fifty meters from where his own ship had touched down. Bane stood impassively, waiting for Zannah to emerge. When she did, there was a young man with her. The Dark Lord could feel the Force in him, though its presence was weak. When he saw that the man was missing his right hand, everything fell into place.

"We were supposed to meet at Ambria," he snarled at Zannah. "Why did you come here? And why did you bring him?"

"I came to warn you," she answered quickly. "The Jedi know you survived the thought bomb."

"Because of him," Bane said, nodding in the other man's direction.

"He was going to speak to the Jedi Council," Zannah explained. "If he vanished, they might dismiss the rumors that you still lived."

"Why didn't you just kill him?" Bane asked, his tone ominous.

"He's a healer" was her immediate reply. "He knows how to free you from the orbalisks."

Zannah's answers came too quickly to suit Bane. It was as if she had already had this argument, likely rehearsing it in her head over and over in preparation for this meeting.

"Is this true?" he demanded of the other man.

"I can't do it here," Darovit answered. "I need supplies. Special equipment. It's dangerous, but I think it can be done."

Bane hesitated. Not because of the potential danger; he had known that any procedure to rid himself of his infestation would be fraught with risk. But now that he knew his failures with the Holocron were not linked to the orbalisks feeding on his power, he wanted to reevaluate the decision to remove them.

The sight of another ship appearing over his apprentice's shoulder, still too far in the distance to make out a model or affiliation, put an end to his deliberations. An instant later he felt the unmistakable light-side power of those on board.

Zannah must have felt it too; she turned and looked in that direction, then turned back to him with a worried grimace.

"Is something wrong?" the young healer asked, noticing the exchange. "What is it?"

"We were followed," Zannah muttered.

The ship was coming in quickly, too fast for them to get into their own craft and take to the sky. If they tried, the other vessel would shoot them down before they took off.

"Inside the fortress," Bane ordered. "The Jedi have found us."

21

THE *JUSTICE CRUSADER*, Master Raskta's ship, was easily the fastest vessel Johun had ever been on. A small, personal attack cruiser, she required a crew of four. Fortunately for Johun, there were four others with him on board, all of them clothed in the simple brown robes that marked them as members of the Jedi Order.

Master Raskta Lsu, an Echani, sat at the controls of her ship. She had the alabaster skin, pure white hair, and silver eyes common to all her species. She was almost as tall as Johun, with the muscles and physique one would expect in a species that valued physical combat as the highest form of art and personal expression. Named in honor of the legendary Echani warrior Raskta Fenni, acclaimed by many to be the greatest duelist of her time, Master Raskta had spent her life honing her martial skills so that she could one day equal, and even surpass, her namesake.

She had achieved the rare and prestigious rank of Jedi

Weapons Master. Eschewing all other fields of study and forsaking the development of her other Force talents to focus exclusively on the lightsaber and combat, she had transformed herself into a living weapon.

Now tasked with training apprentices in the forms of lightsaber combat, Raskta had been part of the campaign on Ruusan. Wielding a blue-bladed lightsaber in each hand, and shunning any form of armor, she was a terrifying figure to behold on the battlefield. Johun vividly remembered her carving great swaths of destruction through the heart of the enemy ranks, leaving a litter of bodies in her wake. It was said that, by the end of the war, as many Sith Lords had fallen under her twin blades as had been killed by the thought bomb.

In the gunner's chair across from the pilot was Sarro Xaj, the human male who had served as Raskta's Padawan on Ruusan. A year older than Johun, Sarro had olive-brown skin and a single topknot of black hair. He was also the largest human Johun had ever encountered. Over two meters tall and 150 kilos of raw muscle, he could easily be mistaken for a hairless Wookiee rather than a man. Yet despite his mass, he was still quick enough to snatch a zess-fly out of the air.

Elevated to the rank of Jedi Knight seven years before, Sarro had chosen to follow in his Master's path, focusing on mastering a massive double-bladed lightsaber measuring almost three meters in length. Johun imagined there were few beings in the galaxy who could stand up under the ferocious assault of his weapon's blue blades.

Handling the navigation in the back of the vessel was Master Worror, an Ithorian. His long, flat neck curved forward and up to a head shaped like the letter T, with his large, bulbous eyes on either end of the cross stroke. This odd appearance had led to his species being commonly called hammerheads by the ignorant and insensitive.

Master Worror's surname could only be pronounced by beings possessing the two mouths and four throats unique to Ithorian anatomy. Johun had heard tales of Ithorian Jedi channeling the Force to transform their multiple voices into a devastating sonic weapon. Master Worror, however, was a healer by training, and his power lay in that direction.

He had been one of General Hoth's advisers on Ruusan, and a key to victory in many battles, even though he didn't even carry a lightsaber. The Ithorian's role was not to engage the enemy but rather to provide support through both his healing abilities and the rare art of battle meditation. Although his talent was not strong enough to single-handedly alter the outcome of a large-scale conflict, in close quarters Worror could draw upon the Force to give strength to the bodies, minds, and spirits of those around him, enhancing the skills and abilities of his allies.

Located beside the navigator in the rear of the vessel, the fourth member of the crew, Master Farfalla, provided support for the pilot, gunner, and navigator. He called up astronav charts, engine readings, weapons status, scanner reports, and anything else the others needed to do their jobs.

Johun was seated up front in the cockpit with Raskta and Sarro, occupying the passenger's chair behind the pilot. Until they reached Tython, his only job was to stay out of everyone else's way.

Using the long-abandoned hyperspace route indicated on the datacard they'd discovered in the Archives, the *Justice Crusader* had penetrated the Deep Core. Master Raskta had expressed her concern at the start of the voyage: According to current records the hyperspace lanes they were traversing had been known to momentarily collapse without warning. A ship traveling anywhere along the hyperspace corridor during the nanosecond before it re-formed would be lost forever. Combined with the other dangers of the Deep Core—including wandering black holes that would rip a vessel apart, even in hyperspace—the instability of the route had led to it falling into disuse and finally being forgotten for well over a thousand years.

Worror had calculated the risk of a hyperspace collapse during their journey at just over 2 percent—more than high enough to make Johun breathe a sigh of relief when they emerged unscathed a few thousand kilometers away from their destination.

"Weapons primed and ready," Sarro's voice told everyone over the intercom. "Any friends we have to worry about?"

"Nothing in orbit," Farfalla reported. "Looks like we're clean."

"I'm taking us in," Raskta told them. "See if you can find anything."

"Picking up an ion trail," Farfalla said as they neared the planet's atmosphere. "Looks like we're right behind them."

"Locking on to the ion trail . . . locked on." Even over the crackle of an intercom, Worror's deep voice resonated through the ship.

"Engaging autopilot," Raskta said. "Let's see where this takes us. Sarro, keep your trigger finger ready."

The autopilot dropped them down into Tython's atmosphere, and for several seconds the only thing Johun could see through the cockpit viewport was a wall of gray cloud. When they broke free their destination was immediately obvious.

"I think I know where we're headed," Sarro mumbled.

Below them was a flat, empty field virtually devoid of life. A dark fortress was visible on the horizon, the only significant structure in sight.

"Picking up two small vessels on the ground," Farfalla told them as they drew nearer. "Nobody outside, though."

They were close enough now that Johun could make out two melted towers rising up on either side of the stronghold's front face.

"Reading life-forms inside the building," Farfalla noted. "Looks like . . . three."

"Only three?" Sarro mumbled, sounding disappointed. "This might be too easy."

"Don't count on that," Farfalla warned him as Raskta brought the *Justice Crusader* in for a landing.

ZANNAH WAS TRYING to concentrate, gathering her mental energies for the coming battle. She was distracted, however, by her Master's own preparations.

Darth Bane was prowling back and forth like an angry rancor, his lightsaber already drawn. She could feel the dark side building inside him, fueled by his rage—his never-ending hatred of the Jedi; his resentment toward Darovit for exposing them; his anger at her for leading the Jedi here to Tython. At any moment she expected to see the bloodlust of the orbalisks unleashed, but Bane kept his fury in check, saving it for the coming battle.

Her Master had led them back inside the stronghold to a large, open room with an exit at either end. A single door would have been easier to defend, but he was wary of getting trapped. If the Jedi cornered them, they would settle in for a long siege and wait for reinforcements to arrive. As the last two surviving Sith, Zannah and her Master did not have the same luxury, so it was important that they keep alternate escape routes open.

The room was empty, completely devoid of any furniture. Based on that fact and its great size—forty meters by thirty— she guessed it had been built as some kind of practice arena or training center. In addition to the exits on either end, there was a small door on one of the side walls that led to a tiny, dead-end room. It had probably served at one time as a storage closet for weapons, targets, and other implements used in drills or training.

At Bane's instruction, she'd stashed the datacard from the Archives inside the closet, and her Master had done the same with Belia Darzu's Holocron. At her suggestion, Darovit was hiding in there, too. He was unarmed, and he would be of no help to either side.

"Don't come out until the fighting's done," she'd warned him, drawing a sour, disapproving look from her Master. "He'll only get in the way," she'd explained as Darovit had closed himself in.

Now there was nothing to do but wait for the enemy to arrive. Fortunately—or unfortunately—they didn't have to wait long.

The doors on either end of the room burst open simultaneously, the Jedi splitting their numbers in two to better coordinate the attack. The first group—a female Echani wielding a blue lightsaber in each hand and a Jedi Master in garish clothes with a golden blade—charged straight for Bane. The other two—a lean, quick-looking Jedi armed with a green lightsaber and a gigantic mountain of a man spinning a massive blue, double-bladed weapon—came at her.

Zannah ignited her own double-bladed lightsaber and threw up a twirling wall of defense, though her weapon looked puny and insignificant set against the blue monster brandished by the larger of her two opponents. Before they could engage her, she backpedaled toward one of the corners, stopping several meters from the intersection of the two walls. This allowed her to protect her flanks, but still left enough space for her to duck, dodge, and evade the weapons of her enemies.

From the corner of her eye she saw Bane take a completely different approach. Protected by his orbalisk armor, he charged forward to meet the two Jedi Masters confronting him head-on.

And then her enemies fell on her. It took only seconds for her to realize that the bigger man was by far the more dangerous opponent. In the time it took for the smaller man to strike at her twice with his green blade, she had batted aside half a dozen attacks from the other. There was a marked difference in the style and effectiveness of their blows, as well. The skills of the Jedi with the green lightsaber were raw and basic. When he struck, it was with either strength or speed, but not both at the same time. His blade came in either high or low, but never altered its plane during the attack. In contrast, the big man attacked her from creative and unexpected angles, the massive blue blades changing course midthrust. Each offensive was a model of lethal efficiency—quick and powerful strikes and counterstrikes that kept an opponent guessing.

Yet as long as Zannah kept her blade spinning to hold its momentum, she was able to ward off both their attacks easily using whirling parries, in large part because the Jedi with the green lightsaber was inadvertently working at cross purposes to his partner. He was attempting to alternate his forays with those of the bigger man, expecting they would take turns pressing forward, then withdrawing, always keeping Zannah on defense. But the incredible reach of the bigger man's weapon made it difficult for him to unleash a sustained volley without fear of injuring or even killing his companion when the other man moved in to join the fray. As a result, the bigger man constantly had to step back, pull up, or lay off his attacks. He was forced into an awkward rhythm of advance and retreat, his timing and strategy dictated as much by his ally as by his opponent.

Zannah noted all this from behind the impassable wall of her spinning twin blades, content to play a completely passive role in the encounter. Were it not for the big man's brilliance, she would have quickly switched to an aggressive sequence and easily dispatched the smaller man. But were it not for the smaller man's mediocrity, her defensive talents would have been pushed to the very limits by her more skilled opponent. The arrangement suited Zannah just fine, allowing her to play them off against each other. She didn't need to kill them; she only needed to hold them at bay until Bane, protected by the invulnerable orbalisk shells, killed his two opponents and came to her aid.

She waited until it was time for the smaller man to attack again, then gauged his painfully predictable incoming stroke. Knowing exactly where it would end by watching where it began, she was able to momentarily divert her attention from the combat to see how her Master was doing.

To her surprise, both of Bane's opponents were still standing: proof they were exceptionally skilled combatants. She also noticed that a fifth Jedi had entered the room: an Ithorian who stood apart from the battle, his eyes closed as if he was meditating. And then she turned her focus back to her own melee, just in time to avoid certain death.

The glance in her Master's direction had lasted only a fraction of a second, but in the brief interval of her distraction the larger man had sprung forward, jabbing the tip of one of his blades toward her eye like a spear. Zannah snapped her head to the side at the last possible instant, hearing the hiss as the blade sheared off a lock of her hair. The sudden movement threw off her timing and balance, and as her spinning lightsaber slapped away the blow she had earlier anticipated from the smaller man's green blade, it lost its centripetal momentum and faltered.

In the split second it took to roll her wrists and start the intricate, whirling patterns of her blades again, she was vulnerable. The big man sliced high at her head, forcing her to duck, then chopped in low at her feet on the backstroke, causing her to jump before she could properly set herself. She avoided the swipe, but landed clumsily on her feet. Another blow rained down on her. With her body out of position, she was forced to block its path rather than deflect it to the side. The power of the impact sent her reeling, and she fell to the floor.

The man with the green lightsaber saved her. He leapt in to finish her off, blocking his companion from doing the same. Against his pedestrian assault she was able to regain her feet and slide into the sequence of moves that were the foundation of her virtually impenetrable style.

There was a brief instant when she saw an opening—but rather than choose to kill the man with the green lightsaber she let him live, knowing he was a greater hindrance to his allies than he was to her.

From across the room one of the other Jedi called out, "Johun! Sarro! We need reinforcements!"

"Go," the big man shouted. "I can handle this one."

And suddenly the man with the green lightsaber was gone.

The olive-skinned giant reared up to his full height; Zannah realized he was even taller and more heavily muscled than Bane. The air sizzled as his long lightsaber carved an elaborate flourish around his body, then another above his head. He smiled down at her knowingly.

Then he leapt forward and the real battle began.

IT HAD BEEN many years since Farfalla had fought while empowered by Worror's battle meditation. He had forgotten how much quicker and stronger the Ithorian's amazing talent made him feel. The Force flowed through him with greater power, filling him with its might. Yet even with their enhanced abilities, he wondered if they would survive the coming battle.

As they burst into the room a man who could only have been Darth Bane charged recklessly toward them. In any other instance the move would have spelled a quick end to the encounter, as Raskta raced ahead of Farfalla to carve the Sith to pieces.

Raskta's blue blades flickered too quickly for the eye to see, neutralizing her enemy's initial, wild attack then landing half a dozen lethal blows to his chest and abdomen. But instead of toppling, the big man kept coming, never even breaking stride. He would have plowed straight into Raskta, trampling her under his heavy boots, had she not cartwheeled to the side at the last possible instant.

Bane never stopped, his momentum carrying him straight toward Farfalla. The Jedi Master had a moment to register the strange armor coat of hard, shiny shells he wore beneath his clothes. Then he, too, leapt to the side to avoid being crushed, surviving only because his reflexes were heightened by Worror's power.

Raskta was already back on her feet and flying through the air toward him. Bane spun and threw a wave of invisible dark side power at her. A Weapons Master was not skilled at defending against enemy Force attacks. The impact of the wave would have plastered her against the wall and crushed her had Farfalla not thrown up a shield to protect the Echani. Even so her muscular body was plucked from the air and hurtled backward, though she twisted and turned so she landed on her feet.

Farfalla saw the Sith Lord turn toward him, sensing the intervention that had saved Raskta's life. Bane unleashed a barrage of Sith lightning, gathering and releasing his power at the speed of thought. The Jedi threw up a Force barrier to shield himself, but the electricity tore right through it and arced toward him. Then suddenly Raskta was there to save his life, repaying a debt that was only a few seconds old as she threw herself in front of him. Fueled by Worror's battle meditation, she switched styles seamlessly, and her arms and blades became a blur as they carved figure eights in the air to catch and absorb the bolts of dark side energy.

Their enemy fell upon them again, following up the lightning with pure aggression. Raskta rushed ahead of Farfalla to meet this second charge. She crouched low, viciously slashing at his thighs and calves, attempting to leave their opponent crawling legless on the floor. Her blades carved through his boots and sliced wide gashes in his pants, only to reveal more of the chitinous shells.

Bane brought his lightsaber down at the Echani, who crossed her blades into an X, attempting to block and trap her opponent's weapon at the point of intersection. But the Sith's move was only a feint meant to distract her, and at the last instant he pulled his weapon back and swung an elbow around to catch her in the ribs. The contact lifted her off her feet and sent her sprawling. Then he was past her, and bearing down on Farfalla.

The Jedi Master dropped into an elegant defensive stance to meet the charge.

"The handle!" Raskta gasped as she scrambled to her feet.

The warning caused Farfalla to notice the hook-handled lightsaber of his enemy, and the unusual grip it required. This would alter the nature of his attacks, causing them to come in from odd and unfamiliar angles. In the regimented and hyperprecise world of Jedi–Sith lightsaber duels, it transformed his style into something unique and unexpected.

Valenthyne recognized, processed, and reacted to this information in a fraction of a second, allowing him to adjust his own weapon's course just enough to block a strike that otherwise would have slipped along the edge of his blade and taken his arm off at the elbow. Even so, the strength behind the attack tore Farfalla's golden blade from his grip, sending his lightsaber skittering across the floor. Unarmed and helpless before his enemy, he was saved by Raskta.

Knowing that her lightsabers couldn't penetrate Bane's armor, she slid in from behind and scissor-kicked his legs out from under him. He toppled over backward, turning his fall into a roll that ended with him back on his feet. However, the distraction allowed Farfalla to look over and reach out with the Force, calling his weapon back into his hand.

He spun back to the fight to see that the Echani Weapons Master had taken the offensive, sending quick flicks of her blue blades toward Bane's unprotected face—the only spot on his body seemingly not covered by the impenetrable shells. Remarkably, Bane was giving ground.

"Stay back!" she shouted at Farfalla. "You'll just get in the way."

Farfalla did as he was told, gathering the energies of the light side to throw up another protective Force barrier should Bane try to unleash his dark side powers against the Echani.

She seemed to be everywhere at once—in front of Bane, beside him, behind him, circling low, leaping to come in high, deflecting his blade with one of her own then stabbing three quick times in succession at his eyes. The big man's head ducked and bobbed, twisting and turning to avoid her blows as he tried to mount a counteroffensive.

Raskta's mastery of her blades was unparalleled, but even with her talents augmented by Worror's battle meditation she wasn't able to land a telling blow on such a small target through Bane's defenses. Still, the ferocity of her new strategy had turned the momentum in her favor . . . or so Farfalla thought.

Bane continued his retreat, circling away from Raskta's blades, then suddenly turned and ran straight toward the un-armed Ithorian standing just inside the door of the room.

Battle meditation required Master Worror's complete focus; there was no chance for him to mount any type of defense. If Bane cut him down, the others would lose the only advantage that gave them any chance of surviving the encounter.

Farfalla released the power he'd been gathering in a single concentrated burst. Bane was suddenly encased in a shimmering stasis field of light-side energy, freezing him where he stood. But his command of the dark side was too powerful for it to hold him for more than a split second. The shimmering field exploded into fragments as the Dark Lord broke free, though the momentary delay had allowed the Echani to place herself between the Ithorian and the Sith.

Raskta's blades hummed and sang as she engaged him again, determined to keep him from reaching Master Worror at all costs.

He's too strong, Farfalla realized, even as he ran to help her. *Both physically and in the power of the dark side. It's like trying to fight a force of nature.*

"Johun! Sarro! We need reinforcements!"

JOHUN TURNED HIS HEAD at the sound of Farfalla's voice.

"Go," Sarro shouted at him. "I can handle this one."

The young Jedi looked over to the far side of the room and instantly recognized what was happening. Master Worror was

in danger; he had to be protected or his battle meditation—
and any hope of victory—would be lost.

He leapt across the room, using the Force to propel him
through the air so that he landed only a few meters from where
Raskta was dueling Darth Bane, desperately trying to drive
him back and away from where Master Worror stood but a
meter or two behind her. He hesitated before attacking, noticing that the Sith Lord's skin was covered with a strange, crus-
taceous growth.

"Go for the face!" Farfalla shouted, arriving on the scene
and throwing himself into the battle as Johun did the same.

Together the three of them held the Sith Lord at bay: Farfalla on the left flank, Johun on the right, and Raskta in the
center. Between blocks and parries they cut and stabbed at his
face, their combined efforts finally forcing their enemy into a
defensive stance.

The young Jedi marveled at the speed and savagery of
Raskta's blades. And while Johun's own clumsy efforts had actually seemed to impede Sarro when they fought side by side,
Raskta appeared to thrive off his presence. When he went high,
she went low. If he came from the left, she came from the right.
It was partly a function of her choice of weapon: individually
each of her lightsabers was more precise and accurate than
Sarro's giant double blades. But it was more than that. Her
reactions were so fast, her combat instincts so pure, that she
was able to sense and anticipate what he was going to do even
as it happened, then use his attacks to her own advantage.

On her opposite side Farfalla struck with clean, elegant
blows, his form perfect as he harried Bane's right flank. Yet
though they were able to hold their ground, they couldn't drive
him back or defeat him.

They were at an impasse, none of their attacks able to con-
nect with the one vulnerable part of Bane's anatomy. Then
Johun caught a glimpse of white flesh peeking out from the
seam between the Sith's armored gloves and the strange shells

on his forearm. The gap was narrow, but it was large enough for a well-aimed blade to penetrate.

He slashed at his new target. Amplified by Worror's power, the Force flowed through him and guided his blade home. The contact wasn't perfect; his lightsaber glanced off the edge of the armored shells so that he only made shallow contact with the skin beneath. Instead of severing the hand, he merely sliced deep enough to sever nerves and tendons.

Bane bellowed in rage as his weapon slipped from his grasp, the wound leaving his fingers limp and powerless. But before Johun or any of the others had a chance to finish off their unarmed opponent, they were blown backward by an explosion of dark side energy, their enemy's power fueled by the sharp, sudden pain of his wound.

Lying on the ground ten meters away, Johun watched in helpless horror as the Dark Lord's lightsaber leapt from the floor and flew back into his hand. Amazingly, his fingers wrapped themselves around the hilt and reignited the crimson blade, his injuries somehow healing almost instantly.

There was no longer anyone standing between Bane and the Ithorian; like Johun, Farfalla and Raskta had both been thrown clear. The Sith Lord raised his blade to end Worror's life, and Johun thrust out with the Force.

He knew he wasn't strong enough to penetrate Bane's defenses, but the big man wasn't his target. Instead, the powerful push struck Worror, throwing him into the corner as the lightsaber strike that would have cut him in two swished harmlessly through the air.

Johun felt his strength and energy plummet. A wave of exhaustion and fatigue overwhelmed him, the beneficial effects of the battle meditation vanishing as Worror's concentration was broken. But the Jedi Master was still alive, and Farfalla and Raskta were back on their feet. If they could hold Bane off for just a few seconds, the Ithorian could resume his meditations and restore their advantage.

ZANNAH SLID TO the side, her spinning weapon redirecting the blade of her enemy away from her throat and harmlessly up over her shoulder. Its twin came in quickly from the other side at her hip, and she threw herself into a back handspring to avoid it, landing nimbly on her feet. Grimly, she realized that she'd never understood the true meaning of the term *martial arts* until now.

The warrior assailing her had elevated the act of combat to its purest and highest form. He moved with the fluid grace of a dancer, his monstrous blade singing the deadly song of battle. He executed his moves with a perfect elegance born of obsession. Zannah knew it left him vulnerable to other forms of attack, but he pressed her so relentlessly that she never had a chance to effectively gather her power.

Had the Jedi enjoyed the same advantages Bane's orbalisk armor provided, their encounter would have ended long ago. Bane could shrug off otherwise lethal blows, forgoing all sense of personal safety in a reckless assault of pure offense to overwhelm her defenses. In contrast, the man before her, massive though he was, would still die if her blades caught him. He had to guard against her counterattacks, his style less aggressive so he didn't leave himself vulnerable. Even though his technique was more refined than her Master's, she'd been able to withstand his assault . . . so far.

He came at her again, his blade changing directions so quickly in midstroke that it seemed to bend and curve. Zannah repelled the assault with a furious defensive flurry, breathing hard. Her style was meant to prolong combat, exhausting her opponents as they tried to penetrate her defenses. But each time she clashed with the olive-skinned giant, she was the one forced to expend desperate, frantic energy. Slowly, he was wearing her down.

It was more than just his talent and training. Zannah sensed some type of greater power at work: the Force flowed through him as if it was being channeled by another, giving even greater strength to her opponent.

Another exchange drove her backward; the man was cutting off the room, herding her tightly into the corner to limit her movement. He was taking away her agility, knowing she was no match for his strength. And there was nothing she could do about it. Taking another step back, she felt her heel butt up against the edge of the wall. There was nowhere left to go; the end was near.

On the far side of the room she heard Bane howl in rage, and she braced herself for a final stand she knew she couldn't survive. Her opponent spun the long double-bladed lightsaber around his own body, gathering momentum for his next attack. And then, suddenly, the power behind him—the Force being channeled through him by another—was gone. Zannah felt it disappear, snuffed out like a candle in a puff of wind.

The big man hesitated, casting a quick glance over toward the others to see what had happened. Seizing the opportunity, Zannah's fingers flickered in strange patterns as she unleashed her Sith sorcery at her foe.

His eyes went wide and he stumbled away from her, his lightsaber swinging wildly at the air around him as he was beset on all sides by imaginary demons. Flailing in half mad terror at the invisible monsters, he ignored Zannah as she swooped in and ended his life with one long, diagonal stroke across his muscular chest.

As he fell to the ground, Zannah turned her attention to Bane on the far side of the room. He was single-handedly battling three Jedi, slowly pushing them back toward where the Ithorian lay crumpled in a corner.

Gathering the dark side around her, Zannah created a concealing cloak to mask her power as she had done at the Jedi Temple. While she did so, she saw the Ithorian slowly rise to his feet and close his eyes in concentration. She felt the surge of light-side energy rolling across the room, as did Bane's opponents. Suddenly invigorated, they backed her Master up against a wall, concentrating their attacks on his face and the joints of his wrist where the orbalisks had left tiny gaps in his armor.

Zannah rushed to her Master's aid, coming up silently behind the Jedi. Her presence hidden by her spell of concealment, they never sensed her coming. She struck the Echani down first, thrusting her blade forward so that it pierced the Jedi's back and ran her through.

The Echani cried out and slumped forward, dropping at Zannah's feet. The men on either side half turned toward her, momentarily forgetting the opponent directly in front of them. Bane took the opportunity to slice off the weapon hand of the man with the green lightsaber. He screamed and dropped to his knees, clutching his cauterized stump. The image pulled Zannah's mind back to the cave on Ruusan where she had taken her cousin's hand.

With a shake of her head, she dispelled the memory. Her distraction had given the young Jedi a chance to roll clear of the battle. Zannah hesitated, uncertain whether to finish him off or help her Master against the man he was still battling. The question became moot a moment later when Bane swatted the Jedi's golden lightsaber aside with his orbalisk-encrusted left forearm, then removed his foe's head from his body with his lightsaber.

In the corner the Ithorian broke his meditative trance, sensing that his companions had fallen. But before he could act Bane leapt through the air and landed in front of him, slashing all four of his throats simultaneously. The Ithorian crumpled to the ground, and Bane turned to finish off the one-handed Jedi.

Zannah felt the gathering dark side power of her Master, but in the instant before he unleashed the storm of deadly purple lightning, the Ithorian reached up from the floor and clutched him by his ankle. A shimmering blue globe surrounded them both as the mortally wounded Jedi released his own power in his final, dying act.

Instead of arcing across the room to destroy the one-armed Jedi, the lightning that flew from Bane's fingers reflected off the inside of the shimmering blue globe encasing him. The bolts ricocheted around wildly inside the globe, creating a storm of energy so intense that Zannah had to shield her eyes and look away. She heard Bane's scream rising above the sharp crackle of electricity, and when she looked back she saw the globe vanish and her Master fall to the ground in a charred and smoking heap.

She started to run to him, then saw that the sole surviving Jedi was crawling toward where his lightsaber had fallen on the ground, determined to fight on despite the loss of his hand.

Her face frozen in a mask of rage and hatred, she stepped forward and spun her lightsaber above her head. He looked at her with pleading eyes, but her only response was to bring her blade crashing down, ending his life.

22

WHEN ZANNAH FIRST reached Bane's side, she was sure her Master was dead. The lightning had reduced his clothes to ash, and his gloves and boots had melted away. The flesh of his face and hands was charred and burned, covered with blisters that oozed a runny yellow pus. Several of the parasites on his chest and stomach hadn't survived, their brown shells turned black and brittle by the lightning's electrical charge. Wisps of still-smoldering smoke crept out from beneath their shells, bringing with it a sickly stench that made Zannah's stomach churn.

Then she saw Bane's chest rise and fall, his breaths so shallow and faint she had almost missed them. He must have slipped into unconsciousness as his body went into shock from the unbearable pain. She paused, half expecting to see his seared skin and tissue begin to regenerate, but his injuries exceeded even the ability of the orbalisks to heal him, and nothing happened.

The sound of a door opening made her turn her head,

glancing up to see Darovit emerging from his hiding place. He looked around at the carnage in the room, then saw Zannah crouched over her Master.

"Is he . . . ?" He left the question hanging in the air.

"He's alive," she said angrily, rising to her feet.

Darovit slowly walked over to her side, cradling Belia's Holocron and the datacard against his sternum with his good hand. Zannah reached out and snatched them away when he drew close. He didn't seem to notice, his eyes transfixed by the charred husk at her feet that was somehow still alive.

"Get the lightsabers," she commanded. "We're leaving."

Darovit had the good sense not to question her orders, but went to gather the weapons of the fallen Jedi: trophies of the Sith triumph on Tython.

Zannah stuffed the Holocron and datacard away in the pockets of her clothing, then took a deep breath to focus her mind. She reached out with the Force and lifted Bane's body off the ground, levitating it at waist height.

She carried her Master this way from the fortress and outside, Darovit following closely behind her. She briefly considered which ship they should use to take them from Tython, then settled on the *Loranda*. In addition to being larger, it was also equipped with a full medical bay.

"Open the cargo bay," she ordered, nodding her head in the direction of the vessel.

Darovit raced ahead and did as she instructed, while Zannah slowly lifted her Master up and into the ship.

Once aboard they hooked Bane up to a bacta pump. His injuries probably required complete submersion in a bacta tank for several days, but she didn't have access to those kind of facilities. A bacta pump was the next best thing; it injected a heavy dose of the fluid directly into his veins, circulating it through the body, then filtering it out, only to repeat the process.

"He's stable," Darovit said. "But he won't be for long. When an orbalisk dies it poisons the host."

"You read the information on the disk," she said. "Get them off him."

"Even if I did it wouldn't help," Darovit told her, relaying what he had learned from the disk. "It's too late. The orbalisks release toxins into the host's tissue the instant they die. It breaks down the cells at a microscopic level. He'll be dead in a matter of days."

"You're a kriffing healer!" she shouted. "Help him!"

"I can't, Zannah," he said softly. "Not here. We don't have the proper equipment or supplies. And even if we did, there's nothing I can do. Once the orbalisk toxin enters the host, there's no way to stop its progress."

You can't die yet, Zannah thought bitterly, chewing on her lip. *There's so much more you have to teach me!*

Her Master's power was still far greater than her own. She had the potential to surpass Bane—he had told her so himself—but right now he still possessed a strength she could only aspire to. There were secrets he had not yet shared with her, keys to unlocking even greater power than she now possessed. If he died, that knowledge was lost. It was *possible* she might one day succeed in discovering it on her own; with Bane as her Master, success was *assured*.

But what he still had to teach her went far beyond her ability to harness the energies of the dark side. For the past decade she had been focused only on learning to control her own power. Over that same time, her Master had begun to assemble the pieces that would one day allow the Sith to rise up and rule the galaxy.

He'd created a vast network of spies and informants, but Zannah had no idea as to its true extent, or even how to contact them. He had put into motion a hundred long-range plans to slowly build their strength while weakening the Republic. Yet she was only just now beginning to understand the scope and complexity of his political machinations.

Bane was a visionary, able to see far into the future. He understood how to exploit the weaknesses and vulnerabilities of the Republic. He knew how to draw the eyes of the Jedi away from the dark side, while at the same time leading them down the first steps of the long road that would end in their complete annihilation. He could manipulate people, organizations, and governments, planting seeds that would lay dormant for years—even decades—before they burst forth.

If he died now, everything he had put into place over the last ten years died with him. Zannah would have to start at the beginning. She would have to find and train an apprentice, even as she was still learning the full extent of her own abilities. She would be stumbling blindly forward, beset by enemies on all sides. It was almost impossible to imagine she wouldn't make a mistake that would lead to her downfall . . . and the extinction of the Sith.

She couldn't allow that to happen. For the sake of their order, she had to keep him alive. And though Darovit might not have the knowledge and power to heal her Master, she knew someone who did. Someone who had saved his life once before.

"Make sure he lives," she said to Darovit, an implied threat in her tone.

Leaving the medical bay, she marched to the cockpit and sat down behind the controls. She punched in a course for Ambria, but she wasn't heading back to their camp. She was going to see a man called Caleb.

THOUGH CALEB'S CAMP was less than a hundred kilometers from their own on Ambria, Zannah had never met him. She knew him only from the tales of her Master. Bane had told her the healer was strong in the Force, but he didn't draw on it the same way the Sith or Jedi did. Light side and dark side had no meaning for him; his was the power of nature.

Her Master's words hadn't made sense at the time, but as they came in to land near the tiny, dilapidated shack Caleb called home, she began to understand. There was power in this place; it called to her, but in a strange and unfamiliar language.

She could smell it in the air when the cargo doors of their ship opened, and she could feel it beneath her feet when she jumped down from the ship. With each step she took, the ground seemed to vibrate, humming with a sound too quiet to hear, but deep enough that she could feel it in the back of her teeth.

Darovit walked behind her, manipulating the controls that guided the *Loranda*'s medical gurney. It floated along beside him, supporting Bane's still-unconscious form. As he had been when Zannah brought him forth from Belia's stronghold, her Master was once again being unceremoniously transported like cargo hovering a meter above the ground. This time, however, he was supported by repulsorlifts rather than the Force.

"This place is amazing," Darovit breathed. "I've never felt anything like this before. So . . . raw."

Zannah recalled that, even though he lacked the power of the Jedi or Sith, her cousin was also attuned to the Force. She briefly wondered if it was possible that he shared the same type of talent as Caleb, then decided it made no difference why she was here. Four days had passed since they'd left Tython, and Bane had grown steadily weaker. If they didn't find help for him here, her Master would die.

Judging from her first glance, she didn't hold out much hope for his salvation. As was common on Ambria, they were surrounded on all sides by a desolate, arid wasteland stretching out as far as the eye could see. The only features of the landscape, other than a few scattered rock outcroppings, were Caleb's shack and fire pit. The camp appeared to be deserted.

The shack was small, a few meters on each side. The walls were angled at forty-five degrees, meeting at a peak in the center, making the structure resemble a crudely built pyramid. Where or how Caleb had acquired the wood was impossible to say, but it was obvious he hadn't replaced it anytime recently. The timber was faded and bleached by years in the sun, and though it wouldn't rot in Ambria's dry climate, hundreds of long vertical cracks had formed in the grain as the moisture was leached away. On the wall facing the fire pit was a small doorway leading into the hut. A tattered blanket hung down across it, fluttering slightly in the desert wind.

The fire pit was nothing more than a small circle of round stones, scorched and blackened from years of smoke and flame. A metal stand supported a large iron pot over the center of the circle for cooking, though the pot was empty and the fire was cold.

Zannah remembered from Bane's tale how Caleb had plunged his own hand into the pot when it was filled with boiling soup, scalding himself to prove to her Master he feared no pain and couldn't be threatened or intimidated.

Ten years ago the healer had initially refused to heal her Master, though ultimately Bane had compelled him by threatening the life of Caleb's daughter. Zannah wondered if, should they find him, he would refuse to help Bane again.

"Hello?" Darovit called out, his voice sounding small in the emptiness all around them. "Hello?"

Zannah moved slowly to the ramshackle hut and drew back the blanket in the door. The only thing inside was a small sleeping mat in the corner. She stepped back from the door, peering out at the empty wastelands around the camp to see if there was anywhere else Caleb might have gone. Darovit mimicked her actions, then offered up the only logical conclusion.

"Nobody's here."

It wasn't just Caleb that was missing, Zannah had to admit. Where were the medicines the healer would use to cure those who sought his aid? Where were the basic supplies—food, water, fuel for the fire—he would need to survive?

She recalled that Caleb had come to Ambria to escape the war between the Jedi and the Sith. Unfortunately for him, the war had eventually followed him even to this remote world. Yet the healer had maintained a steadfast neutrality during the conflict, refusing to aid followers of either the dark side or the light;

only Bane had successfully compelled him to make an exception to his rule. Maybe with the end of the war, he had renounced his solitary ways and returned to the world of his birth, reintegrating himself into galactic society. It was just one of several possibilities that would explain his disappearance.

He could have died. It had been ten years since Bane had visited the camp, and though Caleb couldn't be that old, it was possible something had happened to him in the ensuing decade. Ambria could be a harsh and dangerous world; the healer might have been slain and devoured by the hssiss, the fearsome carnivorous lizards that sometimes emerged from the depths of Lake Natth to feed.

The planet had its share of sentient predators, too. The handful of people who still lived on the world survived by picking through the remains of the battles that had once raged over its surface and in the skies above, finding damaged items and old technology they could restore and sell offworld. Most of the junkers, as they were called, were simple folk just trying to get by. But a few had become desperate criminals, willing to kill over anything of value—like Caleb's missing collection of medicine and supplies.

Or maybe the healer had fallen victim to some disease or affliction even he couldn't cure. If he had died of natural causes, it wouldn't take long until the various desert scavengers carried off the last of his remains, leaving behind no evidence of what had happened.

It was clear there was no help to be found here, but there was no point in going anywhere else. Bane had a day, at most, before the orbalisk toxins reached lethal levels in the tissues of his body. Zannah simply stood there, unable to even think what she should do next. And then she remembered another detail from her Master's tale.

Caleb had tried to conceal his daughter from Bane. Her Master had easily discovered her cowering inside the shack; there was no other place to hide in the small camp. At least, there hadn't been ten years ago.

"Wait here," she said to Darovit, leaving him to watch over Bane on his gurney.

She went back into the shack, kicking the sleeping mat aside to reveal a small trapdoor in the floor. She used the Force to fling it open, and was rewarded with the sight of a man staring up at her from a small cellar.

His expression wasn't one of fear, nor even anger. Not exactly. He looked more like he was weary; as if he knew his discovery was going to lead to a long and tedious exchange.

"Out," Zannah said, stepping back and dropping her hand to the handle of her lightsaber.

Without a word, he climbed up the cellar's small ladder until he stood beside her inside the shack. He looked to be in his late forties, a thin man of average height. He had straight black hair that hung down to his shoulders, and his skin was brown and leathery from a decade of exposure to Ambria's burning sun. There was nothing about his appearance to suggest he was a man of power or importance, yet Zannah could sense his calm inner strength.

"Do you know who I am?" she asked him.

"I've known ever since you and your Master built your camp on this world," he said quietly.

"And you know why I'm here?"

"I sensed you coming. That was why I hid."

She peeked down into the cellar, noting that it contained a number of small shelves lined with bottles, bags, jars, and pouches that held the medicines and healing compounds he used in his vocation. There were also a number of ration kits piled in one corner, along with a handful of small, square supply containers.

"When did you build that?" she asked, curious.

"Shortly after my previous encounter with your Master," he answered. "I feared he would one day come back, and I wanted a place for my daughter to hide."

The man suddenly smiled at her, though there was no joy or mirth in the expression.

"But now my daughter has grown," he told her. "She has left this world, never to return. And you have no power over me."

"Are you saying you will not help my Master?" Zannah asked, not even bothering to put a threat into her voice.

"There is nothing you can do to compel me this time," he replied, and she sensed a deep satisfaction in his tone. She realized he had been preparing for this day for over ten years.

"The war between the Jedi and Sith is over," Zannah told him. "My Master is no longer a soldier. He is just an ordinary man who needs your help."

The man smiled again, flashing his teeth in a feral grin. "Your Master will never be ordinary. Though soon enough he will be dead."

One glance down at the man's hand, permanently scarred by the burns he had given himself plunging it into the boiling soup, made Zannah dismiss any ideas of using torture to change his mind. And she knew that any attempt to dominate his mind with the Force would fail; his will was too strong for her to bend it to her needs.

"I can give you credits. You'll be richer than you can possibly imagine."

He waved his hands around at the austere little shack. "What use are credits to a man like me?"

"What about your daughter?" Zannah countered. "Think of how much easier her life could be."

"Even if I wanted to let my child take your blood payment, I could never find a way to get it to her. For her own protection, I insisted she change her name when she left this world. I do not know what she is called now; I do not know where she has gone."

Zannah chewed her lip, then tried something desperate.

"If you do not help my Master I will hunt your daughter down. I will find her, torture her, and kill her," she vowed, carefully hitting each word for emphasis. "But first I will make her watch as I torture and kill every other person she cares about."

Caleb smirked, amused at her empty threat. "Go, then. Seek her out and leave me alone. We both know you will never find her."

Again, he had her. With no name and not even a physical description, it would be impossible to track down one woman who could be on any of a million Republic worlds.

Scowling, Zannah glanced once more down at his scarred hand. It stood as mute testament to the fact she couldn't break him through raw physical pain, no matter how brutal. But with no other options left, she decided to try anyway.

She reached out with the Force and picked Caleb up. His feet dangled only a few centimeters off the floor, yet his head brushed against the shack's low, slanted roof. She began to squeeze, applying pressure directly to his internal organs, slowly crushing them as she inflicted an agonizing pain few beings had ever experienced. She was careful to leave his lungs alone, however—allowing him enough air to breath and speak.

"You know how to make this end," she said coldly. "Say you will heal my Master."

He grunted and gasped in pain, but shook his head.

"Zannah! What are you doing?"

Darovit had come into the shack, curious as to what was taking her so long. Now he stood in the doorway, staring in horror at the scene.

"Stop it!" he shouted at her. "You're killing him! Put him down!"

With a sharp growl of frustration she released her grip, letting Caleb fall to the floor. Darovit rushed to his side to see if he was okay, but the older man shook his head and waved him away. He rose to his hands and knees, then settled back onto his heels, his hands resting on his thighs as he took slow, deep breaths.

Darovit turned on her. "What did you do that for?" he demanded angrily.

"He refused to help us," she said, her voice more defensive than she meant it to be.

"I will not release that monster on the galaxy a second time," Caleb declared, his teeth still clenched against the lingering effects of Zannah's torture. "There is nothing you can do to make me save him."

Zannah dropped to one knee beside him. "I can use my powers to conjure up your worst nightmares and bring them to life before your eyes," she whispered. "I can drive you mad with fear, shred your sanity, and leave you a raving lunatic for the rest of your life."

Darovit just stared at her, shocked by her words. Caleb only smiled his infuriating smile.

"If you do," the healer calmly replied, "your Master will still die."

Zannah chewed her lip, glaring at him. Then she leapt to her feet and stormed out of the cabin, leaving Darovit and Caleb alone.

23

Fuming, Zannah stomped her way across the sand between Caleb's shack and the edge of the camp, where her Master lay on the hover gurney.

She checked the monitor attached to the gurney's side, getting a reading of his vitals. He was still alive, but fading fast. Soon he would be gone, taking all his knowledge and secrets with him.

She was standing over the gurney when Darovit emerged from the shack several minutes later. He crossed the camp to stand beside her, gazing down at Bane.

"When he goes," he said, offering his cousin words of condolence, "at least he'll go peacefully."

"Peace is a lie!" Zannah snarled back. "It doesn't matter if you die in your sleep or on the battlefield, dead is still dead."

"At least he's not feeling any pain," Darovit replied, tossing out another meaningless platitude.

"If you feel pain," she answered, "it means you're still alive. Give me pain over peace any day."

"I never thought I'd hear you say that, Zannah," Darovit said sadly, shaking his head. "Can't you see what he's made you become?"

He made me become a Sith, she thought. Out loud she said, "He made me strong. He gave me power."

"Is that all you care about now, Zannah? Power?"

"Through power I gain victory, and through victory my chains are broken."

"Power doesn't always bring victory," Darovit countered. "Even with all the power you have, you couldn't make Caleb help you."

Bane would have found a way, she thought bitterly, but didn't say anything.

"I understand what happened to you," her cousin said, placing a comforting hand on her shoulder. "You were just a kid. Scared. Alone. Bane found you and took you in. I understand your loyalty to him. I understand why you care about him."

Zannah shook his hand off and turned to stare at him with an expression of wide-eyed disbelief. "I'm a Sith. I don't care about anyone but myself."

"You care about me."

Zannah didn't reply, refusing to be drawn again into the same argument they'd had on the way to Tython.

"You don't want to admit it," Darovit pressed, "but I know you care about me. And about your Master, too. Your actions prove that, no matter what you say. But Caleb's right, you know. Bane's a monster; we can't let him go free.

"But he doesn't necessarily have to die," he added.

"What do you mean?" Zannah said, suddenly wary.

"I spoke with Caleb. He thinks you're a monster, too. But he doesn't know you like I do. You're not a monster, Zannah . . . but you'll become one if you let anger and hate rule your life."

"Now you sound like the Jedi," she said carefully. Darovit was clearly up to something, but she couldn't figure out what it was.

"I'm starting to realize they're better than the alternative," he admitted. "I know what's going to happen, Zannah. If Bane dies, you'll kill Caleb."

She hesitated, then nodded. "Probably." There was no point in lying.

"You're balanced on the precipice," her cousin warned her, his voice suddenly urgent and intense. "You can still turn back from this life, Zannah. But if Bane dies, I know your desire to avenge him will drive you to murder Caleb. And I'm afraid your Master's death will push you over the edge. It'll turn you into him.

"I don't *want* you to turn into him," he added more softly, nodding down at Bane's motionless form on the gurney. "I have to save you from yourself. I had to find some way to stop you from killing Caleb. So I convinced him to heal Bane. It's the only way to make you turn away from the teachings of the Sith."

"That . . . that makes no sense," Zannah said, her mind reeling as she tried to wrap her head around his logic. "If Bane lives he'll never let me abandon my studies." *And why would I even want to?* she added silently.

"Before Caleb will help," her cousin explained, "you have to dispatch one of the *Loranda*'s message drones. You have to tell the Jedi where we are so they can come and arrest Bane."

"What?" Zannah shouted, taking a half step away from him. "That's crazy!"

"No, it's not!" he said, grabbing her by the arm with his good hand and pulling her back to face him. "Please, Zannah, just listen to me. If you send that message to the Jedi and hand Bane over to them, it will prove you're turning your back on the ways of the Sith. It will show you want to make up for all the pain and suffering you've caused.

"And it's the only way Caleb will agree to heal him," he added a second later, letting go of her arm.

"You saw what Bane can do," she said. "What's to stop him from killing the Jedi when they get here?"

"The orbalisk toxin is melting Bane's body from the inside. Even with Caleb's help it will be weeks, maybe months, before he can even get out of bed."

"So what's to stop me from just taking Bane away as soon as he's healed?"

"Your greatest weapon is secrecy. The Jedi think your Order is extinct. They won't waste their time chasing shadows every time someone whispers the word *Sith*. That's the only reason you've been able to survive so far.

"But once you send off the message drone, everything changes. They'll know the Sith still exist. They'll have the proof they need to drive them to action. Every Jedi Knight and Jedi Master across a million worlds will be searching for you. The Sith won't be able to hide anymore."

Zannah knew he was right. It was the very reason Bane had worked so hard to keep their existence nothing more than an unfounded rumor.

"Besides," Darovit added, "Caleb won't do anything unless we disable the ship first. If you try to run, you'll have to drag Bane out into the desert on foot. Even if he survived the trip, you wouldn't get very far before the Jedi arrived."

"Sounds like the healer doesn't trust me," Zannah mumbled darkly.

"You did almost kill him," her cousin pointed out.

"If I hand him over to the Jedi," she wondered aloud, "what happens to me?"

"I don't know," the young man admitted. "The Jedi might arrest you, too. But I'm hoping they'll recognize your actions as a turning point in your life. Maybe they'll see it as an attempt to make amends.

"Maybe they'll even take you in," he suggested. "I've heard the Jedi believe in the power of redemption. And, like I said, it's better than the alternative."

"What about you?" she asked. "What will you do?"

"I won't be part of this if you choose to kill Caleb and let Bane die," he told her. "But I don't think you will."

"How can you be so sure?"

"I've told you, Zannah—we share a bond. I can tell what you're thinking, what you're feeling. You're afraid of being alone . . . but you're *not* alone. Not anymore.

"You'll make the right choice. And when you do, I'll be there for you."

She weighed the offer carefully, chewing on her lip so hard her teeth drew blood. If she refused, Bane was dead and she'd have to continue the Sith Order on her own. Kill Caleb, find an apprentice . . . probably kill Darovit, too. If she agreed, she had to betray her Master to the Jedi, which would mark the end of the Sith and the first step in her long road of redemption and atonement.

"Bane's time is running out," her cousin prodded. "You have to decide."

The two paths loomed large before her: alone into the darkness, or into the light with Darovit at her side. She spun the problem over and over in her mind until, finally, the answer came to her.

"Tell Caleb I agree to his demands."

BANE OPENED HIS EYES SLOWLY; his lids felt heavy, weighed down as if they were lined with metal filings. He could feel them brushing over his pupils, rubbing like sandpaper as he blinked against the harsh light streaming down on him. The brightness made him squint again as he tried to sit up.

His body refused to move. Legs, arms, and torso ignored the impulses from his brain to rise. Even his head couldn't budge. There was sensation in his extremities: He could tell he was lying on his back, and he could feel the rough grain of a burlap sheet or a coarsely woven cloth against his skin. But he was paralyzed, unable to move.

He let his eyes flicker open once more, and the brightness began to fade as his pupils gradually contracted. He was staring up at a low, sloping ceiling of simple wooden planks. A ray of sunlight beamed through a narrow crack in the wood, shining directly on his face.

Groaning, he managed to turn his head to the side so the light no longer hit his eyes. The change of angle also gave him a better view of the room he was in: small, plain, and strangely familiar. Before he could match the setting to any of his memories, a figure stepped into his line of sight.

From the fact that he was staring directly into a pair of worn leather boots, Bane deduced that he was lying on the floor. The figure stood over him for a moment, then crouched down to look him in the eye.

The face—ten years older, but unmistakable—jogged the Dark Lord's memory. He had lain on this very floor over a decade earlier on the border between life and death, even as he lay now.

Caleb, he tried to say, but the only sound that came out was a soft groan. Like the rest of his body, his lips, tongue, and jaw refused to move. Bane tried to call upon the power of the dark side to grant him strength, but his will was as weak and helpless as the rest of him.

"He's awake," Caleb called out loudly, never taking his eyes off his patient.

From outside Bane heard the sound of approaching footsteps. He tried to speak again, pouring all his strength into a single word.

"Caleb."

His voice was a faint whisper, but this time the word was clear. The healer didn't bother to respond. Instead he stood up, leaving Bane staring at his boots once more. Bane heard the dull thud of running footsteps on the sand outside change to the sharp clack of boot heels on the shack's wooden floor.

"Let me see him!"

He recognized the voice of his apprentice, and his mind slowly began to reassemble the pieces of what had happened. He remembered the battle with the Jedi on Tython; he remembered unleashing a storm of Force lightning at the last of his foes. He remembered the kriffing shield the Ithorian Master had thrown up around him. After that, all his memories were of unbearable pain.

Somehow the Jedi's barrier had trapped Bane inside the center of the dark side storm. The electricity had enveloped him, millions of volts arcing through his body, cooking his flesh from the inside and throwing his muscles into an endless series of violent seizures that threatened to rip his body apart.

The energy had coursed through the orbalisks embedded in his skin, too. The creatures absorbed the power, hungrily devouring it until they became so engorged that the soft, pliant flesh of their underbellies had begun to swell. Squeezed ever tighter against the unyielding chitin of their own exterior shells, they'd begun to burrow deeper into Bane. He remembered screaming as thousands of tiny teeth started sawing away at subcutaneous tissue, chewing through muscles, tendons, and even bone.

But burrowing deeper hadn't stopped the creatures from feasting on the electricity coursing through Bane's frying innards. They'd continued to expand until they had begun to pop, rupturing like overfilled balloons pinched beneath the hard shells.

Bane had stayed conscious through the torture of the electricity cooking him alive and the agony of the teeth burrowing into his flesh. But the indescribable pain from the chemicals released by the exploding orbalisks dissolving his body on a cellular level finally caused him to black out . . . only to wake up here.

A pair of boots stepped in beside Caleb's: the smaller feet of a woman, most likely Zannah.

"He's trying to speak," Caleb said from up above Bane's line of sight.

He tried to tilt his head again, this time managing to look up toward the pair standing over him. Zannah noticed and crouched down to raise his head and shoulders. She slid a makeshift pillow formed by her balled-up cloak underneath his neck to support him. He felt her long, thin fingers on his back as she did so.

The contact brought a realization crashing down on Bane— the orbalisks were gone! That was why he had felt the coarse blankets against his bare skin. That was why he could feel Zannah's fingers pressing against his flesh.

"Orbalisks?" he managed to gasp.

"We had to remove them," his apprentice informed him. "They were killing you."

Bane felt the world going dim again, his body exhausted by the two words he had spoken. As he lost consciousness, he felt a pang of regret for what he had lost.

To ZANNAH'S UNTRAINED EYE, her Master looked much stronger when he opened his eyes again two days later. This time he was able to turn his head slowly from side to side, taking in the surroundings of Caleb's home and the nearby presence of his apprentice.

"What happened?" he asked.

The words were faint, his voice still raw and ragged.

"Caleb healed you," she told him, adjusting the pillow she had taken from the *Loranda* and placed under his head and shoulders to prop him up. "He saved your life."

Four days ago such a statement would have been hard to imagine. Caleb had watched Zannah program the message drone and send it off to the Jedi, then warned her there was a strong chance Bane wouldn't survive the treatment.

She'd thought at first it might be a ploy, an excuse Caleb was giving to cover up his actions if he decided to let her Master die . . . or simply killed him. So she'd kept a close eye on the healer during Bane's treatment. Even though she knew there were a hundred ways he could end Bane's life without her having any clue as to what he was doing, Zannah hoped her presence might dissuade him from trying anything underhanded.

Now she realized how pointless her vigil had been. Caleb

was a man of his word; he was burdened and bound by foolish notions like honor. He had promised to help Bane as long as she alerted the Jedi, and since she had held up her end of the bargain, he had made every effort to do the same.

Zannah had originally suggested moving Bane back to the *Loranda*'s medical bay for the treatments, but Caleb had refused. He'd claimed the powerful energies coursing through the land around his camp gave strength to his medicine. Darovit had agreed, and Zannah, having felt the power of the place herself, had relented.

The healer had started by forcing a foul-smelling liquid he had concocted in his cooking pot down Bane's throat to counter the effects of the orbalisk toxins. Darovit had warned her that the poison was killing Bane, eating away at his body. But it was only when they began to peel away the orbalisks, beginning with the charred shells of those that had died, that Zannah understood the full scope of how badly her Master had suffered.

What lay beneath could no longer be called skin; it couldn't even be properly called flesh. A pulpy mass of green and black ichors released by the parasitic organisms mixed with oozing white pus and bloody red tissue from Bane's own body. Looking at the damage it was obvious, even to someone like Zannah, with no medical expertise, that the only thing keeping Bane alive was his power in the Force. His wounds gave off the gangrenous odor of spoiled meat, and it was all she could do not to vomit.

The next step involved removing the still-living orbalisks. The key, as Zannah had suspected, was electricity. Caleb had brewed a sticky, highly conductive gel over his fire, then used it to coat the exterior shell of each orbalisk. Next he took a long, thin needle attached to a power cell salvaged from the *Loranda* and inserted it into a tiny hole at the very tip of the orbalisk's plated skull. The needle pierced the soft body underneath, discharging a powerful electrical jolt to stun the creature.

This caused the orbalisk to release a small burst of solvent chemicals that weakened the powerful adhesive the creature used to bond itself to the host. With the adhesive bond weakened, the creature could be manually pried loose. The still-stunned parasites were then tossed into a large, water-filled tank hooked up to one of the *Loranda*'s power cells and killed with a final dose of electricity. The process had to be carefully repeated for each individual in the colony that had sprouted over Bane's body, and even with both Darovit and Caleb working on him the procedure had taken several hours.

The flesh beneath the living orbalisks was pale and ragged, with deep, weeping sores where it had been constantly chewed and gnawed by the parasites' tiny teeth. The wounds looked minor when compared with the grisly mess beneath the dead shells.

Once Bane was cleansed of the infestation, Caleb had rubbed a salve over his entire body and wrapped him head-to-toe in bandages. The dressings had been changed every four hours for the first two days, the salve reapplied each time.

Zannah was impressed with Caleb's skill. Bane had been little more than a mass of dead and infected tissue when the healer had begun, and by the time the bandages came off for good Bane's ravaged body had been reborn. His skin was now a bright pink, unusually supple and extremely sensitive, though over the coming weeks she'd been told it would slowly return to a more normal color and texture.

"Caleb saved me?" Bane muttered softly. "How did you convince him?"

Zannah hesitated, not sure what to tell him. Darovit and Caleb were just outside the door; they could walk in at any moment. But even if they caught her telling Bane about the message drone, why would they care? The deed was done. Her Master was still too weak to stand, and by now the Jedi were probably less than a day away from Ambria.

"We had to tell the Jedi you were here. I sent a message telling them a Sith Lord had killed five Jedi on Tython. I told them you were with Caleb on Ambria, injured and helpless. They're coming for you."

Anger flashed through Bane's eyes and he tried to sit up, but only managed to raise his head a few centimeters off the pillow before falling back. Realizing he was helpless, her Master stared at her with accusing eyes.

"You exposed me," he said. "You betrayed me."

"I had to keep you alive," she explained, falling back on the argument she had used to make her final decision. "You still have so much to teach me."

"How can that happen now?" he demanded angrily. "The Jedi will never allow it."

Zannah didn't have an answer she could give him. Bane closed his eyes, though whether in defeat or thought she couldn't say. She could just make out Darovit and Caleb talking in low voices outside by the fire.

Bane's eyes opened a few seconds later, burning with a fierce intensity.

"Darth Zannah, you are my apprentice. The heir to my legacy. You can still claim the destiny that is yours by right. You can still ascend to the rank of Sith Master."

He was speaking louder now, his strength slowly returning. Zannah wondered if the men outside could hear him.

"Take your lightsaber and strike me down! Claim my title as your own. Slay the others and flee this place before the Jedi arrive. Seek out a new apprentice. Keep our Order alive."

Zannah shook her head. Caleb had already considered that possibility, and effectively eliminated it. "Our ship is disabled, and the Jedi will be here in a matter of hours. Even if I flee into the desert, they will find me before I can escape this world."

"I never thought you would fail me so utterly," Bane told her, turning his head away from her in disgust. "I never thought you would be the one to destroy the Sith."

She didn't say anything in her defense, and a few seconds later Bane turned back to face her once more, casting his eyes to the lightsaber on her belt.

"I don't want to live as a prisoner to the Jedi," he said, his voice low, as if he now knew there were others who might over-hear. "You can end this before they arrive."

Zannah shook her head. She hadn't gone to all the trouble of saving her Master's life just to kill him now. "While you live there is still hope, Bane," she said quietly, worried what Daro-vit or Caleb would think if they heard her words. Yet she had to offer some type of reassurance to her Master. "The Sith may yet rise again."

Bane shook his head, though it took a monumental effort. "The Jedi will never allow me to escape. They will sense my power, and keep me under the constant guard of a dozen Jedi Knights until the Senate decides to execute me for my crimes. Kill me now and deny them their justice."

Zannah had spent the past two days by Bane's side, waiting for him to wake again. It had been clear he would live, but she'd wanted to speak with her Master to be certain his mind was still intact. She'd wanted proof that all his faculties—his intelligence, his cunning—had survived his ordeal. She had it now, ironically expressed in his desire to die.

"A Sith never surrenders, Master," she told him.

"And only a fool fights a battle that cannot possibly be won," he answered sharply. "The Jedi will be here soon. Act now. Strike me down!"

She shook her head. Her Master tried to rise, his fury giving him the strength to sit halfway up. And then he collapsed back onto the pillow, utterly exhausted.

As her Master slipped once more into unconsciousness, Zannah realized he was right. The Jedi were coming, and if she didn't act now it would be too late. She stood up and drew her lightsaber, knowing the hum of its blade would alert the two men outside. She didn't care. By the time they realized what she was doing it would be too late.

24

THE *LIGHT OF TRUTH*, one of the many Jedi cruisers that had been incorporated into the Republic fleet after the Ruusan Reformations, landed with a soft thump on Ambria's desolate surface.

"Be ready for anything," Master Tho'natu warned his team as they prepared to disembark.

Back before he achieved the rank of Master, the Twi'lek had served as a Jedi Knight in the Army of Light on Ruusan. He had been assigned to Farfalla's ship, luckily in time to avoid the effects of the thought bomb, but not before he'd had ample opportunity on Ruusan to witness first-hand the kind of atrocities the Sith were capable of. He wasn't about to take any chances here.

They'd been dispatched in response to a message drone that had arrived on Coruscant a few days before. The anonymous message inside had been cryptically short, and somewhat disquieting in its lack of detail. It contained only a set of landing coordinates and four brief lines of text.

A Sith Lord still lives. He killed five Jedi on Tython. He is now on Ambria, under the care of a healer named Caleb. He is badly injured and helpless.

Less than two weeks ago Master Farfalla and four companions had hastily taken off from Coruscant, leaving behind word they were heading to Tython in pursuit of a Dark Lord of the Sith. They hadn't been heard from since. The message drone offered a grim explanation of their fate, and it drew an immediate response from the Jedi Council.

They'd quickly assembled a team of fourteen Jedi, six Masters and eight Jedi Knights, and sent them to Ambria under Tho'natu's command to apprehend the man responsible for the massacre of Master Farfalla and his companions. The journey had been made with all possible haste, but now that they were here they intended to proceed with caution, wary of walking into a trap.

The landing coordinates had set them down a few hundred meters from a small wooden hut and a tiny campfire. A cruiser with the name LORANDA emblazoned on its side was parked nearby.

The landing bay doors opened, and Tho'natu and the others leapt to the ground, ready to draw their lightsabers at the first sign of trouble. The air around them trembled with a strange and unfamiliar sensation of power, though beneath was the unmistakable taint of the dark side.

"First and second units, go check out that ship," he said. "Third unit explores the camp with me."

Nine Jedi rushed off toward the *Loranda*, while Tho'natu and the others approached the camp. What they saw as they drew nearer filled them with revulsion: Someone had been literally chopped to pieces.

Eviscerated chunks of human anatomy littered the ground around the campfire. Arms had been hewn off at the shoulder, then sliced again at the elbows and wrist. The same had been done to the lower limbs, dismembered into feet, legs, and thighs. Even the torso had been carved into quarters. The clean, cauterized cuts left no doubt the butcher's weapon of choice had been a lightsaber.

Only the head remained whole, placed like a trophy atop an upside-down cooking pot resting on the ground. A human male with long, black hair, he appeared to have been forty or fifty years of age. His features were twisted in a gruesome mask of pain and terror; Tho'natu wondered how many of the wounds had been inflicted while he was still alive.

"What kind of madness could make someone do this?" one of the others asked, but Master Tho'natu had no answer.

At a nod from their commander, the Jedi ignited their weapons. They crept toward the small shack, their commander in the lead. As a unit, they stopped when he heard a soft sound coming from inside the building: hard ragged breaths broken by trembling sobs and whimpers of fear.

A tattered blanket hung down across the building's open doorway, obscuring their view. The Twi'lek reached out with the Force to try to sense whoever was hiding inside, but something—likely the strange, underlying power of the campsite itself—blurred his awareness.

"I am Master Tho'natu of the Jedi," he called out, flicking off his lightsaber's blade. "We're here to help you."

A scream of incoherent rage erupted from the shack. A young man burst from the doorway, brandishing a golden lightsaber above his head in his left hand. His right hand was nothing but a stump, and there was a crazed gleam in his eye.

"No!" he shrieked as he charged at them, flailing wildly with his weapon. "You'll never get me! No! No! No!"

Master Tho'natu ignited his blade as the man fell on him with the fury of madness, his cries turning to mindless, beastly howls. The rest of his team reacted on instinct, leaping to their commander's defense. The battle lasted less than three seconds, the raving young man cut down by a swarm of Jedi lightsabers.

When it was over, the Jedi took up defensive positions facing the shack, weapons poised as they braced themselves for another potential attack. For several seconds nothing happened, and there were no further sounds of life from inside. Motioning for the others to stay back, Tho'natu crept forward and pulled aside the blanket covering the doorway.

The room beyond was empty except for five lightsaber handles lying beside the door. The Jedi Master stepped inside the small building, his keen mind quickly piecing together what must have happened.

He recalled that Farfalla had used a golden blade, just like the one the man had attacked them with. The lightsabers here were trophies, taken from those who had died on Tython by their killer. The man outside was young, but the Jedi were taught that the dark side led to quick and easy power—power enough to kill Farfalla and the others, especially if they'd been led into some type of trap. The Sith had slain the Jedi and claimed their weapons, though he must have suffered grievous injuries in the battle, including the loss of his hand.

He had probably tried to call on the power of the dark side to heal himself. But the Jedi Master knew the dark side couldn't heal; it only caused harm. The misguided attempt was likely what damaged the young man's mind. Wounded and half mad, he had come to Ambria to seek aid from the healer. By the time he arrived at this place he would have been near death, and completely helpless.

That's when Caleb must have dispatched the message drone to warn the Jedi.

A Sith Lord still lives. He killed five Jedi on Tython. He is now on Ambria, under the care of a healer named Caleb. He is badly injured and helpless.

He must have sensed who and what the young man was as he healed his horrific injuries. But Caleb had underestimated the Sith Lord's power—and the degenerating state of his madness. Before the Jedi could arrive, the Sith had recovered enough to torture and kill Caleb for exposing him. The healer's prolonged and visceral death must have further fueled the young man's psychosis, reducing him to the raving creature that had lunged at them from the hut.

All the pieces fit. It all made sense.

"Master," one of the other Jedi said, peeking in through the door. "The rest of the camp is deserted."

"What about the ship? The *Loranda*?"

"Nobody on board," he reported. "It looks like somebody sabotaged her before we got here."

Probably Caleb, Tho'natu realized. He wanted to make sure the Sith couldn't escape. If the young man had found out, that could explain the brutality of Caleb's death.

"It would probably only take two or three days to make the repairs," the Jedi informed him.

"Leave it for the junkers," the Twi'lek said with a shake of his head. There were only two things he wanted to bring back from this accursed place. "Collect the healer's remains. We'll give him a proper burial on Coruscant."

The man nodded and scurried off to relay his orders.

Master Tho'natu bent over and gathered up the lightsabers of his fallen comrades from Tython, so they could be given a place of honor in the Temple. The loss of Farfalla and his companions was a terrible tragedy, as was what had happened here. But at least he could go back to the Jedi Council and tell them with absolute certainty that the last of the Sith Lords had died on Ambria.

He exited the small shack and headed back to his ship, knowing that the memories of the gruesome massacre on Ambria would haunt him for the rest of his life. He never thought to examine the small sleeping mat in the corner. He never noticed the trapdoor built into the floor beneath it. And he never sensed the apprentice and her unconscious Master, masked by Sith sorcery, hiding silently in the cellar just below his feet.

EPILOGUE

I T TOOK ZANNAH three days to make the repairs to the *Lo-randa*. She'd loaded Bane into the ship and hooked him up to the bacta pump so he could continue to recuperate while she worked, sedating him to accelerate the healing process. Now that their vessel was ready to leave Ambria, she went in to check on her Master one last time.

He was still unconscious, lying on his back on the gurney as she had left him. She stepped forward to check his vitals and his eyes flew open, burning with rage. His hand snapped out and seized her wrist, clenching it with the strength of an iron claw.

"Where are the Jedi?" he asked in a fierce whisper, fixing her with a look of pure hatred as he lifted himself up onto one elbow. His grip on her wrist tightened, making her wince.

"They're gone," she said, trying to stay calm. "They've gone back to Coruscant."

She could feel Bane's power—whole once more—coursing through his veins. She could feel the heat of his anger, and she knew one wrong word and he'd snap her neck in two with the Force.

"Why?" he growled.

"They think they killed the Dark Lord on Ambria," she replied. "They think the Sith are extinct."

Bane tilted his head to the side, curious. "Caleb?"

"I killed him."

"Your cousin?

"Dead. Killed by the Jedi."

An unwanted vision of the pitiful creature she had turned Darovit into flashed through her mind. She remembered him huddled in the corner, quivering in terror. He clutched the handle of a lightsaber against his chest, his only defense against the horrors and nightmares he saw crawling toward him from every corner. She swept the memory away with a quick shake of her head.

Bane released his hold and lay back in his bed, his anger fading.

"You have done well, Zannah," he said, his ever-cunning mind filling in the blanks enough for him to surmise what she had done. She smiled at the compliment.

"I underestimated you," he continued. "Had I known your plans, I would never have asked you to kill me."

"You still have much to teach me," Zannah reminded him. "I will continue to study at your feet, Master. I will learn from your wisdom. I will discover your secrets, unlocking them one by one until everything you know—all your knowledge and all your power—is mine. And once you are no longer of use to me, I will destroy you."

Bane raised an eyebrow at her words, and she could tell he approved. Her ambition was good; it would give her power. Her talents and abilities would continue to grow. In time, she would challenge her Master for the right to rule, and only the stronger would survive. It was inevitable. It was the way of the Sith.

"One day I will surpass you," Zannah warned him. "And on that day I *will* kill you, Lord Bane. But that day is not today."

ACKNOWLEDGMENTS

This book came together in the space of only six months—an unbelievably short time to transform an idea into a finished work on the shelves. I'd like to thank everyone at Lucas Licensing Ltd. and Del Rey Books who was part of this incredible accomplishment, along with a special thanks to my wife, Jennifer. Without her help and understanding I don't think this would have been possible given the deadlines I was working under. But most of all, I'd like to thank all the fans who bought *Darth Bane: Path of Destruction*. Without your support, this sequel never would have happened. You have my sincere and humble gratitude.

Read on for an excerpt from

DARTH BANE: DYNASTY OF EVIL

BY DREW KARPYSHYN

PROLOGUE

DARTH BANE, THE REIGNING Dark Lord of the Sith, kicked the covers from his bed and swung his feet over the edge, resting them on the cold marble floor. He tilted his head from side to side, straining to work out the knots in his heavily muscled neck and shoulders.

He finally rose with an audible grunt. Taking a deep breath, he exhaled slowly, reaching his arms up high above his head as he stretched to his full two-meter height. He could feel the sharp *pop-pop-pop* of each individual vertebra along his spine loosening as he extended himself until his fingertips brushed against the ceiling.

Satisfied, he lowered his arms and scooped up his lightsaber from the ornate nightstand at the side of the bed. The curved handle felt reassuring in his grip. Familiar. Solid. Yet holding it couldn't stop his free hand from trembling ever so slightly. Scowling, he clenched his left hand into a fist, the fingers digging into the flesh of his palm—a crude but effective way to tame the tremor.

Moving silently, he slipped from the bedchamber out into the hallways of the mansion he now called home. Luminous tapestries covered the walls and colorful, handwoven rugs lined the corridors as he made his way past room after room, each decorated with custom-made furniture, rare objets d'art, and other unmistakable signs of wealth. It took him almost a full minute to traverse the length of the building and reach the back door that led out to the open-air grounds surrounding his estate.

Barefoot and naked from the waist up, he shivered and glanced down at the abstract mosaic of the stone courtyard illuminated in the light of Ciutric IV's twin moons. Goose bumps crawled across his flesh, but he ignored the night's chill as he ignited his lightsaber and began to practice the aggressive forms of Djem So.

His muscles groaned in protest, his joints clicking and grinding as he moved carefully through a variety of sequences. *Slash. Feint. Thrust.* The soles of his feet slapped softly against the surface of the courtyard stones, a sporadic rhythm marking the progress of every advance and retreat against his imaginary opponent.

The last vestiges of sleep and fatigue clung stubbornly to his body, spurring the tiny voice inside that urged him to abandon his training and return to the comfort of his bed. Bane drowned it out by silently reciting the opening line of the Sith Code: *Peace is a lie; there is only passion.*

Ten standard years had passed since he had lost his orbalisk armor. Ten years since his body had been burned almost beyond recognition by the devastating power of Force lightning unleashed from his own hand. Ten years since the healer Caleb had brought him back from the brink of death and Zannah, his apprentice, had slaughtered Caleb and the Jedi who had come to find them.

Thanks to Zannah's manipulations, the Jedi now believed the Sith to be extinct. Bane and his apprentice had spent the decade since those events perpetuating that myth: living in the shadows, gathering resources, and harboring their strength for the day they would strike back against the Jedi. On that glorious day the Sith would reveal themselves, even as they wiped their enemies from existence.

Bane knew he might never live to see that day. He was in his midforties now, and the first faint scars of time and age had begun to leave their marks on his body. Yet he had dedicated himself to the idea that one day, even if it took centuries, the Sith—*his* Sith—would rule the galaxy.

As he continued to ignore the aches and pains that inevitably accompanied the first half of his nightly regime, Bane's movements began to pick up speed. The air hissed and crackled as it was split time and time again by the crimson blade that had become an extension of his indomitable will.

He still cut an imposing figure. The powerful muscles built up during a youth spent working the mines on Apatros rippled beneath his skin, flexing with each slash and strike of his lightsaber. But a tiny sliver of the brute strength he once possessed had been whittled away.

He leapt high in the air, his lightsaber arcing above his head before chopping straight down in a blow powerful enough to cleave an enemy in two. His feet hit the hard surface of the courtyard stones with a sharp, sudden smack as he landed. Bane still moved with fierce grace and terrifying intensity. His lightsaber still flickered with blinding speed as he performed his martial drills, yet it was the merest fraction slower than it had once been.

The aging process was subtle, but inescapable. Bane accepted this; what he lost in strength and speed he could easily compensate for with wisdom, knowledge, and experience. But it was not age that was to blame for the involuntary tremor that sometimes afflicted his left hand.

A shadow passed over one of the twin moons; a dark cloud heavy with the threat of a fierce storm. Bane paused, briefly considering cutting his ritual short to avoid the impending downpour. But his muscles were warm now, and the blood was pumping furiously through his veins. The minor aches and pains were gone, banished by the adrenaline rush of intense physical training. Now was no time to quit.

Feeling a blast of cold wind blow in, he crouched low and opened himself up to the Force, letting it flow through him. Drawing on it to extend his awareness out to encompass each individual bead of rain as it fell from the sky, he resolved not to let a single drop touch his exposed flesh.

He could sense the power of the dark side building inside him. It began, as it always did, with a faint spark, a tiny flicker of light and heat. Muscles tense and coiled in anticipation, he fed the spark, fueling it with his own passion, letting his anger and fury transform the flame into an inferno waiting to be unleashed.

As the first fat drops splattered onto the patio stones around him, Bane exploded into action. Abandoning the overpowering style of Djem So, he shifted to the quicker sequences of Soresu, his lightsaber tracing tight circles above his head in a series of movements designed to intercept enemy blaster bolts.

The wind rose to a howling gale, and the scattered drops quickly became a downpour. His body and mind united as one, he channeled the infinite power of the Force against the driving rain. Tiny clouds of hissing steam formed as his blade picked off the descending drops while Bane twisted, twirled, and contorted his body to evade those few that managed to slip through his defenses.

For the next ten minutes he battled the pelting storm, reveling in the power of the dark side. And then, as suddenly as it had begun, the tempest was gone, the dark cloud scurrying away on the breeze. Breathing hard, Bane extinguished his lightsaber. His skin was sheened in sweat, but not a single drop of rain had touched his bare flesh.

Sudden storms were an almost nightly occurrence on Ciutric, particularly here in the lush forest on the outskirts of the capital city of Daplona. Yet this minor inconvenience was easily tolerated when set against all the advantages the planet had to offer.

Located on the Outer Rim, far from the seat of galactic power and far from the prying eyes of the Jedi Council, Ciutric had the good fortune to exist at the nexus of several hyperspace trading routes. Vessels stopped at the planet frequently, giving rise to a small but highly profitable industrial society centered on trade and shipping.

More important to Bane, the constant flow of visitors from regions scattered across the galaxy gave him easy access to contacts and information, allowing him to build up a network of informants and agents that he could personally oversee.

This would have been impossible had his body still been covered with the orbalisks—a host of chitinous parasites that fed upon his flesh in exchange for the strength and protection they afforded. His living armor had made him nearly invincible in one-on-one combat, yet its monstrous appearance had forced him to remain hidden from the eyes of the galaxy.

Back then, his plans to build up wealth, influence, and political power had been crippled by his physical deformity. Forced into a life of isolation lest the Jedi become aware of his existence, he had worked only through emissaries and go-betweens. He had relied on Zannah to be his eyes and ears. All the information he received was funneled through her; every goal and task was accomplished by her hand. As a result, Bane had been forced to act more cautiously, slowing his efforts and delaying his plans.

Things were different now. He was still a fearsome figure to behold, but no more so than any mercenary, bounty hunter, or retired soldier. Clad in the typical garb of their adopted home-world, he was remarkable more for his height than anything else—noticeable, but hardly unique. He was able to mingle with the crowds, interact with those who possessed information, and forge relationships with valuable political allies.

He no longer had to remain hidden, for now he was able to conceal his true self behind an assumed identity. To this end,

Bane had purchased a small estate a few minutes outside Daplona. Adopting the guise of siblings Sepp and Allia Omek, wealthy import–export merchants, he and Zannah had carefully cultivated their new identities in the planet's influential social, political, and economic circles.

Their estate was close enough to the city to give them easy access to everything Ciutric had to offer, yet isolated enough to allow Zannah to continue her lessons in the ways of the Sith. Stagnation and complacency were the seeds that would lead to the ultimate destruction of the Jedi; as the Dark Lord, Bane had to be vigilant against allowing his own Order to fall into the same trap. It was necessary not just to train his apprentice, but also to continue to increase his own skills and knowledge.

A cool zephyr wafted across the courtyard, chilling Bane's sweat-soaked body. His physical training was done for the evening; now it was time for the truly important work to begin.

A few dozen strides brought him to the small annex at the rear of the estate. The door was locked, sealed by a coded security system. Punching in the digits, he gently pushed the door open and stepped into the building that served as his private library.

The interior consisted of a single square room, five meters on each side, lit only by a single soft light hanging from the ceiling. The walls were lined by shelves overflowing with the scrolls, tomes, and manuscripts he had assembled over the years: the teachings of the ancient Sith. In the center of the room stood a large podium and a small pedestal. On the pedestal rested the Dark Lord's greatest treasure: his Holocron.

A four-sided crystal pyramid small enough to be held in the palm, the Holocron contained the sum of all Bane's knowledge and understanding. Everything he had learned about the ways of the dark side—all his teachings, all his philosophies—had been transferred into the Holocron, recorded for all eternity. It was his legacy, a way to share an entire lifetime of wisdom with those who would follow him in the line of Sith Masters.

The Holocron would pass to Zannah on his death, providing she could one day prove herself strong enough to wrest the mantle of Dark Lord away from him. Bane was no longer certain that day would come.

The Sith had existed in one form or another for thousands of years. Throughout their existence they had waged an endless war against the Jedi . . . and one another. Time and time again the followers of the dark side had been thwarted by their own rivalries and internal power struggles.

A common theme resonated across the long history of the Sith Order. Any great leader would inevitably be overthrown by an alliance of his or her followers. Lacking a strong leader the lesser Sith would quickly turn against one another, further weakening the Order.

Of all the Sith Masters, only Bane had understood the inescapable futility of this cycle. And only he had been strong enough to break it. Under his leadership the Sith had been reborn. Now they numbered only two—one Master and one apprentice; one to embody the power of the dark side, the other to crave it.

Thus would the Sith line always flow from the strongest, the one most worthy. Bane's Rule of Two ensured that the power of both Master and apprentice would grow from generation to generation until the Sith were finally able to exterminate the Jedi and usher in a new galactic age.

That was why Bane had chosen Zannah as his apprentice: she had the potential to one day surpass even his own abilities. On that day she would usurp him as the Dark Lord of the Sith and choose an apprentice of her own. Bane would die, but the Sith would live on.

Or so he had once believed. Yet now there was doubt in his mind. Two decades had passed since he had plucked the ten-year-old girl from the battlefields of Ruusan, yet Zannah still seemed content merely to serve. She had embraced his lessons and had shown an incredible affinity for the Force. Over the years Bane had tracked her progress carefully, and he could no longer say with certainty which one of them would survive a confrontation between them. But her reluctance to challenge him had left her Master wondering if Zannah lacked the fierce ambition necessary to become the Dark Lord of the Sith.

Stepping into the library, he reached out with his left hand to close the door behind him. As he did so, he noticed the all-too-familiar trembling in his fingers. He snatched his hand back involuntarily, clenching it once more into a fist as he kicked the door shut.

Age was beginning to take its toll on Bane, but it was nothing compared with the toll already wrought upon his body by decades of drawing upon the dark side of the Force. He couldn't help but smile at the grim irony: through the dark side he had access to near-infinite power, but it was power that came with a terrible cost. Flesh and bone lacked the strength to withstand the unfathomable energy unleashed by the Force. The unquenchable fire of the dark side was consuming him, devouring him bit by bit. After decades of focusing and channeling its power, his body was beginning to break down.

His condition was exacerbated by the lingering effects of the orbalisk armor that had been killing him even as it gifted him with incredible strength and speed.

The parasites had pushed his body well beyond its natural limits, aging him prematurely and intensifying the degeneration wrought by the power of the dark side. The orbalisks were gone now, but their damage could not be undone.

The first outward manifestations of his failing health had been subtle: his eyes had become sunken and drawn, his skin a touch more pale and pockmarked than was normal for his age. The last year, however, had seen more pronounced deterioration, culminating with the involuntary tremor that seized his left hand with increasing frequency.

And there was nothing he could do about it. The Jedi could

draw upon the light side to heal injury and disease. But the dark side was a weapon; the sick and frail did not deserve to be cured. Only the strong were worthy of survival.

He had tried to conceal the tremor from his apprentice, but Zannah was too quick, too cunning, to have missed such an obvious mark of weakness in her Master.

Bane had expected the tremor to be the catalyst Zannah needed to challenge him. Yet even now, with his body showing undeniable evidence of his growing vulnerability, she seemed content to maintain the status quo. Whether she acted out of fear, indecision, or perhaps even compassion for her Master, Bane didn't know—but none of these traits was acceptable in one chosen to carry on his legacy.

There was another potential explanation, of course—yet it was the most troubling of all. It was possible Zannah had noticed his deteriorating physical abilities and had simply decided to wait. In five years his body would be a ruined husk, and she could dispatch him with virtually no risk.

In most circumstances Bane would have admired this strategy, but in this case it flew in the face of the most fundamental tenet of the Rule of Two. An apprentice had to earn the title of Dark Lord, wresting it from the Master in a confrontation that pushed them both to the edge of their abilities. If Zannah intended to challenge him only after he was crippled by illness and infirmity, then she was unfit to be his heir. Yet Bane was not willing to initiate their confrontation himself. If he fell, the Sith would be ruled by a Master who did not accept or understand the key principle upon which the new Order had been founded. If he was victorious, he would be left without an apprentice, and his failing body would give out long before he could find and properly train another.

There was only one solution: Bane needed to find a way to extend his life. He had to find a way to restore and rejuvenate his body . . . or replace it. A year ago he would have thought such a thing to be impossible. Now he knew better.

From one of the shelves he took down a thick tome, its

leather cover pockmarked, the pages yellow and cracked with age. Moving carefully, he set it down on the podium, opening it to the page he had marked the night before.

Like most of the volumes on the shelves of his library, this one had been purchased from a private collector. The galaxy might believe the Sith to be extinct, but the dark side still exerted an inexorable pull on the psyches of men and women across every species, and a black market of illegal Sith paraphernalia flourished among those with wealth and power.

The attempts of the Jedi to locate and confiscate anything that could be linked to the Sith had only succeeded in driving up the prices and forcing collectors to work through middle-beings to preserve their anonymity.

This suited Bane perfectly. He had been able to assemble and expand his library without fear of drawing attention to himself: he was just another Sith fetishist, another anonymous collector obsessed with the dark side, willing to spend a small fortune to possess banned manuscripts and artifacts.

Most of what he had acquired was of little use: amulets or other trinkets of negligible power; secondhand copies of histories he had memorized long ago during his studies on Korriban; incomplete works written in indecipherable, long-dead languages. But on occasion he had been lucky enough to come across a treasure of real value.

The worn, tattered book before him was one such treasure. One of his agents had purchased it several months earlier—an event too fortuitous to be attributed to chance. The Force worked in mysterious ways, and Bane believed the book had been meant to come into his possession—the answer to his problem.

Like most of his collection, it was a historical account of one of the ancient Sith. Most of the pages contained names, dates, and other information that had no practical use for Bane. However, there was a small section that made a brief reference to a man named Darth Andeddu. Andeddu, the account claimed, had lived for centuries, using the dark side of the Force to extend his life and maintain his body well beyond its natural span.

In the typical fashion of the Sith before Bane's reformations, Andeddu's reign came to a violent end when he was betrayed and overthrown by his own followers. Yet his Holocron, the repository of his greatest secrets—including the secret of near-eternal life—was never found.

That was all: less than two pages in total. In the brief passage there was no mention of where or when Andeddu had lived. No mention of what had become of his followers after he was overthrown. Yet the very lack of information was what made the piece so compelling.

Why were there so few details? Why had he not come across references to Darth Andeddu in all his previous years of study?

There was only one explanation that made any sense: The Jedi had managed to purge him from the galactic record. Over the centuries they had collected every datapad, holodisk, and written work that mentioned Darth Andeddu and spirited them away to the Jedi Archives, burying them forever in order to keep his secrets hidden.

But despite their efforts, this one reference in an old, forgotten, and otherwise insignificant manuscript had survived to make its way into Bane's hands. For the past two months, ever since this tome had come into his possession, the Dark Lord had ended his nightly martial training with a visit to the library to ponder the mystery of Andeddu's missing Holocron. Cross-referencing the manuscript before him with the vast wealth of knowledge scattered across a thousand other volumes in his collection, he had struggled to assemble the pieces of the puzzle, only to fail time and time again.

Yet he refused to give up his search. Everything he had worked for, everything he had built depended on it. He *would* discover the location of Andeddu's Holocron. He *would* unlock the secret of eternal life to give him time to find and train another apprentice.

Without it, he would wither away and die. Zannah would

claim the title of Dark Lord through default, making a mock-ery of the Rule of Two and leaving the fate of the Order in the hands of an unworthy Master.

If he failed to find Andeddu's Holocron, the Sith were doomed.

THE STAR WARS LEGENDS NOVELS TIMELINE

 BEFORE THE REPUBLIC
37,000–25,000 YEARS BEFORE
STAR WARS: A NEW HOPE

c. 25,793 YEARS BEFORE *STAR WARS: A NEW HOPE*

Dawn of the Jedi: Into the Void

 OLD REPUBLIC
5,000–67 YEARS BEFORE
STAR WARS: A NEW HOPE

Lost Tribe of the Sith: The Collected
Stories

3,954 YEARS BEFORE *STAR WARS: A NEW HOPE*

The Old Republic: Revan

3,650 YEARS BEFORE *STAR WARS: A NEW HOPE*

The Old Republic: Deceived
Red Harvest
The Old Republic: Fatal Alliance
The Old Republic: Annihilation

1,032 YEARS BEFORE *STAR WARS: A NEW HOPE*

Knight Errant
Darth Bane: Path of Destruction
Darth Bane: Rule of Two
Darth Bane: Dynasty of Evil

 RISE OF THE EMPIRE
67–0 YEARS BEFORE
STAR WARS: A NEW HOPE

67 YEARS BEFORE *STAR WARS: A NEW HOPE*

Darth Plagueis

33 YEARS BEFORE *STAR WARS: A NEW HOPE*

Cloak of Deception
Darth Maul: Shadow Hunter
Maul: Lockdown

32 YEARS BEFORE *STAR WARS: A NEW HOPE*

STAR WARS: EPISODE I
THE PHANTOM MENACE

Rogue Planet
Outbound Flight
The Approaching Storm

22 YEARS BEFORE *STAR WARS: A NEW HOPE*

STAR WARS: EPISODE II
ATTACK OF THE CLONES

22–19 YEARS BEFORE *STAR WARS: A NEW HOPE*

STAR WARS: THE CLONE
WARS

The Clone Wars: Wild Space
The Clone Wars: No Prisoners

Clone Wars Gambit
Stealth
Siege

Republic Commando
Hard Contact
Triple Zero
True Colors
Order 66

Shatterpoint
The Cestus Deception
MedStar I: Battle Surgeons
MedStar II: Jedi Healer
Jedi Trial
Yoda: Dark Rendezvous
Labyrinth of Evil

19 YEARS BEFORE *STAR WARS: A NEW HOPE*

STAR WARS: EPISODE III
REVENGE OF THE SITH

Kenobi
Dark Lord: The Rise of Darth Vader
Imperial Commando 501st

Coruscant Nights
Jedi Twilight
Street of Shadows
Patterns of Force

The Last Jedi

10 YEARS BEFORE *STAR WARS: A NEW HOPE*

The Han Solo Trilogy
The Paradise Snare
The Hutt Gambit
Rebel Dawn

The Adventures of Lando Calrissian
The Force Unleashed
The Han Solo Adventures
Death Troopers
The Force Unleashed II

THE STAR WARS LEGENDS NOVELS TIMELINE

REBELLION
0–5 YEARS AFTER
STAR WARS: A NEW HOPE

Death Star
Shadow Games

0

─────────────────────

STAR WARS: EPISODE IV
A NEW HOPE

Tales from the Mos Eisley Cantina
Tales from the Empire
Tales from the New Republic
Scoundrels
Allegiance
Choices of One
Honor Among Thieves
Galaxies: The Ruins of Dantooine
Splinter of the Mind's Eye
Razor's Edge

3 YEARS AFTER *STAR WARS: A NEW HOPE*

STAR WARS: EPISODE V
THE EMPIRE STRIKES BACK

Tales of the Bounty Hunters
Shadows of the Empire

4 YEARS AFTER *STAR WARS: A NEW HOPE*

STAR WARS: EPISODE VI
THE RETURN OF THE JEDI

Tales from Jabba's Palace

The Bounty Hunter Wars
  The Mandalorian Armor
  Slave Ship
  Hard Merchandise

The Truce at Bakura
Luke Skywalker and the Shadows of
Mindor

NEW REPUBLIC
5–25 YEARS AFTER
STAR WARS: A NEW HOPE

X-Wing
  Rogue Squadron
  Wedge's Gamble
  The Krytos Trap
  The Bacta War
  Wraith Squadron
  Iron Fist
  Solo Command

The Courtship of Princess Leia
Tatooine Ghost

The Thrawn Trilogy
  Heir to the Empire
  Dark Force Rising
  The Last Command

X-Wing: Isard's Revenge

The Jedi Academy Trilogy
  Jedi Search
  Dark Apprentice
  Champions of the Force

I, Jedi
Children of the Jedi
Darksaber
Planet of Twilight
X-Wing: Starfighters of Adumar
The Crystal Star

The Black Fleet Crisis Trilogy
  Before the Storm
  Shield of Lies
  Tyrant's Test

The New Rebellion

The Corellian Trilogy
  Ambush at Corellia
  Assault at Selonia
  Showdown at Centerpoint

The Hand of Thrawn Duology
  Specter of the Past
  Vision of the Future

Scourge
Survivor's Quest

NEW JEDI ORDER
25–40 YEARS AFTER
STAR WARS: A NEW HOPE

LEGACY
40+ YEARS AFTER
STAR WARS: A NEW HOPE

The New Jedi Order
Vector Prime
Dark Tide I: Onslaught
Dark Tide II: Ruin
Agents of Chaos I: Hero's Trial
Agents of Chaos II: Jedi Eclipse
Balance Point
Edge of Victory I: Conquest
Edge of Victory II: Rebirth
Star by Star
Dark Journey
Enemy Lines I: Rebel Dream
Enemy Lines II: Rebel Stand
Traitor
Destiny's Way
Force Heretic I: Remnant
Force Heretic II: Refugee
Force Heretic III: Reunion
The Final Prophecy
The Unifying Force

35 YEARS AFTER *STAR WARS: A NEW HOPE*

The Dark Nest Trilogy
The Joiner King
The Unseen Queen
The Swarm War

Legacy of the Force
Betrayal
Bloodlines
Tempest
Exile
Sacrifice
Inferno
Fury
Revelation
Invincible

Crosscurrent
Riptide
Millennium Falcon

43 YEARS AFTER *STAR WARS: A NEW HOPE*

Fate of the Jedi
Outcast
Omen
Abyss
Backlash
Allies
Vortex
Conviction
Ascension
Apocalypse

X-Wing: Mercy Kill

45 YEARS AFTER *STAR WARS: A NEW HOPE*

Crucible

ABOUT THE AUTHOR

DREW KARPYSHYN is the *New York Times* bestselling author of *Children of Fire*, *The Scorched Earth*, and *Chaos Unleashed*, as well as the *Star Wars*: *The Old Republic* novels *Revan* and *Annihilation*, and the *Star Wars*: *Darth Bane* trilogy: *Path of Destruction*, *Rule of Two*, and *Dynasty of Evil*. He also wrote the acclaimed Mass Effect series of novels and worked as a writer/designer on numerous award-winning videogames. After spending most of his life in Canada, he finally grew tired of the long, cold winters and headed south in search of a climate more conducive to year-round golf. Drew Karpyshyn now lives in Texas with his wife, Jennifer, and their pets.

drewkarpyshyn.com

Twitter: @DrewKarpyshyn

ABOUT THE TYPE

This book was set in Sabon, a typeface designed by the well-known German typographer Jan Tschichold (1902–74). Sabon's design is based upon the original letter forms of sixteenth-century French type designer Claude Garamond and was created specifically to be used for three sources: foundry type for hand composition, Linotype, and Monotype. Tschichold named his typeface for the famous Frankfurt typefounder Jacques Sabon (c. 1520–80).

A long time ago in a galaxy far, far away. . . .

STAR WARS

Join up! Subscribe to our newsletter
at ReadStarWars.com or find us on social.

 StarWarsBooks

 @DelReyStarWars

@DelReyStarWars